M000207395

Mostly
Murder

Mostly Murder

LINDA LADD

KENSINGTON
Kensington Publishing Corp.
www.kensingtonbooks.com

KENSINGTON BOOKS are published by

Kensington Publishing Corp.
119 West 40th Street
New York, NY 10018

Copyright © 2013 Linda Ladd

All rights reserved. No part of this book may be reproduced in any form or by any means without the prior written consent of the publisher, excepting brief quotes used in reviews.

All Kensington titles, imprints, and distributed lines are available at special quantity discounts for bulk purchases for sales promotions, premiums, fund-raising, educational, or institutional use. Special book excerpts or customized printings can also be created to fit specific needs. For details, write or phone the office of the Kensington special sales manager: Kensington Publishing Corp., 119 West 40th Street, New York, NY 10018, attn: Special Sales Department; phone 1-800-221-2647.

PUBLISHER'S NOTE
This book is a work of fiction. Names, characters, businesses, organizations, places, events, and incidents either are the product of the author's imagination or are used fictitiously. Any resemblance to actual persons, living or dead, events, or locales is entirely coincidental.

KENSINGTON and the k logo are Reg. U.S. Pat. & TM Off.

First electronic edition: December 2013

ISBN-13: 978-1-60183-051-7
ISBN-10: 1-60183-051-3

First print edition: December 2013

ISBN-13: 978-1-60183-137-8
ISBN-10: 1-60183-137-4

Printed in the United States of America

Prologue

A Very Scary Man

The first time the scary man realized that he liked to frighten people was when he was twelve years old. His little sister was his favorite victim because she was only six and small for her age. Late one night, he sneaked into the room where Mandy was sleeping so peacefully, snoring with little whiffs and snorts because of her allergies, and all snuggled up under the covers with her pink stuffed Easter bunny and her three favorite Barbie dolls. Earlier that day, he had waded through the brush lining the bayou until he finally caught a tiny black garter snake. So, now, at last, it was show time.

Grinning, trying not to laugh with anticipation, he opened up the white Kroger's plastic sack and dumped the wriggling little reptile onto Mandy's pink Cinderella pillow. He let out a loud hissing sound so she'd wake up, and then he took off for the doorway. But the snake had already slithered onto her and stopped right on top of her chest. He paused in the hall and waited with tingling nerves. Her *Snow White* night light was on beside her bed, and when she sat up, all flushed and sweet with sleep, she immediately laid eyes on the snake wriggling around on her blanket. The little girl let out a shriek like he just couldn't believe. She probably wet her pants, too, he thought, racing back to his own room, ready to put on the best acting job of his life.

The greatest lesson he learned that night was that if he was very careful and planned ahead, he could escape punishment for something truly horrible that he'd done. So, he was back in his own bed in his own room when his parents came rushing down the hall to see what was wrong with their little darling. He got up again, feigning sleepiness and concern like the little angel he wasn't, but he was laughing so hard inside when he remembered the absolute terror on his sister's face.

Unfortunately, he thought it best to go back to bed and pretend disinterest in Mandy's drama. So he had to miss all the screaming and sobbing and hysterics, not to mention his dad's frantic and comedic efforts to catch the harmless little snake. Truth was, of course, he really didn't want to hurt his baby sister. He loved Mandy a lot; she was just the most precious little thing in the world. But he loved to see the utter fear on her face even better, and that was the Gospel truth. He loved mind-boggling distress contorting anybody's face, actually. As long as they were absolutely terrified and showed it, it was good for him.

Keenly disappointed that he had been robbed of seeing the hour-long ordeal of rocking her back to sleep, he vowed that someday he wouldn't have to hide his secret obsession. Someday, somewhere, he would find someone that he could torment for his pleasure and never have to miss a single tear or shriek or scrambling flight away from perceived mortal danger. He would plan and plan and plan some more, until he could enjoy himself with no fear of capture or punishment or retribution or grounding. Yeah, and that day was gonna be so sweet. Oh, yeah. He could hardly wait.

And that day came a lot sooner than he expected, right after his Aunt Pamela and Uncle Stanley came to visit for the weekend, because they brought along their tiny little baby boy, Donnie, who was only eighteen months old. So the good thing about that was that the baby couldn't talk yet. Not a damn word, except for babbling for his mama and dada. Yep, he was the perfect little victim with his red curly hair and big blue eyes and chubby little cherub's face. His mommy and daddy loved him so much that they doted on him incessantly, snuggling him and spoiling him and kissing him and hugging him, as if he were the greatest kid ever born. Yeah, it was little Donnie this and little Donnie that and little wonderful Donnie, blah, blah, blah. It was downright disgusting.

Hell, his own parents had never treated him like he was their darling little angel. Of course, he wasn't an angel. He was a devil, really, and proud of it, or maybe he was more like the murderous demons he saw in scary movies. He had never killed anybody or driven anyone nuts, not yet anyway, but he didn't really consider that to be out of the question someday in the future. Not little Donnie, though, not right now. He was way too little and sweet and innocent to kill, and he was his cousin, after all.

When the adults decided they wanted to go out for dinner and dancing at the country club, he was elated and quickly offered to babysit the two little kids. His mom and dad and aunt and uncle thought that he was just so loving and kindhearted to offer, which gave him a really big edge on having two little victims to torment, not to mention how he laughed inside his head at how stupid grownups were. For obvious reasons, his sister begged to go along with the adults, but they wouldn't let her, of course. But she wouldn't tell on him; he had put the fear of God into her about tattling a long time ago. So, instead, Mandy ran upstairs as soon as their parents left and found a hiding place under her bed where he couldn't get at her without poking her out with a broom handle. He didn't care. He had somebody even better that he could make cry.

Angelic little Donnie didn't mind being left alone with him, not at all. In fact, he ran over to him and held up his sturdy little arms as if he wanted to be held. So he picked the toddler up and swung him around and made him giggle with joy. But then, within moments, he felt *the need*, the one he just could not resist or control anymore. Laughing, too, he tossed the little boy way up into the air and suddenly screamed up at him like some kind of a crazy banshee. For a second, the little kid just looked startled, but then he puckered up and began to wail. The scary man caught his baby cousin and cuddled him and rocked him until he stopped crying and was content again.

Once the child was calm, he put little Donnie down and left the room to get something to eat. When he came back, the little kid was playing with a toy that had holes where you inserted colorful little balls to play music. He sneaked up behind the toddler and yelled *Boo!* as loud as he could. The baby went completely rigid and then screamed so shrilly that the boy almost had to put his hands over his ears.

"Hey, now, it's okay, little sweetie pie. I didn't mean to scare you, shh, little guy," he crooned, scooping up the child and sitting down in the rocker by the fireplace. The baby settled down quickly; he guessed Donnie felt safe again. So he rocked the little tyke, who was really awfully adorable most of the time. But there was just something in the look in people's eyes when he scared them that he got off on. It was like they just froze into a statue for a few seconds, rigid and stiff and shocked, and then their brain shrieked out, "Hey, kid, run, run, get outta here fast!"

Oh, yes, he had plenty of that *malice aforethought*, like the lawyers on television shows always said. He liked lawyer shows, and he was smart, too, just like those lawyers. Straight A's in every subject. Maybe he'd become a lawyer someday. Still, that particular phrase intrigued him; it rolled off his tongue somehow and made him feel good. He looked up the definition in the dictionary, just to make sure it was apropos, and there it was, laid out for him in black and white. *Malice aforethought: a general evil and depraved state of mind in which the person is unconcerned for the lives and well-being of others.*

Okay, that's exactly what he had, that evil and depraved state of mind. Maybe he should call himself Malice Aforethought, or just Malice for short, give himself a name like the villains who battled the superheroes in the comics. Because that's what he came after people with, pure malice in his heart and mind and soul. Maybe he would call himself that, just for fun, and thus, his new moniker was born.

Malice grinned, thinking about the exact moment when his victims knew they were in trouble, right before they screamed or took off running or wept real live wet-to-the-touch tears. That's when that strange sense of joy erupted deep inside his gut. It was some kind of release, almost. Satisfaction, that's what it was. A burst of great personal gratification. He wondered if that were normal behavior, or if he might be a really bad person, or some kind of psycho, even. Then he decided he didn't care if he was or not, that it felt good and he was going to do it, whenever he knew he wouldn't get caught.

Yeah, he could even make it his hobby all right, just something to pass the time. He could gather scary things to use on people and figure out what kind of things gave people the creeps and watch murderers in movies and read gory books until he had his talents honed down to sublime perfection. Smiling to himself, he rocked little Donnie to sleep and then he laid the tiny boy gently in his portable crib and went to look for Mandy. After all, she was his favorite victim, and even more important, she was way too afraid to tell on him.

Chapter One

It was a beautiful and sunny December day, only a few weeks before Christmas, in fact, and nothing the least bit catastrophic had happened for a change. That was just fine with homicide detective Claire Morgan. So far, so good. She sat behind her new and temporary desk at the Lafourche Parish Sheriff's Office in Thibodaux, Louisiana and watched her new and temporary partner, Zander Jackson, trying to balance himself on a rickety stepladder while he adjusted a gauzy white angel on top of the eight-foot office Christmas tree. She had only been aboard in the law enforcement department in the bayous southwest of New Orleans for a couple of weeks, all after her true love and super psychiatrist to the stars, Nicholas Black, had flown off on his private Learjet to his London hotel/psychiatric clinic to take care of what he fondly described as a particularly rambunctious head case. He was indeed a world-famous shrink and possibly the best-looking guy she'd ever seen in her life, which was a very good thing, actually.

Claire happened to be one of his rambunctious head cases herself, of course, but she was a lot better off now than she had been several months back. Alas, she did have a tendency to find trouble wherever she went, and Black had always been the protective sort, but especially now. Probably because she had barely survived a work-related, eighteen-day coma, and not so long ago, either. He didn't exactly celebrate the idea of her getting back to work as a homicide detective, whether it be in the lazy bayous or at the Lake of the Ozarks in Missouri, where she had worked on the case that had put her in the aforementioned dream world for those three long weeks. But he rarely took it upon himself to tell her what to do, and vice versa, which was why they got along so famously.

Although Claire hadn't known Zander—actually he was Zee to his friends—long, he was a neat guy. Almost as great as Claire's real partner back at the lake, whose name was Bud Davis. Truth was, she missed Bud like crazy, and all her other Missouri colleagues, too. But it was good to get away from the scene of some rather hairy crimes she'd investigated up that way, and the sixty-eight-degree Christmas weather was a good incentive to stay put until the summer heat rolled in. Also, said Missouri friends visited a lot, which was always something to look forward to. Now that she was back in homicide where she belonged, the utter boredom that had veritably sent her climbing the walls was long gone. Now and again, she still experienced some horrific nightmares of ugly cases gone by, but she was handling it okay. So, onward and forward, bring it on.

"Hey, Claire, who you root for? The Saints or the Rams?"

Claire smiled. Zee was football crazy, to say the least. "Saints when I'm here. Rams when I'm in Missouri."

"Well, you better root for the Saints when you're here."

"So says Black, too."

They laughed together. Claire stood up and helped him drape some gold tinsel, which had probably been in the office storage bin since the 1980s, in and out of the fragrant branches. The tree was a spreading cedar that had been cut down somewhere way out in the surrounding bayous, one that nearly touched the ceiling tiles. She liked that, a real tree that smelled fresh and pungent. Black always insisted on getting a real tree, too, usually one big enough to fit into the nave in the St. Louis Cathedral in Jackson Square. And he liked to cut it down himself, hiking into the woods of his property in Missouri with an ax over his broad shoulder, like some kind of big, handsome Paul Bunyan. The guy loved Christmas, what could she say.

Claire just hoped that he fixed up his troublesome patient and made it home by Christmas Eve. That didn't give him a lot of time to work his magic and hightail it back home with her present, and he usually gave her one hell of a good present. What to get him was a whole different story. She had her work cut out for her. But he loved every inch of New Orleans, his hometown, and was having a ball living there again, even temporarily, so she supposed anything she got for him that was associated with his beloved NOLA would please him to no end. He had bought a hotel there, too, and a restored mansion for them to live in, but that was Black for you. He did love his real estate.

When she'd first glimpsed the house that he'd been raving about on Governor Nicholls Street in the French Quarter, it hadn't looked like much from the outside. In fact, it had looked like a dilapidated building in the warehouse district. Once he'd opened the plain black shuttered doors at street level, however, they'd walked straight into a spread out of *House Beautiful*, all modern and comfortable and beautiful. And she was talking big-time glamour.

For instance, there were the marble grand spiral staircase and the elevator. Not to mention the eight large bedrooms, all with their own marble fireplaces, the formal living and dining rooms, a gourmet kitchen, a private courtyard replete with fountains, a small lap pool with a waterfall, a formal rose garden, and a large mimosa tree on which she could hang her punching bag. Black had told her that he'd had his eye on that particular house for years and finally snatched it up when it went on the market. And yes, sir, it had cost him a pretty penny. But he had lots of pretty pennies and was collecting more all the time. Her guy made serious bucks, all right.

While Claire added some silvery strands of icicles, Zee stood back with his hands on his hips and admired their handiwork. "Hey, this thing's lookin' good. I like those gold fleur-de-lis ornaments you brought in. Know what, though? I'm gonna call Nancy and tell her to bring us down some pizzas. It's gonna be slower than a funeral procession today, believe me. Sundays are quiet, and that's good. We can watch the Saints game without interruptions."

Claire didn't like Zee's analogy all that much. She'd seen way too many funerals in her lifetime. He had earned that nickname, Zee, running touchdowns once upon a time out at Tulane University. Zoom Zoom Zee back then—shortened to 3Z, but that was a bit much for her so Zee would have to suffice. She watched him switch on the flat-screen television on the file cabinet and then punch Nancy's number into his beloved white smartphone. Nancy Gill was the Lafourche Parish medical examiner and the main reason Claire found herself sitting behind a Louisiana detective's desk. Nancy had been at the lake last summer on a law enforcement exchange program and had talked Claire into coming aboard for the winter in a similar exchange, way down there in the bayous.

Zee slouched down across the desk from her, the phone to his ear, all muscles and athletic grace, a real good-looking guy with skin the color of Hershey's chocolate and caramel-colored eyes. She knew he'd spent most of his tenure at the New Orleans Police Department, working in their Vice and Narcotics Units. Then he'd gotten in a few more years busting bearded druggies and swamp-based meth labs in Lafourche Parish before he'd made detective grade and been transferred to homicide.

Because of her years of experience, she had been designated lead on the few cases they'd handled together so far, which had entailed one stolen bateau, which is a bayou boat, and a missing child who'd turned out to be asleep in his rickety backyard tree house. Zee had shown some good investigatory instincts. Apparently, they did not run into a plethora of grisly murders in the bayous around Lafourche Parish, which was fine by her and sent Black a few degrees up the ecstatic scale. Maybe the local felons made the drive up to the Big Easy to perpetrate their Louisiana homicides. As Zee had intimated, today would be quiet. Everybody in the state would be watching the Saints play over in Dallas.

"Nancy said to give her fifteen minutes, tops. Hope you like Meat Lover's Pizza."

"You bet. Sounds good."

When Claire's phone sang out the opening chords of Roy Orbison's "Blue Bayou," her brand new ring tone chosen in honor of her new digs, Black's name popped up on caller ID. Her beau was checking in from Ye Merry Olde England.

Claire moved out into the deserted hallway, punched on, and said, "Hey, cheerio, old chap, and all that rot."

"Cheerio, hell. I miss you. Catch the next flight over here and make me a happy man."

"Well, that's good, and glad to hear you miss me. Ditto back to you. So, how's it going over there? Any crazies running amok?"

"I can't sleep without you in my bed."

"Glad to hear that, too. Really, though, how's your patient? Straitjacket on and all is well?"

"He's doing very well. I changed his meds. How about you? How do you feel?"

Black, worrying about her again. Her coma had gotten to him big time and made him hover a whole lot more than necessary. "I'm fine, really. Feel good, in fact. I like it over here at Lafourche. Zee's cool. Nancy's great. It's been pretty quiet, to tell you the truth."

"No headaches? No blurred vision?"

"Jeez, Black, I'm fine," I said. Hey, he was a good doctor. He covered all the bases. And he had one hell of a bedside manner—at least with her, he did.

"No car crashes? Nobody's shot you down? Beaten you up? Knifed you in the back?"

Yes, he had sarcasm down pat, too. Although most of that stuff had happened to her at one time or another, except for the knife thing. She'd never been stabbed, thank God, not unless you counted one rather nasty meat cleaver attack. Black was joking, yes, but not totally. "Well, some jerk cut me off in traffic two days ago. Made me brake hard. That count?"

"I hate to think what you did to him."

"It was a her, and I let her off with a polite police warning."

Quiet ensued for a beat. "So how is the new job, really? Like it? Please tell me you aren't chasing any serial killers."

"I'm not chasing any serial killers. Yet. We've been lucky."

"You just made my day."

"Truth is, the only excitement around here today is the Saints game. And yes, I put it in the DVR for you. Zee's a bigger Saints fan than you are, if that's even possible. See how exciting my life is when you're gone?"

"I don't particularly want you to be excited while I'm gone." Short pause again. "Are you sleeping okay? Any more nightmares?"

See? The guy is overly concerned. She guessed she'd fib a bit about the nightmares, though, just to give him peace of mind. "Nope. I'm definitely on the mend, at least ninety-nine percent and climbing."

"I miss you," he said again.

"Well, come back home then. I'm tired of sleeping in that big round bed in that big palatial house all by myself. The French Quarter's great, but lonely with you gone. What's taking you so long, anyway? Slumming it with Wills and Kate at Buckingham Palace?"

"I wish. My patient is doing much better, but I've got to tie up a few loose ends. I should be home on Tuesday. Take that day off and the next one, too. I've got good things planned for us in that big round bed in that big palatial house."

Claire smiled. Sounded fine to her. Oh, yeah, definitely. "We'll see, Black. Gotta go. Nancy just walked in with pizza and sodas, and the game's about to start."

"Be careful, Claire. I mean it. Juan and Maria are there with you, right?"

Juan Christo was Black's new home security guard/gardener who carried a shotgun, and his wife, Maria, was their cook/housekeeper who probably carried a pistol, too, knowing Black. The middle-aged couple hailed from Guatemala and kept the house running like clockwork and kept Claire company when Black was gone. She liked them both a lot. "They're fine, too, and hover over me almost as much as you do."

"Okay, then. Remember, duck and weave. Stay close to Zee."

The duck-and-weave thing was a private joke, his way of saying be careful. "Quit worrying. I'm fine. This place is a veritable no-crime zone."

They hung up just as Nancy put down the pizzas on Claire's desk and said, "Does this smell scrumptious, or what? I got us some cheese bread, too."

Yes, indeed, it did smell wonderful. Claire opened the lid and chose a nice big piece as Nancy pulled an ice-cold Pepsi off the plastic rings of the six-pack she carried. She handed it to Claire. "Oh, God, look, they're interviewing Jack Holliday. Man, is he hot, or what?"

"Yep, number eleven, Tulane jersey retired," Zee agreed. "Best college quarterback who ever threw a football, in my humble opinion."

"Best looking, too," Nancy added.

Claire took another bite. "So he doesn't play for the Saints?"

"One season, then he blew out his knee. He lives here in New Orleans, though, and was the biggest star Tulane had ever seen, so everybody loves him. Now he represents most of his former teammates and is making tons of money."

Nancy rolled her chair up beside Claire. Nancy Gill was just gorgeous. She looked like some Amazon warrior of old, very tall and beautiful, with long reddish brown hair and eyes the exact same russet color. She was top-notch at her job, too, almost as good as Buckeye Boyd, Claire's ME up in Missouri. Nancy had been trained at the NOPD, too, by some of the best CSI techs in the country and was ultra-meticulous about her crime scenes. She had become a good friend, especially when Black was off jet-setting around the Continent and Claire could actually spend some time with her.

The pizza tasted delicious, and up on the screen, the stadium in Dallas was alive with thousands of insane fans screaming for blood. The Saints were on the field, milling around, all in gold and black, and the Dallas Cowboys were, too, all of them no doubt just waiting for the head-on, bone-cracking collisions to ensue. Claire had run into a few of those, too, and had the residual scars to prove it.

Just as the Saints completed pass one, Zee's cell phone rang. His ringtone was the voice of the suave and sexy Usher, of course crooning a love song called "Here I Stand" that no doubt had caused many a lady's heart to flutter. Zee mumbled a mild curse and kept his eyes glued on the game while he answered. "Yeah, what's up? C'mon, game just started, dude."

Claire and Nancy watched him grimace. Then he hung up and growled, "Patrol's got a body. Down near where you've been staying, Claire."

Claire frowned at that news. She had been spending quite a few nights on a houseboat while Black was out of town, which happened to be something that Black didn't know and that she didn't want him to know. It was down on the bayou in Lafourche Parish where she'd lived for a while as a foster child with the LeFevres family. The LeFevres' house had been partially destroyed by Katrina years ago, but their houseboat had been taken inland and saved. Since Claire had moved to New Orleans and reconnected with some of the remaining LeFevres brothers, they'd offered her the use of the boat when she was down in the parish. She'd jumped at the chance. It was one of the few pleasant memories in her horrific childhood so she cherished the place.

Zee looked mightily perturbed. "We got big trouble. They found a dead girl down there, and they said the scene's real creepy. They want you out there, too, Nancy."

"Okay, let's get going," Claire said, feeling the familiar surge of excitement and realizing that this was what she'd been waiting for. Despite her recent injuries and the dangers she'd faced in the past, homicide investigations happened to be her passion. She was already pumped up and raring to go.

"Where exactly is it?" Nancy asked Zee, grabbing another pizza slice and closing the box.

Zee picked up the whole box to take with them, apparently not one to waste good food. He looked at Claire. "From the sound of it, Claire, it's right there on the property where you're stayin' some-times. In the ruins of that house just up from your boat. You sleep out there last night?"

"Yeah. I didn't hear anything, and I sleep with the windows wide open. Nobody drove up to the house, or I definitely would've heard the car. You know how sound travels out there on the water."

"You didn't see anything this morning when you left, either?"

Claire shook her head. "Nope, and nothing seemed out of the ordinary. You sure it's not some other place? There are several dilap-idated houses along that part of the bayou. Maybe it's one of them."

"He said it's the old LeFevres place." Zee unlocked his top drawer, pulled it open, and retrieved his Beretta from its black leather belt holster.

Claire never took off her weapons, not anymore, not after her last case. Even at night, she kept her weapons handy under her pillow. Being unarmed had not been healthy for her in the past. And that was the understatement of the year. Her trusty Glock nine-millimeter was snug in her shoulder holster, and the sweet little .38 snub nose that her best friend and ex-LAPD partner, Harve Lester, had once given her for Christmas, was strapped to her right ankle. She grabbed her lightweight black hoodie and looped the chain holding the silver Lafourche Parish Deputy Sheriff badge over her head.

"I guess I better call Sheriff Friedewald. He needs to know a homicide's gone down."

Nancy said, "Let's take my Tahoe. I've got my equipment with me. Looks like I'm going to need it."

Claire said, "If it's that bad, we need to hurry it up and get out there."

So hurry it up they did. Minutes later, they were in Nancy's white Tahoe, headed out to the crime scene. Claire's blood was singing. A murder wasn't exactly what she'd expected on such a nice sun-spangled Sunday afternoon, but she was ready, her instincts telling her something wicked had come calling. And Claire always trusted her gut. Especially when it involved murder and mayhem and raving maniacs. More troubling, she was thinking that if the murder had occurred near her boat, and when she was probably there, was it somehow connected to her? Nope, Black was not going to be a happy camper when he heard about this case.

Chapter Two

Ten minutes later they were barreling down a bayou road on their way to the LeFevres property, dust billowing up behind them like a tornado riding their tail. The LeFevreses had lived in a remote corner of the parish, on a bayou stream that most people never got to see, much less dwell on, but to Claire it was a quiet, beautiful sanctuary. Wooded and full of birds and wild animals, true, but she had felt safe there when she was a girl, after living in a host of foster homes where she hadn't felt safe at all.

When the LeFevres brothers offered her a chance to stay on their houseboat, she'd jumped at the opportunity but hadn't used it overnight until Black left for Europe. Fate had brought her back to the swamps again. Now death had returned there as well, probably following her around, which was usually the case.

"There's the turn, Nancy," she said, pointing out a gravel road up ahead.

Nancy took a hard left into a rutted entrance that wound through a stand of two-hundred-year-old live oak trees, all draped funereally with the coarse and creepy, gray Spanish moss so prevalent in the bayous. Once the road opened up onto the grassy yard surrounding the old Caribbean-style house with its wide veranda and open breezeway, she saw the two white Lafourche Parish patrol cars sitting there. Beyond the driveway covered with white shells and down farther on the banks of the slow-flowing bayou, the houseboat sat silent and undisturbed. Other than the police cars, everything looked exactly the way it had that morning when Claire had left for Thibodaux.

They pulled up beside the other vehicles and then got out and walked across the front yard. The house was a big two-story structure, clapboard, once white but now peeling and gray. Some of the roof had collapsed, but most of the bottom floor was still intact. The giant river stone chimney was crumbling some now, but it had been a wonderful home once, full of laughter and love and happy children. Bobby and Kristen LeFevres had made it warm and safe for their own two children and the multitude of foster kids they'd taken in through the years.

Bobby LeFevres had been an NOPD detective then and had found Claire, her face and arms bruised, hiding in a city park pavilion after she had wandered away from her abusive foster family. He had taken her home with him and fought for her to stay there, until Family Services had seen fit to move her to a new family up around Baton Rouge. But the LeFevres house held only good memories. Until now.

Inside the house, they found the first floor was still in pretty good shape, but the second floor, where Claire had slept in a bedroom with the LeFevreses' darling little daughter named Sophie, was in ruins, the roof caved in, the wood floor water damaged. They stopped outside the front door, put on protective booties and blue latex gloves, and then moved carefully through the living room and joined the officers at the dining room pocket doors. They stood there a few minutes and observed the crime scene. It was not a pretty sight. In fact, it was downright shocking.

The victim was a woman. She had on some kind of long white velvet robe. Her hands had been placed in her lap, but were completely hidden inside the robe's wide flowing sleeves. Her face had been painted to resemble a skeleton. White paint had been applied all over her facial skin except for the eye sockets, nose, and chin, which were painted black, but that wasn't the worst part. The killer had pierced a needle through her white lips and sewn her mouth shut with large black vertical stitches. White thread had been sewn in a large X on each of her eyes. The victim's hair was hidden under some kind of white silk turban with lots of charms and feathers sewn on it. Small bones had been thrust through slits cut into her earlobes. Dried blood had run down her neck and now looked black and crusty.

There was a multitude of candles surrounding her, all white and all covered with thick drippings, burned all the way down to the floor. Some of them, the ones encased in tall glass containers were decorated with pictures of Jesus Christ and the Virgin Mary. One was still burning. More religious pictures, small plastic icons as found in Catholic churches, feathers, and bones made a shrine that encircled the chair. Several human skulls were affixed with white candles. And the smell of death permeated the air, cloaking everybody and everything with the sickening odor of putrefying flesh. Bluebottle flies had found her and buzzed and landed and crawled all over the exposed face.

"Holy God," Zee muttered softly, crossing himself and stepping back away from the victim. "That's a voodoo altar. See the cornmeal spread around down there on the floor. That design traced in it? That's called a Veve. They draw that stuff before the ceremony begins. Don't step in it. Don't touch it. Damn, I don't like this kinda shit."

Claire pulled her gaze away from the altar and stared at Zee. "How do you know this stuff, Zee?"

"Hey, I was born out here, remember. And Mama Lulu is into voodoo. She can tell us what all this means. And it all means something bad, I guarantee it."

"Who's Mama Lulu?"

"My grandmama. She lives up this very bayou a little ways, and she's got a voodoo shop over on Bourbon Street in the Quarter. This's serious stuff, Claire. Don't let anybody touch anything, or God knows what might happen."

"Told you this was super creepy," one of the officers said. Claire remembered that his name was Clarence Dionne. She didn't know him very well yet. He was young, slender, with big brown eyes and dark hair longer than the sheriff really liked his patrol officers to wear. He was from the parish, born and bred, and knew nearly everybody who lived in Lafourche. She did know that much about him, and that was probably going to come in handy in the investigation.

Yeah, it was super creepy, all right. More than creepy—bizarre and horrible, Claire thought. She turned to Officer Dionne. "Do you recognize the victim?"

"Can't tell, ma'am. Not with her face painted up like some kinda zombie like that. She looks young, though. I might be able to identify her after Nancy gets her cleaned up."

"You didn't touch anything, did you, Dionne?"

"No, ma'am. I know better'n that. Nobody touches voodoo altars 'cause they might get cursed."

"Who found the body?"

"Don't know. Desk got in an anonymous call to check out this house for a possible homicide. Gave pretty good directions, too. Used a burn phone so there was no trace."

"Are those the exact words the caller used? Told you to check for a possible homicide?"

"Yes, ma'am. That's what dispatch told me."

"That sounds like somebody in law enforcement. Did they get the voice on tape?"

"Operators at 911's got it, if you wanna listen to it, but they said it was muffled and hard to understand."

"Thank you, Officer. You observe anything suspicious at the scene when you first got out here?"

"No. No tire tracks except for one that led down to the boat. Looked like an SUV of some kind."

"That's probably my Range Rover. We'll get casts made, though."

"You got a Range Rover?" Dionne said. He gave an appreciative whistle, impressed, to be sure.

"It belongs to a friend of mine." That would be Black, of course. He just loved big powerful toys, and he loved her to have them, too. And as an extra wow factor, he had fitted her fully equipped SUV with every tracking device known to man, as he had on her phone and computer and the St. Michael's medal she always wore around her neck. In the past, he'd had trouble finding her on occasions when she really needed finding so he no longer took any chances. So the bells and whistles on her vehicles and personal property suited her just fine. There were times when she definitely wanted him to locate her, and the faster, the better.

"You did bring your cameras, right, Nancy?"

"Yeah, but I better call in the whole team and get them out here quick. This scene is going to be a nightmare to process. I don't like this voodoo stuff, either. It scares me, and I'm not afraid to say so. Zee, what does that design in the cornmeal mean?"

Zee shrugged, and nobody else volunteered the information, so Claire knelt in front of the victim while Nancy got out her camera equipment and started filming their every move. She stared at the etchings in the cornmeal, probably drawn with a finger or some kind of stick. Could've even been a knife.

"Okay, this looks like two snakes to me. Drawn upright in vertical positions with large loops at the end of the tails. Look here, at the top. They've got heads with fangs coming out. And this looks like stars, or asterisks, maybe, in between them. And what's that? A plus sign on the far right. See it? Or maybe it's a cross?"

Claire looked up at Zee, who still looked repulsed by the whole thing.

"So what's going on here, Zee?"

Zee shrugged again. "Don't ask me, but Mama Lulu's gonna know how to decipher all this ritual stuff. It probably represents a Loa. That's a voodoo deity. I don't really know much about voodoo shit, and I don't think I wanna know."

"Well, I want to know." Claire stood up. Great, now they had to deal with a *voodoo* killer, for God's sake. What next? A zombie running out of the woods with a machete? She stared down at the body and realized that the poor woman in front of them might very well have been mutilated and murdered while Claire slept peacefully on the houseboat not even thirty yards downhill on the bayou's bank. Could that even be possible? How could he have gotten the victim into the house without Claire hearing anything? Had he come in through the woods surrounding the house? Claire definitely would have heard any vehicle or boat approaching anywhere near the property, and she was a light sleeper. Surely the crime had been committed when she wasn't there.

Zee was obviously thinking the same thing. "You've been stayin' down in that houseboat at night, right, Claire? You sure you didn't see nothin' or hear nothin'?"

"Like I said, nothing out of the ordinary. I've spent quite a few nights here, and there's no way I wouldn't have heard somebody wandering around up here. It's so quiet—nothing but crickets and frogs and an occasional boat."

"He could've done her and set all this up during the day when you were working. When was the last time you came inside the house?" Nancy said, focusing her camera and snapping still shots.

"Black and I came out here once right after we moved to New Orleans. We came in the house then, but I haven't been inside again since I've been staying out here."

"You can stay with me until he gets back, if you want," Nancy offered. "What's your connection with these people, anyway?"

Claire really didn't want to get into that part of her personal past, but this time she was going to have to. "I lived here for a while when I was young. It still belongs to the same family. We visited them at the restaurant on their boat, the *Bayou Blue*, and they said I could use the houseboat anytime I wanted. So I took them up on it. As far as I know, nobody else ever comes out here."

Nancy said, "Oh, I love the *Bayou Blue*. Especially the Cajun Grill up on the second deck."

Not wanting to go any further into her connection with the LeFevres family, Claire changed the subject. "How long do you think she's been dead, Nancy?"

"I'd say several days, maybe less. It's hard to tell. I'll have to do the autopsy to get you anything definitive. There's no obvious cause of death. It could be strangulation. Or, she could have a fatal wound hidden under that creepy robe she's got on."

"Zee, get more officers out here ASAP. I want this entire property grid searched, all the way out to the road."

"You got it." Zee quickly dialed up another detective and told him to bring out his team and a retrieval unit.

As soon as he hung up, Claire said, "Zee, I don't know anything about voodoo rituals, but this looks to me like some kind of sacrifice."

"Could be. I've seen pictures kinda like this."

Claire jumped on that. "You've seen altars like this? With dead bodies?"

"No, just the altars. No dead bodies."

"Give us a little bit of background on voodoo so we'll know what we're dealing with."

"Okay, but Mama Lulu can tell you more. It's kinda a mixture of African religions and Christianity. See the crucifix there? And the pictures of the Holy Mother? And those bottles probably have spells and potions in them. I doubt it's a real voodoo priest or priestess who did this. Might be somebody who wants us to think it is, though."

"Why?"

"Because of the way the face is painted up. That's meant to create fear. Some voodoo priests paint themselves up to look like skeletons for their ceremonies. Some do it to look like zombies. That's a big part of voodoo, or it used to be. I dunno. Like I said, I'm no expert on this kinda stuff. I stay away from it."

"So things like this aren't prevalent around here anymore?"

"Not dead bodies on altars. But people still practice voodoo, and they take it serious, too. It's a religion to them, and nothin' to joke about. There's a bunch of voodoo shops over in the French Quarter, too. Not too far from where you and Nick live. Haven't you been in any?"

"No, I haven't. Guess I'll check them out now, though."

"Mama Lulu's the one we need to talk to," Zee said again.

"And we will, but right now we need to figure out who this woman is." She looked at Dionne again. "Has anybody called in a missing person?"

"Not since I came on this morning. If she's from out here on this bayou, we'll hear about it soon enough."

"Nancy, do you have a portable fingerprinter?"

"Yep, right here. Got it into the budget last year. Let me finish with my shots, and we'll see if we can get us a good one. Her skin looks pretty rough in some places. We'll see."

A short time later, they heard a car approaching. Zee said, "Here comes Saucy and the guys. They made good time."

That would be Ron Saucier. Everybody at the office called him Saucy. But in her opinion, nobody on God's green earth was less saucy than he was. In fact, she bet ten words hadn't come out of his mouth since she'd been in the parish. According to Zee, Sheriff Russ Friedewald had brought him into the office about eighteen months ago, without telling anybody much about him, but had tacitly let everybody know that the where, what, and why of his hiring was nobody's business. Claire decided they must have been old friends. She did figure Saucier had been a sailor because he usually wore short sleeves, and she'd seen the anchor tattoo on the inside of his left arm.

The only other thing she knew about him was that on his lunch hour, he took a sack lunch across the street from the office and sat alone in the city cemetery. Every day, the exact same thing. Bizarre, to be sure. Someday she was going to walk over there and see whose grave he sat and stared at for so long.

A minute later, Saucier walked into the room. Funny thing was, she found the guy strangely attractive, *strangely* being the operative word. He was tall and looked to be in his mid-forties, maybe even in his fifties, with graying blond hair in a buzz cut, his eyes usually hidden by aviator sunglasses, and his face weathered by lots of sun exposure. He looked like retired military, a mystery man, to be sure. Today he had on a camouflage T-shirt and matching utility pants.

"What d'we got?" he said, staring down at the corpse. He squatted down beside the altar, and she saw a long and ugly scar down the side of his neck. It looked almost as if his throat had been slashed from ear to ear. Can't get more mysterious than that. He had some kind of interesting past all right, one nobody knew anything about, and they were all afraid to ask.

"Voodoo?" he asked, looking sidelong up at Claire.

"That's what Zee says. Or, could be a very good fake."

"True, they don't usually have dead bodies on them. This looks like somebody wants us to experience a bit of drama. You live on that boat down there, right?"

Claire wondered how he knew that. "I've been staying out here some."

"And this happened right under your nose?"

Claire frowned. "Yeah, I guess it did. How'd you know I've been out here?"

"I saw your car when I was frog giggin' the other night. I've got a cabin downstream a ways." He stopped, actually grinned up at her. Yes, he had a nice smile, but it was the first one she'd seen. "I heard you playing your violin the other night."

Well, that was embarrassing. Even more than that, she was shocked at his new Chatty Cathy routine. "You could hear me?"

"Clear as a bell. I'm just about a mile downstream. The music just floated down over the bayou like an angel's song."

Claire and Nancy exchanged startled glances. Good grief, that sentence had to total ten or twenty words. That was a record for Saucier. Not to mention that he had even waxed poetic. She had never heard him say so much. Maybe voodoo altars got him all revved up and made him spout iambic pentameter.

"Well, hope I didn't keep you awake. I was out on the upper deck looking at the stars and picked up an old fiddle I found on the boat." *Bored and missing Black like crazy*, she added to herself.

"You've got to be professionally trained, right?"

"Oh, God, no. Learned when I was young, had to practice a lot, but I haven't played for years until recently."

"Didn't sound like you were out of practice." Saucier looked up at her, his sunglasses now pushed atop of his head. His eyes were vivid blue with very dark lashes. She'd never seen them before. "I actually got out of bed and sat on the porch where I could hear you better. What was it? Violin Concerto in E Minor, right? Mendelssohn? I think that's probably the most exquisite violin piece ever composed. And you played it so hauntingly and beautifully that I actually got choked up."

Exquisite? Haunting? Choked up? Good God, this guy was definitely more than met the eye. Maybe he'd never said much until now, but he knew his classical music.

However, Saucier was evidently finished comparing notes on violin music. He said, "Okay, what'd you know so far?"

Back to harsh reality. Dave Mancini and Eric Sanders showed up and tramped into the room. Both were patrol officers that she'd only met once, right after she'd joined up. Dave Mancini was young and green, apparently just out of the academy. He seemed like a serious guy, never smiled, rarely spoke, just listened and learned. Eric Sanders she'd met once and never wanted to meet again. He was a real loud and obnoxious motormouth type. He was tall, with rusty hair in a flat top and wire-rimmed glasses—smarter than smart, especially with computers, but subzero with the social skills.

"Okay, Nancy, let's finish up and try to get her fingerprints."

Nancy had already filmed the video, and she handed the camera to Mancini and told him to continue filming. After she took a couple more photographs of the altar from different angles, she knelt and lifted up the sleeves of the velvet gown and found the woman's hands. They were bound together tightly with black duct tape, the fingers entwined in a prayerful position. Something had been placed in them, making it look almost as if she held a bouquet of flowers. They watched Nancy snap several pictures of the hands and then pull the fingers off the object.

"Oh, my God, Claire, it's a voodoo doll." She stared down at it and then up at Claire, an awful expression overtaking her face. "And I think it's supposed to be you."

Everybody looked at Claire, and then down at the doll in Nancy's gloved hands. Something about the horrified looks on their faces bothered Claire. Go figure. But this was a superstitious group, all born and bred in the bayous, each and every one, and mostly from French Cajun families, to boot. Voodoo dolls upset them en masse. "You're kidding. Let me see it."

Nancy handed the thing over. Frowning, Claire took it, held it flat in her open palm, and examined it closely. It was her all right. No doubt about it. Hard to miss, in fact, since the killer had affixed a close-up shot of her face over the doll's head, one that appeared to have been cut from a newspaper article. It was held in place with two long straight pins, one stuck in each ear. More disturbing, each of her eyes had a big black X marked on it, just like the victim's. And her mouth had black vertical lines that represented stitches. Blond strands of human hair were attached to the doll with what looked like glue, and the killer had colored in her eyes with a light blue marker. Jeez. How sick can you get? And not a little disconcerting, to be sure.

The handmade doll wore dark clothes, and they looked a lot like the black pants and black department polo shirt that Claire wore to work every day. POLICE was printed on the back of the shirt in white letters, and there was a tiny silver badge made out of aluminum foil on the doll's chest, held in place by another pin. There were also pins in each temple, in the heart, in the abdomen, and between the legs. Claire stared it and felt a shudder undulating up from the base of her spine. She forced it down but with not a little difficulty. Okay, she was now officially creeped out to the max, no doubt about it.

Chapter Three

Claire stared down at the voodoo doll in her hands for a moment, and then attempted a stab at humor. "Well, now, I think you might be right, Nancy. This guy knows me from somewhere. Don't think he likes me much, either."

Nobody said a word, certainly didn't laugh, in fact, they were acting as if they were already at her memorial service. Not confidence building, to say the least. Finally, Zee said, "So leavin' the body out here where you happened to be sleeping was not a coincidence."

Nancy jumped up. "You need to get off this case, Claire. Right now. You've been through enough of this kind of crap. This guy is baiting you or warning you off, or both. The sheriff needs to take you off and let the rest of us handle it."

"I don't warn off all that easily. And I don't believe in voodoo."

Zee said, "Don't take this lightly, Claire. Voodoo, either. Looks like this guy's a real lunatic and he's obviously after you."

Claire had to admit that it certainly appeared that way, but that didn't necessarily make it so. One thing she did know for sure, Black was absolutely going to freak out. He was still shaky from the last time a crazy man had stalked her. "Okay, I get it. I've been warned, but that doesn't have to mean this guy's after me personally. It could mean he wants to scare me off this case, just like Nancy said. That's what I think this is all about. I think he did this to scare us. Right now, we need to finish up out here and get her to the morgue."

Everybody continued to stare at her—in a morbid manner, she might add—and nobody looked convinced. In fact, they looked more than a little spooked. But voodoo obviously spoke to their emotions and not in a good way. Claire tried again. "Well, she's out of rigor. Decomp's definitely started. Are the fingertips intact enough, Nancy?"

"Looks like it. I'll give it a try."

They all stood back silently and watched Nancy remove the hand-held device out of her bag and press the victim's forefinger into the slot. The device immediately began scanning law enforcement databases for prints. Claire hoped to hell they got a hit. This case was unsettling, by design, she felt, and the sooner they got the guy, the better they'd all feel. And with this voodoo craziness going on, the newspapers would have a field day. Nobody said anything, just stared at the victim's pitiful painted and stitched-up face. Claire put the doll down on a sheet of evidence paper and tried not to look at it again.

This poor woman had been killed while Claire lay in her bed and slept like a baby. Or maybe when she was playing the violin and waking up Saucier. Maybe the killer had watched her from the window of this very room. A chill rippled across her heart and raised goose bumps down both her arms. *C'mon, get a grip*, she told herself.

Well now, Black had wanted to get her away from the lake so she wouldn't run into any cases like this one. Wrong. Now she was smack dab in the middle of a psychopath's murder scene, and a scarier one than usual. Okay, maybe what Black didn't know wouldn't hurt him. But the thought of having to lie to him went against her grain. One thing she couldn't stand in a relationship was lying. She and Black didn't lie to each other. They were honest, told it the way it was, and gave each other the freedom to do whatever they wanted whenever they wanted, without having to report in.

Putting Black's probable intense overreaction to this new development out of her mind, she tried to think it through. At first glance, she had figured the killer had decided the old house was abandoned and a good place for him to play his deadly games. When her car wasn't there, it certainly looked abandoned. But the houseboat was in good repair and maybe was sometimes used by the LeFevres. Surely the perpetrator had checked all that out before choosing the place. No, it was more likely that this guy knew her, or about her, and it was pretty much a given that he didn't like her snooping around the bayous and getting in his way.

But when had he placed the body on the altar? Some afternoon before she got off work? Or while she slept? That idea was unsettling. Nope, some wacko creeping around and stitching eyes closed with thread while she was snoozing peacefully yards away did not sit well with her. Whatever the reason, this guy wanted her to find the body and the doll. Hell, he was probably the one who had called it in anonymously. *Why me though?* Now that was the pertinent question.

Since everybody else remained hushed, seemingly in a state of tension and dread, Claire didn't say anything, either. At least, they were all serious now. Time to look at things objectively. Okay, they had a voodoo altar, which was rather ridiculous in itself. But she wasn't a Cajun or superstitious or easily terrified. They were. Black was, too, where she was concerned. So that meant he really was going to raise hell. Maybe she should be terrified. But she wasn't, not yet, and she wasn't a basket case, which was a step in the right direction if she intended to run this case.

Okay, there were plenty of candles. Many in glass containers, and that meant possible latent fingerprints. One had the Virgin Mary holding the Baby Jesus. Another had a large cross, another the nativity scene with the star in the east. There had to be ten or twenty of them. All different sizes and shapes. The killer had to tote all this stuff into the house and that wouldn't have been easy. Then again, he probably had all the time in the world, as remote as this property was. That was what she used to like about the houseboat, but she wasn't so sure about that anymore. Okay, she did know that New Orleans and its environs were known for voodoo. She didn't know all the distinctions yet, but she had a feeling she was going to be an expert on everything about that particular religion, and very soon.

"Got her," said Nancy, gazing down at the portable device. "Her name's Madonna Christien. The address is on Carondelet Street. Arrested for prostitution and possession and spent time in NOPD lockup about a year ago. Here's her picture."

Claire took the device and stared down at how the victim had looked before the killer had painted her face and sewn up her facial orifices. She had been a pretty young girl with long dark hair and a heart-shaped face. One who now would never grow old. Claire sighed and handed the device to Zee. He examined the face, and then handed it off to Saucier and the others. Nobody had ever seen her before.

Claire said, "All right, Nancy, let's try to lay her out on her back and get her bagged. Are you done with the photos?"

"Yeah. The rest of my team ought to be here any minute. They usually make good time."

"Ron, you and Zee see if you can get her down on the ground without disrupting the stuff on the altar. I want everything in this room dusted for prints, everything in the whole house. This guy is seriously disturbed. We've got to get him quick before he kills again. And I think he will. He's too dramatic with his crime scenes not to. He wants to play with us, or he would've thrown her to the alligators. That's probably why he put my face on that doll, because I've been in the newspapers lately. He wants the media to pick it up and run with it. So none of us tells anybody the details of this crime scene, got it? Nobody. I'll talk to the sheriff myself."

They all nodded but still looked worried. Saucy and Zee got hold of the victim's arms and legs and managed to get her stretched out on the floor. She looked very small, probably not much over five feet tall. Nancy unzipped the front of the velvet robe and a strong, caustic smell wafted up to them. Bleach, without a doubt. The corpse was completely nude underneath, her skin mottled dark and Claire winced when she saw the condition of the body. "Looks like the killer washed her up pretty good before he dressed her."

Zee gave a low whistle. "Lord God, look at that gal's ankles, see those bruises. He tied her up nice and tight, all right, and then he beat the holy hell outta her."

Rage shot up, boiling Claire's blood at what had been done to the young girl. She was used to seeing dead bodies, true, had seen plenty during her years at LAPD and more recently up at the lake. But this woman had suffered torture before the killer had finished her off and made her the star attraction of his scary death altar. He had taken his time and terrorized her, probably for hours. And now he had made it all about Claire with that personalized voodoo doll meant to frighten her away.

"I think I just heard your people drive up, Nancy."

"Good."

Zee was looking at the body and shaking his head. Claire tried to see it purely as evidence rather than the corpse of what once had been a healthy, vital, lovely young girl.

Nancy said, "If it's okay with you, Claire, I'd rather get her back to the morgue before I remove the robe. I don't want to lose any trace evidence inside it."

Claire said, "Yeah, you're right. Look at those cuts and bruises. They're deep and black and brutal and all over the body. No way did he kill her here. There would be blood spatter all over the place. He cleaned her up some, I think, so he could set her up out here and get the most shock factor out of us when we discovered her. Ron, you and Eric, check out this house for footprints. There's dust everywhere in here. Outside, too. It rained night before last, so we might get something. Nancy, I want the houseboat dusted, too. If he was ever on there with me, I want to know it."

Nancy nodded. "So you're not going to stay out here anymore, are you?"

"Damn right, I'm not. Somehow this place has lost its appeal. Besides it's a crime scene now." Claire glanced back at Zee. "Any thoughts, Zee?"

"She died hard. He is obviously baitin' you for some reason. This guy has something to do with you, that's what I think. Either he knows you or he wants to know you. Either way, it's not good. But if he wanted to get to you, kill you or kidnap you, he probably would've already tried it. You've been out here alone, at night, with nobody anywhere around. So maybe it's a warnin'. Maybe you're right. Maybe he wants you off the case, or out of here. Maybe it's more to do with this house." He hesitated, looked sheepish. "Could this be about one of those guys you investigated before, you know, those serial killers you got tangled up with?"

Claire shook her head. "Most of them are dead or in jail. It's highly unlikely this is something like that."

Ron Saucier entered the conversation. "Remember, Claire, it was your face that he put on that doll. This has gotta be about you. I hate to say it, but that's what makes the most sense. At least, it does to me."

Nobody said anything else, but all of them knew that was the most likely scenario. "Like Zee said, if he wanted me, he's had plenty of opportunities to get me."

Saucier said, "I live just downstream. I never heard any screams or calls for help. And I would've. Just like I heard your violin. Sounds carry over the bayou."

Claire knelt down again. "Some of these cuts look like teeth marks. Once we isolate suspects, maybe we can get a hit on dental records."

Zee wasn't going to let the Claire-doll issue drop. "Why do you think he put your face on the doll? Why did he put her corpse here? Like you said, if it wasn't about you, he'd just've dumped her body out in the swamp where the gators could feed on her."

"That's what we're going to find out." She looked up as the rest of the forensics team carried their gear into the room. She didn't know many of the criminalists yet, but they all nodded, received their instructions from Nancy, and got right to work. "Okay, let's get the body bagged and downtown. I'm going to touch base with Russ." Claire pulled out her cell phone and hit speed dial for Russ Friedewald's private line.

"Yeah, Detective Morgan? Just heard about this from dispatch. You got a homicide out there?"

"It's a homicide. No doubt about it. I'm looking at the body right now. It's a young woman named Madonna Christien and she's been posed on some kind of voodoo altar."

"Oh, God. Are you serious?"

"Yes, sir."

"Well, that's just great. Especially if the local news gets hold of it. Cause of death determined?"

"Not sure about that yet. Her hands and feet were bound. She's was severely beaten." Claire hesitated. "He sewed her eyes and mouth shut with some kind of heavy-duty thread."

"You sure it's connected with voodoo?"

"Zee and Nancy think so. We're all here and getting ready to bag her. Is that okay with you?"

"Yes, go ahead, but let Nancy oversee it."

"The victim lives in New Orleans. Do we have permission to go up there and search her house?"

"Yes. Put a call in to Rene Bourdain. You know him, don't you?"

"Yes, sir." Rene Bourdain had been Bobby LeFevres's partner at NOPD when Claire lived with Bobby and Kristen, but she hadn't known him all that well and she hadn't seen him since she came back. It would be good to connect with him again, though. He had always been nice to her, way back when.

"Okay, call him. Get permission. See what you can find out. And keep it as quiet as you can."

"Yes, sir." Claire punched off. "Okay, let's take her in. Zee, we need to get over to New Orleans before dark and check out her address. If she is Madonna Christien, we need to notify her next of kin."

Notification of kin was not Claire's idea of fun and games. An entire family was going to be shattered by this. They'd never be the same again after they saw the crime scene pictures of what some monster had done to their baby. She hoped they would elect not to view them.

"Zee, you worked at NOPD, right? Do you know how to get hold of Rene Bourdain? That's who Sheriff Friedewald said to contact. We've got to get permission to search this address."

"Sure, Rene and I are pretty tight. We worked together in narcotics, but now he's headin' up the detectives over there. He's a good guy. He'll get us in."

While Zee moved away and talked to Rene, Claire tried to remember exactly what Rene Bourdain looked like. He had visited the LeFevreses often when she'd lived there, but only a vague recollection of his facial features came rolling up out of that misty memory fog. Which happened a lot since she'd come out of that pesky coma. Black told her that she'd remember most things, but that other memories might never come back. She could think of more than one horrible thing she wished she couldn't remember, but Rene Bourdain didn't meet that criterion. Most everything was coming back, slowly but surely, including that short but happy time she'd spent with the LeFevres family when she was around ten years old.

Zee hung up and turned around. "Rene's gonna meet us there."

Claire turned to Nancy. "You coming back with us or going in with the body?"

"If you'll bring the Tahoe back to the office, I'll go in the van with the body. Better to document the transfer myself."

"Okay, let's go, Zee."

Zee spoke up. "This has gotta be a crime of passion, Claire. Beating her up like that, and all. That's what I think."

"Who knows what motivated this lunatic? Jealousy or revenge, probably. Or maybe, it's just one of those If-I-can't-have-you-nobody-can kinda things. Whatever, I want to get him off the streets."

"Well, if I was you, I sure wouldn't hang around out here by myself anymore. He may be nuts, but I bet he put your face on that doll for some crazy reason."

Claire shrugged. "Yeah, probably. We'll find out soon enough. Nancy, wait until I get to the morgue to do the autopsy, okay?"

She and Zee walked through the house, descended the front porch steps, and headed for Nancy's Tahoe. The midday sun was warm on Claire's hair and felt good after the dark and shadowy chill inside the house. Claire wanted to find this guy, whoever he was, wherever he was. She didn't appreciate him putting her face on that doll or leaving a body in her backyard. She was going to get him, and she was going to keep both her weapons loaded and close at hand. If anything, he had given her a warning to be on the lookout for him. And oh yeah, she was going to heed it.

A Very Scary Man

By the time Malice reached high school, he had honed his skills and had a whole bag of tricks to frighten people out of their wits. He had continued to watch scary television shows and movies. He had learned from some of the mean things said and done in books and comic books, and he dreamed of having his own TV show someday, one where he could make lots of money terrifying people and watching their reactions when they thought they had no escape from a terrible fate. Sometimes, he frightened complete strangers at the mall. He would follow them and see if he couldn't find a moment to slip something alive and nasty into their shopping bags so that when his victim rummaged in them, they might find a big hairy spider he'd caught or a handful of wriggling brown night crawlers.

Women especially hated the worms. It was just so funny to watch. He would follow them and wait on pins and needles for the big finale. Sometimes, they would open their bag or tote for some reason, and they would screech with horror and throw the bag as if it were a poisonous snake. The expressions on their faces were priceless. It was hilarious to watch, and he loved trying to do stuff like that on the sly. He liked the sense of power it gave him. Loved it, in fact. He could make people react, tremble and cry out and curse, but they never knew he was behind it. He would just act like the innocent bystander, just as shocked as the store's clerk or the guy waiting on them in the food court. He was getting really good at his tricks, and the thrill was just getting better and better. He always did it on Friday, and called it Fright Night. It was his favorite time of the week.

After a while, he began to watch shows about serial killers and how they abused and mistreated their victims. Sometimes he even got off on the way they murdered people because they killed them in such bizarre and interesting ways. They had rituals and souvenirs and fetishes and things they liked to do with the bodies. He wanted a dead body so bad he could taste it. So, he began to plan how he could get one. He wondered how it would feel to commit murder. How it would feel to stick one of his mom's big butcher knives into somebody's stomach. Maybe the long, sharp one that she cut up chickens with—that would probably do it. He wondered if he would have to push it in really hard, or if it would just slice the skin open real easy, like cutting into butter. He was pretty sure that he'd have to be fairly strong to do it. Especially if he did a lot of stabbing or carried on with the butchering for a long time.

Finally, he got the chance to try out some of his fantasies. He got himself a girlfriend, one he sort of liked. Her name was Betsy. She was real cute with brown hair and freckles but pretty timid and nervous, too, and easy to frighten. So he started out with all sorts of accidental scares just to warm her up for the big stuff. He planned it carefully, wanting to do it just right, maybe at her house when her parents weren't home. That's when she seemed to be the most nervous, especially when she was alone in her house at night. And her parents liked to go square dancing and to the movies and so forth, so they were gone a lot. Every Tuesday they went down to the parish community center and danced their do-si-dos and all that crap.

One night, after a late football practice, he waited until everybody else was gone, and then he showered and dressed in black clothes like a ninja. He'd seen some kung fu movies and the like, and he knew he'd blend into the shadows when he got into the house. Betsy was home alone. She had begged him to come over so he had told her he'd come by later, right after he was done with football practice. They hadn't had sex yet so he didn't want to scare her too bad too soon and risk her breaking up with him. But he loved her smooth little face and big scaredy-cat brown eyes.

He had gotten her all up and terrified with some bugs and driving too fast and pretending the brakes wouldn't work. She screamed and screamed, and then she'd punched him in the shoulder with her fist when she'd realized that he was lying about the brakes. It was so damn cool. He even liked how she hit him and then fought him some when he tried to console her. He got all excited when she was struggling with him. That was the truth, and he really liked that feeling. He wanted her to fight against him again. He wanted to hold her down and force her to do stuff that he'd always dreamed about doing to a girl.

So he left the stadium, real excited, and drove by the community center to make sure her parents' red Cadillac was still there. It was, so he drove to the woods behind her house and parked in some tall bushes. Then he crept through the darkness to her backyard. He found himself a little nervous, too, because if he got caught, they'd kick him off the football team, and he was really good and was going to win a scholarship to Tulane University. And he liked how all the people at school clapped him on the back and said things about his nice passes or his touchdown runs. The girls were all over him and wanted to wear his letter jacket, but he liked it too much to let anybody else wear it, or even try it on.

Once he got into her backyard, the family's beagle, named Buddy, smelled him right off and barked a little bit. But once Malice tossed him an open package of Oscar Mayer cheesy hot dogs and patted his head, the pooch ignored him and chowed down big time. So he moved stealthily and hunkered down under the family room window. Betsy was sitting inside on the couch, studying her algebra book. She was really smart in math, and helped him with his homework, which was another reason he liked her. But he didn't love her. He loved making her scream, and that was about it.

After slipping his black ski mask over his head and adjusting the eye holes, he pulled out the butcher knife he'd brought and got the back door key from under the flower pot on the steps. People were just so stupid to leave keys around like that. He would never do that, and he didn't let his mom do it, either. He let himself inside, very quiet in his black sneakers. His girlfriend had the stereo on really loud, playing a song by the Rolling Stones. He liked those guys. They always had girls hanging all over them, like Betsy liked to do with him, but then when he tried something with her, she'd always push him away, like he was terrible for wanting to have sex with her. He grinned. She wasn't going to push him away this time, no way.

He approached her from the dining room, tiptoeing up behind her, not making a single sound. When he got right behind the sofa, he grinned to himself, and then he whispered her name in a low, threatening growl. When Betsy whirled around, she got that look on her face for a split second, the one that turned him on so much. It did this time, too. Then she screamed bloody murder and threw her book at him and headed for the front door. Very agile and athletic, he jumped over the couch after her and caught her before she could get out of the room. She fought him desperately, but he lifted weights and outweighed her by at least eighty or ninety pounds. She wasn't all that hard to subdue, and he got her down and held both her hands over her head against the floor and sat on her stomach. She struggled and yelled, and then he hit her in the face. He hadn't really planned to do that, but he did like it. Blood spurted from her nose. She lay still a moment, stunned, but then she started fighting again and clawing at his face with her long red nails. To his shock, she was pretty strong in her terror and somehow managed to pull off his mask.

"You? What are you doing? Stop right now and get off me! Why are you doing this to me? Why? Stop it!" She kept yelling the same things over and over, sobbing now, squirming around under him and getting him all excited. He loved it, loved her fear and disappointment, and the way she ended up begging him to stop.

But now he was in a conundrum, to be sure. She was spitting mad, working herself into a full-fledged rage, still trying to scratch his eyes out, really, truly furious that it was him doing this to her. He couldn't let her tell on him, or he'd lose his scholarship. He just couldn't do that. His parents didn't have the money to send him where he wanted to go. He didn't have a choice now, and he had always wanted to kill somebody, now hadn't he? He wanted to see the light gradually go out of her eyes like it did in the movies.

So he got his knees over her arms and held them down. He put one hand around her neck and he put the point of the knife against her throat. Betsy lay very still then, her eyes wide and afraid, so he put down the knife and pressed both thumbs on her windpipe. That stopped all the yelling, and it got real quiet real quick, except for her gasping and the sound of her heels beating against the floor.

While she suffocated, he got to thinking about all the good times they'd had, at the school dances, and how pretty she'd looked in that short pink formal dress at last year's prom and how she'd helped him cheat his way to a ninety-six on his last math test. She wasn't so bad; maybe he ought to kill somebody else the first time. So he let up, and then she tried to claw his face and called him some real bad names. Then he got so angry that he grabbed the knife and just thrust it down into the side of her throat. He must've hit an artery because blood spurted out everywhere, all over him and the wall and the rug. He scrambled away from her and stood up, but within minutes, she was dead. He had killed her, when he hadn't really planned to, and he hadn't gotten to take her virginity, either, damn it.

Then he ran, outside and through the woods. He stopped at the edge of a little pond and washed himself clean of the blood on his hands and face. But it was all over his clothes so he pulled them off until he wore only gym shorts and a T-shirt. Trembling with fear and excitement and sexual gratification, he put the bloody clothes in a Wal-Mart plastic bag and pitched it into a Dumpster behind a garage. Then he went home, went straight to bed, and lay there reliving the whole thing, over and over, and every time he got more and more aroused. Oh, yeah, killing was fun. Killing was his thing, all right. Maybe he ought to be an assassin or a secret agent. Hone his kills, like James Bond. Kill his victims for money or patriotism. Yeah, that would be his perfect profession, a secret job where he could earn lots of money. He lay awake a long time, wondering how he could make it work, because that's what he was going to do with his life. Scare people, then kill them and watch them die. God, he was so excited that he could barely catch his breath.

Chapter Four

Fortunately, Madonna Christien's home address was not hard to find. In fact, it wasn't all that far from the cozy mansion that Claire shared with Black in the French Quarter. There were several apartment buildings on Carondelet Street, but the one they sought sat near the intersection of Carondelet and Gravier with a narrow alley running behind it. The tarmac was in disrepair, grass struggling up between cracks and potholes here and there, but most buildings lining the back alley were in fairly good shape.

Madonna Christien's home looked considerably better than its neighbors. Painted pale yellow with white shutters, it was neat and clean and deserted. The apartment was on the second floor, but had a large enclosed carport space underneath at ground level. A balcony faced the alley, but Claire couldn't see Christien's front door. There was an interior stair that led to a landing unseen from the street.

Various clay pots filled with wilting red geraniums sat on the wide balcony railing. Several more sat on the floor of the deck. A striped yellow cat with a bell on his collar sat on the banister and stared at them with an utterly bored expression. One pot, the largest, lay in pieces in the alley in front of a new-model white Ram truck.

Zee said, "There's Rene. Right on time."

As they pulled up behind the truck, a man got out and strode back to them. He looked about five feet nine or ten, probably a little bit taller than Claire, and he was ruggedly handsome, with the dark hair and eyes of Louisiana Cajuns. He looked a little different from how she remembered. When Zee rolled down his window, Bourdain leaned in, unsmiling and all business.

"Hey, Zee, my man, how you doin'? Been a while, eh?"

"Yeah, you lookin' good as usual, Lieutenant. Sorry you had to come over here and miss the second half of the game."

"You sure this here's your victim's address?"

Claire decided to get things on the road. "We're not certain about much of anything at this point. This's the address we found when we identified the body with prints, but the victim's face was painted up. It looks like the same woman."

For the first time, Bourdain bent down low enough to look at her through the open window. Claire watched his face register surprise, and then he stared at her, as if speechless. "Annie? That you, *chère*?"

Oh, God, Claire thought. He remembered her better than she remembered him. She did not like him using her birth name. It just brought up a lot of unpleasant questions about her past.

"Hi, Rene. I'm surprised that you recognized me. It's been a long time." Claire got out of the car and gave him the obligatory smile, but her mind remained on the case.

"Oh, yeah, I heard you was down here with that Dr. Black fella. Hell, you're pretty near famous now."

"Not really. Who told you I was here?"

"Why, I heard tell from Luc and Clyde and the boys over on the *Bayou Blue*. I go there to play poker and listen to them play zydeco, and they said that our little Annie gal and Nick Black came in and was talkin' 'bout old times when you stayed down there on the bayou with Bobby and Kristen."

"I don't go by Annie anymore," she told him pointedly, but kept the courteous smile. She didn't want to be rude, but she didn't want to discuss any of this in front of Zee, either. She hoped Rene got the message. "It's Claire Morgan now, Rene. Please don't ask me why, that's way too long a story. Right now, I'm working with Zee down in Lafourche Parish."

"Lord have mercy, little Annie, or Claire, I guess. Look at you, girl, all grown up and pretty as a picture, too, with all that blond hair and those big blue eyes of yours. I'd a known you anywhere. Even with you bein' a grown woman now."

Claire sucked in a breath and looked him straight in the eyes. She liked the guy, but the last thing she wanted was to reminisce about the old days. "Well, it's good to see you, too. Good to see all the LeFevreses, but right now, we're really anxious to get inside and take a look around. This woman died real hard, Rene, and we want her killer. You can let us inside, right?"

Interesting expressions flitted across Bourdain's face. He appeared highly expressive and easy to read. But his wide grin didn't falter. He was a nice-looking man, and he had been good to her once upon a time. "Sure thing, no problem. The TV folks are callin' you a super detective, that true? Wanna come over and join us at the NOPD? We sure could use you."

"I'm hardly that. I just got involved in a couple of newsworthy crimes."

"Well, Luc and Clyde and the rest of us are sure glad you're back."

But there was one person that Claire was interested in. "What about Gabe? I haven't run into him yet. He still live around here?"

"Ah, Gabe. No, no, he went bad from what I hear. Got himself into drugs and spent some time in prison. You know, just went down the wrong path."

Zee was just standing there, looking from one to the other, obviously surprised about their past relationship.

"Zee, Rene's a friend of the family I lived with down here for a while."

Rene nodded. "Yeah, Bobby LeFevres was his name, and a better officer you'd never find."

"Yeah?" said Zee. "Didn't know that."

"Bobby and I both rode patrol here in the city. Down in Lower Ninth, mostly."

"Luc says they both died a long time ago," Claire said. "I was sorry to hear it. He and Kristen were really good to me back then."

"Yeah, I still miss them. He was a good friend and a good cop."

Okay, enough of his sentimental drive down memory lane. Claire was eager to get inside and find something that could help them. On the other hand, they were in Rene's jurisdiction and had to play his game, no matter how chatty he wanted to be.

"Bobby and Kristen were just sick when Family Services wouldn't let you stay with them. They tried to get you back legally, but it didn't go down that way."

Claire began to get annoyed. She didn't want to have this conversation and had told him as much. Most of her childhood years had not been pleasant, and a lot of it was fuzzy now, anyway. The LeFevreses had been the bright spot. They'd treated her like a daughter. It had broken her heart when she had been forced to leave them, especially their son, Gabriel. "Okay, Rene, enough about me. Let's go in. It's gonna be dark soon."

"Okay, good enough. Guess what? I already found the key. Right over there on a hook behind the first step."

"Then let's do it."

Rene Bourdain took the lead. Zee gave Claire a questioning glance as they followed him up the inside steps. Few people knew about the things she'd suffered during the years when she'd endured so many foster families, not even Black, and that's the way she wanted to keep it. Her own personal little childhood hell, but it was long over.

The steps were neatly repaired and covered with a fresh coat of gray paint. Claire took in everything outside, searching for signs of struggle or forced entry, but saw nothing out of the ordinary. Rene opened the screen door and tried the handle. The steel front door was painted indigo blue and was locked up tight. He glanced back at Claire. "I can't believe it's really you, Annie. After all this time. God sure does work in mysterious ways."

Feeling like she was lost in an episode of *Lost*, Claire strove to keep things professional. "Think we ought to knock first, Bourdain? Just in case somebody's home?"

"Oh, c'mon now, *chère*. It's Rene to you, always." Grinning, he tapped on the door with one knuckle, and they all waited. No answer. No sound of running feet going out the back door, either, or of a shotgun being ratcheted. All good signs, under the circumstances. They waited some more. Rene smiled at her until she felt distinctly uncomfortable.

Jeez, what was with this guy? He was looking her over like a blue-ribbon steer, for God's sake. She stayed in serious-as-sin business mode and hoped he would kiss the nostalgia good-bye and just get down to the business at hand. "Looks to me like everything's pretty normal. No newspapers piled up. Except for the broken flower pot out in the alley, Madonna Christien kept a tidy place."

"True, but never can tell what goes on behind closed doors." Bourdain knocked again, harder this time. He called out, "NOPD. Open up."

No answer. When Bourdain inserted the key, it turned easily, and the door swung open. He called out again and was met with dead silence. He looked back at them and said, "You want me to wait outside while you clear the place?"

"Whatever you wanna do, Rene. We just appreciate you comin'." That was Zee, the grateful, polite detective, eager to please.

They stepped inside the foyer and glanced around. Directly in front of them, white-draped French doors were closed. Zee and Claire both pulled their weapons, just to be on the safe side. Perhaps still a bit unsettled by all those big black stitches on the victim's face. Rene Bourdain didn't bother. Let them shoot it out all they wanted; he'd just wait outside where it was safe. The front hall led off to their left, and Claire could see the room at the far end. The open door revealed a white iron bed with white bedding. It was barely visible in the interior gloom.

Rene said, "This's your case, detectives. I'm not gonna interfere. Have at it. I'll wait right here."

What is he, anyway, a U.N. Observer? Claire thought, but she pulled out some latex gloves and handed a pair to Zee. They snapped them on, stepped once more into matching paper crime scene booties. "Zee, you take the bedrooms down this hallway. I'll check out the back of the house."

Zee moved off down the hallway, and Claire opened the French doors and stepped inside what appeared to be Madonna Christien's living room. On the far wall, an undraped expanse of plate-glass windows slanted late-afternoon sunlight across the interior. The floorboards were painted white, as were the walls. Except that now there was blood spattered all over everything. Somehow Claire had expected to find neatness and order inside the apartment, just like there was outside, but was she ever wrong. There had been one hell of a struggle inside that room, violent and lengthy and bloody, one that had left pretty much anything not nailed down overturned, broken, or shattered all over the floor.

Sidestepping the mess, Claire edged around the perimeter of the room, weapon out in front, finger alongside the trigger, avoiding pools of dried blood. She was very wary now, although her gut told her that whoever had been there was long gone with the victim in tow and a healthy supply of black and white paint and sewing thread and religious candles. Quickly, she cleared the kitchen and other rooms for more victims or a psychopath holding a voodoo doll with her face on it. After she was satisfied that they were alone in the apartment, she sidestepped her way back through the living room, thinking it looked as if Edward Cullen, that teenage vampire, had stopped lusting after Bella Swan long enough to have himself a hell of a blood feast. She hadn't read those books, of course, but Zee and Nancy had filled her in on every single detail on every single page.

Zee met her outside the French doors. "Neat as a pin in the bed-rooms."

"Look in here, Zee. Madonna Christien was murdered right in there, I'd bet my badge on it."

Bourdain took a careful step inside the living room. "Christ almighty," he breathed out. "Maybe I should bring in my forensics team to sweep this scene? Nancy's probably gonna have her hands full down there at Thibodaux by the sound of it, both with your victim and the old LeFevres place. It'd be quicker, too, if we take over at this end."

Claire considered his offer and looked at Zee for his take. He lifted a careless shoulder and nodded. So she said, "Okay, call them in. There's got to be a ton of trace evidence in here. Look at the blood. It's all over the place."

Rene Bourdain moved back out into the front hall, his cell phone against his ear. "Okay, Zee, let's look around and see what we can turn up. We can't move anything until the photographer shoots this place."

There was a white rolltop desk in front of the windows. The top was up, and a handful of unopened mail was scattered around. Seemed like somebody had already rifled through the letters. Looking for what? Claire leaned down and read the print on the top envelope. "This's a gas bill. Sent to Madonna Christien at this address. She lives here, all right."

Claire found a light switch and flipped it on. The overhead fan with blades shaped like palmetto leaves slowly started revolving, and the lights flared on in a four-pronged light fixture. Several lamps were overturned and broken, the debris scattered around on the floor. A potted palm was lying on its side with dirt spilled all around it, the huge clay pot cracked open. There was a square cocktail table, the glass top cobwebbed with cracks that streaked down to the opposite end.

"Looks like the perpetrator slammed her head down on this glass top. See the impact point, Zee, the starburst thing? I think he choked her unconscious right there on that table and took her somewhere else and painted the body."

Zee squatted and examined the tabletop. "Blood's accumulated down inside the hairline cracks. Lots more leaked down underneath and stained the rug."

Claire took a closer look. The blood in the cracks looked like a scarlet spiderweb lying on top of the table, and it had soaked into the white shag rug in a round puddle the size of a basketball. It was congealed now and looked like sticky black tar. Madonna Christien's all-white décor made the blood spatter easy to detect. Claire found some long dark strands of hair caught in the cracks. "Looks like her hair, Zee. Hopefully, the killer left his DNA somewhere in all this mess. Notice that everything's white in here?"

"Yeah, just like her gown and candles and everything else on that altar." He stood up and looked around. "I think he slammed her up against that wall over there, too. See how the blood ran down to the floor in those little rivulets. Lord have mercy. She suffered some serious pain before she died. Nancy's gonna find all kind of injuries on the body."

Claire moved to the smear of blood. "It's about waist high. Maybe he bent her over and rammed her head into the wall."

"That would've stunned her, if she was still puttin' up a fight. And she was, by the looks of it." Zee frowned. "He showed no mercy, that's for damn sure."

Rene Bourdain was back. "They've got a unit on the way. Want us to take over the whole case? Just say the word, and we'll be glad to."

Claire wasn't about to do that. She had seen the victim's injuries. She wanted this guy herself. The murder scene was inside NOPD's jurisdiction, but they'd found the body in Lafourche Parish. They could cooperate, but no way was Bourdain taking over. "We can handle it. Thanks, anyway. I think he murdered her here, but he took her down our way to dump her. Sheriff Friedewald doesn't appreciate that. We'll get him."

Bourdain's cell phone rang, and he took it, grimaced with annoyance, and walked back out to the foyer. Zee was on his hands and knees looking at a single red silk slipper with a five-inch spiked heel. The matching one lay atop the pillows of a black-and-white checkered couch. "Looks like she was kickin' and fightin' hard. Maybe he's got some injuries, too."

Claire nodded. "No evidence of forced entry. She must've let him in. If she knew him, it's going to help us find him."

"Got to be a boyfriend or lover. And I don't think it's random, or a robbery gone wrong, either."

"She might have a jealous ex-husband with a key, something like that."

"All true, except it doesn't explain that voodoo doll with your face on it."

Claire ignored that. She leaned down beside the couch and found a hurricane glass lying on its side. She recognized it as a souvenir from Pat O'Briens, a popular bar in the French Quarter. She and Black had spent an evening there, just before he'd left for London. "She was drinking with him, Zee. I bet we've got his prints all over that glass."

"So he beat her unconscious, took her down those stairs outside. Nobody would've seen him leave if he parked under the house."

Claire sighed and nodded agreement. This was quickly turning into a really bad case, and she had an equally bad feeling that it was only going to get worse.

Chapter Five

Stepping carefully around the overturned furniture and broken lamps, Claire and Zee progressed into Madonna Christien's kitchen and found it neat and clean, except for one wine bottle lying on the floor in front of a stainless steel refrigerator. Its contents had drained out into a big puddle in the shape of Florida with part of the panhandle under the white cabinet. Off the kitchen, they found a bathroom that had another door leading into the master bedroom. It had one of the new claw-foot standing tubs built to look old, still full of perfumed water. Two fluffy white towels were folded neatly on a red velvet bench beside it. Madonna Christien had probably been getting ready to bathe when the killer showed up, but the bathroom itself looked untouched. There was no bathrobe in sight, which Claire found unusual. Claire always had one ready and close enough to grab. Most women did. There was a white hairbrush on the sink, alongside a small travel hair dryer and a bottle of Garnier Extra-Hold Mousse.

"Maybe she was in the bath and the guy rang the doorbell. She got out and let him in. She had to know him, Zee."

"Yeah, everything was fine at first. They had a drink together out of those hurricanes, talked some. Then something went down wrong, and the guy flipped out."

"Sounds reasonable."

There were two small closets inside the bathroom. Although she'd checked them out earlier, she hadn't turned on the interior lights, just checked for somebody hiding inside. So, when she turned on the switch, she found Madonna Christien's personal wardrobe.

Claire pulled out a couple of hangers and found that Madonna dressed like a hooker, except maybe a mite kinkier. "Look here, Zee, black leather and spiked collars and fishnet hose. Madonna was a hooker, all right."

"Lemme see." Zee came off overeager, but Claire stepped aside and let him scrape back the hangers one at a time. "This stuff has dominatrix written all over it. See any whips or ball gags? She's a prostitute, all right, but I'd say more of a call girl, maybe. Hope she's got a little black book with all her johns listed for us."

"Don't hold your breath, Zee. If she had one, it's probably somewhere in a safety deposit box." Claire pulled open a drawer in a small antique white bureau on one side of the closet and found neat stacks of pricey thong underwear and lace teddies, most of which looked like "come hither, lover boy" garb. "Could be a porn connection. Looks like she had money to spend."

Zee had moved on to the other closet. "Whoa, look at this. Madonna's into a bit of voodoo, too."

Claire joined him at the door. With the light on, she could see that the altar tucked in the back was almost identical to the crime scene. Lots of candles, skulls, and pictures of Catholic saints and angels. Except for one difference: no body. Instead, Madonna had about a hundred pictures of the same guy. "Who's that, Zee? You know him?"

"That's Jack Holliday. He's the guy Nancy and I were talkin' about at the office. The quarterback at Tulane, remember?"

"Well, whoever he is, she was definitely into him. This looks like hero worship to me. Maybe she was concocting voodoo charms and love potions to win him over."

Dozens of photographs of Jack Holliday were on the walls, some cut out of magazines, others eight-by-ten publicity glossies, all pinned up together. Some looked like photos she'd taken in secret, of him getting into his car in front of some big fancy house, of him walking down a narrow street with another guy, even one of him lying on a couch that appeared to have been taken from outside his window.

"Is that a prayer bench sitting in front of the candles? Good grief, Zee, if this isn't a fixation, I don't know what is."

"This here's a freakin' voodoo shrine dedicated to Jack Holliday, all right. She had to be a nut case, too, to put this kinda thing together. Apparently, the killer isn't the only one into voodoo."

"You think Holliday might be into this kind of stuff, Zee? Maybe a black magic cult, something like that?"

Zee only laughed. "From what I hear, he's into huntin' and fishin' and datin' hot women, lots of hot women."

"Madonna was hot."

"Yeah, but he's into Hollywood stars and swimsuit models and famous women athletes. I've read about it all over the place. He can have any girl he wants, believe me."

Zee found a poster of the guy hanging on the back of the door. "Well, Holliday's been up close and personal with Madonna Christien. This proves it."

There was writing scrawled over his impressively tanned abs. *For Madonna. Jack Holliday.*

Claire stared at the slick poster. Nancy had the same one inside her office and mooned over it regularly but Claire had never paid much attention to it. Upon closer inspection, Claire understood why women went for him. He was a fine-looking specimen, all right. The photographer had caught him wading out of the ocean waves, some kind of tropical paradise behind him. The water hit him at mid thigh, and a swath of dark hair arrowed down his chest into dark blue swim trunks. He was holding a snorkel in one hand and a pair of goggles in his other one. He was staring straight into the lens and looked none too happy about being photographed. His expression made him look tough and sexy. Or maybe just highly ticked off. He was hot, all right—thick dark brown hair, five o'clock shadow darkening his jaw, eyes dark, intense. No wonder Madonna had given him his own room.

"Okay, Zee, what do you think? Would this guy take more interest in our victim than just signing an autograph for her?"

"I can answer that for you," came Rene Bourdain's voice from behind them. "Look what we found when we ran Madonna's name." He handed Claire his smartphone, and Claire read the screen.

"This is a restraining order taken out by Madonna on Jack Holliday. Okay, now we're getting somewhere."

Rene said, "Look at the date. Ten days ago."

Zee came alive. "Hey, man, does that mean I get to meet Jack Holliday in person?"

Claire frowned. "Hold on a minute, Zee. Jack Holliday just turned into our number-one person of interest. This says he's been harassing her, making phone calls, and pestering her out in public. That sounds like a stalking charge to me, at the very least."

Zee shrugged. "By the looks of this shrine right here, I'd say she's the stalker. Or maybe they're stalking each other. Anyway, I can tell you right now he didn't kill her."

"And you know this how?"

"Because he's got way too much to lose to be stalkin' some woman like her, especially if she's a hooker. He's a celebrity in this town, and he's still making a ton of money as a sports agent."

"Rich people drink. Rich people snort coke. Rich people go crazy sometimes and do stupid things. Is he into voodoo? That might be a clue we could take to the bank. Ever heard anything about that?"

Zee shrugged. "Never heard it mentioned. I highly doubt it. He's a jock and likes the women. He doesn't need voodoo."

Rene said, "My crew just pulled up. I'm bringing them in and then you're in charge, Claire. That okay by you?"

"Fine. Let's make sure this entire apartment is filmed and dusted, everything catalogued. If Jack Holliday was in this house, I want to be able to prove it. If he's not the one who drank out of that hurricane glass, I'd like to know who did."

"That still doesn't mean he offed her," Zee pointed out. "They could've just been friends. That's more likely."

"Maybe you ought to try to be a little bit more objective, Zee."

"I am objective. I just don't think he did it."

"Well, we'll know soon enough if he's been here."

As the crime scene techs filed in, it didn't take them long to get down to work. Claire snooped around a bit more. Especially inside the Jack Holliday voodoo shrine or whatever the hell it was. She found several small bottles with hearts and flowers on the homemade labels. Love potions, she'd bet her weapons on it. She opened a drawer and found a couple of voodoo dolls similar to the one found at the crime scene. Jack Holliday's face was on one of them but not impaled with pins. Another looked to be the tiny effigy of a female with a straight pin stuck into each eye. Jeez. But it wasn't her this time, thank goodness. There was a small jewelry box inside as well, and Claire lifted the lid with one gloved finger. Expecting to find bling or sacred voodoo pins, she was surprised to find a small pink book. "Maybe Madonna did keep an appointment book, after all, Zee."

Flipping through the pages, she found what appeared to be Jack Holliday's private cell phone number with a heart drawn around it in red ink. Plenty other male names were listed, too—her clients, no doubt—and believe it or not, each was rated with a star system. Holliday's stars covered the entire page, but most of the regular guys just rated two or three. That poor girl was delusional or just big-time messed up in the head.

The only problem—and a big one, at that—was there were no last names. The numbers would probably be enough unless they were throwaway phones, and that meant lots of time and legwork. Holliday, on the other hand, would be the easiest to find, and the most important to nail down at the moment.

Rene took the book from Claire and thumbed through it. "You wanna couple of my detectives to run down these names for you?"

"Yeah, that would be helpful. Zee and I will handle Holliday."

"My guys'll canvass this neighborhood, too, maybe turn up something for you."

"Thanks, that'll save us time."

"Why don't you and Zee stick around and have dinner with me? Give us time to talk about old times."

That was the last thing Claire wanted to do, but she played nice. Rene had been very accommodating, today and in the past. "No, we've gotta head back for the autopsy, but we appreciate the invite. This Jack Holliday guy, he's a big deal around here, right?"

Rene nodded. "Pretty much. He played at Tulane, got a lot of media back then."

"Then I need to interview him, but I want to do it on the QT. No reporters sniffing around, no publicity. Can you arrange that without tipping him off that's he's number one right now?"

"Shouldn't be a problem. I met him a couple of times at charity events. He supports the Special Olympics and Make a Wish Foundation and Wounded Warriors—he's really big in that one. He's well known enough around here to draw in some big donors."

"Yeah? So what's your take on him?"

"He seems okay, I guess. Generous with his time and money. But that restraining order puts a whole new spin on things. Doesn't look good for him. It's a miracle the media didn't get hold of it, considerin' who he is. Somebody downtown must've hushed it up somehow."

"Well, I'm glad they did. The last thing we need right now is a bunch of reporters following us around. But I am curious to see what he has to say about the victim and where he's been the last few days. I'd also like permission to search his house, if the need arises. How soon can you get us an interview?"

"Tomorrow afternoon fast enough? If he's in town. I know he travels a lot. He was in Dallas today, at the game. I know that for a fact. Saw him interviewed."

"Yeah, we did, too. Any time tomorrow's great."

"I'll get back to you."

"Please, make it sound like we just need to talk to him, nothing that would scare him off. Last thing we need is for him to lawyer up and plead the Fifth."

"Well, sorry, but I'm with Zee on this one. Holliday'd be all kinds of stupid to do something like this. And he's not stupid. He's as savvy as they come."

Zee waited for Rene to take his leave, and then he grinned at Claire. "Maybe we could interview him at the Dome? Wow, that'd be way cool."

"I think I ought to take Nancy along, instead of you. Your eyes are beginning to look a little wild."

"Hell, Nan would faint at the mere sight of him. She went to Tulane, too."

That could very well be true, but Zee would probably ask for the guy's autograph. Truthfully, Claire just might want his signature, too. Difference was, Claire wanted it on the bottom of a confession.

Chapter Six

Inside the sterile confines of the Lafourche Parish morgue, Claire found Nancy Gill sitting at her desk, waiting for Claire to show up so she could get the ball rolling. Through the big windows separating the office from the autopsy room, Claire could see the nude body of Madonna Christien lying on a steel table. The bright overhead light illuminated the victim's battered face. Now that it had been cleansed of the black and white skeleton paint, the bruises were more visible, as were the awful stitch marks on her eyes and lips. Her hair was long and dark and spread out behind her head.

"I got a little trace off the body, which pretty much amounted to zero. A few hairs, some fibers I can't yet identify. The perpetrator washed her clean with bleach before he painted her up and put her in that voodoo costume. But I'm ready to go, if you are. Is Zee comin' in for this?"

Claire shook her head. "He's interviewing people out along the bayou. I didn't know anybody lived out there, except for Saucier. And I didn't know that until he told me he heard me playing the other night. But, maybe we'll get lucky and Zee will find somebody who saw something. If the guys find footprints, tire tracks, anything, maybe we can tie them to the killer. But nothing's turned up yet, nothing at all. I've got a bad feeling that we're not going to find much. This guy knows what he's doing, and that probably means she's not his first victim. Or his last."

"He sure cleaned up the victim well enough," Nancy said, shaking her head. "Okay then, you ready? I'm tired. I need to get some sleep if we're goin' out partying tomorrow night. We are still on for a night on the town, right? Let's go to the *Bayou Blue*, okay?"

"You bet. I need some downtime, too. Black's coming home late afternoon on Tuesday. So I'm all yours tomorrow. After seeing what I've seen today, I am definitely ready for some fun."

"Great, me, too. Get on some gear and let's get this done."

Claire was not thrilled, not one iota, but she donned the protective garb and breathing mask and trailed Nancy into the autopsy room. Finding a crime victim, stabbed or burned or strangled to death by some psychopath, was enough tragedy for her, but standing around watching already abused bodies being sliced, diced, and put on little glass slides didn't remotely ring any kind of happy bells. Autopsies were not trips to Disney World. She'd seen lots of horrible, inhumane things done to other human beings during her career. More than she could count. Zee was even more resistant about venturing into Nancy's domain of the dead. He did everything he could not to step into the room filled with its sickening odors of antiseptic and death and chemicals, so this time Claire bit the bullet for him. Next time, it would be his turn to enter the dead zone.

Claire stood across from Nancy at the steel autopsy table. "Okay, I'm ready."

Nancy nodded, settled the microphone headset, and switched on the tape recorder. Claire fixed her own breathing gear more securely as Nancy gave the date and place of autopsy.

"The body is that of Madonna Christien, a Caucasian female homicide victim. Observing is Detective Claire Morgan on lend from the Canton Country Sheriff's Office in Missouri and lead detective in the investigation. Measurements indicate the body weight at ninety-nine and one-half pounds; height is five foot and one-half inch. The body shows signs of progressive deterioration. Eyelids and lips have been sewn shut with heavy embroidery thread. Time of death is not definitive, but is estimated at three to five days."

Nancy continued, each step precise and meticulously documented, but Claire only stared at the severe bruising on the body, distinct and graphic and brutal. Abrasions and contusions mottled the sloughing skin. Along with the serious head injuries, the poor girl had been pummeled with doubled fists or some kind of blunt weapon until she stopped breathing. The extensive injuries fit very well with the disarray at the Carondelet murder scene.

Claire's guess was that the assailant had thrown Madonna's slight body around and slammed her repeatedly into walls and furniture, and her bruises certainly bore proof of it. Which meant whoever the perpetrator was, he had to be strong. On the other hand, Madonna Christien was a tiny little thing. So small that she could have been overcome by a female perpetrator, especially if dazed by an initial head injury. Her fingernails were broken and ragged, indicating that she had fought desperately against her assailant. Nancy had taken nail scrapings, and Claire hoped that the victim had managed to get her assailant's DNA.

Nancy continued her description. "The skull and facial bones are damaged and swollen. A gaping five-inch laceration appears on the back of the head. There is a hemp rope secured tightly around her neck, indicating probable death by asphyxiation."

Picking up a small pair of scissors from the instrument tray, Nancy carefully snipped through the black threads holding the eyelids closed. She put down the scissors and lifted the victim's right eyelid with a gloved thumb. "After cutting away the thread holding the eye together, petechial hemorrhaging is observed, also an indication of death by strangulation, as is the bruising around the throat and the discoloration of the facial skin after the paint was removed."

Claire watched and wondered about Jack Holliday. Was he really capable of inflicting these massive injuries to a woman half his size? Maybe a guy like him could kill a woman in a rage, but taking the time to sew her eyes shut? Good God, that took a sick person, a special kind of monster, one who no doubt hid in the dark and crept around like some kind of poisonous spider. A famous local sports legend did not fit the profile. Then again, desperate people did reckless things. And some celebs thought they were above the law and above getting caught, much less convicted of wrongdoing. Unfortunately, lots of times they were right.

Claire's cell phone vibrated alive, then started to sing. She grabbed it, thinking it was Black checking in for the night. A little disappointed, she saw Rene Bourdain's name. Claire punched on quickly, hoping he had some good news. "Detective Morgan."

Moving into Nancy's office again, she was glad for the interruption, since Nancy had just started the Y-cut incision that would open Madonna Christien's torso.

"Jack Holliday agreed to talk to you tomorrow, but he wants to do it at his house out in the Garden District. He's throwin' some kinda shindig for his Special Olympics kids out at the Dome first and wants to talk to you after that. It's for some kind of organization he's a part of out at Tulane."

Claire sat down in Nancy's swivel chair and watched Nancy through the window. "So he really is into charity work? Doesn't sound much like the pastime of a cold-blooded, voodoo killer."

"You might be surprised. Ted Bundy worked a suicide line, if I recall. I just hope the media doesn't show up. If they do, stay under the radar and don't mention my name, even if you've got to end the interview. If he's got somethin' to do with this, all hell's gonna break loose around here, and your murder's gonna go viral in about three seconds."

"Chill, Bourdain, we don't have anything on him yet. Except the restraining order and the victim's apparent obsession with him."

"I hope to God you're right. Some people around here still worship the ground he walks on. Maybe we'll get lucky, and he can point you to somebody who had it out for her."

"We'll see, I guess."

"From what I've learned so far, your victim isn't any angel. Prostitution charges and weed possession. Also got intel that she did some stripping at a biker bar off Magazine. Lowlife dive called Voodoo River."

"Well, that just fits right in with all the other weirdness, doesn't it? Want us to check it out? Say the word and we're on it."

"Be my guest. But ya'll be careful. The biker gang that hangs out there? They call themselves the Skulls, and they won't like you comin' around snoopin' on their turf. Madonna Christien was into drugs, too, and there's probably gonna be more charges that'll come up on her rap sheet. I'll get back to you when I get the full report."

"What about her apartment? Forensics find anything we can use?"

"Yeah, they picked up a lot of latents. Two unknown, another off one of the hurricane glasses that came up as Madonna Christien,

alias Jilly Johnston, alias Shannon Martin. But the Madonna one is
her real name. She was incarcerated under that name for soliciting
tourists on Bourbon Street about a year ago. Record's clean since
then."

"She works the Quarter?"

"Did the stroll back then. Looks like she turned that gig into some
kind of call girl business, not exactly the high-priced kind, but still
better than working the streets."

"Rene, you said you knew Holliday personally, right? Is he really
hard up enough to pay for a hooker?"

Rene snorted and smothered his laugh. "Hell no. He can have any
woman he wants. Haven't you seen the guy? Women chase him. But
any man would pay for a hooker, given the right circumstances. Men
are men. You gotta know that."

Claire wondered if that were really true. Some guys fit that bill,
true enough. But Holliday wasn't just any man. Just like Rene had
pointed out, he dripped money, fame, charisma, and sex appeal. His
bedroom probably had a revolving door.

Rene said, "Some guys like the power trip. Buy a woman and
force them to do whatever they want. Domination, plain and simple."

"Did you tell Holliday why we want to see him?"

"I told him you had some questions about a case you're workin'
on down in the Lafourche bayous near Thibodaux."

"Did he ask a lot of questions about it?"

"Not really, we talked over the phone. He offered to meet you
tonight as soon as his plane lands out at Louis Armstrong, but I figured you'd need more time to prepare your interrogation. His flight's
due in around midnight."

"You're right, I want to know everything about him before we sit
down. Do I have permission to ask for his prints?"

"You can do whatever you want, as far as I'm concerned. My
advice, though? Ask him to give them willingly. Can't see him being
anything but cooperative, not at this point."

"Do you like this guy, Rene?

"He comes off like the genuine article, but lots of bad guys do.
I'm sure you know that." He paused. "God, it was good to see you
again. Never woulda thought we'd be workin' a case together."

"Yeah. Got anything else for me?"

"Nope, our techs are still running tests. There was a lot of stuff in that apartment, but I'll keep you posted. Want me to fax you what we've got so far?"

"Yes, please. Send it here to Nancy's office. You want to be there when we talk to Holliday?"

"No can do. Got departmental meetings all day tomorrow. You need anything else from us, you just let me know, okay?"

Claire gave him the fax number, and they hung up. Claire rocked back and forth in Nancy's chair and considered everything he'd said. She could hear the buzz of Nancy's cranial saw and was glad Rene had chosen that particular moment to call. Claire would read the autopsy report later. Excised brain matter wasn't exactly appealing right before dinner. Across from the desk, Nancy had tacked up posters of some of the Saints players. Holliday had the place of honor.

And Claire was right. It was the same poster that Madonna had on her closet door. At the bottom was the title. She hadn't noticed that before. *Stone Angel.* Oh, God, how embarrassing was that? Black would absolutely croak if anybody called him that, even though it described him, too, lucky for her. Yeah, she missed him and all those hard-packed muscles of his. Might as well admit it. Nobody could hear.

She stared at the poster some more, wondering if he could really be the homicidal murderer she was looking for, a beast who could beat a woman black and blue and strangle her and sew up her body parts. Claire suddenly got a visual image of a man bent over a body in the flicker of dozens of white candles, his sharp needle piercing the thin skin of her eyelids and pulling them tightly together. She shivered.

Nancy's flat-screen television sat on top of a filing cabinet and was tuned to ESPN's *SportsCenter*, the sound muted. Jack Holliday's face flashed up on the screen, and Claire scrambled for the remote. He was praising the scoring ability of one of his clients.

"Hey, Claire, they beat the crap out of Dallas. You hear the score? Hey, there's Jack. Does he look good, or what?"

Claire glanced over at Nancy. "Sorry to tell you this, Nancy, but your hero there is our main person of interest at the moment."

"No way."

"Afraid so. Rene says the victim is a known prostitute, and she has a special closet in her house that's a virtual shrine to him. If we find his fingerprints in her house, he's got a lot of explaining to do."

"Nah, he's a smart guy, and he's got way too much to lose to kill a prostitute."

"Funny you said that. So did Rene and Zee."

"Are you going to get to meet him? Can I go?"

Claire sighed and then had to laugh. How would it feel to be worshiped and obsessed over by everyday people, people who were normal and productive in every other way? Bizarre, she suspected. She would hate it. She hated the little bit of media coverage she'd gotten. She hated it even worse when people recognized her name. "I call it interviewing a person of interest. But hey, Nancy, cheer up, you might get to meet him if we throw him in jail."

"Not gonna happen, trust me. And guess what? I found an identifier on the body. A little homemade tattoo, one I think you're gonna find very interesting."

Claire jumped up and trailed Nancy back into the autopsy room. Nancy pulled over the armed and lighted magnifying glass and positioned it down close to the inside of the victim's left wrist. "See it? You tell me what that looks like."

Claire stared at the tiny blue marks. "It's the same symbol the killer drew in the cornmeal at the crime scene. Zee called it a Veve."

They stared at each other for a moment. Claire said, "She was caught up in something, all right. What? A voodoo cult or some kind of black magic?"

"Oh, yeah, that's what I'd say."

"Oh, boy, this case is gonna get messy."

"I'm going to finish and then close her up, okay? Anything you want to see?"

Claire shook her head, and when she heard the fax machine click on, she headed back to Nancy's desk. It was Rene's reports. Madonna Christien's mug shots were on the first page. She wore a tank top, low cut and provocative, but she had been a pretty girl. Small and pixie-ish with waist-length dark hair and a scattering of brown freckles across her nose that made her look really young.

Wanting plenty of ammunition for the next afternoon, Claire turned to Nancy's computer and Googled Jack Holliday's name. About a zillion hits popped up. She clicked on the first site, and it showed his head shot, in which he was grinning confidently. The article gave his stats as six feet eight inches tall and two hundred and thirty pounds. Whoa, he definitely could throw just about anybody up against a wall, and it wouldn't take long to wrap those giant hands around a little woman's throat and squeeze the life out of her.

Even though Jack Holliday had been out of the game, there were all kinds of stats about yards rushed in his Tulane heyday and his short stint with the Saints some time ago, and other stuff like that, but very little about his personal background. She found another site, one run by fans, that had an unauthorized biography of him. She skimmed through all the gossipy stuff, mainly about celebrities that he'd either dated or been photographed with, of which there were plenty. Then she found what she was looking for.

According to the website, he had been born in Colorado, a suburb of Denver called Arvada. Had played high school football there and been given a full scholarship to Tulane University. Had gotten a first-round draft pick with the Saints and led them to a Super Bowl victory before he blew out his knee in the big game. After that, his bio got real sketchy, except for his sports agent status.

For the next thirty minutes, Claire found out with some difficulty that he had no living family, but one fan site said he had an unnamed grandmother somewhere. Not much else. Most bios included his prior prowess at throwing the football and/or sleeping with beautiful women.

Not as much info on him as Claire would have liked to have before an interview, but probably enough to catch him if he fed her a bunch of lies or avoided her questions. Tired and ready to crash and get some sleep, Claire gave Zee a call and told him to pick her up at her house tomorrow and they'd go interview Holliday. He reacted with unbridled, hero-worshipping joy. She knocked on the window and waved good-bye to Nancy, who was now doing her thing with internal organs and placing slivers of tissue on glass slides.

Outside, she stood and breathed in the cool night air. Her cell phone sang, and she opened it quickly, hoping it was Black this time.

It was, and she picked up quickly. "Well, I thought you'd forgotten about me."

"Yeah? You're just about all I think about anymore."

Yes, that was pretty damn sappy, true, but she liked it, not that she'd ever admit it. "So how are your patients tonight? Sleeping peacefully or on a hatchet rampage?"

"All's calm. I'll be home before you know it. I miss you."

"Same here, so hurry up. Jules Verne and I get lost in that huge bed."

He laughed softly. "I'll find you, don't worry. How is that little pooch? Still cooling off in the courtyard fountain?"

Black loved the little poodle he'd brought Claire from Paris almost as much as she did. But Jules was good company at night when Black took off on his business trips. "Oh, yeah, he likes to wade around in it while he gets his drink. But he keeps me company."

"Good. Hey, I've got a surprise for you. It's all arranged so you can't say no."

That was Black. He always had a surprise for her, sometimes very, very good, and sometimes not so hot. "So, what is it?"

"I've got a crew of carpenters lined up to rebuild that old house you like down on the bayou. I'm going to totally remodel it and put in a security system so you can stay there any time you're too tired to drive home. Luc LeFevres already gave me permission to do anything I want with it. He said he'd deed the thing over to you if you want it. They're just letting it fall into ruin."

Uh-oh. Any other time, she'd like that surprise a lot, but not right now. And she didn't want to tell him what was going on, or he might go bananas. She waited a second longer but couldn't think of any other good reason to call off the carpenters. "Uh, Black, maybe you should hold off on that for a while."

"Why?"

She frowned and heaved in a bracing breath. "Because it's a crime scene at the moment."

Dead silence. "What the hell does that mean? Are you okay? Are you involved in something bad?"

Ah, the guy knew her well. "Yes, a case, but I'm fine. We found a body in the house and we're investigating it as a homicide now. Looks like some kind of voodoo thing, maybe."

"Voodoo thing? Are you serious? What kind of voodoo thing?"

Being a New Orleanian by birth, Black sounded almost as spooked as Zee and Nancy. "Surely you're not scared of voodoo stuff, Black."

"I'm not scared, but I know they take their rituals seriously and don't like people messing with them. I'm just glad you haven't been staying out there. Maybe I'll nix those carpenters for good. I don't want you anywhere near that place if that kind of stuff's going on."

Uh-oh, again. "Well, not to worry. I'll be at our house with Jules tonight, all by our lonesome in that big empty bed."

As she suspected, that got his mind fixated on something else. He had been sleeping alone for more than a week, after all. At least, she hoped he had. His next words reassured her.

"Better expect to spend a lot of time in that bed on Tuesday. I'll meet you there for dinner and then you can show me how much you missed me."

Claire smile was anticipatory, too. "Sounds pretty good to me. Getting reacquainted is gonna take a while, so you better not show up with jet lag."

"Not a chance. I'll sleep on the flight."

"Well, get some sleep now, too. What time is it over there anyway? It's got to be late."

There was a momentary pause. She frowned. "Black? You still there?"

"Yeah. It's well after midnight, I guess."

"Well, sleep well, and I'll see you on Tuesday."

"You be careful. Wish you were here."

"I've wished the same thing a time or two this week."

"Well, stay away from that boat and take off Wednesday, all day Wednesday."

Claire laughed and they hung up. Okay, she had fudged a bit to Black, and he wasn't going to like it when he found out the truth, especially the part about the voodoo doll. But he'd get over it. Right now, she needed to hit the sack. It had been a very long day, and she had the drive back to New Orleans ahead of her. What she wanted now was something good to eat, a good night's rest, and a list of pertinent questions designed to make Jack Holliday squirm like a worm on a barbed hook.

What she really wanted, of course, was Black back home and waiting for her in that aforementioned big soft bed with a tray of coconut shrimp and Pepsi on crushed ice, but that wasn't going to happen until Tuesday, so a quick stop at McDonald's for a Big Mac and fries to share with Jules would have to suffice at the moment. One thing for sure, she dreaded going to sleep because she had a bad feeling that her dreams were going to be filled with voodoo zombies and stitched-up eyes and lips and faces painted like skeletons and her face pinned to a voodoo doll.

A Very Scary Man

After Malice killed his girlfriend, he had to keep a low profile. But he found that he was quite an actor, too. He wept at the funeral, even sitting alongside Betsy's grieving, sobbing family. Her mother kept patting his knee and telling him to be brave. It was really pretty fun. He had even gotten all teary-eyed when he thought about how pretty Betsy had looked on Valentine's Day when he'd given her a little gold necklace with a heart on it that he'd stolen from JC Penney. She wore it around her neck in the casket, and he thought that was a sweet gesture of her mother but a real loss of good jewelry.

For months he didn't scare a single soul. He was watching his p's and q's, all right. Even his mother noticed his quiet demeanor and worried about him mourning so long and hard for his poor murdered little girlfriend who had died so young. So, he bided his time, and surreptitiously gathered all sorts of weapons to use when he became an assassin. He broke into houses on weekends and stole handguns and shotguns and filched hatchets and knives from his mom and aunts and killed dogs and cats for practice. It was all pretty easy. When he read in the newspaper about a garrote used in a particularly gruesome Mob-related murder, he fashioned one for himself out of wire and wood dowels. His problem was that he had no privacy and had to hide his stuff out in the woods behind his house. His little sister was sneaky now, a real brat, and was watching his every move so he had to be careful. She wasn't going to tell on him, though, because he'd told her that he'd kill her if she ever told on him. She believed him, and kept her mouth shut. He would, too. Just let her try to get him in trouble, and Mandy would just mysteriously disappear, never to be found again, just like their neighbor's black Lab.

Once he got some books that told about World War II death camps and prison camps and all the cruel stuff that had been done to the prisoners locked up inside them, and he spent long hours upstairs in his room poring over them. He still practiced football and was a star quarterback, and all that, but the terrible things that had been done to people in those books fed his hunger for inflicting pain and fear. He read other books, too. Some were set in the olden days of England when they used to draw and quarter people and had put their severed heads on spikes and impaled them with sharp sticks.

He read about the Spanish Inquisition, too, and what had been done to the people who they had thought to be witches. They had all kinds of torture devices back then, but the worst one had been called the Iron Maiden. It had been a hinged iron box with razor-sharp spikes inside. They had put the accused witches inside and slammed it shut so that all the spikes stabbed into their bodies. He'd never read anything so cool. And he particularly loved one book that he'd found in an old bookstore downtown. It told the true story of some crazy lunatic guy that had put his victims in a maze of dark rooms and hallways and then jumped out and hacked them to pieces with a machete. That book had given him cold chills the first time he read it, but he still loved how the victims screamed and ran and were chased around and finally shot in the back of their heads.

That was when he decided he needed to build a Maze of Terror of his own, a place of horrors where no one could ever, ever escape, where he could chase people all day long and watch them through hidden peepholes and trapdoors. It was exciting to think about that and plan for the future. And he knew exactly where he would build it. Way out in the deepest, darkest part of the swamp where nobody ever went, on an island, where only alligators and snakes and nutria rats lived. Yeah, that would be a perfect place. So he began to search the bayous and find secret routes in and out of the swamp from every direction, just in case he ever got caught playing his games and had to run for his life.

It was fun when he stole off by himself. He wondered sometimes if his friends on the team would like to help him, if they, too, had the urge to hurt people and scare the shit out of them. But he was too careful to involve others. He acted the carefree senior in high school, winning games with his friends, dating popular and pretty girls, making his grades, learning to weld and to build houses at his uncle's construction company, and all the while he was building his own house of horrors, way out in the swamp with the materials he stole from what was left over at his uncle's building sites. He designed it himself, and it was as complicated and evil as hell, but that's what he liked about it.

After he won the football scholarship, he perpetuated his dream, all the while building and planning and scaring people. He began to spend his weekends in the swamp, honing all the scary things, just so. It was during this time that he discovered voodoo and all its creepy rituals. He found the altar by accident, just happened to see the flash of a crucifix, where it was hanging in a tree and swinging in the wind. It was daytime and deserted, and he had never seen a single person within miles of this part of the swamp. It was too dark, too dangerous, and too alligator infested. But he'd heard the beat of drums a couple of times, late at night, and that had spooked him a little.

He nosed his boat onto dry land and waded out toward where he'd seen the glint of silver. There he found the crucifix and lots of other stuff. The altar was fresh. There were all kinds of candles and jars of strange-looking things. Some looked a lot like human body parts. Intrigued, excited, and a little frightened, he held them up to the sunlight filtering down through the cypress trees. One was a human ear in a jelly jar, cut off with ragged edges that fanned out in the formaldehyde when he shook it. Creepy as hell. There was a big bowl of blood, some not yet congealed, and human skulls were sitting all over the place. Many had candles set inside of them, and there were framed pictures of the Virgin Mary and Jesus Christ and angels surrounded by clouds and trumpets.

There were little bottles hanging off the trees with unknown liquids in them, but he knew it was probably bodily fluids. Fascinated, he wandered there among the symbols of death and destruction. He stole some of the skulls and other stuff and later read everything he could find about voodoo rituals. He learned about voodoo queens who tortured and killed and caused people to turn into zombies. He saw gruesome photos of a body that had been dug up and had body parts removed. He found stories of people who had been cursed and died horrible deaths and disappeared into the swamps never to be found again. Wow, he didn't think he'd ever been so excited. This was it. This was his destiny. He would become a voodoo doctor, and he would use spells and terrifying rituals to scare his victims. And he would do it out in the swamp, where it was dark and sluggish with hanging veils of gray moss and alligators sliding into the water and gliding around. The alligators would be his garbage disposal units, after he'd gotten all the fun he needed out of his victims. It was perfect. It would be his perfect little Garden of Evil.

Chapter Seven

Jack Holliday's house was indeed located in the world-renowned Garden District, on St. Charles Avenue, in fact. He lived close to where the nostalgic streetcars still clanked by. Wow, talk about an exclusive abode. Claire and Zee found his primo address with no trouble and parked in front of a stately home built circa early 1830s, about half a block down the street from the Holliday house. They walked slowly up a magnolia-shaded sidewalk, admiring one Christmas-decorated, beautiful old home after another. Great evergreen wreaths hung on every door, with velvet ribbons and expensive gold and glass ornaments. None of the historic houses had anything on Holliday's domicile, however. He had an elegant old mansion, well kept, with lots of dark green wrought iron fashioned into intertwined roses and ivy.

Two long galleries graced the front, upstairs and down, entwined with lights that would probably be beautiful when turned on. Garlands of fresh greenery and wreaths were tastefully displayed in swags tied with huge red velvet bows. Claire and Zee stopped at the front gate and stared up at the house. The sidewalk fence matched the balustrades, ornate with medallions of roses and ivy and another huge wreath, this one plain except for one large red bow.

"I cannot believe we are going to walk right in there and meet Jack Holliday in person," Zee said reverently. "Nobody back home's ever gonna believe me. I'm nervous as hell."

Claire stopped there, her hand on the gate's latch. "Do you think you can control yourself around this guy, Zee?"

Zee revealed openly that he was offended. "Man, Claire, lay off. Anybody'd be excited to meet him. He's a legend around here."

"This is not about meeting a football hero. Don't forget that, and please, let me do the talking."

Now Zee looked annoyed. "You're sellin' me short, Claire. I ain't exactly some rookie officer who never interviewed a suspect before."

"No, you are not. But I can see that wowee-I-get-to-meet-the-big-Tulane-super-star gleam in your eyes. It's a little unsettling, to be perfectly honest."

"Aww, c'mon, I'm not all that excited. Get real."

"Well, I hope not. Let's go. Remember, I'll do the talking."

"Okay, whatever you say."

Zee was miffed, but Claire had meant what she'd said. He was a little too enthralled with Holliday to remain neutral. On the other hand, she was not enthralled with him at all.

Claire opened the gate, and they walked up a red-bricked sidewalk laid in a herringbone design and climbed the front steps. She could smell citrus and found lots of real oranges and apples in the large floral arrangement beside the front door. She considered picking a few pieces off to snack on later, but decided that would be tacky. They stood in front of the most beautiful cut glass door with more facets than the British Crown Jewels. Zee lifted the gold knocker that was shaped like a fleur-de-lis and let it clang down and proclaim their very official presence.

Claire was surprised when a butler opened the door, but then again, who else would open a sports god's portal? More surprising, the elegant servant wore a black tailcoat, white starched shirt with ruffles down the front, and a black bow tie. White haired and dignified, he looked to be in his mid to late sixties. But he also looked physically fit and able to repel hysterical sports fans and tittering women trying to get to his boss. His skin was abnormally pale, as if he'd never been out in the sun one minute or was a vampire. Claire stared at him and felt like an extra in *Gone with the Wind*.

"May I help you?" Said butler's accent was not Southern, not even a little bit. Oh, no, he was oh-so, *ooh-la-la* French.

"We're here to see Jack Holliday on police business." Claire and Zee presented their badges and stated names and titles, and Mr. Supercilious Servant examined them for a whole lot longer than he needed to. Something about the man's staid manner gave Claire pause. He wasn't exactly creepy, but he gave her the willies. Why, she couldn't quite fathom. But she did not like him, not at all.

"Yes, madam and sir. Mr. Holliday is expecting you. He's in the drawing room."

Yeah, she bet he was. Probably with Scarlett O'Hara and Melanie Wilkes and that sissy guy named Ashley that they both had the hots for. Rhett Butler was more Claire's cup of tea, probably because he was manly like Black. Scarlett must've been blind or had a thing for weaklings with wavy blond hair.

The butler preceded them with his über-formality, and they followed with their usual not-impressed-by-you-buster posture. She did feel a bit irked, if only because he seemed so uppity and scornful. They strolled through a beautiful foyer, which contained the expected curved and highly polished staircase entwined with more fresh greenery that smelled heavenly and a ten-foot-high, expensively decorated Christmas tree that would impress Black to no end. They passed under a glittering chandelier that looked as if it had been filched out of a medieval cathedral or the White House. Frenchie walked with the brisk step of a much younger man, and then stopped and slid open a pair of well-oiled, white double pocket doors. They were announced, not by name but as the police officers the gentleman had been expecting. Okay, she guessed that pretty much summed them up.

Frenchie disappeared, and they stood in the doorway. The parlor did indeed look like a room where Jack Holliday's purported octogenarian granny would serve tea to her hoop-skirted old cronies, all right. Claire sure couldn't picture Holliday sitting on those little gold and red velvet chairs with knotted fringe and crocheted doilies. Now that would be a big bull in an antique china shop. But he was doing just that, and he did look like the aforementioned bull. He sat on a hump-backed, gold and white striped brocade sofa in front of a pink veined white marble fireplace. The mantel was carved with beaucoup angels and cherubs playing harps and floating on clouds. The logs in the hearth were crackling and snapping up a storm, despite the warm weather outdoors. Hell, it probably felt the stuck-up coldness of that butler, too.

Way across the room, Jack Holliday rose quickly, with all the good manners of devotees of *Pride and Prejudice* movies. He wasn't wearing a starched cravat or stovepipe hat, though, just khaki pants and a red polo shirt and black Nikes.

"Okay, show's on, Zee," Claire muttered under her breath to her partner. "Now keep your cool, and I mean it. No groveling or drooling on this guy."

Zee gave her a look of mock hurt, but he was whispering. "Ha ha. You are so funny. Give me a break, will you? I can be as professional as you can."

"Okay, now's the time to prove it."

Jack Holliday strode quickly across to them, and then he was there, right in front of them, towering over them, and she meant *towering*. Claire hadn't been around all that many men who were four inches shy of seven feet. Black was six-four, which was pretty good size in her book. She had to look way up at Holliday, which she didn't like much, and which somehow made her feel at a disadvantage, right off the bat. She was five-nine and felt like a six-year-old looking up at her daddy. A glance at Zee told her that he was maybe a half degree away from the forewarned idol drool. Actually, she watched a second longer to see if he staggered with the sheer delight of meeting his Fabulous One.

Claire showed the big guy the badge hanging around her neck, hoped he could see it from way up there. "We're with the Lafourche Parish Sheriff's Department, Mr. Holliday. I'm Detective Morgan. This is my partner, Detective Jackson."

"Nice to meet you," he said, all easy and calm and rife with confident charm. Smiling, he held out his hand. And then Claire felt it, too. Like a blow in the solar plexus, an immediate physical attraction to the sheer masculinity of the man. Now, this just wasn't gonna do. In fact, it made her angry with herself. Black better get home in a hurry, though. She put her hand in his, just to show she could, and his long tanned fingers closed around hers. She shook it like she meant it, with a grip like she meant it. He had the biggest hands, aka bear paws, she'd ever seen on a guy, but all she could think about was how easy it would be for him to press those self-same long, strong fingers around Madonna Christien's neck and slowly squeeze the life out of her. That pretty much put a damper on her appreciation of his massive sex appeal.

Holliday stared down at Claire for an instant too long, as if he read her distrust of him, and then he released her hand and offered a handshake to Zee. Claire's unaffected, purely professional Louisiana law enforcement partner then said, "Oh, man, you got on your Super Bowl ring. Wow, man. You were awesome when you played that last game, the one where you blew out your knee. I got all your games on video." Then he grinned, all white teeth and gridiron-crazed eyes.

So much for Zee's promise not to wallow in the man's greatness. She bet Bud, her trusty partner up north, wouldn't react like that. Oh, well, on second thought, maybe he would. Yeah, he definitely would. And yes, Zee was young and a football fanatic so she guessed she had to take that into account.

Holliday was mighty gracious, yes, ma'am. "Thanks. We had a hell of a good day when we won that game. Wanna try it on?"

When Zee actually squeaked out a peculiar little noise than sounded suspiciously like a man giggle, Claire took back the reins. "We're here to ask you some questions, Mr. Holliday, if that's okay with you."

"Yeah, I know. Rene told me. No problem. Ask away." He took off the ring and handed it to Zee, who put it on his finger and gawked at it in a really goofy way. It was way too big and hung on Zee's finger like the class ring of a teenage girl's boyfriend.

"Please, Detective, call me Jack." He smiled down at her, but he was watching her closely, really looking her over, and she wondered why. "You know what, I've got some good food left over from the charity event I hosted today. You guys want to help me eat some of it? There's plenty."

"That sounds good," said Zee, reverently cradling the ring in his palms.

Claire said, "Thank you, Mr. Holliday, but I don't think we'll have time for that. Do you want to talk to us here, or did you have somewhere else in mind?"

He looked surprised by the question. "Here's fine, I guess.

Whatever. You sure about the food? There's some good stuff out in the kitchen. Barbecue. Seafood. Jambalaya. You name it."

"Man, I love that jambalaya," said Zee. The two men grinned at each other, in love already, she guessed. Jeez. But her stomach growled, just to mock her.

The three of them sat down. Holliday took a seat beside her on the sofa and turned slightly to work his magical smile on her. This guy was indeed the phrase *hot as fire* personified, a real chick magnet, as Zee liked to describe himself. Holliday knew it, too, and he was waiting for Claire to melt into a puddle of goo like the Wicked Witch of the West. She might be a witch sometimes, but she wasn't about to melt down when a great big hunky guy gave her the come-on. Unless, of course, it was Black, who happened to be equally as hot as, if not hotter than, Jack. But she was not always meltable, even then, depending on the circumstances. Nancy, on the other hand, would be all liquid and soaking by now into the priceless Persian carpet under their feet. Good thing they'd left her at the morgue.

"So, what's this all about, Detective Morgan? You really look familiar somehow. Have we met before?"

Claire didn't like the familiarity of that, either. Claire was rapidly starting not to like anything that was going on. He was playing her—she could feel it. "No, we haven't. Now, if you don't mind, we don't really have a lot of time." They did, of course. They had all the time in the world, in fact, but he didn't need to know that. Time to make that big self-satisfied, Crest-white grin fade away and make lots of deep frown lines wrinkle up that handsome brow of his. The smile did falter a bit. He searched her face, openly puzzled at her giant-chip-on-the-shoulder attitude.

"Okay, Detective. What can I do for you?"

"Are you acquainted with a woman named Madonna Christien, Mr. Holliday?"

Well, now, lookee here, the mighty one's expression just changed, and in a nanosecond at that, the very moment she mentioned their victim's name. In fact, Jack Holliday was showing her what his most massive frown looked like.

"Oh, yeah, I know Madonna Christien. Unfortunately for me."

"Unfortunately for you," Claire repeated slowly. "What exactly do you mean by that, Mr. Holliday?"

"Madonna Christien is as crazy as a loon, that's what. She's been stalking me for three months and making my life into a living hell."

Okay. Claire scribbled something on her notepad, most of which looked like scribbles because it was. But it looked official and gave her time to think and hopefully would make him worry some more.

It didn't make him worry some more. "Your handwriting looks like chicken scratches," he said, grinning at Zee. Zee grinned back, of course, rather maniacally, too. Claire tilted the notebook so Holliday couldn't see what she wasn't writing.

"How did you meet Ms. Christien?"

"I met her through one of the Saints cheerleaders. Wendy told me a friend of hers wanted my autograph for her little boy, so I said okay. I like little kids."

"Where did you meet her?"

"At the Superdome, down on the field, right after a game. I was down there congratulating some of the guys I represent. Madonna had one of those stupid posters some paparazzi jerk took of me down in Miami when I was on spring break."

"You were saying about Ms. Christien?"

"She said it was for her son, and that he was too sick to come to the game. We talked for a minute or two, but then she started acting a little weird, so I made an excuse and took off. Later, I wondered if she really even had a kid."

"How was she acting weird?"

Holliday hesitated and looked at Zee. "Weird, as in coming on to me. She wanted me to come over to her house, actually started insisting that I had to. She said she had something for me, kept on about that, and then she said some voodoo doctor told her that the gods were pushing us together and that we'd be getting married inside a year's time. That's when I knew I was in trouble."

"What voodoo doctor?" That was Zee, apparently afraid Mama Lulu's name might come up.

Holliday shrugged. "She didn't say. After that first day, she started sending me all kinds of gifts and cards and flowers, you name it. Addressed to her true love."

Aha, Claire thought. "And did you keep any of these gifts?"

"Are you kidding me? I gave most of them to Wendy to give back to her and to tell her to leave me the hell alone. I might have a few things lying around that I overlooked. I sure didn't want to encourage that woman."

"And who exactly is Wendy again?"

"Wendy Rodriguez. Rodriguez is her married name. She's divorced. She's the cheerleader who introduced us."

"We'll need to talk to her, too."

Holliday shrugged again. "She's not hard to find. What's this all about, Detective?"

Claire ignored his question. Something about his story didn't quite add up to her, something about the way he said it, as if it had been rehearsed. "So you are saying that you hardly know this woman, Madonna Christien?"

"That's right. Just that one meeting and a couple of times she was waiting for me outside this house. She tried to talk herself inside, but my butler wouldn't let her in the door."

"What happened when you did encounter her?"

"Nothing much. That's when she gave me the gifts. When I refused to take them, she'd throw them over the fence out there in the yard. Sometimes she'd just leave them on the hood of my car or at the gate for me to find. What's this all about, Detective?"

Claire remembered the photos in Madonna's voodoo closet, the ones of Jack Holliday that appeared to have been taken without his knowledge. That fit. One point for him. "What you're describing sounds like the work of a stalker, Mr. Holliday. Is that what you're telling us? That Madonna Christien was stalking you?"

"Damn straight. That's exactly what she was doing."

"Was?"

"I haven't heard from her in a couple of weeks. I hope that means she's finally given up. That woman's unstable, I'm telling you. You know, she's not right up here." He tapped a forefinger against his temple.

Claire wrote some stuff down. Then she met his eyes, and they locked on hers, as black as India ink. There was definitely a concerned look in them at the moment. So, okay, time to get down and dirty. "If she was stalking you, sir, can you explain to us why she was the one who took out a restraining order on you?"

Frown. Massive meeting of straight dark eyebrows. So much confusion in that expression, or was that just guilt? "I don't understand. I'm the one who took out a restraining order on her."

Well, now. Claire hadn't been expecting that one, if it were true. But Rene would have told her if that were the case. "Mr. Holliday, we have obtained a copy of an official restraining order issued by the NOPD, prohibiting you from approaching within one hundred feet of Madonna Christien."

Holliday just stared in disbelief, first at Claire, then at Zee. Zee remained suitably sober, thank goodness. Finally, Holliday said, "Well, that's news to me."

Claire wondered if that was true. She said nothing, hoping to fluster him some more. He didn't seem to fluster all that easily. He just looked like he didn't understand where they were going with all this. "Again, Detective, I'm asking you what this is all about. Frankly, I don't like the direction your questions are taking."

Okay, maybe he did know where she was going with all this. "Can you account for your whereabouts for the last four days, sir?"

Holliday stood up. They cricked their necks looking up at him. "I'm not answering any more questions until you tell me exactly what's going on."

"Madonna Christien was found dead inside a deserted house on a bayou in Lafourche Parish."

His mouth actually fell open, just slightly and just for a second, but she had to say that his look of utter shock did not appear to be manufactured. Maybe that meant he didn't have a clue what they were talking about. Or maybe that meant he hadn't expected them to zero in on him so fast.

"Am I being accused of something? If so, I think my lawyer would like to be present."

"I haven't accused you of anything, sir." Well, actually she had, tacitly, in a roundabout, tacky sort of way, of course, but she wasn't going to admit it. "Can you tell us your whereabouts for the last four days? Or would you like to borrow my phone and put in a call to your attorney?"

Holliday looked at Zee, then back at Claire. He didn't look all that friendly anymore. Probably didn't want to share his charity leftovers, either. "I've been in Dallas for the last two days, and I have about a hundred media people and seventy-five thousand eyewitnesses to prove it, not to mention millions of people who watched my interview on Fox Sports."

"I think we can accept that. What about the day before you went to Dallas? Were you here in New Orleans?"

"No. I was in New York."

"And you have witnesses who can verify that assertion, I assume?"

"Of course. I met with my private investigator and an old friend of mine. They can both vouch for my whereabouts."

"And their names are?"

"John Booker and Nicholas Black."

Okay, it was Claire's turn to drop her jaw. She and Zee looked at each other. Her partner looked as surprised as she did. "You were with Nicholas Black? In New York City?"

"Yes, you may know of him. He does a lot of television talk shows. He's a psychiatrist, a famous one. He treats lots of celebrity patients."

Well, there was Blatant Big Lie Number One, since Black had been and was still working in London. But usually where there is one lie, there is a whole truckload of lies. Maybe she could catch him in the one he was weaving around himself. "Is he treating you for some kind of psychological defect, Mr. Holliday? Is that why you were in New York?"

Holliday laughed, amused by the silly old detective. "No, ma'am, he's an old friend. I've never needed his professional services, but I'd trust him with my life."

Me, too, Claire thought. She had, in fact.

Claire met his eyes and tried to make him wonder what she was thinking. But the Black thing was throwing her, big time. "And you don't mind providing us with their telephone numbers?"

"No, I don't mind, but they're gonna be back in New Orleans on Tuesday. I can arrange for them to meet with you, if you like."

Okay, now, Hunk Holliday obviously didn't know she and Black were a couple and for going on several years now, so how close a friend to Black could Holliday possibly be? Their pictures had certainly been plastered in the newspapers a time or two. And why hadn't Black ever mentioned him to her? Maybe Holliday was just trying to arrange a meeting so he'd have time to call and brief them on what lies to tell her. Now that would put her own special true love in a very uncomfortable position, but so be it.

"Can you tell me the airline and flight number you took to and from New York?"

"I flew myself. I have access to a plane. My flight plans are probably still on record."

"You're a pilot?"

"That's right."

Claire's phone started to sing "Blue Bayou." Holliday smiled. "Cool ring tone. I love Roy Orbison."

"Thanks."

Claire moved a few steps away. "Detective Morgan."

"Hey, girl. This is Rene. Where are you?" He sounded a mite breathless.

"Conducting an interview. I'll call you back."

"Jack Holliday's listenin', I take it? I was hopin' I could get you before ya'll got there."

"That is correct."

"Well, get this. We ran the fingerprints on the wineglass we found in Madonna's house, and they came back to Jack Holliday."

Claire moved farther away and turned her back on Holliday and Zee. "He's in your database?"

"Yeah, believe it or not. Nothing serious. Disorderly conduct during Mardi Gras when he was in college. He and some of his Tulane college buddies got into a scuffle on Bourbon during a parade. No charges were pressed against them, though, and they were released the next morning. But they were printed and put into the NOPD database."

Claire finished the conversation and hung up. Holliday and Zee were staring expectantly at her. She said, "You better call that lawyer, after all, Mr. Holliday. Your fingerprints were found at the murder scene inside the victim's apartment."

Chapter Eight

After Claire's announcement concerning Holliday's fingerprints, the big football agent finally began to look concerned. "That's impossible." He hesitated, and then he said, "I've never been there. I don't have a clue where she lives."

"How do you explain your prints being found there?"

"I can't explain it. But I can prove that I wasn't anywhere near New Orleans since last Tuesday night. That ought to clear me, right? That should cover the window of opportunity?"

Law enforcement speak, that was. "If I were you, sir, I would call that lawyer right away. Until I can talk to and verify your alibi witnesses, you're going to be a person of interest to us."

Holliday already had his own phone out, speed dial pressed, giving a quick SOS to his lawyer. "He's on his way," he said after he hung up.

"Do you have John Booker and Nicholas Black on speed dial, too, Mr. Holliday?"

"Yes, ma'am, be my guest. Use my phone. They're both still in New York."

Au contraire, Jack. On the other hand, his offer was an encouraging sign. A guilty man would first want to brief his cronies on what to say. Maybe he was innocent. Or maybe he was just crafty. He didn't look or act like a guilty homicidal maniac who liked to sew, and Claire had seen lots of guilty homicidal maniacs. The sewing part, not so many.

She moved into the adjoining dining room, which had one giant chandelier dripping with plenty of sparkling crystal prisms over a big shiny oak table, one that sat twenty, at least. She found the number for John Booker first. Booker just happened to be one of Black's best friends, not to mention his go-to private investigator. She knew Booker pretty well herself, and had even worked alongside him. She pressed the button for his number and waited. Somebody picked up on the other end after the first ring. "Hey, Jack. Saw you on Fox yesterday. You still got the magic."

Claire said, "Well, hello there, Booker."

Dead silence. "Claire? Is that you?"

"This is Detective Claire Morgan with the Lafourche Parish Sheriff's Office."

"What's going on? Is Jack in trouble?"

"You could say that. I need to ask you a few questions."

"Okay. Is he all right? Are you working homicide again?"

"Holliday's fine. Tell me, Mr. Booker, have you seen Mr. Holliday in person any time recently?"

"He flew up here last Tuesday night and stayed with us at the Ritz-Carlton for a couple of days."

This time it was Claire's turn to frown. "Us?"

"Nick and me. Didn't Nick tell you where we were staying?"

"In London?"

"London? No. We're in New York."

"Have you been in New York the whole time?"

"Yeah. Why?"

Okay, that was not the answer she was hoping for. Black had told her he was working in London, had called her from there several times. Last night, in fact. She felt her jaw began to tighten. What the hell was going on?

"Which days did you see him?"

"C'mon, Claire, what's this all about?"

"I'm waiting, Mr. Booker."

"He got here around noon on Tuesday. We picked him up at LaGuardia, and he stayed with us here at the hotel until he left for Dallas on Saturday."

"And why was he there with you?"

"We were discussing something. A case. I'm a private investigator, remember?"

"A case concerning what?"

"Good try, Detective, but that's confidential between Jack Holliday and me, and I think you know it."

Well, slap me down and make me cry. "Right. And you say that Nicholas Black was also with you during this time?"

"You know he is. Come on, Claire."

Right, she should have known, but she didn't. "Is he there now?"

"Yes, he's in the living room. Would you like to speak to him?"

If Black turned out to be a material witness and got her kicked off this homicide case because of his lies, she was going to pin his face on a voodoo doll. "Oh, yeah, I sure would. That would be just peachy keen, Mr. Booker."

"I'll go get him."

Claire listened to sounds of Booker walking with the phone, of a door opening, a few muffled words, and then a different man's voice, one that she usually heard between her bed sheets, all gruff and deep and sexy and turned on. It was gruff this time, but not sexy or turned on. "What the hell's going on, Claire? Why do you have Jack's phone?"

Black also sounded a bit upset, guilty, even. "I understand you can verify Jack Holliday's whereabouts in New York during the past week, Black. Which is interesting to me since you're in London."

Silence again. Very guilty, very long, Black no doubt thinking, *Oh, shit, what should I say, what should I say?* The rush of anger that shot through her did not help matters.

"I can explain."

"Well, be my guest, Dr. Black."

"You're angry, I can tell."

"I always said you were a genius."

"Claire, I really can explain all this."

"So you said. So, go ahead, explain it."

Claire glanced back at her two companions. Holliday looked like he was trying to eavesdrop on what she was saying. Zee looked like he wanted to kowtow, kneel down, and kiss his hero's ring.

"I'm going to, but not right now, not over the phone. It's . . ." Black paused there, thinking up his very own Blatant Big Lie Number One, no doubt, and then he finished quickly with, "I'll fly in tomorrow around dinner time. We'll sit down, have a nice dinner, and work this out, but right now, let's talk about Jack."

"Was Jack in New York with you?"

"Yes. Tuesday through Saturday. He was here at the Ritz. Booker, too. Jack and I are old friends from college, out at Tulane."

Well, that held up with the French Quarter altercation. Black's prints were probably on file at NOPD, too. Great, just great, and getting more so by the minute. "And you were with him continually during this time?"

"Well, I didn't go to the bathroom with him, but I've got a Royal Suite on the twenty-second floor, and he and Booker stayed here with me the whole time. We didn't go out at all."

"Would you be willing to sign an official police statement to that effect, Dr. Black?"

"Damn it, Claire, cut the Dr. Black crap. Of course, I'll sign it. In fact, I can get you about twenty other eyewitnesses that'll tell you he was here Friday night. We had a little get-together for Jack's birthday. Jack's in some kind of trouble, I take it?"

Black had lost his calm, unruffled shrink demeanor for a moment, said *crap* and everything, but he got it back pretty quickly. But, in a nutshell, not only was Black not in London, he was throwing *little get-togethers* at the Ritz with his college drinking buddies. The hole he was digging just kept getting deeper. Soon, it was going to be over his head. Not that she tried to control him. She didn't, and she didn't want to, or need to, but something about all this was very disturbing.

Black wasn't a liar, didn't have reason to be either, not with her. She gave him free rein to do whatever he wanted, not that he wouldn't do it anyway, with or without her permission. And vice versa. Neither of them would put up with anything less. Black was a bit controlling when it came to her, especially her safety, but he knew better than to order her around. There could be a good reason for all this—probably not, but there could be. Hell, she wasn't unreasonable. Sometimes. But she was mightily ticked off at the moment and wasn't shy about showing it. "We're conducting a homicide investigation, sir, and Jack Holliday's name has come up so we're checking him out."

"Okay, I get it. This is an official call. Listen, I've got the Lear, and I better come back early." Pause and then a heartfelt testimonial. "Claire, I've known Jack for years and I can tell you that he is incapable of cold-blooded murder." Then he sort of laughed, just to show her how totally absurd the idea was.

"Well, thanks for the vote of confidence, but votes of confidence just don't hold up in court. Especially in homicide cases. Truth is, you've pretty much already proven yourself to be a bald-faced liar."

Several beats of dead air. Probably a good thing in her present mood. He must have thought so, too, because he said, "Has Jack talked to his attorney?"

"Would you like to speak to Mr. Holliday, sir?"

A heavy sigh. "Yes, I'd like to speak to Jack."

"Thank you for your cooperation, sir. Please let us know when you plan to arrive in town. You can contact me at the Lafourche Parish Sheriff's Office in Thibodaux, Louisiana. Number's in the book."

"Oh, for God's sake, Claire!"

Maybe, but guess what, she didn't like to be lied to, especially giant lies that had lasted over a week now. However, if what they asserted turned out to be true, Jack Holliday was pretty much off the hook. And, if that turned out to be the case, how the hell did his fingerprints get on that glass?

Claire walked back to Holliday and handed him his phone. "Dr. Black would like to talk to you."

He said, "Satisfied, Detective?"

"Not by a long shot, Mr. Holliday. I advise you not to leave town."

"I didn't touch Madonna Christien. She was the one stalking me, and I can prove it. Check it out with the NOPD. They issued my restraining order against her. I'm telling you that I haven't seen her since. That's why I thought the whole thing was over and done with."

"I'll check out your allegations. Our investigation is just getting started. The fact that your friends can alibi you will make a big difference."

"Jack, wait, don't say another word!"

Mr. Slick Lawyer was heading across the room toward them as if the seat of his expensive custom-made, pinstriped suit were on fire.

Carson Lancaster himself, in the flesh. Claire had met him once, not long after they'd moved to New Orleans, at the grand opening of Black's new pride and joy, an exclusive and pricey boutique inn inside the French Quarter that he'd christened the Hotel Crescent. She'd seen Lancaster on the local news, too, usually smiling and gloating over his latest victory in court. He was the most famous defense lawyer in Louisiana.

"It's okay, Carson. I've got a rock-solid alibi. The detective is only doing her job. We can't fault her for that." Holliday gave Claire a magnanimous smile.

Claire said nothing, and Holliday kept those black eyes on her for an extra-long moment, and then he showed her his even white teeth and übercharming smile. "I bet you're one hell of an investigator, aren't you, Detective?"

"I believe your friend is waiting on the telephone," she said to him, and then looked down at her notes and ignored his question. "Well, I guess that's it for now, Mr. Holliday. Will you be willing to talk to us again, if the need should arise?"

"As long as I'm with him," said Carson Lancaster, aka Suspect's Ace Attorney.

Holliday put his hand on Lancaster's shoulder. "I'll look forward to it, Detective."

Maybe that flirty come-on wouldn't look so good to him once he had a heart-to-heart chat with his old bud Nicholas Black, Claire's so-called lover/liar. "We'll be in touch, Mr. Holliday. Thank you for your cooperation."

"I'm happy to help. Yannick will show you out."

Outside in the hallway, Yannick, aka Snooty-Nosed Butler, appeared out of nowhere and deigned to show them out with a look on his face that intimated some very strong "good-bye and good riddance, peons" vibes.

They took their leave, and Zee trailed her to the car and didn't speak until they were both inside. "Thank goodness he's got alibi witnesses, Claire. And, hey, did you know he was up there with Nick the whole damn time?"

Claire just shook her head. She did not want to talk about that, not until she had cooled off. But Holliday was not sweating it. Not if Black and Booker came through with hotel records, witnesses, and verifying flight plans. If that happened, his alibi was pretty much written in stone. Now all she had to do was figure out how his fingerprints had gotten on that hurricane glass and who had killed Madonna Christien and stitched up her mouth and eyelids and how Claire needed to deal with Black's Blatant Big Lie. Fun, fun, and more fun.

"Okay, Zee, how about us visiting your Mama Lulu's shop on Bourbon Street and seeing what we can find out about that Veve thing?"

"She'll be there today. Let's go. I haven't seen her in a while."

So off they went to Bourbon Street and its crowds and impossible parking problems. But Zee lucked out, especially after he pulled up in a loading zone and propped his POLICE OFFICIAL BUSINESS placard on the dashboard. Claire didn't care. They were getting nowhere on this case and had no time to waste. She had a bad feeling that their voodoo psycho was making up another creepy doll and sharpening his pins as they continued to run headlong into high brick walls.

Chapter Nine

Mama Lulu's voodoo shop was appropriately named Mama Lulu's Voodoo Shop. Couldn't get more to the point than that. It was tucked in a tiny building between a boisterous rhythm-and-blues bar with blaring music and plenty of customers and a nostalgic little old-fashioned bookstore where people could sit in easy chairs and read old classics by Charles Dickens, or somebody else nerdy like that. The patrons probably smoked pipes, too, and wore patches on the elbows of their tweed jackets like college professors. Not her thing, at least not until she was ninety years old and walked with a cane. Even then, she'd leave the elbow patches to Black.

Out front, Mama Lulu's shop had a rather spooky-looking skeleton dressed in a suit that faintly resembled Mr. Snooty Butler's attire, but with a matching top hat and less meat on the bones and a friendlier expression. Said skeleton had on lots of Mardi Gras beads and gaudy jewelry around his neck, too. Claire followed Zee through the front door, where a cheerful tinkling bell greeted their arrival. Inside the establishment, however, it was rather dark and appropriately creepy with signs hanging around everywhere warning customers not to touch anything, including several large ones that read: No Photographs Of Charms Or Amulets Allowed, No Cameras Of Any Kind Allowed Inside Store, No Handling of Merchandise Blessed and/or Cursed by Voodoo Priest, Management Not Responsible for Evil Spirits Attached to Inventory, and last but not least, Visa, Mastercard, American Express, and Discover Card Accepted. So there you go: buyer beware, but do pull out the plastic.

Patrons were taking heed of the fear factor, too, hands stuffed in pockets, avoiding any brushing up against infected goods. There was no shoplifting going on; that went without saying. There were at least a dozen people browsing around the glass counters, admiring skulls and snake heads and wind chimes made out of fake human bones. At least Claire hoped they were fake. Otherwise, they just might have to arrest Zee's granny for grave robbing. All the browsers looked very serious and intent on reading the small print on the labels. Claire decided to follow suit in that regard. All she needed was a bunch of clingy evil spirits going home with her to Governor Nicholls Street. A little boy sat behind the counter, one who looked amazingly like an eight-year-old, miniature Zee. He was dressed a lot like the skeleton and snooty butler, miniature top hat and all. Cute as could be, too.

"Hey, Etienne, how's it goin'?" Zee said, rounding the counter and doing some fancy high and low fives and bumping of hands and other bodily parts with the child.

"We been real busy, Zee Man. Mama Lulu's back there, makin' up those good-luck amulets for Christmas stockings. Sellin' lots of love potions today, too."

Claire could use one of each at the moment, and so could Zee. He had a hot date tonight, and Claire was just hot under the collar where Black was concerned. A lady who was obviously a tourist from New York, considering her accent, came up and demanded that they come down on the price of a jar of bat wings, which Etienne answered with calm and polite respect. "Can't do that, ma'am. They is hard to come by."

Claire smiled to herself and followed Zee through a curtain of clicking black beads into the back of the store. There they found his granny, sitting on a tall stool at a worktable doing God knew what with what looked like lots of dead critters' body parts. She wondered if PETA ever picketed the place.

"Hey, Mama Lulu, Etienne says you been too busy to think."

"Well, now, look at dat, de big po-lice detective, come to see his grandmama at last. Where you been at, Zander? Forget about who raised you up and put de food in yo' mouth?"

"Nah, Mama, you know I haven't. We got a big case that's keepin' us busy."

The old woman had to be in her eighties, and spoke in an unusual accent and cadence that appeared to be pigeon English with a lot of French patois and some kind of native Caribbean dialect thrown in, too. Very distinct and different, and it made Claire wonder where the old woman had grown up. When Mama Lulu suddenly jumped down off the stool, she appeared spry and sassy and wore some kind of a bizarre gypsy outfit that would no doubt wow tourists, especially coupled with the handsome little boy in his miniature tuxedo. Quite an outfit it was, too. A red and yellow paisley skirt, long and full. A gold shawl was knotted over a long-sleeved black silk blouse, and a fringed purple turban and huge gold hoops finished the eccentric getup. Apparently, some tourists were real suckers, but Zee said that Mama Lulu made enough off them to keep food on the table and to send Etienne to a private Catholic school in Thibodaux. So good for her. Everybody needed to find a way to make a buck these days, unless they were Black or Jack Holliday. They had plenty of cash just lying around and getting dusty.

"Who dat? You got a pretty gal you ain't tole us 'bout?" Mama Lulu demanded, looking Claire up and down with a critical eye.

"Now, Mama, she ain't my girlfriend. She's my partner. You know that. Claire Morgan's her name."

Mama Lulu put some very dark eyes on Claire for a very long time and made Claire very uncomfortable. It seemed as if the old lady could read her mind or was implanting strange voodoo commands in her brain, but maybe it was just the vibes in the slightly sinister shop that were freaking Claire out.

"How do you do, Mama Lulu?" Claire said, mainly to break their uncomfortable eye lock.

"You best be careful, girl. You got dark gris-gris all 'round you."

Well, that was just great. Damn it. "And that means?"

"Dat mean you better watch out for evil t'ings."

Double greats. "Thank you. I try to, but sometimes it just gets tough out there."

"I got amulets that'll protect you. I will sell you two for one. Five bucks."

Claire felt a little better for a moment, thinking the gloom-and-doom prophecy was just a sales tactic. Until Mama Lulu turned, picked up two necklaces with little leather pouches on the end, and draped them around Claire's neck. "I give you dese two. You need dem worse'n me."

Crap. Claire was beginning to feel sorry that they came. But she shook it off and opened the manila envelope she carried, chock-full of ugly crime scene photos. She chose the close-up shot of the Veve with the two snakes and stars. "Thanks for the amulets, Mama Lulu, but we really need you to look at this picture and tell us what it means. Would you mind doing that for us?"

Mama Lulu looked accusingly at her grandson. Zee made nice. "It's nothin' evil. Just a picture of a Veve."

"You be wearin' de charms I gave you, Zander?"

Zee looked like a subdued child in his grandmama's presence, but Claire had a feeling she looked a little hangdog herself. It had to be the shop and the peculiar smells and human skulls and snakeskins, not to mention the bat wings. They had both been fine before they'd walked in.

"Yes, ma'am. They're tucked inside my shirt, next to my heart, just like you told me."

Mama Lulu nodded sagely and looked satisfied. She took the photo of the spilled cornmeal and tracings that Claire was holding out. She laid it on the table under the hanging light. She studied it very closely, *very* closely, for at least three minutes. Claire wanted to drum her fingers on the table but stood still, the rather unpleasant and less than aromatic scents emanating from her necklace charms wafting up to her nose. Not exactly Estée Lauder but Estée Lauder couldn't stop a bullet, either.

"Dis be a Loa named Damballah-Wedo."

"Shit," said Zee.

Not a good sign, that. "Now what exactly again is a Loa?" Claire asked quickly.

"A Loa is a voodoo deity. Damballah-Wedo is a deity in Loa family of Rada. He is male."

"Good or evil?" Claire thought it best to know that right off, but she had a feeling she already knew.

"Either and neither."

Hocus-pocus, anyone? But then Mama Lulu suddenly became more forthcoming. She pointed to the symbols in the photograph.

"We know him by de sign of de serpent or de snake. Humans possessed by him do not speak but dey hiss and whistle. Dey move like snakes and slither along de ground and flick de tongue and climb up de walls and writhe about on de tree limbs. He be associated with St. Patrick."

Zee nodded. "Yeah, makes sense. St. Patrick drove the snakes outta Ireland, didn't he?"

Oooookay. Yep, a hissing, slithering murder suspect writhing around on a tree limb should be quite easy to spot. "Why are there two snakes? And what do the stars mean? And is that a cross or a plus sign?"

"Damballah-Wedo is deity of creation and loving father to de world. He bring peace and harmony and water and rain. Dat's a cross. Voodoo use many Christian symbols. I do not know what dis here picture in de Veve mean with dese t'ings. Only he knows, de one who make it."

"Well, that peace and harmony stuff's a lot better than hissing zombies," Claire remarked. Zee gave her a warning look, obviously buying into all the mumbo jumbo. Somehow Claire wasn't quite convinced yet. Maybe it was the slithering up a live oak tree thing. "Do this god's priests ever kill and sacrifice human beings?"

Mama Lulu stepped away from her as if Claire's hair had suddenly burst into flame. "Do not talk such evil t'ings."

Well, Claire guessed that was that. She sorted through the photos until she found one depicting the highly bizarre altar. Hesitating, she looked at Zee. "What about the actual crime scene, Zee? That too much?"

"I will look at it," Mama Lulu answered for him.

Claire handed it over. Again, Mama Lulu took a *verrrrrrry* long look at it, and then finally said, "Dis will summon Papa Damballah. His color is white. Dat is why woman is dressed in white with de white flowers and candles. Dis is offering."

"Does this look like the work of a real voodoo priest or somebody trying to give that impression?"

"Voodoo priests don' leave dead bodies on dere altar places," Mama Lulu told her in an accusatory and offended tone. She might've well as said, *You stupid idiot girl,* because that was what her tone clearly implied.

"Okay, that's what I figured."

"Maybe long ago in de old and bad days. Dis will disturb Papa Damballah. He will rise and be angry at de sacrilege."

"Well, that's all we need. We've got enough trouble. Tell me, Mama Lulu, what does it mean when a picture of a person is pinned on the face of a voodoo doll, stuck on with pins, you know, in the eyes and heart and between the legs, and placed in the corpse's hands?"

Mama Lulu quickly crossed herself and looked frightened as all get out. "Dat means dat dey will suffer a horrible death soon."

Wonderful. Maybe Claire would keep wearing the smelly amulets, after all. Black would just have to get used to the less than pleasant odor. She sighed. "Do you have a book on all this stuff, Mama Lulu? I think I need to brush up and see if I can figure out some kind of motive here."

Mama Lulu nodded and led them out into the front of the shop, which was now even more crowded with customers. Many of them were staring at Etienne, who was holding a human skull with a burning candle stuck in a hole in the top of its head. As it turned out, Claire found several books on voodoo and the god who liked white so much—to the tune of $57.14. She wondered if Russ Friedewald would reimburse her if she left them at the station as research materials. Her salary wasn't exactly Paris Hilton comparable, and she did have to buy Black something nice for Christmas, not that he deserved anything at the moment. Hell, maybe she'd give him some books on voodoo and a truth-telling amulet to tuck into his shirt. But now, she was going to go home, get some sleep, and pore over all this weird stuff and figure out what their hissing, slithering voodoo murderer might do next.

A Very Scary Man

Malice's dream was fast becoming a reality. He continued to pilfer building supplies from his uncle's business and tote them out to his secret place deep in the bayous. He had started his Maze of Terror and it was going very well, but it was slow work. He had already built all sorts of metal tunnels made out of barrels and big plastic tubes for his eventual prey to crawl through so that he could hit the metal with a hammer while they were inside and terrify them. He made all sorts of trapdoors with hinges over deep pits and hidden doors and barred cages so that he could jump out and scare the devil out of his screaming captives. It was all going extremely well, and nobody suspected a thing. He was just ecstatic.

Even at school, everything was most excellent. He had met the most wonderful girl in the world, and she loved him back. She wasn't anything like Timid Little Dead Betsy. She was strong and smiley and smart and beautiful and a good athlete like him. He found himself downright intrigued by her, almost as fascinated with her as he was with honing his terror tactics. Strange thing was, though, he had no desire to scare her. He just wanted to look at her and be with her and breathe in her perfume that smelled like lemons, all the time, every day, and she wanted to be with him all the time, too. He even gave her his letter jacket with all its medals and chevrons and let her take it home and wear it whenever she wanted. And it only got worse. He adored her to the extent that he didn't want to do anything else but be with her every single minute of every single day.

He rarely worked on his Maze of Terror, until he decided that maybe it could be a place for them instead, just the two of them, the only ones who knew where it was and how to get there through all the stagnant sloughs and flooded cypress trees. Maybe he could make a beautiful lover's bower for them there, where they could take off their clothes and make tender sweet love and nobody would ever find them. The thought appealed to him, and he started work on the maze again. He gave her his class ring with the big red stone as soon as he got it. She wore it on her finger with a rubber band around it because her hands were so small and dainty though they were strong too. She could throw a softball harder than he could.

Then calamity struck. The police caught him stealing stuff for his maze out at his uncle's construction site and arrested him. His parents and his uncles came to the station to see him but would not give him bail so he had to stay in jail for thirty days. He hated it there, and for the first time in his life, he felt truly frightened. He was terrified to go outside his cell and into the bullpen for exercise because of all the drug addicts and big muscular criminals who hung around in there. He was as scared as all his victims had been. He understood how they felt for the very first time. But it made him angry, too, furious, and filled him with a vindictive thirst for revenge. Even worse, his girlfriend's parents decided she couldn't go out with him anymore because he was now a jailbird. That nearly killed him because he loved her so much. And then, the worst thing of all happened. She began to date another boy, one with whom Malice had played football during all those years when they were growing up.

Both of them betrayed him, and he hated them for it. He hated them so much, in fact, that as soon as he got out of jail and graduated, he joined the Merchant Marine. Maybe then he could forget her and not cry into his pillow anymore when he was alone in bed or out in the swamps working on his maze. He despised himself for that, the weakness she brought out in him. And he despised the other boy for taking her away from him. Someday they'd pay for what they'd done; he swore that to the depths of his soul. He wouldn't rest until they did. He even went to a voodoo queen in the French Quarter and asked her to put a hex on them and their marriage and their children. He asked her to make them suffer and die with her evil charms and poison potions.

Then he went to New York for training, and then in time, he finally shipped out on his first tour at sea and left behind everything and everybody who had hurt and betrayed him. But he didn't leave behind the pain and anger and viciousness and vengefulness. He tucked it away for when he came back. That's when they would be the ones who suffered, not him. They would pay for what they had done to him, and they would pay with their lives.

Chapter Ten

Zee and Claire spent the next morning at the office in Thibodaux preparing written reports on the Madonna Christien homicide for Sheriff Friedewald, who was off attending a law enforcement seminar in Metairie. By eleven-thirty, she was in good enough shape time wise to drive back home to New Orleans. After lunch, Zee would drive over to the city, and they would seek out a certain cheerleader by the name of Wendy Rodriguez.

Claire decided to leave her vehicle at the *Bayou Blue*'s parking lot because she was supposed to meet Nancy there later for their girls' night out and she didn't particularly want to see Black beforehand, so Zee picked her up at the docked steamboat. On their way to the interview, Claire sat silently and listened to Zee's excited minute-by-minute account of the latest episode of some campy HBO vampire show that he never, ever missed.

Black had called several times the night before to explain himself, but she hadn't picked up. She did text him back and tell him that she was all right and to please quit calling and that they'd talk when he got home, but she'd only done that because he worried about her all the time and had saved her life on several occasions. She would see him later tonight, and that was soon enough to hash things out. Besides, she was still sitting on simmer over the fact that he had lied to her. He had better come up with some damn good reasons, which she suspected he would. She had dreamed about him, too, a lovely little tidbit in which he'd turned into a hissing snake and slithered up a palm tree and thrown coconuts down at her. Somehow, she thought that symbolic. But she was used to bad dreams—well, not used to them, but she'd had enough not to panic when she woke up alone and sweaty in the middle of the night. At least Jules Verne had been there to lick her face and make her feel better. And beefy Juan Christo had been on guard downstairs with a very large shotgun and a pricey security system that did everything but pull the trigger. Meanwhile, she'd concentrate on the case and worry about Black later.

Midday traffic was going strong in downtown New Orleans, and Claire opened Zee's laptop. "I researched our cheerleader when I got home, Zee. Wanted to find out something about her that I could sink my teeth into."

"You sank your fangs into Jack Holliday pretty good yesterday. Sucked him dry, I'd say. He probably had to get a transfusion today."

It appeared that Zee still had his mind on the undead. "Well, cheer up. I think you're going to enjoy this interview. Take a look at Wendy Rodriguez."

Zee glanced over at the screen and gave a low, appreciative whistle. "Whoa now, she is smokin' hot."

"What did you expect? She's a Saints cheerleader, isn't she? She's awfully skinny, if you ask me. Needs to eat a couple of po'boys now and again."

But it is the truth about her being beautiful, Claire thought. *Exactly Jack Holliday's type.*

As it turned out, Wendy Rodriguez lived in a pretty nice apartment complex, not far from Tulane University and just off Magnolia. Zee pulled in the main entrance, where a big sign made out of cypress heralded the words, *Mimosa Circle*. A black-uniformed security man ensconced inside an eight-foot-square, cypress-planked booth asked them what business they had with the denizens of his domain. They showed him twin shiny badges, then continued on their way through serpentine, mimosa-tree-lined roads, looking for number 541. Ten minutes later, they found the home of Wendy Rodriguez. A cypress-sided apartment with only one differentiating factor from the other two hundred young adult/yuppie cribs of Mimosa Circle—her giant black and gold New Orleans Saints flag hanging on the front porch.

Zee said, "We gonna give her a call first, let her know we're comin'?"

"I don't want her to know we're coming. I want to catch her off guard."

"Okey doke. This's gonna be a pleasure for a change."

As they walked up the short sidewalk to Wendy's front door, Claire said, "Now try not to gawk when she opens the door, Zee, like you did with Holliday. Sometimes you remind me of my other partner."

"Hey, now, Bud's cool."

Yep, Zee and Bud had hit it off big time when Bud had been down visiting at Thanksgiving. In fact, she had felt like a fifth wheel at times when they were talking football with Black.

"Yeah, you liked Bud almost as much as you liked Holliday. Then again, you tried on his ring, which gave him an extra point."

"Hey, I was just takin' the edge off those needles you was stickin' in him. The poor guy didn't have a chance."

On the front door, Wendy had hung a big silver Christmas wreath with red-and-white candy canes hanging all over it. There was a little pair of scissors tied to it with a red ribbon. Zee helped himself to one while Claire found the doorbell, all shiny brass and lit up. Claire pressed it, and soon signs of life appeared at a narrow aperture window beside the front door, just a faint stir of white silk drapes. Gorgeous cheerleader checking out uninvited guests. By the looks of this girl, she would have a whole queue of males lining up to ring her doorbell and other kinds of bells, too.

Then came clicks and rattles, as locks were disengaged and chains slid out of their grooves. The door cracked two inches max, stopped short by one last, extra-duty heavy security chain.

"Yes?" Female voice, wary and husky and sexy.

"Hello, ma'am. We're looking for a Ms. Wendy Rodriguez. Are you she?"

"Yes. Who are you?"

"I'm Detective Claire Morgan with the Lafourche Parish Sheriff's Office. This is my partner, Detective Zander Jackson."

"Lafourche! Oh, my God, is Mama okay?"

Claire and Zee looked at each other. "I have no knowledge of your mother, Ms. Rodriguez."

"Oh, thank God. She lives down there around Golden Meadow so I thought ya'll were comin' out here 'cause something awful happened to her."

"No, ma'am, as far as we know she's fine. But we do need to talk to you. Maybe we could come in?"

"Well, I'm not dressed yet."

"That's okay," interjected Zee, very understanding when he wanted to be.

Claire frowned a warning at him. "We can wait out here until you get some clothes on," she said, the considerate partner. Zee was the leering partner, or would be, as soon as Wendy opened the door all the way.

"I guess I'm gonna have to see your credentials."

Now that was a good sign. A sexy young Saints cheerleader who has a cognitively functioning brain in her head and probably a can of mace in her hand. A better combination there could not be.

Claire held up her badge around her neck but not the plethora of aromatic amulets she still wore just for safety's sake. "Here you go. Zee, show her yours."

Zee grinned, and then he obliged.

Wendy's pretty face appeared in the crack of the door. She looked at Zee. "You got a cool name. Zee. I like it."

"Yes, ma'am," he drawled out, pleased as punch she liked his name.

They shared a gooey smile. Zee certainly had a way of bonding with their interviewees within the first two seconds. Zee and Wendy were going to get along fine and dandy, Claire just knew it. Unfortunately, Claire also felt it necessary to crash their mutual admiration society. "This is very important, Ms. Rodriguez. We can wait while you get dressed, if you'd like."

"Well, I don't mean to be rude, but maybe I should call your office down there in Thibodaux, just to make sure you're cops." She laughed a little, and yes, it sounded nervous. She looked at Zee some more.

Okay, talk about tedious. "I think that's a good idea for a single woman such as yourself. I can give you the number for the sheriff's office, or you can get it out of the phone book, if you prefer."

"Well . . ." She drew it out for a second and then apparently had some more welcoming inclinations. "I guess I can let you in. You both look okay and have those badges, and all."

"We're legitimate law enforcement officers, I assure you."

So the doubting damsel's portal swung wide open with no more hesitation, and alas, without enough pause for her to get decent. Zee didn't seem to mind what she had on, which happened to be a tight black camisole top and a scrap of black lace she probably thought of as underwear. Claire looked to see where Zee's tongue had landed. His smile was almost as pleased as it was when scarfing down his garlic and shrimp po'boys. Good grief, he was acting more like Bud every single day.

"Lemme get my robe on," she said quickly, dashing Zee's enjoyment.

Zee watched her sashay off down the hall, and then dug frantically in his pockets for the peppermint candy cane. Claire smiled and lowered her voice. "Okay, Zee, take a deep breath."

"I can handle this."

"Guess we'll see."

Wendy was back, stopping at the far end of the entry hall. "Okay, guys, I'm ready. Please, come on back to the kitchen. How about a cup of coffee? I just got up so it's hot and fresh. I had a late date last night. Didn't get in till around two o'clock."

Claire said, "Coffee sounds great." And it did. She could hear the perking and smell the aroma, strong and fragrant and full of caffeine. A definite siren call.

"Sure does," Zee agreed with great admiration and appreciative warmth. Nothing compared to a scantily clad cheerleader who brews a great cup of Folgers.

Claire sat down on a chair that looked like it had been designed for one of Snow White's dwarves. Dopey, maybe, and made out of white tree branches somebody stole from a Colorado aspen grove. Zee took his seat on the brown-and-white striped couch so he could sit closer to Miss Wendy. Claire then got a visual of Peter Pan and Tinker Bell but didn't see any pirate ships or Disney cups or bags of magic dust, so this Miss Wendy evidently had never visited Neverland.

The beauteous Wendy rounded a long black and white granite bar, holding a white wicker tray by leather handles. Three black coffee mugs emblazoned with fleurs-de-lis sat atop it. She was a very good-looking woman all right, pretty much a clone of all cheerleaders who could land gigs at pro football franchises. All the same type, young, gorgeous, impossibly skinny, dark tans, bleached-blond hair hanging way down their backs with dark roots showing along the part like aging pop singers liked to do, lots of smoky gray eye makeup and shiny lip gloss. Oh, yeah, and the obligatory large breasts. She had donned a very short black silk robe, one that was cinched tightly around her small, very anorexic waist. But she was turning out to be a good hostess with a nice smile and a most agreeable manner.

"Here you go, guys. I do have to have my cup of coffee when I get up. I'm addicted to this stuff, plain and simple, can't get enough of it." She gave them both another very nice smile that indicated she'd seen an abundance of teenage braces and Crest White Strips, despite her dependence on coffee.

Then they all sat around and genially agreed that caffeine was indeed a necessary morning ritual and then took synchronized and cautionary first sips. Claire's swallow went down hard. Wendy did make some incredibly strong coffee. Chicory, oh yes, black as swamp mud, oh yes. Then Wendy leaned back against a couple of fuzzy white couch cushions that looked as if they were made out of Pekingese dog fur and gave them yet another sunny smile. Obviously a morning person, so Claire couldn't relate. "Now, what can I do for you?"

"Did I understand you to say that you are from Golden Meadow down in Lafourche Parish?" Claire thought that was an interesting coincidence, might even amount to more than that, if they got lucky. She gauged Wendy's skinny musculature and found it well developed strength-wise, despite the lack of even one fat globule. Wendy obviously knew her way around a workout. She could take on a girl of Madonna Christien's diminutive size, subdue her even. Claire would bet on it. Actually, a ten-year-old, underfed orphan from Sri Lanka could take on somebody Madonna's size.

"Yes, ma'am—oh, I guess I should call you detective, huh? Anyway, I was born smack dab down there in bayou country. Golden Meadow. You know, where my mama lives."

Claire placed the fleur-de-lis-embossed coffee mug on the little round cork fleur-de-lis-embossed coaster on the big fleur-de-lis-embossed coffee table. The woman did love her Saints. But time to get down to brass tacks.

"Are you acquainted with a woman by the name of Madonna Christien, Ms. Rodriguez?"

"Yeah, sure. I know her real well." She looked from Zee to Claire then back to Zee, seemed like all their interviewees did that, but Wendy might've just been concerned about the way Zee's pupils dilated as she crossed her legs and her robe fell open, not enough to be obscene but enough to be admired. She said, "I bet this is about Doc, isn't it?"

"Doc?"

Uh-oh, was she going to bring Black into this case, too? That would just be the last straw. Yes, it would.

Wendy said, "Doc Holliday—you know, Jack Holliday, that good-looking sports agent from Tulane."

Wendy examined Claire curiously, and then she said, "I've heard him called Black Jack, too, but he's not the skirt chaser everybody makes him out to be. Most of his clients in the organization call him Doc now."

The organization meaning the pro football team, Claire surmised. Or maybe Wendy meant the Mob. One thing for sure, Holliday had a whole slew of nicknames.

Zee said, "Yeah, I get it. Doc Holliday, the guy who hung out with Wyatt Earp, right?"

Wendy smiled at him, picked up her mug, cradled it with both palms, looked cute as a button doing it. "Well, truth is, they like to tease him about him gettin' that doctoral degree, and all that junk."

A doctoral degree? Claire couldn't wait to follow up on that one. "Jack Holliday has a doctoral degree?"

"Yes, ma'am, and isn't that just a hoot? He went to school for most of it, right here at Tulane. I think he said his degree's in aviation engineering, or something real brainy like that. Everybody gives him grief about it when he comes around. Call him Einstein and all those geeky names."

It seemed to Claire that Miss Wendy knew a heck of a lot about Jack Holliday's personal business, which made her wonder if Wendy might just be some of Jack Holliday's personal business.

Wendy elaborated further. "Oh, yeah, that airplane thing's got something to do with his family's business."

Then the connection dawned on Claire like the proverbial cartoon light bulb. "Do you mean he's part of Holliday Aviation Enterprises?"

"Yeah, that's right. I never can remember the name of that place."

Seemed pretty easy to remember to Claire, considering the spot-on Holliday name in the title, but then again, Wendy was a blonde and a cheerleader. Claire didn't know much about the company, but she'd seen the hangars when they flew in on Black's Lear out at Louis Armstrong. "I didn't realize he was connected to that Holliday family."

"He's really something," said Wendy.

"That he is," Claire agreed, and meant it, sort of. "Now, Ms. Rodriguez, we've established that you are acquainted with Madonna Christien, is that correct?"

"I know her from high school. We were best friends back then. She lives here in the city now. Somewhere down on Carondelet. Off Gravier, I think."

"And you introduced her to Mr. Holliday?"

"I sure did. She was a fan of Jack's when he played in college and wanted to meet him once she knew I was talkin' to him, and stuff. I guess she thought he was hot, too."

Well, that checked out with Jack's version. "Madonna asked for the introduction, not Jack?"

"Yes, but he was fine with it until she started driving him nuts and chasing him around all over the place. He didn't get pissed at me about it, but he finally had to get a judge to get her off his back. You know, one of those restraining things. I mean, we're talking stalker city, you know, the old *Fatal Attraction* rabbit-cooking-on-the-stove-and-drowning-in-the-bathtub kinda obsession."

"I love that movie," said Zee.

"Me, too," said Wendy. "Especially the part in the elevator."

Well, even Claire remembered that part, but who wouldn't recall that wild sex scene that probably bruised up Glenn Close pretty good in some intimate places. But it was a young and hunky Michael Douglas doing the business so she probably didn't mind too much at the time. By Zee's expression, Claire decided that he remembered it, also, and only too well.

"What can you tell us about Madonna's alleged stalking of Mr. Holliday?"

"Are ya'll gonna arrest her for stalking? Like I said, we're BFFs, and I hate to be snitching on her like she's some kind of stranger and getting her in trouble, and junk. Especially after what we went through when we were little. Did Doc tell you to come out here and look me up?'

"He mentioned that you introduced him to Madonna." But Claire was curious about the other thing Wendy had just mentioned. "What did you and Madonna go through when you were little, if I might ask?"

Wendy went sober really fast. She sat up straight, avoided their eyes, and acted extremely uncomfortable. "Well, we were kidnapped by this crazy guy."

"Kidnapped? When?"

"When we were little, both of us." She shivered all over. She remembered it all right.

"Can you tell us what happened?"

"I can hardly talk about it now. Madonna can't at all. I was spending the night with Madonna, you know, at her house, and he came there in the middle of the night and killed her parents, and then he tied us up and threw us in the back of his van. See, he had on this really scary mask, like voodoo guys wear."

"God, that must've scared the hell outta you," Zee said.

"It sure did. Jack thought the same thing. Asked me all about it. But it made us both real careful about things. Like all those chains on my door. We were lucky he didn't kill us."

But Claire knew this was important and somehow fit into the Christien murder. And she wanted to know how. "So you got away? Did they catch him?"

Claire waited for Wendy to answer, but the kidnapping had to be significant, considering the voodoo mask.

"We didn't get away right off. He put us in a boat and took us out in the swamp to this big voodoo altar kinda thing. He laid us in front of it and lit up a bunch of candles, but then a boat started comin', thank goodness, and he took off and left us there. The fisherman saw

the candles burning and came and saved us. It was the scariest day
of my life. We never got over it, either one of us."

"How old were you then?" Claire asked.

"Around ten. Well, Maddie wasn't ten yet, but I was."

"And Jack asked you all about this incident, you say?"

"Yeah, he thought it was a real terrible thing and wanted to know
if I remembered anything about the guy."

"Do you?"

"No. It happened so long ago. Truthfully, we were both so scared
that we couldn't remember much. Except for the altar and the mask.
That mask was terrifying. It was red and had snake scales and
feathers and bones all over it."

And once again Papa Damballah slithers back into the picture.
"And they never found your abductor?"

"No, ma'am, but he's still out there in the swamps. Everybody
who lives out around there knows it, too. It's almost a legend now.
The snake man. And poor Madonna. She got real, real superstitious
after that. You know, started studying voodoo and all that stuff. She's
even made a voodoo love altar for Jack. Isn't that just pathetic?"

Well, that explained the altar at the Carondelet Street crime scene,
but there were lots of voodoo rituals going on here, too, too many to be
coincidental. Not that Claire ever believed in coincidences. Yep,
Wendy's kidnapper could be the guy they were looking for. But why
wait until now? Why murder Madonna now, after so long? Or, was
this another member of some cult? Maybe an initiation ritual? Wow,
everything was getting unreal. She looked at Zee. He was frowning,
too. Jack's interest in the kidnapping was something they couldn't
overlook. "Okay, let's go back to Jack Holliday. You said he showed
a big interest in your abduction?"

"Yeah. He was real sympathetic to both of us. Thought it was a
bad thing for little kids to have to go through."

"And you introduced him to Madonna, is that correct?"

"Yeah. Maddie told me she thought he was real good-looking."
Wendy shook her head. "Lots of girls like Jack. You've seen that
poster of him coming out of the water. It's sort of old now, but he
really looks good now, too."

"A friend of mine has it."

"He's like some kind of glorious Greek god, don't you think? Just like Apollo, or Adonis, or Superman."

Claire was impressed with Wendy's classical analogies until her last hero shattered the illusion. "And he didn't like Madonna's attention?"

"He was okay with it at first when he felt sorry for her because of us getting kidnapped, but then she just kept on pushing him, giving him stuff. Gifts and love letters, even roses. She's got it really bad for him; I've never seen anything like it."

"Did she give him anything else?"

"Oh, yeah. Once it was this key ring, sterling silver with his initials on it." She thought about it some more, while taking an extra second to exchange sappy smiles with the very attentive Zee. "Once she got him a black cashmere sweater with a little fleur-de-lis on it. Right here." She tapped on her left breast. "But he gave it to me to give back to her. He gave most all that stuff back to her."

Wendy stretched her neck from side to side, then lifted the back of her long hair up into the air as she stretched out her arms in a most languorous pose. "He didn't want anything from her. He was pretty cool about me being the one who introduced them. I'm still real embarrassed that she's acting this way."

"I see."

"Is she in trouble? I was pretty sure Jack was going to end up havin' her arrested, or something. I guess that restraining order didn't do much good, huh?"

Zee gave Claire a significant glance. Unfortunately, it was her cue to ruin Wendy's day. "I'm very sorry, Wendy, but I've got some bad news concerning Madonna."

"Oh, God, what?" Now Wendy looked scared. Terrified, actually.

"She was found dead on Sunday. Murdered."

Wendy's face actually went white under her spray-on tan, and her hands went up to cover her mouth. Yeah, she was flabbergasted, all right. She was awfully open with her feelings. "Murdered? No way, no way. Who did it?"

"That's why we're here. We're trying to figure that out."

Wendy's big mocha-colored eyes burned a hole in Claire's face, so wide and shocked that it wasn't hard to read the exact instant when the truth dawned inside those heavily lined and mascara-drenched depths. "Oh, my God, ya'll think Jack did it, don't ya? Oh, no, uh-uh, he's not like that, I swear to God. He'd never hurt her. She's dead? Really? Dead? Are you sure she's dead?"

Claire envisioned that poor girl, dressed all in white, posed on that altar, eyelids and mouth stitched together, and the way she'd looked stretched out naked on the cold steel table, dozens of ugly bruises and contusions all over her flesh. "Yes, Wendy, we're one hundred percent sure."

Wendy's straight white teeth nibbled at her full, coral-tinted bottom lip, liquid spilling over her eyelashes. Some suspects could weep on cue, veritable Meryl Streeps, in fact. But Wendy's tears were the real thing, no doubt about it.

Wendy said, "That poor little thing. She was tiny, you know, barely five feet, and she was okay, a pretty good girl, except for that sick thing she had for Doc." She kept running splayed fingers through her silky hair. "Does her brother know yet?"

Claire perked up. Zee perked up. Claire said, "Madonna Christien has a brother?"

"Yes. He's a few years older than her."

"What's his name?"

"Rafe. That's short for Raphael. Christien."

"Do you know where we can find him?"

Wendy hesitated. Did that hair-stroking thing some more. "Well, okay, he's a junkie, if you must know. Crystal meth, usually. Maddie worries about him all the time. He's got friends down in the Quarter. Some really bad guys."

"Was Madonna into drugs?"

Wendy looked down a little too long, maybe thinking through whether she wanted to vilify her recently deceased friend. "Yeah, she was. Just weed, mostly, but other stuff, too. I'm telling you she was constantly upset about Rafe and those guys he smoked dope with. They're real dirtbags. His friends, I mean. You know, those Skulls in that biker gang. They're dealers and lowlifes, all of them. But she still hung around with them a lot."

"Did Madonna ever mention to you that somebody was threatening her or that she was afraid of anybody in particular?"

She shook her head. "No, never. She dated lots of men, though. You know what I mean? Lots."

Dated was one way to put it. Not exactly the way Claire would describe Madonna's relationships, but it did sound better than whoring, especially when referring to an old high school BFF.

"Were any of these men into voodoo?"

"Not that I know of. But, hey, I don't mean she's some kind of voodoo priestess, or nothin' like that. She just got all involved with that junk after that guy took us. Said it protected her from that snake monster. She called him Papa something or other. I handled getting abducted a lot better than she did. I'm not sure why, but I just put it behind me, as much as I could and tried to concentrate on other things. You know?"

Claire did know, but she was having trouble burying some of the demons she'd met up with, just like Madonna had.

Zee decided to join the party. "You know anybody who's got a reason to want her dead?"

"No, except for Jack, who has a pretty good one, if you want to know the truth, but like I said, that's downright ridiculous. All he wanted from the beginning was for her to leave him alone, once and for all, and she pretty much did that, I reckon, after he got that restraining order. She sure didn't want to end up in jail. She told me that. Said she'd been there before and wasn't ever going back—no matter what she had to do, she wasn't gonna end up in jail again."

"Where did she go to jail?"

"Downtown. It was just thirty days for possessing weed and prostitution; they went easy on her on the first offense. She toed the line after that. Said she nearly went nuts in that jail cell. She said she was scared of some of the girls locked up in there with her, and some of the cops, too."

All that she just said fit in with the info Rene had sent to them. "Did she ever tell you that she took out a restraining order on Jack?"

Wendy actually laughed at that one, but then she stopped herself when she remembered that this was serious business. "Why in the world would she do that?"

Yeah, why, indeed? It didn't make a lick of sense to Claire, either, especially since Jack didn't seem to know about it. Unless he was lying to them, which could very well be the case. On the other hand, Rene had faxed a copy of that restraining order to Claire, which pretty much made it official. "Does Madonna have any other relatives that you know of?"

"I don't think so. Like I said, her parents got killed. She and Rafe ended up living with their grandma. Now it's just Rafe and her, I'm pretty sure, but maybe her grandma's still around. You need to ask Rafe."

"And her parents were murdered by this man in the mask, right?"

"It was awful. They just came in their house and shot them dead. We were there, too, Maddie and me, but we didn't hear anything. Not until he woke us up, and then we were scared to move. We just did whatever he said."

"Did they catch the perpetrator?"

"The what?"

"The guy who killed her parents?"

"No, the detectives never could find him. They did say they thought that guy who took us was gonna kill us, too."

Claire had been thinking the same thing. And all of this was connected. She knew it. She just had to line up the dots and draw the lines between them. Easier said than done, unfortunately. "Was that the Golden Meadow detectives?"

"Yes, ma'am."

"Was her brother there when his parents got killed?"

Wendy shrugged. "Yes, but he was older and got to sleep in a room he liked out over the garage. He said he didn't hear anything that night. He just slept right through everything."

"Where can we find him? We've got to notify him about his sister's death. It'll be bad if he reads it first in the newspapers."

That idea seemed to horrify Wendy. "Oh, no, no. Wouldn't that just suck?"

Silence reigned as we all considered that remark, but it would suck, big time, of course. Then Wendy piped up again and became a veritable font of knowledge. "I think I remember Maddie sayin' something about him getting a job as a bouncer down at that biker dive in an alley somewhere off Magazine. Voodoo River, I think the name is, but I'm not positive. All I know for sure about Rafe is that he deals lots of drugs. That's where Maddie always gets her stash. I tried to get her off it, but I never could get her to stop. Wish I had, though. That's probably why she hung out with those guys."

Zee and Claire nodded with sympathy, and Claire took some notes on all the information. Bourdain had mentioned Voodoo River, too, said Madonna might've done some hooking down there. Claire put that down as a target on her places-to-shake-down list. So, all said and done, and as it turned out, Wendy the Cheerleader had been more than helpful, more so than Claire had expected. Now Rafe Christien was in her sights, and his lowlife, dirtbag, druggie friends, who just might be into voodoo and killing his little sister and dumping her down on the bayou in Lafourche Parish. Whoever had set up that scary little altar was going to find out that he had discarded his murderous handiwork in the wrong neighborhood.

Chapter Eleven

The new information about Madonna Christien's brother was the best lead they had at the moment, so they jumped on it and headed straight down to Magazine Street in search of the Voodoo River bar. As it turned out, the establishment was a real nasty little dive halfway down a real nasty little alley in a real nasty little part of town not too awfully far from the French Quarter. Not that Claire usually minded real nasty little dives down real nasty little alleys. She'd been in more than a few such places on official business. And she'd been in a few having some fun, too, and nearly always came out alive and kicking. Usually, however, at such times, she was more apt to be hauling off to jail some brutal, drunken guy who had used his wife as a punching bag and called it sport.

Zee had told her that he rather enjoyed rousting wife batterers, too, especially if he got to subdue the guy with a baton. But he only did that if absolutely necessary, of course. Sometimes, though, after seeing such a man's beaten and bloody wife, lying on her couch with an ice bag on her lumps and bruises and two black eyes swollen shut, he tended to really, really want to teach the guy a lesson. But he was a good cop; she'd found that nobody walked a straighter line than Zee did. Just like Claire, he went by the book. Unless the perpetrator resisted arrest and threw a punch—then the guy might get as good as he dished out to his helpless, frightened wife.

Zee pulled up across the alley from the sleazy bar and shut off the engine. They got out. Claire made sure Zee zapped his door locks. Not that she expected somebody to steal his pride-and-joy red Jeep Cherokee, but such things happened a lot in these sorts of environs. That and/or a broken passenger window and the ever-popular grab-and-flee crime.

Zee bopped along beside Claire, busily punching apps on his beloved smartphone.

"You got all your phone apps up and working, Zee?"

"Yeah, and I'm gettin' me some more. This phone is awesome. What apps you got?"

"I've got a cheap little Samsung TracFone, that's what apps I got. I can call out and text and people can call in. That's it."

"No way. No games or music, no nothin'? No camera?"

"There might be, but I haven't seen it. I have better things to do than stare at a little screen on my telephone all day and poke in abbreviated words that take longer than dialing a number and talking straight into somebody's ear."

"Yeah? Like what?"

"Like rounding up Rafe Christien."

"Okay, I get it. Let's go in." He turned off his phone, but Claire sensed his keen reluctance. Those things were way too addictive. Black was almost as bad except that he had half a dozen for various and sundry reasons. He had given her one a couple of times, but she had a tendency to lose them. So she'd bought one at Wal-Mart for herself, one without all the bells and whistles and installment plans. Now if she lost the thing, no big deal. Zee glanced over at the pack of Harley Davidsons and other powerful motorcycles crowded together just down the alleyway. He said, "You got your weapon loaded, right? Looks like we might be crashin' in on some major thugs and felons."

"I'm sure you're right. Keep your hand near your weapon, and so will I."

Zee stopped outside the entrance. "Okay, I heard about this bar on one of my vice cases. These guys deal outta here and they kill outta here. Just sayin'."

"Then like I said. Proceed with caution."

Okay, granted. The place was a rowdy bar, lots of brawls, lots of assaults, lots of arrests, lots of cretins and morons and worse. So they had to be vigilant and put some impressively serious expressions on their faces as they stepped inside the dark, dank, crowded, smelly bar. They had to act as if they weren't the least bit scared of all the big, black-leathered, chained, tattooed guys with Yeah-I-killed-a-guy-last-night-and-so-what patches on their denim jackets. Inside, a plethora of Skulls were coiled around every table. Claire could smell weed in the air. Weed and spilled booze and filthy bathrooms and sweat and testosterone. Especially testosterone. No low T going on in Voodoo River.

Wary, Claire observed the scene first, took a second gander at one particular Skull associate that she knew rather well, but hadn't seen in a very long time. She hid her shock, hesitated, and then decided this was not the time or place to renew their acquaintance. Maybe he wouldn't remember her. He was sitting at the far end of the bar, and she let her gaze sweep past him as if she didn't know him from Adam and didn't want to. That would be better for both of them— oh, yeah, and for Zee, too. She hoped he had enough sense not to approach her with malice aforethought, or trouble would come calling and soon. She kept her hand on the butt of her weapon, just in case anybody felt the need to assault her.

Long and L-shaped, the bar was made out of scarred, burned, and punctured oak, said imperfections probably created by boozy bikers and other similar ilk that had missed their victims and stabbed their Bowie knives into the wood instead. It also looked to be stained with something grossly unpleasant and had seen nary a Clorox wipe in a month of Sundays.

Claire's previous acquaintance had one arm draped around a— how should she describe the gal? Scuzzy but slightly attractive hooker, perhaps? Yes, indeed, the woman did show signs of being a genuine, fully initiated biker babe. First clue? How about the tattoo proclaiming ROCCO'S SLUT in big red letters on her bulging left breast? Yes, her major attributes were barely contained inside a tight, white nylon tank top. Claire did hope those delicate bosoms were held up with reinforced, double-stitched, industrial-strength bra straps. If the dam broke, it wouldn't be pretty.

Rocco's Slut appeared to be his girlfriend, since the name Rocco was embroidered in curly gold script across the breast of his sleeve-less black denim vest. Nothing underneath but bare skin and jailhouse tats and lots of muscles. Rocco wasn't the name Claire knew him by, of course, but she had a feeling he had lots of names and lots of jackets with lots of highly imaginative, embroidered aliases. A quick glance alerted Claire that Rocco was still as tall and tough and intimidating as he had been the last time she had run into him. His black hair was longer now, tied back at his nape with a leather strap, and he had grown himself an incredibly silly-looking Jack Sparrow mustache and goatee.

Even worse, he'd braided his chin hair, which struck Claire as rather juvenile and immature, even for a Skull. A Confederate-flag scarf was tied around his forehead, also ala *Pirates of the Caribbean.* He was wearing the aforementioned sleeveless denim vest designed to make sure everybody knew how big and bulging his biceps were. And was that black man-cara on his eyes, just like Johnny Depp's? Oh, my, Rocco did have an affinity for swashbuckling. Claire looked for his cutlass and turned-back, high-heeled boots like Puss in Boots wore, but didn't see any.

Claire did notice that there were a couple of blood-dripping knives and sharp hatchets added as cutesy curlicue embellishments around the name Rocco on the vest. He had numerous patches sewn on, lightning bolts and stars, stuff like that, their biker meanings something Claire shuddered to think about. She didn't see the skeleton death patch earned when somebody died painfully by one's hands, but maybe he was just shy about mentioning his murder rampages.

Rocco saw Claire grimacing at his attire and glanced away, which was a good thing. He kept his face averted and appeared so completely bored that she almost believed it. She stared at his companion, Ms. R. Slut, until the girl shifted her eyes away, too. It took the woman a few seconds longer though, pretty much until right after she saw the badge dangling on the chain around Claire's neck and the loaded Glock in her holster.

The bartender was beefy and red-faced. Why were all bartenders beefy and red-faced? Now the center of attention, Claire and Zee strolled over to the bar and sat down on a couple of swiveling stools where their backs wouldn't be such an open invitation for sharp knives and/or prison shivs. Claire avoided looking at the pool of something rather black and rancid on the bar. Whatever it was, it smelled really bad. But she preferred clean air and the smell of Downy and flowers. So there you go.

The barkeep was leaning against the wall, staring at them, chewing on a toothpick, or maybe it was a nail. "What can I get for you, Officers?"

So everybody saw the badge. Well, good. Zee was being watchful, hand on his hip, very near his weapon, too. Claire was pretty certain that nobody was going to accost two police officers, but bikers never talked to police officers, and didn't snitch on each other, either, so she didn't expect to get much information without a couple of strategically inserted deadly threats.

Claire met the bartender's stare. "How's it going?"

"What's it to you?"

Enough small talk. "You know a guy named Rafe Christien?"

"Rafe Christien? Let me think." He pressed his fore and middle fingers up to his forehead as if contemplating. A real card.

Zee said, "Somebody told us that he mops up around here. That true?"

The Real Card swiveled his gaze to Zee. "Maybe."

Claire said, "Maybe you should tell us then."

He shrugged and idly wiped a dirty dishrag over the dirty counter with his dirty hand. Again, the place did not appear to be a *Good Housekeeping* test kitchen. No casseroles, no cucumber and cream cheese sandwiches, no million-dollar-winning recipes, no mop, no anything that equated with clean.

"Yeah, he mops sometimes, bounces sometimes, too. That's all I know."

"That's not much. Is Christien here now?" Claire glanced around and decided that everybody in the place looked like bouncers. She also found about thirty pairs of beady, mean, and possibly whiskey-fogged eyes boring into her. Luckily, she'd seen other cop haters before so she wasn't inordinately upset. Zee was trying to be friendly now. He smiled and nodded to a bald-headed guy, the one who'd sidled up and claimed the bar stool right beside him. His new friend displayed a rather skillfully rendered skull-and-crossbones tattoo on his scalp, just above his right ear.

The bartender finally decided it wouldn't hurt to answer her question. "Nope. Ain't seen him."

"Know where he is?"

"Yep."

"And where would that be?"

"My guess is he's sittin' in jail since a couple of your NOPD buds came in a coupla nights ago and roughed him up. Last I saw they was shovin' him into the back of a cop car."

"Gee, poor guy. I bet he missed Communion Mass, and everything. What'd they charge him with?"

He shrugged. "I didn't see him do nothin'."

The bar was suddenly quiet, pin-dropping silent in fact. Even the jukebox shut itself off.

The friendly bartender must've decided it wasn't such a healthy choice to cooperate further, not with everybody hanging on his every word. He said, "Ain't none'a my business."

"You better make it your business, or you can come down to the Lafourche Parish Sheriff's Office and talk to us there. So, I'll ask again, Christien work here long?"

"Three, four months, I reckon."

"What about this week?"

"He ain't been here much. He done some crabbing somewheres down around Chauvin. Hell if I know. I ain't his mama."

"You didn't see him earlier this week?"

"I ain't keepin' track."

A few more questions got a few more disingenuous and evasive answers. Claire took a casual gander down at the end of the bar and found Rocco nuzzling said slut's neck. Lucky gal. She better check for fang marks.

Old Skull and Crossbones beside Zee decided to stand up and glare down at Zee, arms akimbo, frown rather intimidating.

"Quit starin' at me, asshole," he sweet-talked Zee. The guy was clenching and unclenching his fists, as if fantasizing about Zee's neck.

Unfortunately, Zee decided a reply was in order. "My pleasure, man."

It appeared that Zee didn't particularly like people messing with him. He didn't appear to be a man to take insults lying down either, giant ugly biker, or not. But Zee could take care of himself—at least she hoped so. She did know he had won trophies for karate and jujitsu. And he did have that great big loaded gun to pull out.

The tension was so thick that it felt like a heavy fog pressing down on her head. She took a deep breath, now fairly certain that the situation would soon escalate into a rather unpleasant, nuclear evening. Them's fighting words, and all that. Several more tough guys scraped back chairs and flexed inked muscles. Including Pirate Beard and his lovely companion. Rocco's Slut slid away from the bar and the probable onset of physical violence, which only proved that she was probably smarter than she looked.

"Yeah," growled Rocco, walking slowly toward them, calm as could be, but the menace was there, and everybody could see it. "Who do you think you are, bitch, coming in here and bustin' our balls?"

"I think I'm an officer of the law. You interested in doing something about that, Rocco?"

Zee turned to face all their newfound friends, leaned his back against the bar, but kept one eye on the man behind the bar, who had lots of bottles at hand to break over their heads. Rocco was close enough now for Claire to smell the whiskey on his breath. He said, "You busted me once, bitch. Ain't gonna happen again."

Zee decided it was time to pull his weapon. He did so. Everybody noticed.

Nobody moved for a couple of beats. Claire decided to defuse the situation. Couldn't hurt. She preferred to avoid shootouts.

"Don't be stupid, Rocco. I'm not hassling you. I'm asking questions about Rafe Christien and his whereabouts."

His big brown eyes were focused on her face. Now that they were up close and personal, Claire could see that he absolutely did wear black eyeliner and man-cara, lots of it. Gross.

"Maybe what we need here is some one-on-one, Rocco. How about you take a little ride with Detective Jackson and me down to bayou country? You can tell me where you've been and what you've been doing for the last week, or so."

Rocco didn't appear interested in her offer. "You think you're hot shit, don't you?"

"Aw, stop, Rocco, you're hurting my feelings."

Quiet, extreme quiet. Glares, stares, gritted teeth, everybody quivering in anticipation of the first fisted blows. Then Rocco gave a tight little laugh, one with no trace of amusement. Claire heard a few nervous charity snickers. She kept her eyes on Rocco, and let Zee watch everybody else. Rocco narrowed his gaze and looked at her as if she were the most disgusting little cockroach that he'd ever stepped on. He didn't blink. He said, "Let's get outta here. I don't like the way cops smell."

Halfway to the door, he turned back and gave Claire another hard stare. "Better watch you back, bitch. We might meet again down in the bayous one of these days."

"That sounds vaguely threatening. Is it?"

Rocco held her gaze in a vaguely threatening manner, and then he strode out, macho leader of the pack, black leather boots scraping across the floorboards. His busty bimbo fled her hidey-hole and scurried after him. The rest of the Skulls spent a few more seconds nursing their disappointment over the lack of a bloody, knock-down-drag-out and then stomped out behind him, but with just enough nonchalance to show they weren't intimidated by the likes of two detectives from Lafourche Parish. Outside, a dozen choppers fired up all at once, engines loud and revved to ridiculous decibels, to scare them, she supposed, and then the lot of them roared off down the street, off to no good.

"Thanks for clearin' out my bar," said the surly bartender.

Claire said, "We'll be back. If Rafe Christien happens to show up, tell him we want to talk to him. Thanks for your cooperation."

Outside, Zee stopped, sucked in some air, and looked at Claire. "Well, that was interestin'. Can you believe those guys? I mean, who lives like that anymore? Grown men ridin' around together on big loud bikes and gettin' tattoos all over their heads. It's childish and absurd."

Somehow, that struck Claire funny. "Childish, huh? You saying you never ran into guys like this when you worked narcotics? Who'd you run in on Saturday nights? Sunday school teachers?"

"Yeah, sure I ran into this kind of lowlife scum. But not this many at once and not in their favorite waterin' hole. Tell me about this Rocco punk. What's up with you and him?"

"Nothing much. I ran into him once a long time ago. No big deal."

"He seems to remember you fairly well. Enough to hate your guts. You better watch your back like he said. That was definitely a threat he tossed at you."

"He took off without throwing a punch. He's not as tough as he looks."

"It got a little hairy in there, don't you think?"

"They're stupid men, but they know better than to assault cops in broad daylight."

Shaking his head, Zee pulled open the driver's door of the Jeep, and Claire walked around the front and slid into the passenger's seat.

"Hey, Zee, how about us going down to lockup to see if Rafe Christien's still there? Think we can get Rene Bourdain to give us the go-ahead."

Zee pulled out his phone. "You read my mind. Let's do it."

A Very Scary Man

Malice ended up liking the Merchant Marine a lot. In fact, he loved it. He loved being at sea. He loved shore leaves in exotic places that he'd never seen before. He loved the hardness and callousness of some of his shipmates and the crudeness of their words and actions. He loved being able to find prostitutes in the slums of the cities they visited, and he loved pretending they were the bitch who had betrayed him with his best friend and hurting them the way he wanted to hurt her. He beat them, took them by force, slapped them around, bit them until he drew blood, and nobody said a word, not if he gave the pimp a little extra cash.

After a couple of years of service, he met his new best friend. He was an older guy on the crew, a lot older than Malice was. He was from Algiers, a town just across the river from New Orleans. He, too, was of Cajun birth, and they had a lot of stuff in common. They both liked to be violent and cruel and fed off each other when they had opportunities to find victims they could abuse. But he learned a lot because the older man finally admitted one day when he was drunk that he worked for a Louisiana crime family out of Algiers, that he did contract hits for them, and had actually murdered people for money, lots of money. He was a cold-blooded killer for hire, an actual hit man, and he fascinated Malice. He told Malice how he committed his murders when he was home on shore leave so he could ship out right afterward so no one could connect him to the crimes. It was a good and lucrative job. The hit man said that he was willing to put in a good word for him with the Mob bosses, but only if Malice was willing to study hard and learn the ropes. He said time would tell if Malice had it in him to kill people for money. But he did. Of course, he did.

As time went on, the hit man taught him to murder with precision without leaving incriminating clues. They began to practice their skills in other countries, sometimes killing some drunk they picked at complete random. His new friend taught him to stalk and watch and plan and then swoop in and stick the knife in, so to speak. He learned a lot about the art of assassination and he learned it fast and he learned it well. More important, he liked it, even better than scaring people and killing somebody by mistake like he had with Betsy.

As soon as he served a few stints, he decided he would return home. He would get a reputable job first, so he'd have a good cover, and then he could start his shiny new life as a professional hit man, earning lots of blood money and spilling lots of blood. He grinned at the idea. If only that betraying bitch at home knew what he had become, she would be terrified of him, and fear his return. And for very good reason. He intended to kill her and the man who had taken her away from him. But she wouldn't know that, no way, uh-uh, not until he stabbed the knife into her heart, cut her jugular, and then stepped back and watched her blood flush out of her, red and sticky and slick, just like his new best friend had taught him.

Chapter Twelve

Downtown, two uniformed NOPD officers manned the front desk. Rene Bourdain had paved the way, so they didn't give Claire and Zee much grief. Looked like a friendly relationship with Lieutenant Rene Bourdain went a long way in New Orleans. A tall sergeant named Chris Makowski escorted them to a small interrogation room with hospital-gray walls, a scratched-up black steel table with four uncomfortable black folding chairs, two on each side. The guest of honor had not yet made his appearance.

Fifteen minutes dragged by, and then Rafe Christien clanked in, all scruffy and bleary-eyed, dressed in white jailbird togs with NOPD JAIL in big black letters across the front and back. His chains dragged the ground as if he were the Ghost of Incarcerations Past. He sat down across from Claire. Mr. Docile, now that he was hooked up nice and tight to a floor ring, nursed a swollen black eye, a painful souvenir from his resisting-arrest charge, no doubt.

"Mr. Christien, we're Lafourche Parish detectives. My name's Claire Morgan, and this is Zander Jackson. We need to talk to you about a homicide case."

They also needed to tell him that his sister was dead, which was not something she coveted. Even with a reprobate and criminal like Rafe. Wendy of cheer fame had intimated that Rafe and Madonna had been fairly close, at least in their drug-dealing/using, sibling/symbiotic sort of way. But blood was thicker than water, or so it was said.

Rafe wasn't one to waste time on idle chitchat. "What case? And what's in it for me?"

Rafe Christien was a small man, not much taller than his diminutive little sister, probably not much over five feet four or five. Hair more orange than red, brown freckles, a bouncer he did not look like. He had to be either super wiry or carry a large weighted sap, take your pick. Claire would bet on the sap or an equally big gun. And he was apparently all set up to be the primo jailhouse snitch for the right incentive, of course. Claire decided to hit him with the bad news first and judge his reaction. He could be involved with his sister's death, but somehow she doubted it.

"I'm afraid this case concerns your sister. Madonna Christien is your sister, isn't she?"

All right, that did surprise him. He revealed shock, very clearly, and his bloodshot blue eyes latched on to Claire's face and held there. "Maddie? What's goin' on with Maddie? She's okay, right? Nothin's happened to her, right?"

Beside her, Zee shifted uncomfortably. Claire shot a glance at him. She had told Wendy what had happened to Madonna. It was Zee's turn to take over.

"We got some bad news, man," Zee started off, voice really gentle. Claire was finding that Zee was a nice young man, more sensitive than most. Then Zee sighed. "There just ain't no good way to say it, man. She's dead. Viciously murdered down in the bayous."

Now that was not exactly the degree of sensitivity Claire had in mind, nor the way she would've broken the news, but she'd found that men, even compassionate ones, didn't like to beat around the bush with bad news.

Rafe's face paled to the color of cold ashes, his jaw went slack, and he looked at Zee as if he were a hideous apparition. Then he swiveled horrified eyes to Claire. But he wasn't breaking down or showing unbridled emotion yet, so maybe Zee did know how to break sad tidings to his fellow man. "She didn't OD?"

Claire said, "No."

Rafe scrubbed rough, calloused hands over his face. "What happened to her? I mean, how'd she die?"

Rafe wanted details so Claire gave them to him, except for the voodoo crime scene. She was keeping that under her hat. "We believe the cause of death was strangulation, but we haven't received the official autopsy report yet."

Now that information hit him hard. All kinds of emotions, fleeting and painful to watch, flitted across his face. Suddenly, he put his forehead down on the table and started an awful, low-pitched keening. Then he began, his words muffled against the table. "Our Father who art in Heaven, hallowed be thy name . . ."

Neither of them said anything. Claire felt bad for him. Zee looked disconcerted. Rafe continued the prayer to the end, signed the cross as best he could shackled in handcuffs and leg irons. But he didn't cry, at least not on the outside.

"I'm very sorry for your loss, Mr. Christien. I truly am. Do you have any idea who might've wanted to harm your sister?"

Rafe's head jerked up. Anger flared inside his eyes, and she could see the flush rising under his whiskered cheeks. "That boyfriend of hers, that bastard Holliday, probably did it."

"Jack Holliday?"

"That's right, the big-shot sports agent—you know, he used to play football."

Claire played dumb. "Jack Holliday was your sister's boyfriend? You sure about that?"

"Yeah, and she had it real bad for him. God, he treated her like crap. Like garbage."

"How do you mean?"

"Well, he took out a restraining order. Led her on first, and everything, and then he sicced the cops on her when she tried to do nice things for him."

Claire digested the different versions of the Holliday/Madonna relationship, or lack thereof. "Did you ever observe the two of them together? Go out with them, anything like that?"

Rafe frowned, looked at Zee. "No. Maddie told me how much he liked her. He just got tired of her. He thinks he's better'n her."

"How do you know that?"

"Because he let Wendy introduce them and then he told Maddie to get lost. She bought him all kinds of stuff—she loved him, I tell you, she did. A lot."

So Rafe had not seen them together. That was a bonus point for

Jack, one to add to his alibi witnesses if he was going to beat this rap. "Okay, Rafe. Anybody else you know who wanted to hurt her?"

Rafe balled his fists and rubbed his eyes. He looked like he'd just come down from a drug high and hadn't slept for the last six months. The whites of his eyes were the color of strawberries, including the seeds. "Guys hung around Maddie all the time. She's so damn pretty. But he's the one she loved."

"Okay. Who were these other men?"

Rafe thought about it, licked dry, cracked lips. The bottom one was split just under his right nostril. His scuffle with arresting officers was one-sided, it appeared. He didn't show a lot of brilliance assaulting cops like that, but she had a feeling he didn't ever show a lot of brilliance.

"She went out with biker dudes the most. You know, the Skulls. Guys she met at Voodoo River. I got a job there; she used to come see me. Guess I still got it when I get outta here. I dunno."

"I need names, Christien."

"Most of 'em. She hooked some, but that don't make her bad. There was one guy. Name's Rocco. Don't know his last name. His old lady hangs out with him, but he messes with Maddie some, too. Nobody crosses him. He'd just as soon stab you in the eye as look at you. Keeps a stiletto in his right boot." Claire filed that back as an important tidbit to remember, but then Rafe stopped and shook his head. "Them Skulls are all bad news, but they ain't got no reason to go and hurt Maddie. They liked her, thought she was sexy. Tell me who did it. I need to know. When? When did she get killed?"

Well, well, Madonna Christien had hooked up with Rocco the Pathetic Pirate Impersonator. Interesting and disturbing and nasty. Maybe that's why he'd backed off at Voodoo River before she could question him about the victim. Rafe was watching Claire closely, no doubt trying to second-guess her. More pertinent, he still hadn't wept any real tears. Somehow Claire knew he was the kind of guy who had probably stopped crying a long time ago.

Claire said, "We found her on Sunday. She's at the morgue in Lafourche Parish. Somebody's got to go down there and claim the body."

"I guess I gotta find somebody to carry her back down to Golden

Meadow. I can't." Rafe looked bereft now, the finality probably sinking in.

"Somebody's got to sign for the remains and make funeral arrangements, Mr. Christien. You have any relatives who might want to do that?" Claire hated that word, *remains*—it just sounded like nothing much was left of the deceased. Disrespectful, somehow. One last and final slap in the victim's face.

Rafe put both hands over his face again. The handcuffs clanked. Jail music. "I guess Granny's gonna have to. She's all the family we got. Her name's Leah Plummer. I need to call her and tell her. You gotta phone I can use?"

Well, Zee didn't offer the guy his precious new white smartphone so Claire pulled her cheap and does-nothing-but-call-people Trac-Fone off her belt. "Give me the number and I'll dial it for you."

He did, and Claire did. She held it up to his ear but didn't let it touch him. He was pretty grubby, and she didn't know where his hands had been. Just a rule she went by.

This time Rafe had to tell the sad story in his own words and hear his granny crying at the other end. That made him break down and cry, too. Zee and Claire sat there and listened and wished they were somewhere else. In time, Granny Plummer agreed to claim the body and make funeral arrangements. Claire let them talk a few minutes about arranging bail before the funeral, and then she motioned for him to end the conversation. He did, and she closed the phone.

"We talked to Wendy Rodriguez, and she told us that she and Maddie were kidnapped when they were little girls. What can you tell us about that?"

"Yeah, that happened. Maddie was never the same again, either. Got all hung up on voodoo shit and started takin' drugs. They never got the guy."

"Do you think he could have come back for her?"

Rafe raised bloodshot eyes. "After all these years? Why would he?"

"What about your parents? Wendy said they were murdered. Were you there the night they died?"

He began to shake his head. "I didn't have nothin' to do with that. I was out in my room in the garage. I didn't know nothin' about it till I woke up the next morning. You can't pin that on me. I was just a kid back then. Barely thirteen."

"We're not blaming you for anything," said Zee.

Mollified, Rafe took a deep breath. "I can't believe Sis's gone."

Claire said, "Anything else you want to tell us, Christien?"

Mopping his wet cheeks with the tail of his prison smock, he nodded. "Yeah, I want you to find out who did this to Maddie and make sure they get the needle up in Angola."

"We're sure gonna try," Zee assured him.

"Oh, God, Maddie was just the best. She's been through so much, and now this. That abduction was what threw her off. She wasn't never the same, never was."

"Do you know anybody else around her who was into voodoo?"

Rafe sobered instantly, appeared as if he was choosing his words. "Don't you go thinkin' she's some kinda kook, or somethin'. She just made up that little altar to get things she wanted. She was still scared. That snake guy used voodoo on her and Wendy when they was little. She just tried to protect herself, in case he ever came back to get her."

Actually, Claire wondered if that could be true. First, Wendy, and now Rafe had mentioned how traumatic Maddie's childhood abduction had been. Maybe everything was connected to that whacked-out sociopath in the devil mask from long ago. Or was it a ruse set up by the perpetrator to make it look that way? Stranger things had happened. "So, Rafe, when's your hearing on the meth and resisting charges?"

"In the morning. Nine o'clock. And the judge's gonna find out that those cops planted that bag on me. I ain't done nothin', just done my job over at Voodoo River, mindin' my own business, and they come in and beat the shit outta me. Look at my face, if you don't believe me. I can barely breathe no more. Police brutality."

"You're talking to the wrong people," Claire said, standing up. "Sorry for your loss, Christien. We may be back, so be thinking about all this and see if you can come up with anything else that'll help us find your sister's killer."

They walked out, glad to get out of that stuffy, closed-in, claustrophobic, and cruddy little room. Rafe Christen stayed where he was, moaning and mourning his murdered little sister, his head down on the table. Or, maybe he was weeping for himself and his busted-up face.

Chapter Thirteen

About the time Claire and Zee decided to call it a day, she received a text from Black telling her that he was due to land in New Orleans by dinnertime. Not particularly chomping at the bit to see him yet or disappoint Nancy on their prearranged night out, Claire texted him back and told him something important had come up that she had to do and she would see him later. All true, she did need more time before she saw him, she did have something else to do, and she had promised Nancy that she'd meet her at the Cajun Grill aboard the *Bayou Blue*. Maybe it would distract her a few hours from the Christien case and Black being a liar and put her in a better mood before she met up with him again.

So, after she and Zee had enjoyed the lovely tête-à-tête with Rocco and other various and sundry Skulls at Voodoo River, as well as the depressing visit to NOPD lockup, she was glad when Zee dropped her off at her car in the steamboat's parking lot. She invited him to join Nancy and her for some fun, but he had a date with a Tulane senior majoring in criminal justice who was hot and who was also hot to spend time with a real live homicide detective and pick his investigative brain. Probably a match made in heaven.

Claire watched him drive away and then looked up at the three decks of the impressive paddle wheeler, replete with all the ginger-bread curlicues and adornments of Civil War steamboats of old, and owned and operated by the LeFevreses. She and Black had dined there several times since they'd come to town. What memories she had of them were pleasant, and that was saying something, considering her sordid formative years. But they'd been as glad to see her as Rene Bourdain had been, and that made her feel pretty good. Tonight, she needed to feel good about something. She certainly didn't feel good about Black or her case or that voodoo doll with her face pinned on it, so she headed for the gangplank and a night of good cheer, and maybe even a little fun, if she was lucky.

A restaurant called The Creole was located on the main deck, a fancy-schmancy one at that, with plush maroon carpeting with a gold paisley pattern and gold velvet drapes and white linen tablecloths and sparkling chandeliers and a Creole cuisine to die for. Black loved it.

The second deck stern held the Cajun Grill, which was way more Claire's cup of tea with its po'boys, crawfish gumbo, jambalaya, fiery hot wings, juicy cheeseburgers, and homemade pizza, not to mention jeans and sweatshirt attire. The gangplank was down and hung with silver tinsel and blinking colored Christmas lights and swags of greenery, and the boat looked crowded. It was a bit early for the formal dinner crowd, so most of the customers were upstairs enjoying the Cajun Grill's zydeco band. Claire searched the parking lot and espied Nancy's Tahoe right off, so her friend was already inside.

Things had been super intense all day long, and it had been a very long day. Claire welcomed some downtime, even one hour, and she had better take advantage because it wasn't going to last long. Tomorrow she had to figure out who'd killed Madonna and why, and last but not least, she had to meet up with Rocco, if and when she could find him and she had a pretty good idea where he might be. And she had to do that by herself. She was looking forward to it, sort of.

As it turned out, she was right about the bar. The place was jumping, all right. It was also all decorated up with several sparkling artificial Christmas trees with ribbons and angel ornaments and twinkling white lights as well as lighted wreaths on every window and door and twigs of mistletoe hanging over every table. People were taking advantage of that mistletoe, too. Lots of kissing and groping going on under those seasonal twigs of romance, oh yeah. The band was on the stage, having a rip-roaring good time. Uncle Clyde was going strong on the washboard, and when he saw her come in, he motioned for her to join them.

When she reached the side of the dais, he stopped playing,

stepped down, and gave her a big bear hug. A Cajun through and through and proud of it, he looked like a skinny Santa Claus, sans the red suit and furry hat. He had been a fisherman and a true man of the sea when she'd known him all those years ago, but Hurricane Katrina had destroyed his shrimper so he'd taken the insurance money and bought and refurbished the steamboat, much to the delight of the people now dancing and clapping to the strains of "Jolie Blon." He was the one who owned the houseboat she had stayed on until they'd found Madonna Christien, battered and posed on that creepy altar. Now he lived aboard the *Bayou Blue* with his brothers and most of their families.

"Hey, li'l girl, you be just a sight fo' sore eyes, you. How 'bout takin' a turn with the fiddle whilst I make sure the waiters done turned up fo' the downstairs crowd?"

Claire smiled at his Cajun brogue. She really wasn't in the mood, but she took the violin and greeted Luc LeFevres, who was pushing his accordion for all it was worth. Luc was tall and slim and dressed in denim overalls, but the shirt he wore under it was snowy white and crisply starched. Cousin Napier was on the bass fiddle, portly and full bearded and strong as an ox.

Claire didn't know any of them well, not anymore, but she liked having people around her, especially people who treated her like family. Black was the only other person she considered family, except Bud and her colleagues at the lake. She felt a streak of guilt that she was avoiding Black. She wasn't really angry with him anymore, more curious than anything, and she knew he would explain everything away and they'd be fine again. She just needed some time to think it all through first. It wouldn't hurt him to reflect on it, either.

The guys started out with a second rendition of "Jolie Blon," always a crowd pleaser, and Claire joined in. She was still a little rusty, but she could play that song. Since she'd started playing again out on the bayou, to Saucy's delight, she guessed, she had been enjoying it. Excited patrons crowded the dance floor, and Claire felt herself relax, despite the fact that she hit a bad note once in a while and made her fellow musicians laugh. Everybody in the place was talking and dancing and having fun, and that's what she needed to do, too. Forget voodoo altars and stitched lips and lies and death and blood spatter, just for a few hours of mindless frivolity.

As she ended the song to enthusiastic applause, Claire caught sight of Nancy Gill where she stood having a drink at the packed bar. Nancy waved and then pointed behind her to the entrance. And who should be standing there but the great Jack Holliday himself, all big and impressive and studly, wearing a black nylon Saints warm-up jacket and black jeans. To Claire's annoyance, he was watching her and quickly motioned her over to him, as if they were the best buds in the world all of a sudden. Had he lost his mind, or what?

Frowning, Claire ignored him. Holliday was still a person of interest in the Christien case, perhaps even the *numero uno* suspect, which meant he was case related, big time, and any kind of social interaction was just not going down. Not here, not anywhere.

Claire put down the fiddle, waved good-bye to the LeFevreses on the dais, and headed toward Nancy. Nancy was still watching Jack when Claire reached her, and a quick glance around told her that lots of other people recognized him, too. After that, came a spattering of applause and a few autograph seekers. Great, now he was playing the popular-celebrity-with-nothing-to-hide role.

"Lord have mercy, Claire, he looks even better in person."

Claire watched Holliday stop at a table and scribble his name on a napkin, smiling and chatting as if he wasn't worried one bit about being under suspicion in a murder investigation. He seemed incredibly comfortable and at ease and unconcerned.

"Remember that poor, beaten girl stretched out cold on your table, Nancy? Remember her eyes and her mouth? Your hero there just might turn out to be the one who did all that. Just look at his hands. Nice big murder weapons."

"Yeah, all that's true. But he didn't do it."

Nancy was teasing, of course. She was laughing at Claire's serious warning. "Tell me he isn't hot. Make me believe it."

"He's okay."

"Are you kidding me? Oh, that's right, now I get it. You've got a guy like Nick panting after you, don't you? And he's even better looking than Jack, I have to agree. So guess I'll have to take Jack."

"We're professionals, Nancy. Please don't forget that. You're acting just like Zee did about that guy."

"Have you ever seen me act in less than a professional manner?"

"No. But Holliday hasn't come over here yet."

Nancy laughed. "Don't worry. I'll keep my head. Maybe."

It didn't take Holliday long to disengage himself from his adoring public. Then he headed straight for Claire. She watched him approach, football fans reaching out to touch him. Jeez! The Big Easy was one heck of a football-lovin' city, all right.

"Don't forget to introduce us when he gets here," Nancy said. "I mean it. I just wanna meet him, shake that big weapon of a hand, that's all."

"Get a hold on your hormones, Nancy. I mean it."

"I'm not gonna jump his bones, Claire. At least I don't think so."

Then Holliday was there, towering over them, and the rapt expression on Nancy's face made Claire want to laugh.

Holliday said, "Hey, there, Detective. Fancy meeting you here."

"Yeah, fancy that. Are you following me, or what?"

"Actually, I am. We need to talk."

"How'd you know where I was?"

"I called Zee. He said you were here."

Damn, Zee knew better than that. She felt her phone vibrate so she jerked it out, expecting it to be Black and glad for a reason to ignore Holliday. Maybe she'd go home and deal with Black sooner than she thought.

"Hi, I'm Jack Holliday," the big former jock was saying to Nancy.

Nancy took the hand he held out and smiled. "Nice to meet you. I'm a huge fan. Have been ever since your Tulane days. I'm a Tulane grad myself."

Claire moved away. Caller ID said Zee Jackson.

"Just a heads-up, Claire. Jack Holliday called me and asked where he could find you."

"And you obliged him."

"Well, yeah. He said he's gotta talk to you about the case. Said it's real important."

"How'd he get your number?"

"I gave him my card."

"Okay, he found me. And it better be important. Talk to you later. Have fun tonight."

Claire punched off, and yes, she was a tad peeved. But if a suspect suddenly had some new information to add to his initial statement, she was all ears. She turned back to Holliday. "I guess you know that Nancy's the Lafourche Parish medical examiner, Mr. Holliday."

Momentarily, he looked startled, but then it turned into interest. "No kidding? I'd never of guessed that. Want to join me for a beer, Nancy?" Nancy nodded, and Jack called over the bartender and ordered two cold Turbodogs. Then he turned to Claire. "How about letting me buy you an Abita, too, Detective?"

"You really think I'm gonna do that, Mr. Holliday?"

"No. I was just being polite. I take it that you're still on duty?"

"No, I'm definitely off duty. But I'm not going to sit around and drink with you. You are a person of interest in this case until I can rule you out as a suspect in the murder of Madonna Christien." That was all rather official-sounding, yes, but all true, too.

"What about after that?"

Holliday had to be smarter than this. If he was coming on to her, Claire considered what his motives might be. Other than to charm her into going easy on him, she couldn't come up with anything much that made sense. And some friend he was to Black. She placed her attention on the band.

Nancy was being hit on by a good-looking guy standing on the other side of her, so Holliday swiveled his chair around to face Claire and became quite the chatterbox all of a sudden. "You're really good on that fiddle. You play zydeco like a born Cajun."

"So?" Okay, that was rude. But Holliday was not taking the hint to get lost.

"I meant it as a compliment. I like Cajun music."

"Really? I thought you hailed from Colorado."

"Ah, you've been checking me out."

"That's why they call me a detective."

"So you're with Nick, huh? I was surprised I didn't put that together. He talks about you a lot. I guess I just didn't expect you to be working as a deputy down there in the bayous. The connection just didn't click at first. I should've recognized you, though. I've seen pictures of you in the newspapers."

"So, Zee said that you have information pertinent to our case, Mr. Holliday."

"Call me Jack, will you?"

"Well, no."

"Is there somewhere around here where we can talk privately?"

Claire wondered if he really did have something important to tell her. Maybe he was just going to hit her with some cockamamie, made-up story that put him in a better light.

Holliday suddenly waxed serious. "It's important, Claire."

Now that was irksome. They were not on a first-name basis. They looked at each other, did some sizing-up, followed by a rather challenging eye lock.

"Okay, I'm game. Give it to me."

"I want to show you something. In private."

Now she was curious. She glanced around. "There's an empty booth over there. That private enough for you?"

Holliday trailed her to a window booth overlooking the Mississippi River, the water of which looked very dark and cold in the December evening. The plate glass was foggy, and outside the deck railings were wrapped with more tiny white twinkling Christmas lights and fake greenery and red plastic bows.

"You haven't worked down there in Lafourche Parish long, have you?"

"Mr. Holliday, please, let's just keep this professional, okay?"

Holliday kept up the staring, his eyes crawling all over her face like she was some kind of exotic Syrian butterfly he'd just discovered. Claire stared back without blinking. She could ogle with the best of them.

She spent the time wondering if he was really capable of strangling Madonna to death. She visualized his hands around her throat, those big fists of his beating her black and blue and throwing her down on that glass coffee table and pressing on her windpipe until the light went out of her eyes. Then she thought of him hunched over that poor little woman, inserting a sharp needle into her eyelid. Okay, nope, he didn't seem the type, but sometimes non-types killed people, too. Sometimes killers were just as handsome and easygoing and polite and rich as Jack Holliday. Sometimes they wore warm, friendly smiles like the one he was giving her right now. Sometimes they even smiled all warm and friendly-like while they choked the life out of their victims.

He said, "Why are you looking at me like that?"

"I'm just waiting for you to tell me why you really came down here."

"So you and Nick are together?"

What? Somehow, that really grated on her nerves, too, even when she was slightly irritated as hell with Black. "Yes, we are. So why are you so interested in Black and me?"

"Exclusively?"

Claire could only stare at him. "Please tell me that you're not trying to hit on me, not when Black's sticking his neck out to alibi you. Because that would make you a colossal jerk."

"I'm not hitting on you. You're just so different than I thought you'd be. Booker told me that you and Black are seriously committed."

"You know what, sir? None of this is any of your business, and it's none of Booker's business. Look, I don't discuss my private life, especially with suspects. So I'm outta here. It's in your best interest to stay away from me while I'm investigating this case. Are we clear on that?"

After that, Holliday decided it was time to declare his innocence again. "I didn't kill that girl, I swear to God, and I'm going to prove it. Then I hope we can become friends."

"I've got all the friends I need. This is getting downright tedious. Now, one last time, do you have something to show me concerning the Christien case, or not?"

Holliday smiled and pulled out his ace in the hole. "I've got a DVD of that party we had in New York. I put my video cam on the buffet behind the table, and let it roll. You'll see everything that happened the entire night." He retrieved it from the inside pocket of his Windbreaker. He slid it across the table. "Watch it. You'll see. It's dated and everything. Lots of witnesses were there who'll alibi me. There's no way I could have been down here and killed that girl. Talk to all of them. I want you to."

They both glanced up as a gaggle of giggling young women came in the front door, their arms full of shopping bags. Christmas shopping with the BFFs. Something Claire needed to do. What to buy Black?

That was a perennial problem. Maybe a portable lie detector machine would be nice, at least for her.

"Listen, Detective, I got a call from Wendy Rodriguez today. She told me that you and Zee had been out to her house grilling her."

"That's right. But I wouldn't exactly call it grilling. We're questioning everybody associated with Ms. Christien."

"She said you were asking about the gifts that Madonna gave me."

"You want to add something to your statement about that?"

Claire listened to him start talking again about Madonna and her fixation on him, and wished he'd just leave. He had already given her the video. All she wanted tonight was to enjoy herself for a single hour, and he had to show up and ruin everything. She was going to kill Zee for telling him where she was. And she was going to get rid of Holliday right now, even if she had to walk him out to his car at gunpoint.

A Very Scary Man

Malice and the professional killer came off their life on the sea and settled back into their prior lives in New Orleans and the deep bayous. They rarely met except at the Maze of Terror, which he was reinforcing now with his new knowledge of welding that he'd perfected through his shipboard duties, in anticipation of some scary fun and games. He did find a job, the perfect vocation for someone who intended to break the law in truly horrific ways. So he worked diligently there, made a good impression, and pretended that he forgave his old girlfriend and his former friend for betraying him. But he hadn't. More than anything in his life, he wanted to kill them. He wanted to see the lifeblood leak slowly out of their veins. Indeed, he would kill them. All he had to do was bide his time, plan carefully, and do the deed so well that he would never get caught. The professional killer had taught him well, indeed.

Then the day came when he got the perfect opportunity. One

sunny, clear day, during Mardi Gras, he followed his two coveted victims out to a remote bayou. They were fishing there and having a picnic with their two children. They were laughing and playing games, having a good time celebrating their little girl's birthday. He watched the happy little family, thinking it should have been his family, his children, his life, damn them all to hell. But it wasn't his. He had no family and never had. Their children were getting older now, the boy almost twelve and the girl a little younger. So he hid himself in the bushes with his serpent Mardi Gras mask in place and watched and waited for the exact right moment.

When the children moved up the bank toward his hiding place, he waited until they were out of sight of their parents, then moved quickly. When the boy entered the woods, looking for a place to dig worms, he grabbed him and subdued him. It only took seconds. Then he taped his hands and feet and mouth and went after the little girl, still sitting on the bank with her fishing pole, but well out of sight of her parents. She was even easier, freezing in terror when he ran at her. She didn't make a peep. It all happened within a minute or two, and he taped her up securely, and then left them hidden there in the bushes. He took off the mask and headed down the bank toward the two people who had filled his dreams with visions of bloody murder every night for months on end.

His old girlfriend and her rotten husband got up from the blanket when they saw him. She was straightening her clothes, embarrassed he'd found them making out. His blood ran cold with fury. They waved at him, and he smiled and waved back. He had played his part well; they didn't know how much he hated their guts. They thought he was still their friend. That was the way to murder people: make them think you loved them, disarm them with kindness, and then cut their throats. But Malice knew her husband always carried a weapon so he had to be careful. When he got right up to them, he glanced around and found the bayou still deserted. Then he pulled the .45 out of his coat pocket and fired a slug point-blank into the man's forehead. Bam, you're dead. His only true love screamed and tried to run away, but he caught her easily and held her tightly against his chest. She was struggling hard, but he forced a brutal good-bye kiss on her mouth as he had daydreamed of doing for years and years and years, and then he pressed the gun against her breast and fired. She fell backwards, writhing and groaning in agony, and he stood above her and told her how much he loved her and how much he had always loved her. Then he squatted down beside her and fired a bullet into her forehead to end her suffering.

Heartbroken, now that she was gone forever, that he'd never see her again, he sat on his heels, watched her bleed out, and wept hard for a while. Once Malice regained his composure, he took time to remove the dead man's gun from the holster he wore at the small of his back and then arranged the body in the exact position in which Malice wanted it to be found. A nice little suicide/murder scenario was always a nice touch, and something the police usually took at face value. After he was satisfied with every detail, he walked back to where he'd left the dead woman's two beautiful children. He hated her boy the most. When he returned from the Merchant Marine, he had found out the real reason his true love had never come back to him. She had gotten knocked up with his best friend's baby, the boy who was lying limp and frightened at his feet. If that hadn't happened, she would have come back to him, and they would've eventually married. He knew she would have. It was the kid's fault, and he needed to suffer for what he'd done. Suffer greatly, and so did the little girl.

Squatting down, he took the hand towel and chloroform out of his knapsack, saturated the towel, and pressed it over the little girl's face. It didn't take long. When she was unconscious, he picked her up. She was as light as a feather, and he carried her quickly to his boat, still bound and gagged. Then he went back for the boy. He was big and strong for his age, like his father had been as a kid, so he chloroformed him until he lay limp and unmoving, and then he carried him down to the bank and threw him into the bottom of the boat with his sister.

Climbing into the stern, he headed straight for the deserted old house where his murder mentor was staying. The Maze of Terror wasn't quite finished yet. They might get away from him out there, but not in the cellar of his fellow assassin. So, finally, at long last, he had his own helpless little victims to torment. Victims that he really detested for what their parents had done to him. He couldn't wait to start the fun and games.

Chapter Fourteen

Nicholas Black pushed through the front door of the Cajun Grill, right behind a bunch of silly girls, just about as pissed off as he had ever been in his life. It didn't help when he caught a glimpse of Claire getting cozy in a booth with Jack Holliday. Nope, he did not like that, not one bit. He was not happy, and he intended to show it for a change. He threaded his way through the tables, nodded at Nancy at the bar, then stopped beside the booth. Claire and Jack glanced up at him. They both looked startled to see him, as well they should.

"Am I interrupting anything important, Claire?"

Jack immediately appeared embarrassed and looked down. Then he said quickly, "Hey, Nick. No, no, I just came down here to give the detective a DVD of my birthday party at the Ritz and tell her a couple more things that I thought might help exonerate me."

Not smart, that, Nick thought. "Well, I'm surprised to find you here, Jack. Your lawyer would be, too, trust me. Scoot over," he ordered Claire, and not in any lovey-dovey tone, either. "You should've told me that we were eating out tonight, sweetheart. And I would've joined you about an hour ago instead of sitting around waiting for you to show up at home."

Claire frowned, but she did make room for him, and Nick slid in beside her. He tried to control his anger. Flying off the handle was not his style. Truthfully, it was a rare occurrence for him, especially where Claire was concerned. His profession necessitated him to remain calm, cool, and collected at all times, and he'd learned how to do it, but Claire could push his buttons like nobody else. He did not like or appreciate her giving him the cold shoulder. He didn't like what she said next, either.

"Yeah, Black? I guess I figured you were still over in London Town. You know, hard at work in the clinic, changing your patient's meds, and all that kinda stuff."

Miffed by that, to be sure, Nick didn't respond to her jibe. Which was probably the best way to go with Claire. Jack looked slightly embarrassed as ice pellets began to form in the air around the booth. He glanced from one of them to the other. "Okay, I think I'll take off and let the two of you enjoy your dinner. We can talk about this later. I have your number, Detective. I'll call you."

"Sure you don't want to join us?" Nick offered tightly, but he sure as hell didn't want his old friend sitting there and witnessing the argument they were going to have. "On the other hand, sometimes three is a crowd, Jack."

Claire took umbrage to his remark. "Whoa, Black, no need to be rude. I'm the rude one, remember? Maybe Jack and I aren't done talking, ever think of that?" Claire gave him a long, dead-eyed stare, apparently so as to reveal her true feelings about what she thought he'd done. Unfortunately, she still looked damn good to him, so good, in fact, that he could barely keep his hands off her. He'd been gone too long this time.

Claire turned back to Jack. "Okay, go ahead and tell me what you came down here to tell me, Mr. Holliday, and tell me now, if it's really pertinent. What about Madonna's gifts? Black can hear this, I guess. After all, the two of you attend secret birthday parties at the Ritz together."

Nick gave her a sour look. Holliday was quick to respond. "I've still got some of those presents. Most of it, Wendy returned to her for me."

Now that's pretty good news, Black thought. For Holliday's case, at least.

Claire said, "Did you bring them with you?"

"No."

"Well, why not?"

"They're out at my river house."

"Oh, but of course, they are. You rich guys, you just slay me. Tell you what. Bring them down to the Lafourche Sheriff's Office as soon as possible and don't come looking for me again. You've got my number if you want to add something to your statement."

Nick said, "And you're calling me rude, Claire? Listen, Jack, don't take offense. She's like this with everybody."

Before Claire could retort to that unkind remark, Nancy joined their happy little soiree, looking pretty damn sober herself. "Hey, sorry to interrupt, but I need to talk to you, Claire."

"Black, you wanna let me out?"

He didn't want to, but he obliged and stood politely while she exited the booth. Claire hurried after Nancy into a back hallway and out of sight. Then he sat back down. He and Jack needed to have a little chat or Jack just might end up behind bars before the night was over.

"Okay, Jack, listen good. Don't mess around with Claire while she's working your case. I found that out firsthand and the hard way, not so long ago. I know you didn't do this, but she doesn't know it yet. She'll think you're trying to play her, believe me."

"Yeah, I'm beginning to see that. She's something else, isn't she?"

"She's good at what she does. Remember that. You were with us, and you can prove it. Back away and let her prove it to herself, and you'll be free and clear."

"She's just so—man, she's just so . . ."

"Yeah, I know. I'm a lucky man, but she's annoyed with me at the moment so why don't you clear out, and let us patch things up."

Jack nodded, and they both looked at Claire when she arrived back at the table. She didn't waste words.

"Mr. Holliday, I just received word that Madonna Christien was pregnant when she died. Are you willing to come in to our office in Lafourche Parish and take a paternity test?"

First off, Holliday just looked stunned. Nick decided that he was going to have to coach Jack on better veiling his reactions, especially around Claire.

Nick said, "Call your lawyer, Jack. Now. You should never have come down here without him. She's like a dog with a bone when she's after somebody."

Claire didn't retort. Hell, she probably liked that description.

Holliday ignored Nick and said to Claire, "Absolutely, I'll take that test. I never touched Madonna that way. Never. Not once. I'll take the test right now, this minute, if you want. Just say the word."

Now that sounded like the protestations of an innocent man. Nick felt relieved, too, and vindicated.

Claire said, "We appreciate your cooperation, but going in for the test tonight is unnecessary. Would it be possible for you to come in sometime during the next few days?"

"Just give me the date and the time. I'll take a polygraph test while I'm there, too. Just set it up, and fingerprints, or anything else you want me to do. I didn't hurt that girl, I swear to God, I didn't."

"Black's right, you better ask that slick lawyer if he's copacetic with all this stuff you're offering up to us, Mr. Holliday. I predict he'll put the brakes on it quickly enough."

"He'll do what I tell him to do."

"Then we'll see you then, Mr. Holliday. Thanks for bringing me the DVD. Maybe you can bring those gifts from Madonna Christien with you when you drive down to Thibodaux for those tests."

"I'll do that, Detective. Thanks for your time. Nick, take it easy. I'll see you later."

Jack Holliday got up in a hurry and headed for the exit, getting the hell out of Dodge before the fireworks began, no doubt.

Nick looked up at Claire. "Have a seat, Claire. We need to talk this out, don't you think?"

Claire didn't particularly like Black's bossy behavior, but she sat down across from him. Truth was, she was pretty damn glad to see him back in New Orleans, safe and sound. And did he ever look good tonight, like some kind of male model, a big, tough, angry one, maybe, with ice-blue eyes and thick black hair and sexy-to-the-max dimples. He had on a red pullover sweater under a black leather jacket, and dark jeans. He was probably the best-looking man she'd ever seen. Too bad he was a liar.

"How did you even know I was here?"

"Zee told me. He also told me that a voodoo doll at the crime scene had your face on it. I guess you forgot to mention that to me, right?"

"Zee's got a big mouth tonight. I'm gonna have to talk to him about keeping the facts of our case confidential to non-law-enforcement people."

They stared at each other until Black sighed, and then he said, "Look, I don't like it when we fight. And I don't like it when you don't let me know where you are."

"Oh, my God, are you kidding me? Now you want to keep tabs on *me*? Okay. Well, I guess I'm in London with you."

"You've been refusing my calls. Don't you think that's a little childish?"

"Maybe. So what?"

"So I don't like it."

"You're supposed to like everything I do? Sometimes things happen that I don't like, either. Deal with it."

Black blew out a frustrated breath, frowned darkly, and watched the band for a few seconds. Claire watched them, too. She and Black hadn't had an argument in a long time, but Black wasn't a man who groveled for forgiveness so she didn't expect that to happen. Not in the kind of mood he was exhibiting at the moment. And what was with that? He was the one who had lied to her, not the other way around.

"I missed you, Claire. A lot."

"Really? All the fun times and parties at the Ritz didn't help you cope?"

"I go to cocktail parties all the time when I'm out of town on business. You've never minded before."

"You never lied about it before. Not that I know of, anyway."

"I'm sorry I didn't tell you the exact truth, Claire. I should have."

The *exact* truth? What the devil did that mean? But he had offered an apology, sort of, and Claire appreciated it, sort of, but he wasn't getting off that easy. "Tell me why you felt the need to lie to me. I've never tried to put you on a leash, and you know it."

Now Black began to look a mite uncomfortable. He shifted in the

Linda Ladd

booth, picked up a menu but didn't open it. "I can't tell you right now. But there's a very good reason."

Claire could not believe her ears. "Know what, Black? I've got a very good reason not to want to be with you tonight, too. Think I'll just take this DVD, pop me some popcorn, and see what kind of parties you throw when I'm not invited."

"There's something else you need to know before you watch that video."

Oh, God, what now? He did not look like he wanted to tell her, whatever it was. "Yeah? So hit me with it."

Black usually didn't say anything he didn't want to say. He was pretty strong willed himself. But he had nursed her back to health and hovered over her bed for three long weeks when she had been in a coma and ever since, too, so Claire was usually willing to let a lot of things slide. This time he was being secretive, which was unusual and made her curious, more than anything else.

"Are you in trouble, Black? Rob a bank, wake up with a dead hooker in your bed, something along those lines?"

"Very funny." Finally, he came out with it. "Just so you know, Jude was at that party in New York."

At first, Claire could only stare at him. "Jude, your ex-wife and famous supermodel?"

"Come on, Claire."

"Come on, Black." Now that was frosting on the disgruntled cake, to be sure. Not only was Jude gorgeous and sexy, she still acted like she was in love with Black and didn't mind anybody knowing it.

"She needed to talk to me about some personal problems, and I couldn't fit her into my schedule so I invited her to have dinner with us. It was as innocent as that."

"You are just such a prince among men. No wonder she married you."

Black had now reverted to his unruffled shrink-composed self. Mr. Sangfroid Personified. "You're being unreasonable. It was nothing. You know good and well that it's over between Jude and me. It was over for years before I even met you. We're old friends now. That's it."

"Tell you what, Black. I'll be reasonable after I watch this video and see what went on at that party."

"Fine. And then you'll see that nothing happened." Small silence. "Okay, Claire, what if I told you I was working on a special Christmas surprise for you while I was in New York?"

"I'd say that sounds pretty damn fishy, and that I don't like surprises and you know it."

"It's not what you think."

"And what do I think?"

"That I was with another woman. Or Jude."

"You *were* with Jude."

"We were with a group of friends, and it was purely professional. She just wanted to talk to me about a personal problem. As psychiatrist and patient."

"What about?" Oh, man, she was beginning to sound jealous and petty and that was the last thing she ever wanted to be or wanted him to think. Maybe she was, though. A little.

"Her thirteen-year-old stepson's into drugs and she doesn't know what to do."

"Okay. That's a problem, all right. I can believe that."

Black studied her face and looked skeptical. "So everything's all right between us now?"

"I wouldn't say that."

"What would you say?"

"I'd say that if you lie to me and keep secrets, then you can't complain if I do it to you, too. Starting now."

"Now wait just a minute, Claire. What secrets are you keeping from me?"

"Seriously, Black? Seriously?"

He stopped, looked annoyed, and then just resigned. All anger fading away, just like that. "I missed the hell out of you, babe. I just want to go home and make love to you. We can talk about this there where we have some privacy. I'm tired. It was a long flight, and I spent the whole time worrying about you."

"Go on ahead. I'll catch you later. I promised Nancy I'd hang with her and have some dinner, and I don't want to disappoint her."

Black's jaw tightened and a muscle worked in his cheek, giving away his true feelings, but he nodded. He was not going to beg, and he wasn't usually overly controlling, either. "Okay. I'll see you at home in a little while. Don't forget to show up. If I'm asleep, wake me up."

Claire watched him thread his way through the tables and disappear out the door and began to feel fairly down in the dumps herself. They rarely had cross words, much less a fight. She didn't like it any more than he did. But he certainly hadn't given her a good reason for lying about where he'd been. It made her wonder how often he had been off having good times with his friends when he'd told her he was working. She sighed, and then headed to the bar and Nancy. She'd have a good time with her friend, too, damn it, or die trying.

Chapter Fifteen

After a fantastic dinner of a fried-shrimp-and-mayonnaise po'boy and Cajun cheese fries and a Pepsi and some fun with Nancy Gill, Claire decided to bid her friend farewell and drive back over to Lafourche Parish. She had something important she had to do there, and she wanted to take a look at Holliday's video before she went home to Black. The roads were dark and relatively free of traffic, and once she reached the bayou crime scene, she drove straight past the house, still surrounded by crime scene tape, her headlights spearing the black velvet night. She turned off the engine and sat there alone in the dark, listening to the tick of the cooling motor. She thought about the brutal murder that had gone down and the abused body found just up the hill and felt an urge to turn the car around and go home posthaste. But she couldn't, not quite yet, so she got out. She smelled the cigarette smoke first, and then she saw the shadow move across the aft deck. Her nine-millimeter was in her hand instantly, and she went down behind the car door and held it on the dark figure moving around on the boat.

"Who's there? Don't move, you hear me? Don't move a muscle! I've got a gun on you."

"Claire! Don't shoot. It's me, Ron Saucier."

Claire recognized his voice, so she re-holstered her weapon and walked quickly to the lamppost that housed the covered outside light switches. She flipped all of them on, and the boat was flooded with light.

Ron Saucier still stood on the aft deck, not far from her, a lit cigarette in his left hand. He had a rifle in his right fist, pointed down at the ground. What the hell was he doing on the boat?

He didn't give her time to inquire. "Sorry if I scared you. I was out fishin' and came by here. I just pulled in to check out the place and see if you were still stayin' out here alone. There's a night light on inside, and I just wanted to check, that's all. You know, just to make sure you were okay."

"Didn't you see my car wasn't here?"

"Yeah, but I just wanted to be sure. Honestly? That voodoo scene up there in that house pretty much freaked me out. So I decided to sit down here in the dark and watch the crime scene. Thought maybe the killer might come back and revisit the place once the police were gone. They do that sometimes."

"Yeah, that's true. I guess you haven't seen anything?"

"No. I'm really sorry if I scared you, though," he said again. "I didn't know it was you. Too dark, and I didn't want to give away my position."

"That's okay. Thanks for checking on me. I appreciate it."

"So why are you out here? Anything wrong?"

Claire didn't want to tell him the truth, a little embarrassed about her spat with Black, so she only said, "I guess we're thinking on the same wavelength. I wanted to check the place out."

"Yeah. It's really creepy down here in the dark. The floodlights make it better."

An uncomfortable silence ensued as he made his way down the narrow, roped gangplank, still holding the rifle. Claire decided to be gracious. After all, the guy had gone to the trouble of checking on her. "Want a beer, or something, before you go?"

"Nah, I need to get home. It's late. You're not stayin' out here tonight, are you?"

"Oh, no, I'll hang around a while, then I'm heading home."

"Okay, see you tomorrow at the office."

She watched him climb into his boat. It was a big brown-and-gold bass boat with a built-up seat in back, a nice one that looked fairly new. He got the motor started, gave her a quick air salute, and took off. Saucier was truly a weird dude, to be sure, she had to admit. Pretty nice, too, but definitely on the peculiar side.

When he faded into the darkness, headed downstream to his own place, she climbed the gangplank and looked around for anything out of place. After all, and despite his story about worrying about her, she didn't know Ron Saucier all that well. But the houseboat looked no different from the last time she'd spent the night there. She shivered in the cool air, thinking about what had been done to Madonna Christien's body. She drew her weapon again and thoroughly checked out the boat, turning on overhead lights in every room, but found nothing disturbed. Satisfied, she slipped out of her faded denim jacket, walked to the DVD player, and slid in the disc. It came on as she collapsed in the worn brown recliner facing the television, with the sound of multiple male voices, loud and boisterous in overlapping conversations. Then there they all were, with smiles and toasts and laughter and great good cheer. About fifteen or twenty people sat around a formal dining room table set with lots of crystal goblets and fancy gold-rimmed plates and one giant silver candelabra sitting in the middle of the table and burning with a multitude of white tapers. Male hotel waiters in starched white shirts and black vests hovered around unobtrusively, topping off wine-glasses and serving delicious-looking food.

Wow. Black knew how to throw a birthday party sans her, all right. But, hey, this was how rich shrinks and famous sports agents celebrated stuff. Hell, just the other day their department had Zee's birthday party down at the office with red Solo cups and a sheet cake Nancy had picked up at Winn-Dixie. Nope, and there hadn't been any candelabras on his desk, either. In fact, there hadn't been any candles at all. Claire had forgotten to buy them. But the cake had been milk chocolate with fudge icing and sugar sprinkles and had probably tasted just as good as the three-tiered, magnificent white cake with Holliday's name on it sitting on the buffet. Jack's cake was decorated with fleurs-de-lis, too. In fact, there were lots of fleurs-de-lis decorating the table. Tulane graduates, all, and through and through.

On the screen, the hijinks commenced, a good time being had by all, it seemed. Bone tired all of a sudden, Claire kicked back the footrest and watched her honeybun have a spanking good time with all his friends. It was turning out to be a friendly, good-natured roast, with lots of teasing about Sigma Chi and all their wild shenanigans in their college days. They even mentioned the night in jail during Mardi Gras so they were probably telling the truth and not exaggerating everything.

Claire's attention sharpened considerably when Black's old love, Jude—no other name, just Jude, because she was such a superfamous fashion model, bless her skinny little heart—was escorted into the room by a maid. And yes, she looked just like a modern version of Scarlett O'Hara entering and wowing all the menfolk in her über-slinky scarlet sequined dress. She was also wearing a gaudy display of emeralds around her neck. Yep, all decked out in red and green. Guess she had gotten into the Christmas spirit. No *To/From* tag hung off her come-hither holiday package, however, unless she had it attached where no one could see it without opening it up first. Claire would bet it had Black's name on it, though, and in capital letters. Upon her appearance, the rowdy men all stood up like even wealthier versions of Rhett Butler or Mr. Darcy, but without top hats or male scornful attitudes. Well, maybe some of the attitudes.

The lovely-beyond-compare Jude sat down beside Black, of course, making one of the other guys give up his chair. She was all over him immediately. Black wasn't encouraging it, but he wasn't exactly throwing her hand off his arm like it was a scorpion, either. The party progressed, with toasts galore, and the two of them had their heads together at times, smiling at somebody's joke once in a while, but mainly talking seriously in low tones. Black didn't look like he was nailed to the floor, but he didn't kiss her or look like he wanted to drag her into the bedroom and unwrap her, so Claire gave him a pass on that.

After a while, Black, as the host, stood up and made some toasts, and the party went on, through the meal, through the dessert and the singing of "Happy Birthday." Jude stuck like glue to Black's side the entire time, but when she left early, he didn't go with her, didn't walk her to the door, didn't kiss her good-bye, not even a peck on each cheek for old times' sake. In fact, he acted relieved to get rid of her so he could get back to drinking and kidding around with his Tulane buddies. Okay, he hadn't had a quickie with dear old Jude, no matter how hard she'd tried to get her lips on him. So, okay, nothing untoward had happened. No need to get bent out of shape.

More important, Jack Holliday was there with him, having fun and laughing and not strangling a small woman to death on Carondelet Street. It looked to Claire like Holliday was off the hook. Still, some inconsistencies in his story nagged at her. If somebody had attempted to frame him with the murder by planting a glass with his prints on it, they were either inept or they'd done it in a big hurry. Either way, they'd done one crummy job since he had a whole passel of eyewitnesses to corroborate his alibi. Once, not so long ago, somebody had tried to frame Black for a murder and done a much better job of it. Even she'd had her doubts on that one for a while, but at the time she'd recently hit her head in a car crash and hadn't remembered if Black was a good guy or a bad guy, so there you go.

A distant sound filtered through the trees, somewhere way out on the bayou road. Concerned, with visions of sewing needles and black thread and white candles and the smell of death erupting in her head, she walked outside and stood on the aft deck under a string of white lights and realized soon enough that she had company coming down her road, all right. Recognizing the roar of a big, souped-up Harley Davidson when she heard it, she pulled her weapon, held it down alongside her right leg, and stepped back into the shadows where she couldn't be seen. She kept her eyes peeled on the dirt road up near the house. When the motorcycle came into sight, jouncing down the hill toward her over ruts and gravel, it didn't take long for her to identify the rider. Well, well, her friend Rocco hadn't had any trouble finding her, after all.

Rocco stopped the bike at the bottom of the gangplank beside her white Range Rover, turned off the motor, and sat there staring up at the boat. Claire didn't move a muscle. She watched him swing a leg over the seat and set the kickstand. Tonight he was dressed in a faded denim jacket, black jeans, and a gray sweatshirt, actually almost looked like a regular human being, except for the giant red swastika painted on the front of the shirt. He didn't have a gun in his hand, which was always a good sign.

"Hey, anybody home on there?" he yelled, but he still didn't step foot on the gangplank. Probably afraid Claire might jump out and shoot him.

"Over here," she called out, and when he saw the business end of the Glock in her hand, he raised both his hands in the air. "Don't shoot. I come in peace."

Claire re-sheathed her weapon. "So, Rocco, tell me, what's up with the skeezy Blackbeard impersonation?"

Rocco grinned. "Jack Sparrow's my man. Admit it, Annie, he's a cool dude. Or, wait a sec, I gotta call you Claire now, right?"

When he grinned, looking as devilish as always, Claire was just so glad to see him that her throat clogged up and she couldn't speak for a second. It had been years since she'd seen Gabriel LeFevres before she'd run into him at Voodoo River. His parents were the ones who had lived up the hill in the house when she'd been with them. Gabe had been her best friend and confidante when they were both ten years old. His family had taken her in and treated her like one of their own children. Back then, she had absolutely worshipped the ground Gabe walked on. Still did, in fact.

"Well, c'mon, now, Annie, don't I get a hug or a kiss, or something good like that?"

Gabe strode up the gangplank, and Claire went quickly into his arms. She clutched him, just so glad he was safe. He led a dangerous life, but he'd always had a wild and reckless streak inside him. One that often got him into trouble, even when they were little kids.

"Damn it, Gabe, what the hell are you doing, riding around with those cretins?"

He laughed softly. "Tell you one thing, for sure. I couldn't believe my eyes when I saw you and your partner waltz into that bar. I thought you were gonna shoot up the place there for a minute."

Claire stared up at him and examined his handsome face, and then she shook her head. "That dumb little beard braid is weak, Gabe. Pretty sucky, actually."

"Makes me look tough, and you know it."

"It makes you look stupid, is what it does. By the way, I don't appreciate your calling me a bitch. Three times, if I recall."

Gabe perched a hip on the aft railing. "Your partner shouldn't've messed with Manny. That guy's psychotic and stupid, and not afraid to show either one."

"I think you're psychotic for hanging out with him. They'll kill you if they even get a hint that you're undercover."

"Not gonna happen, unless you poke your nose in Voodoo River again and try to start something. I got hell for defusing the situation. They wanted to beat you and Zee to shit. Still do. And they will if they ever see you again, trust me. So watch out for them. You're on their radar now."

"*You* just be careful. You always did take too many chances." They smiled at each other. Claire shook her head. "So how long have you been back home? Rene spun us the usual cover story—you know, that you'd gone bad and spent time in prison. Last I heard, you were working undercover narcotics in Seattle."

"Six months."

"Thanks for coming by and saying hello."

"Hey, I'm risking my neck right now, coming out here. Yours, too. But I wasn't followed. I made sure of that."

"Well, I need to talk to you about a case. It's important."

"Yeah, that one-on-one remark came through to me loud and clear. And I'm sorry to hear about Maddie. She was a good kid, messed up in the head for sure, but sweet, in her own way."

"Yeah, well, guess what? Your name's already come up as a suspect. In fact, it was Rafe Christien who told us that you liked to mess around with her. He's sitting in NOPD lockup, by the way."

Gabe frowned and stood up. "That's because I put the local cops onto him."

"You been sleeping with her, Gabe?"

"Hell, no. Why?"

"Because she was pregnant when she died. Which might turn out to be the motive. You may have to give us a paternity test, unless your DEA boss can fix it with my sheriff."

"She can fix it. I'm getting close to taking down the entire Skulls outfit. But I've got no problem taking the test, if you want me to. The kid's not mine. She slept with nearly all the Skulls, one time or another. She turned tricks at Voodoo River. It could be anybody's baby."

"Any of those guys into voodoo rituals?"

Gabe smiled. "They like to wear the skulls and crosses and all that shit, but none of them practice it. Why?"

"Because Madonna's body was found right up there in your old dining room, smack dab in the middle of a voodoo altar."

Gabe glanced up at the dark house. "Man, Mom and Dad would've hated that." He looked back at her.

Claire said, "Do you still miss them and Sophie?"

"Yeah. I've felt all alone for a long, long time. It's hard not having a family, especially right now at Christmastime. I've got my uncles and aunts, though. They try to be there for me when I need them. And I've got you every five years or so."

Claire smiled, but she knew all about not having a family. She didn't like thinking about it. "I heard about your parents' car wreck, but not until a long time after it happened. I'm sorry I wasn't around to help you get through the funeral. I can't believe you lost them all at once, even poor little Sophie. That's just awful, Gabe."

"Clyde and Luc and the other guys kept me sane, somehow." Gabe wouldn't look at her, obviously not wanting to talk about the deaths of his parents and only sister because he quickly changed the subject. "How bad was it for Madonna?"

"Horrendous. She was beaten black and blue. The killer sewed her eyes and mouth shut with heavy-duty thread."

Gabe looked repulsed. "No shit? Sounds like a whack job's on the loose."

"Yeah." Claire sighed. "And we aren't getting much yet, either."

"You will. A scene like that should give up lots of evidence. Any suspects?"

"Jack Holliday's a suspect."

"The Tulane football star? No way. He was a great quarterback when I went there."

"You ever see him with her?"

"No, but I remember her talking about him all the time. She had it bad, but I was pretty sure she was makin' all that stuff up. From some of the stories I heard, I figured she was stalking the guy."

"You're probably right. He's got alibi witnesses all over the place. Problem is, we got his prints on a glass at the murder scene, and he says he's never been there."

"Could've been planted, I guess."

"Yeah, I thought of that."

"I'd believe him, if I were you. Like I said, Maddie was fucked up, big time. Her brother didn't help, either. Rafe gave her anything she wanted to get high on, and she wasn't particular about what she took. Anything that numbed her to her life did it for her." Gabe hesitated, looked away, out over the slow bayou current just barely visible in the boat lights, and then back at her.

"I hate to tell you this, but Madonna was one of my confidential informants."

"She was a CI? Are you kidding me?"

"Why'd you think I sweated her taking drugs so much? She started using more after I recruited her."

"You're damn lucky DEA's gonna back you up, Gabe. Otherwise, you'd look pretty damn guilty. They're gonna say you wanted to get rid of her because she was going to blow your cover. You're playing a dangerous game here."

Gabe shrugged. "I'm used to it."

"Would anybody in the Skulls kill her?"

"Sure. Hell, they give out special patches for murdering people. But none of them have the intellect to think of leaving her on an altar with her orifices violated."

"Well, did anybody get a shiny new kill patch this week?"

Gabe laughed, and he did look good when he smiled, even with that stupid chin braid. "Nope, and I would've heard about it. They get drunk and run their mouths. Most of them are fine with her. Unless they found out she was a CI. If that's why they killed her, I'm next."

Claire wondered how he could stand being part of such a sleazy, violent, disgusting world. "What about voodoo? You sure none of them are into that?"

"Pretty sure it's all talk."

Claire said, "When are you getting out, Gabe? They're gonna find you out, sooner or later. You do know that, right?"

Gabe shrugged again. "I've got almost enough on them to shut it down. I'm gonna make sure that every single one of them goes down on drug charges." He glanced inside the galley windows. "I came out here once to see if I could find you. You had beer in the fridge. How about a drink before I take off?"

"You've been coming out here looking for me?"

"Yeah, heard you were back and wanted to see you. I think a lot about the good old days when we were little and you lived with us. You ever think about it?"

"Yeah. A lot's happened since then."

"True. We went our separate ways, that's for damn sure."

"God, Gabe, it's good to see you again."

"I've read about you in the newspapers, y'know. You're quite the famous detective. You still dating that shrink?"

"Yeah, but I'm kinda ticked off at him at the moment. C'mon, let's sit down and catch up."

Gabe walked inside and got them cold bottles of Dixie beer. They sat down across from each other at the round picnic table on the upper aft deck. They just talked for about an hour, smiling and remembering all the times when they'd fished off the bank and shot at birds with slingshots and stolen the best sugar cookies in the world out of his mother's pink-and-white-flowered cookie jar.

"So, Gabe, tell me, who's your squeeze with the classy tattoo on her boob? You get married and not tell the family?"

"Bonnie's FBI."

Well, that shocked the hell out of Claire. "No way."

"We work together. She's good, but she's reckless and takes way too many chances. That's why I keep her so close to me. If she's my old lady, the other guys won't bother her."

"Sexually assault her, you mean?"

Gabe didn't answer, which probably meant yes.

"How'd you come up with that ridiculous name? Rocco? Come on."

"Had a nice ring to it."

"What's the last name?"

"Ramone."

Claire leaned back her head and laughed out loud. "Rocco Ramone. That is just downright pitiful."

They drank and talked and listened to the night sounds of the bayou for a while. Finally, Gabe said, "I'll see what I can find out about Maddie. Just don't expect much. I don't think the Skulls were involved. I would've heard something by now."

"Thanks. Things just aren't adding up very fast. Madonna was with lots of men, but we haven't found anybody with a real motive. Except for Holliday, because of the stalking. And now we got the CI thing, which could be a reason. I don't think Holliday did it. He's way too eager to prove his innocence. But maybe he's slick. Using voodoo as a distraction sounds more like him than your biker buddies."

"Some killers come off as white as snow. He had a motive. She was driving him crazy. I can attest to that. Could be she was accusing him of fathering her baby. He sure wouldn't want the press to get hold of that."

"He was in New York with lots of eye witnesses. So he could've hired it done. The Skulls are all thugs for hire. And the Montenegro family's into lots of criminal activities."

Claire stiffened at the Montenegro name. Black had a closer association with the Montenegros than anyone knew, not that he was ever involved with their underworld dealings, true, but very few people knew about the connection. And she didn't want Gabe to know about it, either. Fortunately, the sound of a car approaching interrupted their conversation. They both stood up. Gabe looked at her.

"Who's that? Your partner? You didn't tell him who I was, did you? You can't tell anybody. You gotta promise me."

"No, of course, I won't. It's probably Black out looking for me. We had a little disagreement. He's determined we're going to talk about it tonight."

"Good, I'll get a look at him. See if he's really good enough for you."

"Well, just keep your mouth shut and let me handle it. He's a shrink, and he's good at it. He'll see right through your biker act. He's jealous sometimes, too, but he's too polite to attack you outright. But he can handle himself, trust me, so don't sell him short. I've seen him in action."

Gabe gave a low laugh. "I was jealous over you, too, once a long time ago. 'Member the time you went fishin' with Freddy Sabattein at his secret fishing hole and didn't tell me? Boy, was I ever pissed at you. Especially when you caught a whole string of crappie to fry up for supper."

"Yeah, you wouldn't speak to me for two days. Okay, just sit right there, look tough, and say nothing. It'll go better, believe me."

Gabe merely grinned, apparently enjoying her predicament. Ignoring
him, Claire watched Black's Range Rover appear just as she pre-
dicted. She walked down the gangplank to meet him and to keep him
away from Gabe.

A Very Scary Man

Once back at the assassin's condemned house where Malice planned
to keep his victims until the maze was complete, he carried his old
girlfriend's two children inside and laid them in front of his impressive voodoo altar. He had prepared it earlier and with the sole intention of scaring the hell out of anybody unlucky enough to be trapped
inside the house with it. He tied the two kids to lawn chairs first off,
binding their legs and feet with tape. They were still sleeping peacefully, poor little drugged sacrificial lambs. He hated them, almost as
much as he hated their dead parents. But at least they were going to
provide him with some pleasure. But, first things first. He got out
the battery-operated tattoo gun he'd purchased for a pittance in the
slums of Mumbai and started with the little girl. Her arms were taped
palms up on the arms of the chair so he started inking the tattoo of
his Veve at the inside of her wrist. He drew it carefully freehand, just
as he intended to draw it on every one of his future victims. It was
his gift to the Loa he had adopted. Papa Damballah would be pleased
to see his symbols worn upon such a young and innocent person and
would bless the kills sacrificed to him.

But he had special plans that day for the boy, the child whose birth
had ruined his life. He pulled off the boy's sweatshirt, laid him on
the floor, and carefully tattooed his thin wrist. Now he belonged
solely to Malice, and so did his little sister. And they would belong
to him for as long as they lived, which might be a very long time or
might just be a few more hours. It depended on how much fun they
turned out to be. He was all-powerful, like his patron Loa.

After he was finished inking his tribute to Papa Damballah, he

bound the boy's hands together and tossed the end of the rope over
one of the cellar's ceiling beams. He hoisted him up far enough so
that he would be able to stand after he came to. Both of them were
still deeply unconscious and had not moved a muscle throughout all
his preparations. Good, that's what he wanted. He took his cigarette
lighter and began to light all the white candles around his altar and
then took time to go behind the screen and slather his face with black
and white paint.

After he molded his face to look like a smiling skeleton, he
poured a good amount of cornmeal on the floor and drew the same
Veve in it that he had inked onto the children's arms. Still, neither of
them moved, which was beginning to get on his nerves. Impatient to
start his fun and games, he almost woke them, but decided against
it. He didn't want them to be groggy. He wanted them to feel fear
and terror and despair, wanted to see them shake and tremble and
suffer and beg him to stop.

Moving behind a screen, he sat down and watched them and ate
a package of barbecue potato chips and a can of Vienna sausages.
He was starving. He had been so eager to finish his vendetta that he
had skipped lunch. He got a Coke out of the crushed ice in his cooler
and leaned back and waited some more.

At long last, the boy came to and struggled desperately to free
himself, but that was futile. Malice watched him swing on the ropes
and heard all the muffled yells of panic underneath the duct tape
covering his mouth. Most of all, he enjoyed the absolute terror in the
boy's eyes, reflected in the mirror he'd set up so the boy could see
his own predicament, especially when the kid managed to twist
around enough to see his little sister taped to the chair. He started
trying to wake her up, his cries muffled and pathetic. The little girl
still did not move.

Malice slipped on his red devil mask and stepped outside, where
the kid dangling on the ropes could see him. The boy went rigid, eyes
huge and shocked. He approached the twelve-year-old, reached out
and grabbed his hair. His young captive tried to jerk free and kicked
out hysterically at him. This one was going to be a handful, but he
liked that. The boy had guts, just like his daddy; he'd give them both
that. He picked up the cat-o'-nine-tails rawhide whip that he had

bought in Shanghai and slapped it in his open palm. He came up close and stared into the boy's bulging eyes. He made his whisper low and gruff and impossible to recognize.

"Meet your new daddy, kiddo. You and little sis over there are gonna live with me from now on. And we're gonna have all sorts of fun. Know what else? You're gonna do every single thing I tell you, or I'll make your little sister pay for you bein' obstinate. Got that? I'll string her up here instead of you, understand me, boy? Understand what I'm a sayin' to you?"

The boy struggled impotently and looked frantic, but after a few minutes, he stilled and just hung there.

"Ever heard anybody say 'the sins of the father,' sonny? That's what we got here. That's why I'm a gonna whoop on you until you bleed. Got that? Okay, hold still now, it's time for your very first whoopin'."

Smiling in anticipation, Malice pulled back the whip and sent it slicing through the air. He'd been practicing his aim on stray dogs, and the practice had done him good. The leather lash hit the boy's in the middle of his back and cut a long red streak across it, exactly where Malice had intended. The boy jerked but didn't scream. So he flicked it against him again, harder this time and with more sting.

Malice stopped and watched the blood now dripping down the cut on the kid's back, like water oozing over a wall. The kid moaned some, but he still wasn't pleading and whimpering the way Malice wanted him to. So he hit him again, and then again, and then again, crisscrossing the blows in a nice neat little tic-tac-toe pattern. Smiling, he stopped for a moment. He felt a great satisfaction well up inside him. Yes, it did feel good to wreak his revenge at long last. Really, really good, in fact. And the boy would eventually beg for mercy. Oh, yes, he would. Malice wouldn't stop until he did.

For the next week, he kept them locked in the dark, dank cellar, pretty much drugged up during the daytime while he worked. His double murder of their parents was all over the front pages of the parish newspapers, and the New Orleans television stations were all over it. Everybody in town was upset and afraid, so the police went on high alert and put out a curfew for all young kids. They were searching all over the parish for the perpetrator so he had to play that game along with everybody else and pretend that he felt sad for the family. How ironic was that? They had search teams from all over the state coming in to look for the two kids, but he wasn't worried.

There was no way they would ever find them. The assassin's old house was on private property and was boarded up and isolated and overgrown and very few people knew it was behind the tall brick wall edging the river. Even if someone came around, the kids were in the root cellar secure in a hidden wooden box with air holes, unconscious and silent. He was not worried in the least. He would just have to wait until things cooled down some, and then he would take them upstairs where he had built a mini maze for them to play in, one that was just as terrifying as the real one. But in the worst case scenario, and even if the search parties did manage to locate the children someday, they could never pin him to the murders or to the kidnapping. He made damn sure of that. The kids would never get a look at his face.

Then at night, when he got off, he would return and force them upstairs where he would chase them around inside the boarded-up first floor and jump out and catch the little girl. Her big brother was very protective and took her whippings for her. That was fine by him. His true love would've come back to him if she hadn't gotten pregnant by the boy's father. Then the boy had been born, tying his true love to the other man forever.

Sometimes, he'd take the girl upstairs and pull her hair or shake her violently, just to make her scream and cry, because he knew that tormented her brother even more than the daily beatings, but he rarely ever really hurt the little sister much. She was a pretty sweet little thing, to be sure. Just a slap now and then to shut her up or make her mind him. She would just cower and cry and plead, and that was no fun for him. He liked her brother better. He had so much grit and gumption. Brave as the day was long.

Although he still hated the boy, he had to respect his courage. No matter how many times he hit him, the boy set his jaw and refused to beg. It was really something to see, all right. He wasn't even sure that he would be able to do that if his back were being lashed. But he always stopped before the boy passed out. And then he doctored him carefully and gave him painkillers and didn't touch him for a time, so that he wouldn't die. He didn't really want to go that far. In fact, he might even let both of them go, since they'd ended up giving him so much enjoyment.

One night he forced them into a tunnel he'd made out of barrels positioned end to end, so that he could beat on the metal and listen to the girl scream and cry. He could see them through tiny holes he'd drilled in the barrels but they couldn't see him. He had other holes on the sides, where he could thrust in sticks to prod them in one direction or the other, depending on what he wanted to do to them. He was having a ball, and they were becoming more docile with each passing day.

After about a month without detection, he no longer worried about being found out. The investigation was running into dead ends, and nobody suspected him, not a single soul. So elated with the success of his very first double murder and abduction, he went back out to the house by boat in the middle of the night. Eager to see his playthings again, he opened the cellar door and went down the steps, wearing his devil's mask, his heart racing with excitement. He had a new experience for them tonight. A cold water drenching that he'd jerry-rigged up out of odds and ends.

To his utter shock, the two kids were gone. Oh, God, they had escaped! He finally found where a board had been pulled off a window. The boy must have found something with which to pry it off. Malice leaned out and got a quick glimpse of them running through the moonlight back toward the old graveyard on the edge of the swamp. He ran back upstairs and grabbed his shotgun and headed out after them. He could see their silhouettes in the distance, running for all they were worth. They wouldn't get far, not with the boy nursing the lashing he'd given him the night before. Malice couldn't believe he had actually been able to get up and run so soon after his injuries. Then, suddenly, they just disappeared into thin air.

Frantic, he searched everywhere and heard nothing, no splashing of water, no panting or thud of running footsteps. Then he realized they were probably hiding among the gravestones. He moved into the cemetery and stood very still, listening in the quiet night. He could hear the wind in the trees and the distant rush of the river. But then another sound came to him, a low whimper, and it came from somewhere very close by. They were hiding in one of the crumbling burial crypts. He followed the sound and jerked open the wood door and flashed his light inside. The little girl was in there all right, huddled in the corner and hiding her face, but the boy wasn't. He had gotten clean away, probably thinking he had hidden his sister well enough while he ran for help.

Cursing, he grabbed her out and dragged her back to the house. Damn it, now he'd have to get rid of her. The boy probably wouldn't make it through the swamps alive, not in his condition and with his back dripping blood, and not with so many alligators swarming in the stagnant water back there. He would never make it to town. He'd end up on the bottom in a gator's nest, or what was left of him. But he couldn't take that chance. So he put his hands on both sides of the girl's head and gave it a sharp jerk. Her fragile little neck snapped easily with a crunch of bones but no pain. He walked to the side of the bayou and tossed her out into the still and murky water. It didn't take the gators long to discover her. He watched a moment until the biggest gator got a good hold on her body and took her down under the water. Damn it, he hadn't wanted to kill that cute little girl. He liked her. She was a real sweetie pie. It was her brother's fault that Malice had been forced to do such a terrible thing.

So Malice went hunting. Big brother would have to die, too, as soon as he tracked him down. That was fine with him. He had grown tired of the boy's stubborn resistance, anyway. The kid couldn't have gotten far, not in the shape he was in. Malice headed out into the swamp, following the boy's trail with a flashlight, shotgun in hand. He needed to find the boy before dawn and finish him off, because he had to be at work in the morning at nine o'clock sharp or risk getting his pay docked.

Chapter Sixteen

Still irate that he had to drive all the way down to the bayous in the middle of the night to find Claire, Nick Black pulled his black Range Rover up beside Claire's white one and shoved the gearshift into park. Not that he was surprised to find Claire holed up on the houseboat. She loved the place, and he figured she was looking for a sanctuary where she could be alone and think things out.

However, it was also dark and isolated and the scene of a recent grisly murder so he thought he better show up and make sure she didn't end up as victim number two. One thing for certain, though, he hadn't expected to find her out there alone with another man. That didn't particularly sit well with him, either, not at all, but he knew her well enough not to get up in her face about it. She would just bull up and take off with the guy, whoever the hell he was.

Climbing out of the SUV, he walked to the gangplank, where Claire stood waiting for him. Her unknown companion stayed where he was, slouched in a deck chair on the top deck. Which was probably a good idea, considering Nick's present infuriated state of mind. The guy was watching them, though, with an amused expression on his face. He didn't appear to be too shaken up by Nick's sudden appearance.

"Hello, sweetheart. Thought I'd come out and make sure you were all right. Seems like you have lots of guys interested in keeping you company tonight, though. Guess you weren't as lonely as I thought while I was out of town."

"How did you know I was out here?"

"Guess I just know how your mind works." He glanced up at the guy sitting at the deck table. The other man looked completely ridiculous, as if he were going to a costume party. "So, who's Johnny Depp up there? I don't believe we've met."

"He's an old friend."

"How about introducing us? You know how much I like to get acquainted with your old friends."

"Go home, Black. And quit thinking what you're thinking. We'll talk later, but right now, you need to just go away. I'll be home in an hour or two."

Like hell. "What is this, Claire? Some kind of payback for Jude being at the party? That's not like you. Or, are you hiding something out here that I need to know about?"

Claire looked annoyed and lowered her voice. "Okay, Black, listen to me. He's an old friend from way back who looked me up tonight. I wasn't expecting him. He just showed up. We're talking about old times when we were kids. That's it. No ex-husband I'm getting cozy with."

Nick felt the dig in that barb. He stared down at her and quieted his voice, too. "Jude and I were over a long time ago, and you know it. Just like I said, she was all torn up about her stepson's drug habit and wanted advice. That's it."

Claire frowned and appeared embarrassed that her mystery guy was listening to their conversation. Nick didn't care much. Something was going on, and that usually meant Claire was putting herself in danger. So he wanted to know what. He didn't think she was cheating on him, or even thinking about it. And neither was he. They were in too deep with each other for that, and had been for a long time. But the guy looked downright bizarre and maybe a little dangerous, and Nick didn't like the way he kept staring at him with that knowing smirk. He brushed past Claire and strode up to the aft deck, then took the stairs up top. When he reached the table, he extended his hand to Claire's secret pal. "Hi. I'm Nick Black."

Up close, the man was big, muscular, confident, and relaxed. But he looked like an idiot in the pirate getup. He stood up, looked at Claire, who was right behind Nick now, and said, "Rocco. Glad to meet you."

"Rocco who?"

"Rocco Ramone."

Nick turned around and gave Claire a look that said as plainly as he could make it: *A pirate? Really? Rocco Ramone? Really? You expect me to believe this shit?*

Rocco sat back down. "Have a beer, Nick. Claire's got plenty of Dixie longnecks down in the fridge. Ice cold, too."

"Yeah, I know. I bought them. So help yourself. Really. I try to keep this place well-stocked."

At that, Rocco shifted his eyes to Claire, a slow, crooked grin overtaking his face. Nick realized that he sounded jealous, and then with some dismay, he realized that he *was* jealous. The concept was a trifle alien to him; he was not the jealous type. But he felt a lot of things about Claire that he'd never experienced with any other woman. He didn't really think she was doing anything wrong with this guy, but he didn't like her being out there alone with him. Claire only sighed and looked resigned.

"Well, go ahead and sit down, Black. Since you've already crashed the party. Want a beer?"

Nick nodded, and after she headed down to the galley at the front of the boat, he sat down across the table from Rocco. "So I understand that you're an old friend of Claire's?"

"Yep."

"How long has it been?"

"Long time."

Nick leaned back against the chair cushion. He glanced around the deck and listened to the slow, rippling bayou current and was fairly certain that he and Rocco weren't going to hit it off. He leaned back, nowhere near as relaxed as the other man, and enjoyed dead silence for a moment. The galley windows were open, and he could hear Claire opening the fridge, bottles clinking as she got out their drinks.

"So, Rocco. Who the hell are you really?"

"Your girl down there? We were close once, but not anymore. I'm leaving when she gets back. Don't want any trouble with jealous boyfriends. Just don't ever hurt her or I'll come after you."

Nick had never in his life been described as a jealous boyfriend, didn't like it at all, and he sure as hell hadn't ever been threatened to his face. Rocco's accent was distinctly Cajun but well-educated, a whole lot like his own. Rocco was trying hard to hide his true persona. He wanted to appear dumb and/or violent and dangerous, but Nick would bet that he wasn't either. Well, he might be violent and dangerous under the right circumstances. Thus, the pirate beard and fake tough biker mentality.

On the other hand, Rocco looked like he could hold his own. And he carried a weapon under his jacket on the right side, probably a .38, and probably some kind of dagger in his black leather boot. Nick had seen such men before and he'd pegged Rocco Ramone right off. Most likely he was an undercover cop. What the hell was Claire into now? And why wouldn't she tell him about it?

"No trouble. Stick around. I usually like Claire's friends. As long as they don't get her shot or put her in a coma. Then I have a tendency to look them up and take care of it. Guess we're alike in that way."

Rocco placed a steady gaze on him and dropped his lowlife, I-can-kill-you-before-you-blink act like a hot rock. "I won't get her shot. You don't have to worry about that. And I'm not putting moves on her, either."

That was all he was going to get out of Rocco, Nick was pretty sure, but he had gotten the answers he wanted, so he didn't push it. He got up and headed to the steps, wondering what was taking Claire so damn long. He stopped at the top of the stairs and turned back when he heard the buzz of a motorboat, very loud in the quiet night. It seemed to be going fast and headed up the bayou toward them. As it neared, Rocco stood up, too, and watched it approach. The boat passed them on the opposite side of the bayou, about twenty yards distant, near a stand of flooded cypress trees.

It was dark, and all he could see was a figure in the stern, working a powerful outboard and wearing a dark hoodie against the chilly night. There was a single light in the prow, but it was too dark to see the driver clearly. The boater waved as he passed, a friendly Cajun out frog gigging, probably. Nick watched him a moment, and then glanced down below when he heard Claire come outside.

A low thud behind him told him something had hit the deck, and he spun and crouched quickly, his first thought that Rocco had come up fast behind him, perhaps more dangerous than Nick had thought.

But it wasn't Rocco. Rocco was staring at the object rolling across the deck toward where Nick had been sitting at the table. Both of them froze for the first second, until a second grenade was lobbed onto the boat and landed, not a yard in front of Nick.

"Grenade!" Rocco yelled and tried to jump over the rail into the bayou.

Nick took a flying leap down onto the lower deck. He landed wrong, fell down on his shoulder, rolled back up onto his feet, near where Claire was standing, three beer bottles in her hands, looking stunned by his gymnastics. He threw himself toward her and took her over the railing with him. They hit the water about the time the first grenade exploded. The boom rocked his eardrums, and he felt splintered wood and shattered shards of glass raining down in the water all around them.

The second grenade went off almost simultaneously as they plummeted deeper and hit hard against the layer of mud at the bottom of the bayou. Then they fought their way back to the surface, gasping, choking, just as the gas tank in the stern blew up with a thunderous boom and a fiery explosion that lit up the night sky as bright as day. The houseboat disintegrated into rubble and orange flames that shot high in the air like hellfire loosed on earth.

Claire was treading water. In the glow of the flames, she looked shocked but okay. She was bleeding from the nose, but she was still breathing and her arms and legs were functioning. Black looked out over the debris-littered surface for Rocco. He saw him about six feet out, floating face up in the water. Nick felt a little stunned himself, ears stopped up and vibrating, eyes aching, and he was blinking away blood from some kind of gash over his left eye. He headed out to Rocco, found him still alive but unconscious. He and Claire grabbed him and somehow fought their way back to shore.

After they'd dragged him out, they rolled onto their backs for a moment, panting with exertion. Claire appeared too dazed to speak. He got up on his knees and did a cursory check of her arms and legs and found a gash on the back of her head, but it wasn't bad. He jerked off his shirt, ripped it up, and tried to wrap some of it around her head, well aware they'd both been extremely lucky they'd been blown off the boat or they'd have been caught in the fire of the explosion.

Then he checked out Rocco, who had taken the brunt of the first blast, probably hit with debris before he made it down to the water. He was covered in shrapnel wounds. It looked like his left arm might be dislocated, maybe even broken, and he might have internal injuries as well. It was a good thing he was unconscious or he'd be in agony. Nick's head was pounding, blood pouring down his forehead, and he checked himself over and found another fairly deep laceration on his right thigh. He bound it up with what was left of his shirt. He felt dizzy for a moment, like he was going to pass out, and got on all fours and hung his head down until it stopped spinning.

"Black, Black . . ." Claire tried to sit up, then groaned and dropped her head back into the mud.

"Don't move yet. You might've hit your head. We've got to get an ambulance out here."

"You're bleeding," she managed in a slurred voice, frowning and trying to focus her eyes on his face. The whites of her eyes were bloodshot, the shock of the blast wreaking havoc with the capillaries. His probably looked the same way.

"Yeah, a few cuts and bruises. Lie still. Does your head hurt?"

"It's killing me. What happened?"

Nick glanced at Rocco again. He was still breathing, but he was in bad shape. "That boat that passed by? He tossed a couple of grenades in on us."

That got her attention and she roused up big time. "What? Grenades?" She stopped and then remembered her friend. "Is Gabe all right?"

"Rocco's in bad shape, if that's who you're talking about."

She pushed herself up, and immediately cried out and grabbed her head with both hands. "Where is he? How bad is he?"

"He took the worst of the blast. I need to call an ambulance from the car." Nick's head was slamming against his skull as if trying to knock his brain stem loose, and it felt like it was about to get its way. He was weak, but he was the one in the best shape to get them to the hospital. Rocco, or Gabe, or whatever the hell his name was, needed medical attention and needed it fast. His left arm was not in good condition, and he was bleeding from both his nose and his ears. Nick used a shattered piece of plank off the boat to splint the arm as best he could, which wasn't very well.

Still woozy, Claire managed to sit up and stare at the flickering flames, still roaring and crackling and consuming the houseboat, Nick watched her crawl on her hands and knees and cradle the other man's head in her lap. At that point, he knew that this guy, whoever he was, meant a lot more to Claire than some casual old friend. But all that would have to wait. He staggered to his car, got the hospital in Thibodaux on his satellite phone, identified himself as a doctor, described their injuries, and instructed the ambulance to meet them on the highway to Thibodaux.

When he got back, he pulled Rocco up and onto his shoulder, trying to avoid further injuring Rocco's bad arm and hoping to God Rocco didn't have internal injuries bleeding out inside his head or chest. The ensuing pain was severe enough to bring Rocco half conscious, and he groaned in pain. Claire tried to help Nick with him, but stumbled herself and went down to her knees, still groggy and disoriented. He left her there and hurried ahead, got Rocco in the backseat of the Range Rover, and then went back for Claire and settled her in the passenger seat. She lay her head back and shut her eyes and lapsed into semiconsciousness.

More than anything, he feared she'd sustained a second concussion, and he knew all too well what that could do to her, right now, when she had only just recovered from a head-injury-induced coma. Cursing inside, angry at himself for not realizing the danger and getting her out of it before the blast, he turned the ignition, slammed the car into gear, and backed up, spinning gravel in a sliding one-eighty turn and driving hard for the highway and the dispatched ambulance. Because now he knew, and all too well, that the grenades that had hurt Claire and her friend might have been thrown onto that boat to kill him, not them.

Chapter Seventeen

Four hours later, all three of them were back inside Black's walled mansion on Governor Nicholls Street in the French Quarter. They had been bandaged and checked out at the hospital in Thibodaux, and Gabe had indeed suffered the worst of the blast. At the moment, Claire stood alone beside Gabe's bed in the largest and most elegant of their seven guest bedrooms. Gabe lay there in the ornate mahogany antique canopy bed with its magnificent royal blue velvet hangings, very still, very pale, looking like a corpse. She sank down into a cushioned gold-and-white-striped empire chair beside the bed and massaged her temples. Her headache felt like some kind of out-of-control jackhammer. Black had been wonderful, just like he always was when she needed him, and he still hadn't asked her any questions about Gabriel LeFevres. But he would, and she would tell him everything he wanted to know. And there was no way that Gabe could ever go back undercover, not with the Skulls. It was completely out of the question.

Claire turned her head and watched Black where he stood across the room. He was giving orders to the private nurse he'd summoned. Julie Alvarez was an old friend of his from Charity Hospital, a pretty woman with short brown hair and green eyes and very good ER skills. At the moment, Black was swearing her to secrecy. The doctors had set Gabe's arm, which turned out to be a severe dislocation of the shoulder as well as a cracked wrist and elbow. They'd also stitched up dozens of ugly shrapnel wounds on his arms and chest. But he was breathing fine and resting comfortably now. He would be all right, but he had not regained consciousness.

All three of them had been extremely lucky to escape the blast alive. Gabe was terribly wounded, and Black had a deep gash on both his forehead and leg. She had fared better because Black had shielded her from the blast with his body. He was fine, though. Even with his head and thigh bandaged, he was up and walking and talking and giving orders. Thank God. A wave of anger swept through her, and she sat very still and swore that she would get whoever had done this to them. No matter how long it took. Gabe shifted slightly and made painful grunts, but he was heavily sedated and quieted at once.

When she looked back across the room, Black was gone. Julie was sitting in a white easy chair beside the window watching Claire hover over Gabe. Claire had a feeling that Black had reached his limit. She didn't blame him, either, but she was surprised he hadn't demanded some answers out of her before now.

"Don't worry, I'll take good care of him," Julie said softly. "You probably need to get some rest. Nick's beat, too. I suspect he's waiting for you."

"It's very important that no one knows Gabe is here. You do understand that, don't you, Julie?"

"Oh, yes. Nick made that crystal clear."

Claire looked down at Gabe again. The ER nurses had washed off his eye makeup and cut off his braid when they were working on a laceration on his chin, and he looked more like he used to.

"He must be very special to you," Julie whispered softly.

"He's the closest thing I ever had to a brother."

"That's pretty much the way I feel about Nick. Please forgive me for saying this, but you might want to tell Nick that. He didn't say so, but I sense he's pretty upset about what happened tonight."

Claire stared at her. Julie was right, of course. "You'll come and get me if he wakes up and calls for me, won't you?"

"Of course. Nick gave him quite a heavy sedative. I don't think he'll come around until morning. That's a good thing. He's going to suffer a lot of pain when he comes to."

Claire took one last look at Gabriel, and then she walked down the long white marble hallway to the round master bedroom she shared with Black. She found him there, sitting in a large maroon leather wingchair in front of the fireplace. He still wore the green scrubs provided to both of them by the hospital staff after they'd showered and washed off the bayou mud and the blood from their stitched wounds. He was in profile to her, staring motionlessly into the fireplace grate, where a roaring fire was snapping and popping like crazy. He had a short glass of Chivas in his right hand and held it propped on the arm of the chair. It was almost empty. A little blood had seeped through the bandage over his eye, a tiny spot of scarlet, the size of a dime. He sat utterly still. If he had not shown up and come aboard when he had, she and Gabe would probably be dead. Or injured a lot more severely than they were.

She stood there in the threshold for a moment. Jules Verne was curled up asleep in the middle of the round canopy bed after having yapped incessantly when they'd rolled Gabe in on the gurney and settled him in the guestroom. Poodle stress. It was extremely quiet now, except for a bird chirping outside the open French doors and the breeze fluttering the sheer white curtains and filling the room with cool fresh air. She could hear the distant tinkling of the fountain in the middle of the large and private walled courtyard below their balcony. Juan and Maria had helped them situate Gabe in his room, but then Black had told them they should go back to bed and get some sleep. Dawn was beginning to break now. She could see the graying sky through the giant fanlights over the row of tall French doors leading onto the gallery, but there were few sounds yet of the city bustling awake in the French Quarter outside the tall walls.

She just stood there, head still aching, looking at Black, very glad he was home with her again, very sorry that he'd been injured, and because of her again. She wondered if he had about had it with her and the dangers of her job. But he hadn't asked her to quit, and had even said he would never do that. He had saved her life, and Gabe's. Moving across the room, she stopped in front of him. He looked up at her, his eyes bloodshot from the blast, a black five o'clock shadow darkening his cheeks. He looked so tired, so spent, that her heart clenched. She straddled his lap, careful to avoid his injuries, her knees on either side of his thighs, and encircled his head with her arms. She brought it up against her breasts and kissed his hair.

"I'm sorry, Black, I'm so sorry that you got hurt. I'm so sorry I involved you in all this."

His next words were muffled against her, but they touched her heart. "No matter how hard I try, no matter what I do, I can't seem to find a place where you'll be safe."

Claire put her palms on his cheeks and gently raised his face. "You are my safe place, Black. You are, right here, right now, always."

His arms tightened around her, and he pulled her closer. She threaded her fingers through his thick hair and told him how much she loved him, something she did not say to him very often. They didn't speak for a little while after that, just held each other, and then he pushed her back where he could look into her eyes. "We can't keep doing this, Claire. You do know that, don't you? Someday, if this keeps up, one of us is going to get killed. Do you even realize how close we came to dying in that blast?"

He was dead serious, sounded almost defeated. They had barely escaped a horrible death, and she knew it all too well. "I do know that. And I know that if you hadn't come out there, Gabe and I would both likely be dead right now. What I don't know is why this happened. I wasn't expecting any kind of danger out there, I swear. But I think it's got to do with Gabe, not me. I think you and I were just in the wrong place at the wrong time. He's been riding undercover with the Skulls. That's a biker gang here in New Orleans." She stopped and took a deep breath, shut her eyes a moment against the pounding in her temples. "They must've found him out and been suspicious enough to follow him or something. We didn't expect it. He hadn't even been there very long before you drove up. I swear it, Black. He was a friend to me a long time ago, when I was a child and really needed somebody I could depend on. That's all, that's all it is, all it ever was."

Black nodded, just a bare shake of his head. "Okay, I don't want to talk about it anymore right now. I want to get in bed and hold you and try to get some sleep. Tomorrow, when we're rested and can think straight, we need to talk about what we're going to do. Right now, let's just go to sleep. It's been a long day for both of us."

"That sounds good to me."

So they got up, undressed, and slipped under the soft sheets. He put his arm around her waist and pulled her in close against his chest, and then he fell asleep almost immediately, his cheek on the top of her head. Claire was not so lucky, and she lay there warm and content inside his arms, very glad to just be there with him, listening to his steady heartbeat, and feeling safe again. Finally, long after dawn peeked through the fanlights, she closed her eyes and slept like the dead, too, her dreams dark and disjointed and full of flames and falling glass and Gabe's groans of pain.

When she awoke again, it was early afternoon. They still lay entwined together in the bed, but her head no longer ached. She pulled back and raised herself on one elbow and studied Black. He was still sleeping, his right arm flung over his head as he was wont to do. But she vaguely remembered rousing up not too long ago when he'd left the bed and gone into the bathroom, and then down the hall, probably to check on Gabe. She had gone back to sleep before he returned, but now she eased quietly out of bed and tested her arms and legs and found out that her whole body felt as if she'd been stretched for hours on a torture rack. She made her way to the bathroom and washed her face and brushed her teeth, thinking she should go ahead and take a shower and get dressed. But she didn't really want to, not yet. She still felt sore and exhausted, and she didn't want to face the day, or the serious conversation Black wanted to have.

Claire had a feeling he had reached his breaking point with what she unintentionally but repeatedly put him through. She didn't know why terrible things happened to her so often, tried not to think about the reasons. But she did know that right now the idea of being without Black was the worst thing she could think of. She had let him in, let him get closer to her than anyone ever had. He was her life now, and she could finally admit that. So she slipped back under the covers and lay there close beside him and watched him breathe and tried not to think about anything.

After dozing awhile, she decided that it was time to shower and get dressed and check on Gabe's condition but her efforts to slide out of bed were brought up short when Black's fingers tightened around her arm. "Uh-uh," he said, eyes still closed. "He's fine. Julie's with him. Come back here. I want us to pretend that last night was an extremely bad dream."

Claire smiled and snuggled back in against him. His arms tightened around her, and he leaned his cheek against her hair. "So? You ready to tell me who the hell that guy is?"

He definitely had a right to know, but she'd promised Gabe she wouldn't tell anybody about him. On the other hand, some maniac had tried to kill them all. Black needed to know, for his own safety. She trusted him. Gabe would understand. He wasn't going back with the Skulls, anyway.

"He trusted me to keep his cover. That's why I didn't tell you about him and why I had to go out there alone last night to meet him."

"What is he? DEA or FBI?"

"DEA."

"So what's his connection to you? You work undercover together before? Or was it really a childhood thing?"

"It's a childhood thing, just like I told you. We've never worked together."

"That outfit he wears? It's a dead giveaway."

"Well, it worked well enough for him the last two years riding with the Skulls."

"The biker gang out of Algiers? I've heard about them and none of it is good. They're into drugs and prostitution and God knows what else."

"He earned their trust, and they respect him. He's tougher than you think."

"Oh, I think he's tough, all right. But why all this intrigue with you? Is Lafourche working with him?"

"No." It went against Claire's grain to betray a confidence, but this was different. Gabe owed Black his life. "We told you the truth. It's just like I said. He's an old friend of mine. His name is Gabe LeFevres, and I lived with his family when we were kids, for about a year. It was the only foster home where I ever felt like part of the family. He protected me back then. He was like the brother I never had."

"Then I guess I owe him, too."

"You'll like him. He's a great guy."

"Was it a romantic thing?"

Claire laughed at that. "We were ten. He was nicer to me than anybody I could ever remember, and I adored him. He taught me to fish and shoot a BB gun."

"What about now?"

"C'mon, Black. It happened years ago. We were just little kids."

"What were you doing together last night? Was he bringing you in on his case?"

"No. He wanted to make sure I didn't blow his cover. Zee and I ran into him the other day, just by a crazy coincidence. When we went into a bar named Voodoo River looking for our victim's brother, he was in there. It was a little dicey for a minute, but Gabe managed to get those creeps out of there before anything bad went down."

"How dicey?"

"No blows were thrown, if that's what you mean."

Black shifted slightly until they were lying on their sides and facing each other. He examined her face a moment, appeared to be thinking about what he was going to say. "And you think those bikers found Gabe out and tossed those grenades at him?"

"That makes the most sense to me. We know you're not the target, and it's unlikely anybody's after me this early in the investigation. My face was on that doll, true, but I was out there alone several times, all night long. He could've gotten to me a lot easier than lobbing a damn grenade on the boat and risking killing other people."

Black frowned. "What the hell were you doing out there alone at night?"

"I didn't want to make the drive up here every night so I slept on the boat a few times. Who would've thought something like this would happen out there?"

"You told me that you were staying here with the Christos."

"Anyway, so that leaves Gabriel. They must've made him and decided to get rid of him. He told me Madonna was his CI, and that she was shaky. She could've let it slip to one of the Skulls, for all we know. So they killed her and went after Gabe. He told me he's been out at the houseboat looking for me." She stopped and took a deep breath. "Maybe they followed him out there before and were lying in wait to get him. But it could be me, I guess. The Christien case is getting weirder by the day. And I'm talking voodoo altars and skulls on sticks and mutilated women and spooky emblems

drawn in cornmeal. We're questioning a lot of people, including Jack
Holliday. Maybe we're getting a little too close and making somebody nervous."

"What makes you think it couldn't have been me?"

That brought Claire up short. She hadn't been expecting him to
say that. "What do you mean? Do you think this is about you?"

Black looked so intense that Claire knew that was exactly what
he thought.

"Last night I realized that we need to get everything out in the
open between us. I mean that. So, I'm telling you now that it could've
been me. Actually, it probably was aimed at me."

Astonished, Claire could only stare at him. Then she sat up cross-
legged and looked down at the serious expression on his face.
"What's going on, Black? Tell me. What kind of trouble are you in?"

"I lied about going to London for a reason. I didn't like doing it,
and I haven't liked doing it in the past."

"You've lied to me before?"

"Not exactly. I just didn't tell you the whole truth."

"Well, tell me the whole truth now. Are you in trouble?"

"Not exactly." He sighed deeply. "You're not going to like this,
but I can't tell you everything now, either. In fact I can tell you very
little, and there's a good reason for that. I will say that I'm doing
some covert work and it's made us some enemies."

"Oh, my God. You're not saying you're a secret agent?"

"No, I'm not a spy." He laughed a little at her expression, but cut
off his amusement pretty quick. "I just help out certain people sometimes, with my areas of expertise. I can't tell you more than that."

"Oh, my God, you're talking about psyops, aren't you?"

"Maybe. Maybe not. That's all I'm saying."

"Are you a specialized interrogator?"

"No, definitely not that. Please quit asking me questions. Nobody
knows about this, Claire. You understand that, don't you? And nobody
can know about it. So that's why I didn't tell you, and that's why you
can't tell anybody, not ever. It's imperative that you don't. For your
own safety and mine."

"Is that all you do?"

Black actually squirmed a little, and Claire knew then that it wasn't all he did. "You said *us* a minute ago. Who's in this with you?"

"I can't say."

"I want to know. I have to know, Black. You're not being fair."

"There's a group of us, trained in certain areas. We work together as a unit sometimes, but not so much since I met you. That's it. No more, Claire."

"Let me guess. Booker and Holliday. Anybody else?"

"I'm not saying they're involved. I'm not saying they're not. Good God, Claire, you don't want to know this. Trust me."

"Is that what you were talking about with Booker last summer at the lake? When I walked into your hospital room and you said he would look into somebody wanting you dead?"

Black just stared at her.

"Are you in danger on these little covert psychological operations?"

"Not really."

Claire had a feeling that wasn't true, but his startling revelations out of the blue gave her a lot to think about. She couldn't say she was all that surprised, not after the first shock receded. She had observed how he handled weapons, how watchful and careful he was all the time. He knew what he was doing, and he had an arsenal of sorts in his private gun collection at the lake. She'd seen it. But Jason Bourne escapades? James Bond stuff? She never would have imagined that. Black was more the James Bond type, to be sure, every bit as suave and sophisticated as the fictional British spy, and he wasn't an assassin like Bourne. Or was he? Lord have mercy. He had thrown her for a loop this time.

"Do you assassinate people?"

Again, Black laughed at her. "Oh, yeah, you should see all the notches on my gun."

"That isn't funny. You hit me with all this stuff and then laugh it off?"

He sobered instantly. "You wanted the truth so I gave it to you. I'm rarely in danger. You're the one who's always in danger, not me. But I'm glad to get this off my chest. I don't like hiding things from you. I trust you. You've got to know that."

Claire listened to him, but one phrase stuck out in her head. He was *rarely* in danger. That sounded good to her, kind of. "Wow, Black. I don't know what to say. I'm going to have to get used to all this."

As far as Black was concerned, she was pretty sure he felt the subject was now closed, and probably forever, too. Especially when he said, "Well, I think you've still got a lot you need to say to me. It's your turn. So tell me about your case and don't leave anything out this time."

Claire eyed at him, still bowled over by what he'd told her about his little secret excursions. Man, Black was into covert operations? What the hell was going to come at her next? She took a deep breath and ran the Christien case for him. Halfway through, she realized there wasn't much to tell. They hadn't made a lot of progress on finding the killer. It also reminded her that she needed to put in a call to the office and let them know what happened out at the boat.

"I've got to call Zee. And Sheriff Friedewald needs to know that there's a second crime scene out at the LeFevres place."

"Oh, no, you don't, not yet. Look, you owe me, Claire." Black hugged her closer and pressed his lips against her temple. "Like I said, I missed you. Right now, I'm going to show you how much, and you're going to let me."

His hands were roaming under her clothes and over her naked flesh, in places Claire wanted him to go unhampered, oh, yes, she sure did. But she needed to tell him something else first, something she didn't want to. She shivered a little as his hand slid up her spine and his fingers closed on the back of her neck under her hair, his mouth seeking hers, warm and gentle and eager. "Black, wait a minute."

"I don't think I can."

"Can I trust you, Black? Really, no matter what?"

That got through to him. He stopped kissing her and drew back where they could stare into each other's eyes. "Oh, God. What now?"

"You didn't answer my question."

"Of course, you can trust me, and if you don't know that by now, you're never going to. I just spilled my guts to you, for God's sake."

"Even if it concerns your brother?"

That took him aback, she could see it clearly inside his keen blue eyes, but then they turned wary—very, very wary. Black had changed his last name years ago in order to distance himself from the crime family run by his older brother, Jacques Montenegro, but very few people knew of their family relationship. And that's the way Black wanted it, for obvious reasons.

"What about Jacques?"

"Gabe thinks the Skulls might deal drugs for your brother's organization. If the blast wasn't about you, the Montenegros might've been the ones who put the hit out on Gabe."

Black shook his head, emphatically. "Jacques put a stop to all that kind of thing. He's trying to go more legit. No Mob hits, either. And certainly not if they knew you were out there on that boat. Jacques and his wife are very fond of you. In fact, they've invited us over for dinner on Christmas Eve."

Claire thought: *No way, no way, nooooo way*. But she said, "Nobody knew about my relationship with Gabe or that we'd even end up out there last night. You just guessed right, thank God. What if they didn't know I was with him?"

Black frowned. "You've got to sit on this, Claire. Let me see what I can find out. I'll inquire around, see if Jacques has any interest in Gabe. Is that his real name?"

"Yes. Gabriel LeFevres, just like I told you. What if Jacques did put out the hit?"

"Like I said, that's not Jacques's style anymore. He's trying to tone down the violence. There are other crime families in the state— maybe they're working with the Skulls. But I'll protect Gabe, if I can. And I can, if Jacques does know anything about all this stuff. But Gabe's got to go into hiding for a while until we can find out who's behind the hit, if he even was the target last night. He runs with dangerous people. He's got to lay low until we smoke them out."

"They'll find him. No matter where he goes. He's not going to be safe anywhere."

Black hesitated. "He'll be safe, if he stays here. Or he can have one of the suites next door at the Hotel Crescent." He frowned. "Damn it, here would probably be the safest place for him. Although I was looking for some downtime with you, and alone for a change. It's been over a week. We have things to catch up on."

Claire smiled, couldn't help it. Yes, they did, indeed. Black did not want her old puppy love to hang around, either, but he was willing to let him. That told her a lot. She went back into his arms and pressed up against him. "It means a lot to me. He was good to me when I was alone and in trouble."

"Just be careful, okay?"

"I will, but I really do need to get down to the office. I've got a lot of work to do."

Black only laughed, and yes, it sounded arrogant and very alpha male. "Get real, Claire. You just survived an explosion. If that's not a reason to take a sick day, I don't know what is. For God's sake, it hasn't even been twenty-four hours."

Claire couldn't argue with that so she didn't argue. "Then I have to get on the phone with Russ Friedewald and Zee. I've got to get a new phone, too. Mine was sitting on the deck table."

"You can have one of mine, a decent one. That phone you bought at Wal-Mart was pathetic."

"You got some extras lying around?"

"You have a tendency to lose them as fast as you get them. I try to stay ahead of the game. I like to be able to get hold of you."

All that happened to be true. "Okay, I'll take it. We'll call it my Christmas present."

"Oh, I've got other things planned for that, which involve long airplane flights away from here. After last night, I want to get you as far away from the bayous as humanly possible."

"Sorry, no can do, but it's a nice thought."

"Well, sorry right back to you. You're not going in to work today. I've got a bad feeling, and I trust my gut."

"Yeah? Me, too. But I'm in the middle of a case. Since I don't have my car, I'm going to get hold of Zee in a little while and have him bring it back over here. And until he does, I want you to kiss me and never stop."

Black apparently liked the sound of that. "No problem."

The first one was very soft and tender, at least long enough to get her all worked up and considering they were both nursing recent injuries. But it didn't take long for the fires to start burning inside them and the flames to start streaking along their nerve endings, and she was glad to surrender to him and let it happen for as long as he wanted it to happen. Maybe a day off was in good order. She had missed the hell out of him, too.

A Very Scary Man

For a long time after his little playmates escaped, Malice had to lie low and be very careful. The search for the two children was still going strong, so the fun and games inside the cellar with new kids ground to a halt. He had been forced to kill his true love's little girl, even though he hadn't really wanted to, so he didn't have to worry about her bringing the law down on him anymore.

Unfortunately, and despite the fact that he'd tracked down the boy out in the swamp and practically beaten him to death and dumped him in the sluggish water for the gators, the kid had survived, thanks to some duck hunters who'd happened by and found him muddy and bleeding where he'd somehow crawled out and collapsed on the bank. That pretty much scared the hell out of Malice. As it turned out, however, the boy's head injuries had affected his memory, and he couldn't identify his kidnapper or lead the cops back to the house, so all was well. Finally, after months and months, the notorious case faded unsolved and forgotten and went cold. He felt safe to strike again.

He did manage to obtain a couple of sanctioned hits when his assassin friend was tied up with his own out-of-town kills. One assignment he got was in Muncie, Indiana, where he just ran a guy off a deserted road and then shot him in the head and chest while he was slumped unconscious in the front seat of his truck. Then he doused the body and vehicle in gasoline and burned it unrecognizable. Malice got paid some big bucks for that one.

The other hit was down in south Florida around Naples, where he just shot the guy point blank right in his own backyard when the man went outside before bed to have a smoke. Both murders were quick and simple, which really wasn't Malice's style, but he guessed he couldn't have everything he wanted all the time.

So, the years passed, with a steady stream of hit jobs assigned to him. The payments were large. It was a lucrative profession indeed, and gave him the ability to buy anything he wanted. Then, one day he got an assignment in his home state. After he murdered the parents in their bed with his silenced .45, he found two ten-year-old girls sleeping just down the hall, all alone and defenseless and ripe for the picking. He just couldn't help himself. He really, really wanted them so he woke them roughly at gunpoint, and the two girls were so scared that they just fell on their knees at the side of the bed and waited, trembling and shaking and praying. He tied them up and taped their mouths and told them he would kill them if they made a single peep but would let them go if they cooperated and did exactly what he said.

That was a lie, of course. He had no intention of letting them go. They were going straight into his maze out in the swamp, as its very first victims. This time nobody was around to see him take them out to where he'd hidden his boat. He could make it to the maze quickly and easily with them bound and gagged and blindfolded in the bottom of his boat, an old moldy tarp spread over them.

But first, he decided to mark them as the property of Papa Damballah. So, he took them to the edge of the bayou and then he got out his battery-operated inker and climbed into the back of his van with them. He quickly drew his Veve on the inside of their wrists. They lay paralyzed the whole time, especially the smaller one. She was so scared that she wet her pants. The other girl moaned when the needle pierced her skin but did not move a muscle. After he was done and satisfied with his artwork, which was rather good, he carried one girl under each arm and dumped them into his boat.

Halfway to the maze, he decided to stop at the old voodoo altar on Skull Island, as he had recently christened it, mainly because it was spooky there at night with all the creepy moss hanging almost to the ground and lots of human skulls scattered all over the place. So he laid the two girls out on the ground in front of the altar, put on his mask, and lit some of the candles. Then he took off their blindfolds so they could see the scary stuff all around them. He was getting aroused, thinking about how helpless they were, ready to take the prettiest one off alone and see just how brave she really was. But then he heard the buzz of an outboard headed fast in his direction. He froze where he was, hands on the frightened girl's shoulders, but he could see a light filtering through the trees, one that was affixed to a boat. He couldn't take a chance on being caught red handed, so he had no choice but to run. He took off in his boat and left the girls lying bound and gagged on the ground.

Furious at being disturbed just when things were getting good, Malice pulled his boat into a thick stand of cypress trees and shut off the motor. He floated there a moment, nervously watching to see if the boat would come in his direction. Chances were the fisherman would not see them, and he held his breath as the boat neared the voodoo ritual island. But the guy did see them, apparently drawn closer by the candle flames. Cursing to himself, Malice watched the man pull up to the bank near the altar, and then jump out and run to help the girls. Malice could hear them screaming and screaming when the fisherman pulled the tape off their mouths, the sound echoing for miles out over the bayous.

And then he sat there, absolutely terrified, too afraid to even move. If the fisherman decided to look for him, there was no way he could get away fast enough. He lifted the shotgun carefully out of the bottom of the boat, not wanting to kill the man, or the girls, not out in the open like this, but he was ready to, if it came to that. But Papa Damballah was with him again, protecting him from harm, because the man just got the two hysterical girls into his boat and took off toward town, probably pretty damn spooked himself.

After that, Malice waited a long time, just in case they circled back, and then he finally started up his boat and headed out in the opposite direction. He needed to put space between himself and that island. Damn it to hell, he was just getting started with those girls. He wanted them so much he could taste it. He should never have stopped there. He should've continued on out deeper into the swamp and trapped them in the maze. This time, it had been a little too close for comfort. He had gotten way overconfident, and this was the second time he'd let his victims escape. He'd better get his act together and get it together quickly, or he was going to end up in a jail cell, or lying in a death chamber with a needle stuck in his arm.

Chapter Eighteen

When Claire checked in with Sheriff Friedewald, who was still at his conference in Metairie, she alerted him to the new developments in the case. He also insisted that she take a day off while his forensics team combed the blast site. So Claire did get to pursue idle pleasures with Black, and a very enjoyable day it was. Black was feeling good again and smiling, obviously relieved to get his guilty secrets off his chest. Gabriel was going to be okay, but he was still sleeping a lot and Julie Alvarez was staying with him 24-7. So Claire and Black took advantage of their downtime and spent most of it in their huge round bed, recuperating and calming their nerves in the best way they could think of while getting reacquainted after a week apart and enjoying it immensely.

That evening, the weather was pleasant, and they sat together out in the courtyard, enjoying fresh fried shrimp and lobster and delicate croissants sent over from the chef working next door at Black's Hotel Crescent. Unfortunately, their idyllic day together ended abruptly when Claire's new smartphone vibrated itself around her waterglass. She picked it up and saw that it was Zee. She punched on quickly.

"Claire, where the hell are you? I've been trying to get you for hours. I couldn't get hold of Nick, either."

"We both lost our phones in the explosion. Just now got our new ones up and working with the old numbers. Sorry. What's up?"

"You remember Wendy? The Saints cheerleader we interviewed?"

"Of course. Did she come up with something new about Madonna?"

"She's dead, Claire. I'm standing in her apartment right now. NOPD is taping off the scene as we speak. Rene called me this morning. He's here, too, lead on the investigation. And she's posed on a voodoo altar, same M.O., same perpetrator. No doubt about it."

That news shocked Claire almost as much as Black's reluctant confession had. She was struck mute, something that didn't happen very often. Then she caught her breath. "Oh, my God. She's dead?"

"She's hangin' from the balcony, you know, that white iron one in her foyer. Rene's got to go back downtown in a minute, but he's gonna hold the body at the crime scene for us because it's related to the Christien case. How fast can you get out here?"

"I'll borrow Black's vehicle and be there in fifteen minutes."

"Hurry it up. God, this is so sick. She was a nice girl. She didn't deserve to die like this."

Black was listening intently and showing extreme interest in her end of the conversation. "Now who's dead?"

"A Saints cheerleader named Wendy Rodriguez. We interviewed her about Madonna Christien. And she's a friend of Jack's, too. I've got to go. Zee's waiting for me at the crime scene."

"What happened to her?"

"Don't know the details. Zee said it's got another voodoo altar."

Black frowned. "We never hear about that kind of stuff around here anymore. Not with dead bodies."

"Yeah, that's what Zee's grandmother told us, too. I've got to borrow your car. Mine's still down at the boat. That okay?"

He didn't look particularly pleased, but he hadn't looked pleased since the phone had rung. He handed over the keys to his Range Rover. "I wish you'd take another day off. I'm going to."

"Good, maybe you and Gabe can get to know each other. I don't know when I'll be back. Don't worry about me."

"Yeah, right, like that's going to happen. Why don't I come along? Maybe I can be of some help."

"I don't think so. You're an alibi witness in this case, remember? Try not to worry, really. There's gonna be all kinds of NOPD detectives working that crime scene. It's right here in New Orleans, not too far from here. I'll be back as soon as I can."

Then she headed for the garage, on her way to the apartment of the pretty cheerleader, a woman who probably didn't look so pretty anymore. She got into the car and backed out, feeling sick to her stomach. She did not want to see what that psycho had done to Wendy Rodriguez, but she had to.

When she arrived at Wendy's apartment complex, there were three NOPD cruisers blocking off the entrance gate. They waved Claire through when she flashed her badge, and she followed the winding road back to Wendy's unit. The crime scene was taped off, but thankfully, authorities outside the gate had stopped the media. And there had been plenty of them, and they had kept their cameras on her SUV. That also meant this murder was probably going to be on the morning news. Reporters would start digging and what they would dig up was Madonna's murder and Jack Holliday's involvement, which would really start a feeding frenzy that would never stop. If they got wind of the explosion at the boat with a guy as famous as Nicholas Black being one of the injured, it would really hit the national networks. Sometimes her life just sucked. The last twenty-four hours fit the bill, to be sure. And to think Black had told her that they would thrive and be safe in Louisiana's slow and lazy Southern rhythms. Wrong, wrong, and more wrong.

Three police officers stood outside the yellow tape at the apartment, talking together on the front sidewalk. Lots of neighbors were standing across the street, watching and talking excitedly into cell phones. The NOPD officers greeted Claire and raised the tape so she could duck under. She stopped at the front door, not exactly eager to go inside. It was always that way when she knew the victim. Wendy had been so alive and vital and friendly, and not all that long ago, either. Claire wasn't looking forward to seeing the beautiful young woman, cold and dead, eyes wide and empty and staring. Or stitched shut.

Sucking in a bracing breath, Claire snapped on gloves and stepped into the paper booties the guys at the gate handed to her. The door stood wide open, and she walked inside and found Zee all alone in the entry hall. Her gaze latched immediately on Wendy Rodriguez. She was hanging from the upstairs banister, just as Zee had described. She was naked and had been beaten, almost as badly as Madonna. Claire wanted to close her eyes and not think about how much the girl had suffered. The killer was sick and brutal and soulless and cruel. They had to get him.

"Hey, Claire. This is not good, not good at all."

"No, it isn't."

"The media's gathering at the gate. Did you have to talk to them?"

"I pretended I didn't see them." She stared at the paint that turned Wendy's face into a black and white skeleton, wincing at the X stitches holding her eyes shut. Candles were everywhere, on the floor under the hanging body, on the steps, all white, and the pictures of saints were sitting around, and the cornmeal on the floor had the same Veve scratched into it. "Oh, God, it's the same perp. There's no doubt about it."

"Yeah. And Jack Holliday's connected again. We found a note on the coffee table in his handwriting."

"Damn, I thought we could rule him out." Frowning, Claire moved down the hall to the den and squatted down. Rene's forensic people were still everywhere, dusting for prints and taking photographs. The folded note was on the table outside its envelope. She lifted the front flap with her forefinger and read: *Thanks for all your help, Wendy. Sorry you had to deal with the police, but I'm grateful. I'll be over later to talk. Jack.*

Well, that's just hunky dory, Claire thought. "Who found her?"

"Next-door neighbor was supposed to go to a late movie with her, and when she couldn't get Wendy to answer the door, she thought she better call the police, just in case something was wrong. The officers got here approximately eleven minutes later and found her like that, candles still burning and everything. Rene called me in when he saw the similarities to the Christien case."

"So she hadn't been dead long when the neighbor called it in?"

"We assume she hadn't. Not sure yet."

"What time was that?"

"Around eleven o'clock last night. They've been processing here ever since. They're waiting for us to get done before they remove the body."

"Then we might be able to rule Jack Holliday out. He was with Black and me last night. I saw him myself."

"Where?"

"On the *Bayou Blue*. You sent him over there to see me, remember? And he gave me a video that proved he was in New York at the time of Madonna's death, but it was lost in the blast. Offered to take a lie detector test and give a DNA sample. Big-time cooperative."

"Well, that's good for him. If he was with you once we get the time of death nailed down, he'll be clear and free."

"Have forensics found anything significant yet?"

Zee shrugged. "They'll be wrapping up here as soon as you give the say-so."

"I need to examine the body first."

"Climb up the steps. You can see her better. Man, she was so young and so nice and so pretty, and she has to end up like this. It's a damn shame."

Claire made her way up to the first landing and tried to study the body objectively. It wasn't easy. Wendy's face was eggplant purple. There were trickles of blood at the needle's puncture points around her eyelashes and lips. That meant she had still been alive, her heart pumping, when he'd stitched on her. God, this killer was a true psychopath. And then she saw the voodoo doll taped to Wendy's hands, one identical to the one Madonna had been clutching, including Claire's picture pinned to its face. The guy was consistent, if nothing else.

Then she wondered if he had been the one to throw the grenades. She could have been the target, and that seemed a lot more likely scenario to her now than someone wanting to eliminate Black or Gabe. A cold shudder started somewhere at the base of her spine and undulated all the way up to the roots of her hair. She turned around and went back down the steps, not wanting to look at the corpse anymore.

"Anybody see anything?" she asked Zee.

"Nobody saw nothin'. The neighbors said that Wendy slept a lot durin' the day so nobody thought much of her not being out and about. They said it was real quiet around here last night, not much goin' on."

"Doesn't look like much of a struggle went on, not like at Madonna's house."

"No, everything's as neat as a pin. And Wendy was strong and physically fit. Rene said they think she was killed upstairs in the bedroom, but it's been cleaned up, too. Nothin' much to see. You really think you can alibi Holliday?"

"We were with him. So was Nancy. So were lots of customers on the boat who asked for his autograph. He was there for a while. Like you said, it depends on what time the ME comes up with."

"He could've been setting you up for the alibi. It's hard for police to argue with a cop's statement."

Surprised, Claire jerked a look at Zee. "So the guy isn't such a hero to you anymore?"

"No, just sayin'. It sounds pretty lucky. For him. He's the one who called me, lookin' for you. Maybe he planned it."

All that was true, of course, but she still wasn't sure that Jack Holliday had it in him to beat a woman to a pulp like this, much less kill her. Especially not if he ran some kind of missions with Black and Booker. That would make him one of the good guys. And Wendy had been his friend. Claire had a pretty good hunch that Jack did work with Black. Then again, lots of killers kept an aura of innocence until they stretched out their arm for the lethal injection. If Holliday was indeed some kind of psychopath, he also was a very good actor. Black was gonna have a cow. He thought he'd gotten his pal out of trouble.

"Maybe somebody's trying to frame him."

Zee said, "Yeah? Who? Why?"

"I don't know." She looked around. "Seems like he took time to clean up and set the scene. Or he subdued her quickly upstairs. But she's beaten black and blue. How did he do it without any blood spatter or overturned furniture like at Madonna's? It doesn't add up."

"He could've knocked her unconscious and used her as a punching bag when she couldn't fight back. And then cleaned up with the bleach."

Claire envisioned that scenario in her mind, and then wished she hadn't.

"And you can smell bleach big time in the master bathroom. We aren't gonna find much trace. Could be he beat her unconscious, strangled her, cleaned her up and then the apartment, did his creepy paint job, then hung her up there over the altar. But he had to have all the time in the world to do all that."

Whoever killed Wendy was very good at his game, and probably had lots of kills under his belt with victims they had yet to find. So how come this time out he had left two bodies for them to discover and made the crime scenes so bizarre? And how had he gotten out of Wendy's house without being seen? How had he gotten past the security guard manning the gate into Mimosa Circle? On foot? There were tons of people living in this apartment complex. Somebody had to have seen something. She just hoped they had the guts to come forth. Or could the killer live nearby, too?

Claire and Zee hung around until Wendy's battered body was removed, and then had to face the reporters clamoring around with their lights and cameras outside the entrance gate. Several TV stations filmed Claire inside her car again as she pulled out, and she cursed under her breath because the last thing she needed was her picture plastered all over the evening news. Or, maybe that's why the killer had put her image on the dolls—to use her past notoriety to gain more publicity. Maybe he wanted to be remembered as the Voodoo Killer or some other moniker equally grotesque, and all the celebrity that kind of thing would bring to him. Lord have mercy, they could not let the particulars of the crime scene get out, not under any circumstances. She hoped Rene knew that and had done enough to prevent it.

Chapter Nineteen

"So, what you two are telling me is that you've pretty much come up with nothing, other than probably ruling out Jack Holliday as a suspect since his paternity tests came back negative and all his alibi witnesses turned out to be telling the truth. Not to mention that he was with you and Nicholas Black and about a hundred other witnesses around the time the second victim was murdered with the same M.O.? Is that about it, Detectives?"

Sheriff Russ Friedewald leaned back in his swivel chair and leveled his piercing gaze at Claire, then gave another measuring stare to Zee, which caused Claire's young colleague to shift uneasily in his chair. Claire was used to such eyeballing. Charlie Ramsay, her sheriff in Missouri, was a lot more intimidating and used a heck of a lot more cusswords. They sat together in the departmental conference room, the slats open on the mini-blinds. Russ liked to hold his meetings there instead of inside his own spacious office, which usually remained pretty much sacrosanct for him, and for him alone. He sat at the head of the table with Zee on his right and Claire on the left. They all had unopened bottles of water in front of them, in case the grilling got too hot and Zee and Claire had to douse each other. On the other side of the conference room windows, where only she could see him, Eric Sanders stopped and blew them a kiss. Quite a comedian, he was, oh yeah. An annoying comedian, too. He was on his way outside to have a smoke, no doubt.

The sheriff continued, "And these murders are being splashed all over the newspapers as we speak with our office front and center and empty handed. And somehow the New Orleans press has dug up enough information to christen our perpetrator as the Voodoo Doctor. Do I have my facts in order?"

Claire answered for the two of them. "Yes, sir. I'm afraid that pretty much sums it up."

More silent facial examination of them ensued. Russ Friedewald was a really nice man, a transplant from Springfield, Illinois, in his mid-sixties, turning gray but still a youthful-looking, handsome guy and a real whiz at computer technology. According to Zee, he had been married for many years to a wonderful woman named Rita, had some kids and grandkids that he adored, was honest and straightforward, and ran a clean operation. He didn't like loose ends, he didn't like controversy, and he didn't like the media climbing on his back when former celebrated sports figures got themselves publicly involved in his murder cases.

"I don't suppose either of you have been watching the news programs."

"No, sir," said Zee.

Claire had. She had seen a news report on one of the New Orleans stations that had pretty much been a mishmash of unsubstantiated half-truths and half-conjectures indicating that, seeing that Wendy had been one of their cheerleaders, unnamed players on the Saints team could possibly be involved in her murder. The report had also included a liberal dose of Jack Holliday's name as the man who represented most of them. Claire didn't want to admit she'd seen it, though, much less discuss its ramifications with Russ. So she kept her mouth shut, which ten times out of ten was the best thing to do. And Russ hadn't missed the fact that Claire, Black, and an undercover DEA agent had almost been blown to smithereens near the first crime scene.

"There was a really nice shot of you, too, Detective Morgan." Russ aimed that comment at Claire. "Leaving Mimosa Circle. Somehow you forgot to mention to me that you visited the crime scene on the day that I told you to stay home and recover."

"I'm sorry, sir. Rene called us as a professional courtesy, because the crime scene held a voodoo altar identical to the one we found in the Christien case and felt the two murders were connected. He wanted our input on the scene."

"And I guess you didn't think I'd be interested until the next day about a houseboat blast where one of my detectives got blown into the bayou, either. Seems to me everyone knew about that before I did."

Claire swallowed hard at that one because she *had* put off calling him. "I called you, sir, as soon as I could. We were at the emergency room most of the night. We were all fairly shaken up."

Claire watched his jaw flex into a tight line, astute enough to realize he was not a happy camper. She hadn't been aboard his team long, but she already knew that he rarely ever showed what he was thinking. He said, "I thought once we ruled out Jack Holliday we were home free, but that appears not to be the case. For your information, Rene Bourdain called me and informed me of the particulars and indicated there's a note addressed to the victim in Holliday's handwriting. I take it that's true?"

Well, thank you, Rene. Russ was ticked off, all right. "Yes, sir."

"Why didn't you apprise me of that instead of leaving it for Bourdain to do?"

"I was gathering facts, trying to find the parallels in both cases so I could fill you in with a comprehensive overall picture as soon as you got back from the conference." She had used this reason before with Charlie to good avail and hoped it would work again.

"But in the meantime, you took time off to get yourself nearly blown to hell?"

"That may or may not be connected with Christien's murder. Gabriel LeFevres was on the boat with me, and as you know, he's been working undercover in the Skulls biker organization."

"Yes, and he is a very good undercover officer. I'm sorry to see him have to give up this assignment before he was ready to."

Well, I'm not, Claire thought. "We do have a few leads that might help us find the killer, sir. Would you like to hear them?"

"Please, Detective, feel free."

Flipping open the manila folder on the table in front of her, Claire took out the enlarged pictures of the tattoos on Madonna Christien's inner wrist and slid them across the table. "This same tattoo was found on both victims left on the voodoo altars so we're trying to determine when and where they got it. Here's the photo of Wendy Rodriguez's wrist that Rene faxed to us. We have already discovered that this symbol is a voodoo Veve dedicated to the deity called Papa Damballah."

Russ picked up the photos and examined each one in turn. "So they are exactly the same? Any progress on this really being a legit voodoo connection?"

"That's what we need to find out. When we go down to Golden Meadow for the funerals, we can question the victims' families about it. The two victims grew up together—you know, a BFF thing. And Wendy told us that they were both abducted as children. We think the tattoo might be linked to that. Maybe even the same perpetrator, getting rid of survivors of his crimes."

"Well, did Wendy tell you it was linked to their abduction?"

"No, sir, because we weren't aware she also had that tat until we found her body."

"What the hell's a BFF thing?"

Zee spoke up, obviously feeling he could handle that one. "You know, Sheriff, Best Friends Forever, like on Facebook."

"And that's supposed to mean something to me? What the hell's Facebook?"

Claire explained that it meant they were lifelong friends and told him what she knew about social networking, which wasn't much. Then she said, "Now we think it's his signature. The same image was scratched in cornmeal in front of the two bodies. Serial killers sometimes mark their victims, as you know."

"Oh, that's all we need. This thing just keeps getting worse. Okay, just get on this fast. The media's all over the Rodriguez murder because of her cheerleader status, and they're not going anywhere, trust me on that. I got a call from Jack Holliday's attorney this morning, wanting to know why they haven't been apprised of the Rodriguez homicide and warning us that they don't want Jack hassled anymore."

Claire said, "There's no proof that he was ever in Wendy's apartment, just the note he sent her and it was stamped and went through the U. S. postal system. Rene hasn't given us all the forensic reports yet. Besides, Jack was with us at the Cajun Grill. Lots of other people noticed him there, too. Time of death was estimated to be somewhere between six and nine on Tuesday night. I don't believe it could've been him. Neither murder, actually. However, we have yet to explain

that hurricane glass with his prints, since he swore he's never been
to Madonna's apartment."

"Well, finally some good news. Maybe the firestorm will die
down if we can announce that Jack Holliday is no longer a person
of interest in either case. He's had the good sense to stay out of sight
and keep his mouth shut so far, and his lawyer says he hasn't given
any interviews, and isn't going to."

"Yes, sir."

"Okay, go on, get back to work, and I want frequent updates on
this from now on, and written reports. Do you understand me,
Detectives? Don't leave me in the dark again."

"Yes, sir," they both said as one.

They headed out of the building quickly before Russ could come
up with something else to berate them about. Once outside in the
parking lot, Claire stopped. "Madonna's funeral starts in an hour,
Zee. You ready to go?"

"Let's do it. Even a funeral is better than gettin' chewed out
like that."

Golden Meadow turned out to be a representative slice of small-
town America. Madonna Christien's funeral was held in a tiny
clapboard Catholic Church with a square bell tower off the beaten
path, and there weren't that many beaten paths. The sanctuary was
full of people, more than Claire had expected. To her surprise, most
of the Skulls were there, too. They all sat hunched together in the
back pews like a gathering of leather-clad black crows. The rest of
the mourners sat as far away from them as they could possibly get.
Zee joined the fastidious townsfolk on the other side of the central
aisle. Claire sat down in a pew next to Manny of tattooed head fame,
just to show them she wasn't afraid of them. She also wanted to get
a few questions answered about who the hell had blown their friend
Rocco off that boat.

"Hey, Manny, how's it goin'?"

"I ain't answerin' none a your questions."

"Gee, you're a friendly guy, aren't you?"

He gave her a blank, yet surly look. He was as dumb as a stump,
no question about it. All eleven of the bikers were now looking at

her. Ever heard of eye daggers? That was the case at the moment. "So, where's the fearless leader of your motley little pack? I heard he was tight with Madonna. He not like funerals, or what?"

Manny tensed up, shoulders hunched. "What d'you care what Rocco do?"

"I don't care."

The Skull sitting in front of them was a tad more interested. He turned around and showed Claire his scarred-up, unpleasant face. "We thinkin' maybe you done got him locked up. He ain't been around nowhere."

"Yeah." That came from Rocco's Slut, aka Bonnie, the reckless FBI gal, who looked about the same as she had in Voodoo River. "He went off and didn't come home. You got him in your jailhouse up in Thibodaux, just like you said you was gonna do, don't ya? Why you got him in there? He didn't do nothin'."

So Bonnie was sending her a message. Claire deciphered it right off as the Skulls didn't know where the hell Gabe was, which meant they hadn't thrown the grenades to get rid of him. The fact that Bonnie was still with them and not floating face down in the bayou, also pretty much verified they hadn't found out her true identity, either. She needed to get out now, while she could still walk around in one piece.

"Maybe he got up in the wrong cop's face and started making threats," Claire told them calmly, giving the band of morons something to think about, if they were even capable of logical reasoning, and then she got up and joined Zee across the aisle on the other side of the tracks.

"What are you, crazy?" Zee muttered in a low voice. "All we need is a brawl to break out at the memorial service. Friedewald's pissed enough already."

Claire glanced at the cameraman and blond reporter standing at the back of the church. She leaned close to Zee's ear. "I just found out they don't have a clue about what happened to Gabe. The girl tried to tell me that in so many words. She'd be long gone if she thought they had any inkling that he was a cop."

"You couldn't pay me enough to infiltrate that band of idiots," Zee informed her.

Then the music began at the front of the church, loud and mournful organ chords that engendered a lot of weeping and sniffling in the front pews. She glanced at the Skulls, who all looked bored. They'd probably had their tear ducts removed.

After the Funeral Mass, they sought out Grandma Leah Plummer, who looked about a hundred years old, as white as a Hilton hotel's sheet, and unsteady on her feet despite a cane. Apparently, Rafe hadn't made an impression on the judge at his hearing because he was nowhere in sight. After the graveside prayers, they approached Ms. Plummer and she agreed to sit down inside the church and talk to them.

"Thank you for speaking with us, ma'am. We know this is a hard time for you."

"Yes, it is. Little Maddie, such a terrible life. That poor child was never the same after that evil man killed her mama and daddy and took her off. Just couldn't get over it, poor baby girl."

"I'm very sorry to bring up unhappy memories, Mrs. Plummer, but could you tell us about that snake tattoo on her wrist?"

"Oh, yeah, he marked her up good. Her and Wendy, too. They were his then. They didn't have a chance."

"Who marked them?"

"The snake man. He took 'em, and they was lucky to even get away. He been watchin' them all these years, just waitin' to finish what he started."

"Did he contact them again? Or was there ever a second attempt to abduct them?"

"No, but those li'l girls got real careful after that. I begged Maddie to get that awful mark taken off her, said I'd find a way to pay for it, but she said it reminded her to be careful. And that's why she took that terrible meth poison—she was always scared to death, yeah. When she hooked up with that big football fella, I thought it'd be different." She kept shaking her head.

"Jack Holliday, you mean?"

"Yeah, but now I think that was all made-up stuff, just in her mind is all. She told me they was gonna get married and be real happy.

That he was gonna pay off my house and get me a new Ford Fusion, all that stuff she always said she'd do when she got big money. Poor baby. She was as kindhearted as they come, and now she's out there in the cold ground, God bless her soul."

She started crying after that, heartbroken. They got a few more questions asked, but she really wasn't in any shape to be interviewed. But Claire wanted to know one more thing before they wrapped it up. "What about the voodoo, ma'am? Was she in some kind of secret cult, or something? Anything like that?"

"Oh, God, no, that would've scared her plumb to death. She wanted him to love her, so she got some love potions from those voodoo shops over in the Vieux Carré. But it was so she'd be safe, that's what all those charms and potions and that altar at her place was all about. She said the snake man was comin' back to get her someday, and she was right, too."

"Why'd they call him the snake man?"

"He got that snake mask he scared her with, and the tattoo had snakes, too. That's what she always called him. The snake man."

"Goddamn, can this thing get any more creepy?" Zee said as they left the church and got into his Jeep.

"Yeah, and I think that tattoo is the key." She thought about it a minute as Zee fired up the ignition. "Didn't you say Mama Lulu's shop was closed today?"

"Yeah, it's a saint's day. She'll take Etienne and go in to church."

"Think she'd mind if we paid her another visit? Maybe she knows something else about these tattoos. She's lived around here a long time."

"Sure. It's close enough. She lives out in the bayous not far from here."

As Zee headed for his grandmother's place, Claire sat back and thought about everything. It was all centered on the voodoo stuff, she felt it. But there was so much that didn't fit together. If they could only get a break, a clue that would make all the loose ends tie up nice and tight, that would crack the case. Somehow, though, she felt it wasn't going to be that easy. Nothing else had been.

A Very Scary Man

Several years passed before Malice was offered a really lucrative hit out in Colorado. The designated family lived in a small town outside Denver, and he was supposed to get rid of both the husband and the wife. That was a bit trickier than a single kill assignment so it required a lot more watching and double planning. But he was very good at that. In fact, it was his strong point.

So, on a snowy night in December, Christmas Eve, as a matter of fact, he drove down his victims' tree-lined street. There were lots of big houses with huge yards full of Christmas decorations, and all lit up with lots of expensive light displays. Neighbors were moving from house to house, giving and receiving gaily wrapped packages, big shopping bags full of presents. Nobody knew him. Nobody had a clue that Malice had invaded their exclusive neighborhood, ready, willing, and able to kill two of their own.

He had chosen the night before Christmas, because he knew full well that all the happy people he was watching would soon be snug in their warm fancy houses, tired and sated with food and drink and good cheer. And the local cops would be holiday staffed and slow to respond if somebody noticed him lurking around. He cased out the street and getaway routes several times, casually driving by the large Tudor house in the swanky subdivision. The family did all right, it appeared. The man he sought was a witness to a crime against an accused Chicago mobster who was now sitting in a jail cell awaiting trial. The organization wanted the witness to go away for good. His wife, too. She had been there when the guy had shot down his victim in cold blood just outside a steak house. They'd just happened to be in the wrong place at the wrong time, but they had agreed to testify and thereby signed their own death warrants. No skin off his nose. The more people he killed, the merrier, and the more he got paid. He was inching up now on fifty kills, and truly enjoying every single minute of it. It was easy and gratifying, now that he had his tactics down pat and rarely made mistakes. Disposing of troublesome people was a damn fine way to make a living. And he got to see the fear in their eyes sometimes, up close and personal.

As he parked his car under an isolated and thick stand of pine trees and climbed out, snow was still spiraling softly to the ground as it had been all day long. It was beautiful against the streetlights, very quiet and serene and magical. The inclement weather was a stroke of good fortune because it cut down on people getting out and going somewhere. It was bad luck in that he might leave footprints behind. But he had thought of that in advance and fixed the problem by strapping climbing spikes to the soles of his boots, which would be impossible to trace. It was very late now, well after midnight. The family had enjoyed a fun evening together inside by the fire, having a big dinner and playing games. Charades, it looked like, and then they'd opened an absolute ton of presents. They were wealthy, all right. They were getting another gift, too, one they wouldn't exclaim over with such delight.

The father of the family, his primary target, appeared rather nerdish in the photograph he'd been given, with horned-rim glasses and longish brown hair, which fit perfectly with his career, one of those pompous university philosophy professor types. The woman was well educated, a physicist even, but at the moment just a regular housewife, pretty as a picture, tall and slim and blond and sedately sexy. They had two little girls, three-year-old twins, and were they ever cute. He had spoken to one of them once when he was following the family through the Cherry Creek Mall. Just a casual smile and hello, and she had responded with a beatific little smile of her own that had made Malice want to scare her.

That's when he'd decided he was going to take the twins home with him. He hadn't abducted anybody for several years, and he had begun to kill and dispose of the ones he did abduct so they couldn't identify him. He craved that lovely release, the one he got when he saw people so terrified and panicked and trying to fight their way outside the maze. There was nothing like that to soothe his restless soul. He deserved some fun. He worked hard at both his jobs. And he'd grown a lot more careful during the last few years. He would never let another victim escape.

He had been damn lucky he hadn't been caught a couple of times in the past. But that was one reason he chose the little ones for his abduction victims. He could handle two tiny little twins just fine by himself, carry one under each arm if necessary, and he had duct tape in his pocket that would keep them quiet. They were very small for their age. They couldn't get away, even if they weren't too scared to try.

But there was one problem. A very big problem. There was another grown-up in the house. One he hadn't seen before that night and that hadn't shown up in his target dossier. The guy was very tall, very strong looking, and he would be hard to handle. He'd have to surprise him when he was least expecting trouble. He would probably have to kill him, too. But he had a suppressor on his weapon, which should do the trick. After all, they would all be asleep when he got to them. The children were already in bed, of course, and he'd watched the upstairs light come on in their room so he knew where to find them.

He settled back, concealed in some cedar trees in their backyard, glad that he had bundled up properly. He wasn't used to mountain weather; it rarely snowed in Louisiana. He watched through the window when the adults finally said their good-nights and hugged and kissed and wished each other Merry Christmas and trailed off upstairs after one full and exciting day of celebration. More bedroom lights came on, but the big stranger remained in the living room beside their Christmas tree, sprawled in a big recliner while he talked on the telephone. He was the last one to retire. He walked across the living room to the hallway, and then the downstairs lights died out, one by one.

Stamping his feet and chafing his hands together, Malice waited a bit longer, just to be on the safe side, and kept himself well hidden among the trees. The night stayed quiet, all the stars twinkling brightly above him, and it seemed such a peaceful place to live and raise a family. But that wouldn't last long, not for this particular family. It was almost time for him to make his move. But then he detected someone at the back door, and he quickly stepped farther back into the shadows. The big guy came out, all bundled up in a dark green fur-lined parka and gloves and hiking boots and carrying a red shopping bag. He walked quickly out to the street, where a large black SUV was sitting at the curb, got in, let it warm up a moment, and then drove away.

Smiling, Malice waited for the sound of the car to fade in the distance and continued watching the house, in case anybody else decided to leave. After about fifteen minutes, he decided the big guy was not coming back for a while, so he moved up the driveway, staying on the shoveled parts so he wouldn't leave any kind of trail. The back door's lock was easy to jimmy, and the big guy had obviously turned off the security system, which saved time.

Then he was inside, standing in the family's big modern red and white kitchen, the warm air feeling really wonderful against his cold face and hands. He kept on his ski mask and gloves and moved stealthily to the bottom of the back staircase, where he stood listening. There were no sounds from upstairs. He wondered where the big guy had gone so late at night. Maybe he didn't live there. Maybe he was just a good friend of the family, invited over for the festivities. Again, he waited, just to make certain. He had become quite cautious and careful, much more so than he had been in his early years. He rarely made mistakes anymore. That's why he was still alive and killing.

When he felt everything was optimal and everyone was asleep, he moved silently up the steps and down to the end of the second-floor hallway. Enough of the street light filtered through the sheer draperies for him to see the mommy and daddy asleep, snuggled close together in a giant king-sized sleigh bed, their door left open in order to hear their twins if they should cry out during the night, no doubt. He walked across the plush carpet to the bed, quickly fired a silenced slug once into each of their heads and then another straight into to their hearts, just to make sure. It had become one of his trademarks. He liked having trademarks, giving his victims or the police something to remember him by. Afterward, he moved quickly back out into the hall. He stopped there and listened again. Nothing. Silent as a grave.

The little girls were sleeping peacefully, too. There were two white canopy beds in their large bedroom but they were lying close together in one of them. There was a small ceramic Christmas tree between the beds that they used as a night light. He moved over to it and switched it off. He carefully folded down the big soft down comforter. They had on matching red Christmas nightgowns with Rudolph the Red-Nosed Reindeer on the front. God, he was going to have some fun with the little darlings. Double the pleasure, double the fun, as they used to say in that old commercial. He hummed that old tune in his mind, and then he laughed to himself.

Watching them sleep for a moment more, he took out the chloroform bottle and poured a good dose of it on a hand towel and then pressed it against the first child's face. She barely struggled before she was totally out. Then the other kid, same thing with no problem whatsoever. It was a piece of cake, a lot easier than most of his abductions. Then he wrapped them both up together in a pink-and-white-flowered Disney Princess comforter and carried them out of the house and out to his panel van where it was parked down the street. He laid them carefully in the back, still wrapped up in the comforter. Then he got into the driver's seat and started the car and turned the heater on full blast.

Merry Christmas to me, he thought as he drove off, very satisfied with his night's work. Merry Christmas to all, and to all a good night. Then he laughed, more pleased with himself than he'd been in a very long time.

Chapter Twenty

As they drove through the streets of Thibodaux, Claire stared out the window and watched a pretty, black-haired preschool teacher supervise her little ones on an outing in a grassy public park. The children were walking in single file, all with kiddie backpacks strapped onto their backs. When one little girl stopped suddenly, the next three all bumped into her, just like a *Three Stooges* skit. Claire smiled, and then sobered quickly. Hell, that looked a lot like them working their case. Regular Keystone Kops, for sure. Frowning, she considered everything. She didn't want to ask Zee what she was about to ask him, but she had to. She decided a preamble wasn't a bad idea. "Please don't take offense to what I'm about to say, Zee."

Zee glanced over at her as he stopped at an intersection. He looked wary. "What?"

"Okay. I heard somebody say that Mama Lulu might know some wise guys over in Algiers. That true?"

"She's clean, Claire. All that was a long time ago when she was young and growing up on the other side of the river. Yeah, some guys outta her old neighborhood got caught up with the Montenegro crime family, that's true, but none of us are involved with the Mob anymore. You tryin' to offend me now, or what?"

That's more than Black could say, since his older brother ran the Montenegro organization. "I didn't mean to offend you. I just thought maybe she could remember something that would help us, some kind of new lead. We're going nowhere right now. I'm grasping at straws here."

"She already told us she recognized the Veve. She goes way back with the Montenegros."

"We need to tell her it showed up on Wendy, too, don't you think, as a tattoo? That might mean something different to her."

"She might know something. If she's cool with it, I'm cool with it."

Twenty minutes later, they pulled up and parked in front of Mama Lulu's house. Zee's diminutive grandmother was on the front porch, wrapping Christmas lights around the posts by the front door. This time she was dressed normally, in a brown sweatshirt and jeans. She had a whole string of lights, already plugged in and blinking. Claire did not have the Christmas spirit, and probably wouldn't have it any time soon. Not the way things were going. The big evergreen tree Black had brought back from the forested upper New York environs was still bound up and leaning against the wall in the chandeliered foyer at the base of the grand spiral staircase, just waiting for some holiday cheer to show up.

Little Etienne was asleep, stretched out under a red-and-black patchwork quilt in an old lime-green metal glider at one end of the front porch. Zee led the way and unlatched the gate. Mama Lulu straightened up and twisted around, stretching her back as they approached the porch. "Well now, dis heah be a surprise, yeah," she said to them.

"Hey, Mama Lulu," Claire said. "It's good to see you again."

"Mama Lulu, we got some questions to ask you about that Veve we talked to you about." That was Zee, getting to the point.

"Both our victims had that Veve tattooed on the inside of their wrists, right here," Claire said, showing the old woman. "You know, the one we asked you about, the one that was on the floor in corn-meal at both crime scenes. You've lived out here in the bayous for a long time, Mama Lulu. You know anything about people getting that Veve tattooed on their wrist?"

The old woman stared at Claire. She nodded. "I reckon I seen it done a time or two. Bad gris-gris. Nothin' but bad gris-gris in dis here Veve, yeah."

"What d'you mean you've seen it?"

"I seen it put on dead people."

"Who? When?"

"I done seen it on a body dey pulled out de bayou, seen it two times like dat." She stopped, shook her head. "Bad gris-gris."

"Could it be some kind of signature? Of an assassin or a killer, something like that? Ever heard anything along those lines?"

Mama Lulu started winding the lights again. Zee picked up the end and helped her. Claire waited. "Could be I heard dat a time or two," the old woman finally said.

"Mama, this's real important," said Zee. "Two innocent girls have been killed already."

Mama Lulu sighed. "I do know somebody dat stay over in Algiers, he might know somet'ing 'bout it."

Claire jumped on that quickly enough. "Will you go there with us? Ask him to talk to us about it?"

"We gotta all go to church and light candles 'fore we see 'bout dis bad gris-gris."

"Now we're getting somewhere," Claire whispered softly to Zee a few minutes later, while they sat on the front porch steps and waited for his grandmother to change into her church clothes. Etienne was inside now, too, loudly complaining about the bath Mama Lulu was making him take. When he came out on the porch again, he looked scrubbed clean and wore a starched long-sleeved white dress shirt and clean black pants. His black leather shoes were shiny, too. Zee and Claire both wore jeans and matching black department shirts and would have to go casual.

Nobody said much along the way. Etienne played with the Nintendo DSi that Zee had given him for his birthday. Mama Lulu was asleep, her head lolling back on the seat, or maybe she was feigning sleep so she wouldn't have to talk about something she didn't want to talk about, which Zee had admitted that she did on occasion.

Once they reached the city limits of Algiers, Mama Lulu roused up and told Zee to head for the Sacred Heart Catholic Church. Claire had been there before, for another funeral, on a long-ago case when she'd had Black in her crosshairs, not very long after they'd met. She had kept to herself her knowledge of the bayous back then, just to see if he was trying to play her. That seemed a century ago now. A lot of stuff had happened since then, some of it good, a lot of it bad, at least as far as her homicide cases went. Inside the old stone church, Zee and Claire sat down together on the back pew while Mama Lulu knelt, crossed herself, and approached the altar to pray, leading Etienne forward by the hand.

"I guess I better get down there, too," Zee said. "Say hello to Jesus, or I'll never hear the end of it later."

Claire smiled at his grumbling, but hey, she might need to say a couple of Hail Marys herself. Maybe a *Thank you, God*, for getting the three of them off that houseboat alive and in one piece. So she did say a few prayers, even lit some votive candles for keeping herself and the two men she loved relatively unscathed. She lit two more, one for Madonna Christien and one for Wendy Rodriguez, and then she returned to the pew and waited, about as impatient as she could possibly get.

Only a few old women, their heads draped with black lace mantillas, graced the church, sitting around at various places, some kneeling and saying their rosaries, but no one else was in the church. After a very long half an hour, a wizened, white-haired black priest appeared from somewhere behind the altar, shuffling his footsteps, head bent, hands folded prayerfully. Eventually he reached the confessional booth behind the pillars to the left of the nave. Once he was inside and the door closed behind him, Mama Lulu waited for the green light to come on, and then she opened the supplicant's door and disappeared inside. Claire couldn't imagine what the old woman could possibly have to confess. What? She'd cut off too many bat wings this week, she'd accidentally stuck a pin in the wrong place in a fake voodoo doll, or maybe she'd simply forgotten to say her rosary.

As it turned out, she must have been pretty good or confessed her sins at warp speed because she was out of there in under a minute. She walked back up the side aisle, again grasping Etienne's hand, her footsteps a lot more spry than the aforementioned priest's had been.

"You, now," she instructed Claire as she sat down in the pew in front of her and turned slightly to look over her shoulder.

"I think I'll do it later, Mama Lulu, back at home. Thanks, though."

"You t'ink again, girl. Father Gerard is de one you want to talk to. Go, take dat picture of de Veve tattoo dat you got. See what he got to say 'bout it."

Well, okay now.

Zee was already inside the confessional, doing his spiritual duty. Claire waited. He came out and nodded to her, as if he knew the score. Claire went inside. She hadn't been to confession in a long time, hadn't been to Mass, either. Maybe because she wasn't Catholic. Black was, though. On the other hand, maybe she ought to get a few things off her chest while she had the opportunity.

"Detective Morgan?"

"Yes, Father. Mama Lulu told me I could ask you some questions. I didn't expect to do it in here. Is that all right with you?"

"It's all right, my child. I prefer it this way. There are people who would not take kindly to my speaking to a police officer."

Uh-oh and holy cow. Serious intrigue incoming. "I appreciate your time, Father. Can you tell me who these people are who've got you so intimidated?"

"I think you know who they are, my child, but I will say it, if it pleases you. Jacques Montenegro has far-reaching tentacles."

Claire actually cringed, couldn't help it. She'd met Black's brother, Jacques. He wasn't intimidating to look at. He was slight and thin and sophisticated and unthreatening, in fact. Maybe it was the huge herd of muscular thugs he kept around him. "And you are a thorn in his side, I take it?"

Claire heard him sigh. His voice sounded old, tired, and world-weary. "Alas, I was a part of the Montenegro family at one time, but it was a very long time ago. And then I found my savior, Jesus Christ, and opened my heart to Him. Mama Lulu helped me to do this. We grew up together as children here in this city, a long, long time ago. She is a sainted woman and will reap her heavenly reward."

"Are you saying that you were in the Montenegro organization?" Her voice sounded incredulous. She couldn't help it.

"Yes, my dear. I was a very unprincipled man back then. I did bad things that I shudder now to think about. I have killed men in terrible ways for money."

Whoa, slow down here. Who was taking confession, him or her?

"I've got a picture of a tattoo that I want to show you." Claire took out the photo and pressed it up against the grilled screen, which was fashioned with entwined fleurs-de-lis.

"Yes, Mama told me about it. Let me get my spectacles on."

Seconds passed. "Do you recognize it, Father?"

"Yes, I do."

"Please, Father, tell me everything you know about it."

"I know it is the mark of an evil man, a hired killer. They called him the Snake back then because of this tattoo. Even the Montenegro enforcers like me, we whispered when we talked about him."

"Do you know his real name? What he looks like?"

"I'm very sorry that I cannot tell you either of those things. He has been around here for many years—decades, I fear—killing and abusing others. This thing you show me. It is how he marks his victims as possessions, subjects, if you will, of Papa Damballah, of the voodoo Loa. He always signs his evil work with this Veve to honor his voodoo god. Look at the symbol. Some have said he takes children of his victims and torments them for amusement. Then he is said to kill them and throw them to the alligators that surround his lair. He is thought to be possessed by a voodoo demon that has eaten away any vestige of his humanity. He is evil personified."

"And no one knows who he is?"

"No one. He is very careful. Many think he is of Cajun birth and lives here with us, doing his evil among us."

"Is there anything else you can tell us about him, Father?"

"Once I knew a parishioner, who swore this demon lived deep in the swamps, took his captives there, killed them there, and sank them with rocks in the deep bayous or tossed them to the gators. This man said there were times when he heard drums and screams somewhere faraway in the night. But I cannot say that for the truth."

"Do the Montenegros still use this man for contract hits?"

"I do not know. I no longer have any connection with Jacques's organization. It is not as brutal as it was in the old days, I hear. Jacques is trying to reform and become godly. He attends Mass here, and they say he mourns the death of his only child and wishes to atone before his own death."

Claire knew that only too well. Jacques's young daughter had been a part of the case in which she had met Black. It had been the beginning of Claire's own personal nightmare, too, with the demons from her past catching up with her.

"She didn't die by the hand of this assassin, Father."

"No, that is true. Another evil man killed that child of God."

"Did the witness ever say where he heard the cries in the swamp? Was it down our way? Around Thibodaux? Napoleonville? Chauvin? Where was it?"

"It was down around those places, but no one knows where he dwells. I have heard he is still out there in the darkest depths of the swamp. Was this mark found on a murder victim?"

"Yes, two different women. Both bodies were beaten and strangled and left on voodoo altars for us to find."

"Then I fear he is still alive and doing evil deeds."

"Father, there's something else. Did you ever hear that this killer tried to frame others for his crimes? Plant false evidence, anything like that?"

"No, he is a professional hit man. Usually he kills with execution style, a bullet to the head and another to the heart. But I have heard of cases when he used other methods and when he took children of his victims into his lair. Most were never heard from again, and nobody ever knew what happened to them. They may still be his captives somewhere out in the darkness."

"What families?"

"There was a case I recall when the child survived and it was hushed up by the family. I understand he abuses these children in terrible ways. It was whispered by some that one survivor told tales of being terrified by him, for his sadistic pleasure."

"And he's never been caught? Nobody's ever gotten close to him? Not the police, no one knows who he is?"

"He is very good at what he does. He has many years of practice."

"We're good at what we do, too. We're going to get him this time."

"That's why I agreed to talk to you, but only here, in secret. I wish I could tell you more."

"You've helped us a lot, Father. At least now I know who I'm dealing with."

"God help you," he said. "I will pray that you find this evil man. Go with God, my child."

Claire stepped out of the booth and looked at the back pew, where Zee and his family were kneeling together in prayer. *God better go with her*, she thought, because now she was pretty sure she wasn't just chasing Madonna's and Wendy's killer, but a devil incarnate who walked among them and had for a very long time. Maybe even someone she knew, someone who passed her on the street and nodded a friendly hello. She headed for the back of the church. If this guy did tie into her case, if he was the one who had killed her victims, a sadist who terrified little kids for fun, he was going down, and she was going to find him and make him pay for all the death and destruction he'd wreaked on the innocent. And now she had a pretty good idea what the killer was. She just had to find him.

Chapter Twenty-one

For the rest of the day, Zee and Claire spent their time interviewing old timers and bayou dwellers in and around Lafourche Parish about this mysterious assassin who supposedly roamed the bayou swamps, unknown and undiscovered and unpunished. They went so far as to show the photograph of the killer's Veve to people living on Bayou Corne and Bayou Lafourche, Lake Verret, and even as far away as Bayou Teche. Most of the people crossed themselves and looked afraid, but none of them admitted to knowing a single thing about any sicko snake man that haunted the deep swamps. Whoever this guy was, he had put the fear of God into his neighbors, or maybe it was the fear of the devil.

After a long day and a pounding headache that just would not stop, she and Zee decided that they could do no more. It was getting dark and raining hard in the French Quarter when she finally got back home, and she hit the remote to open the garage door, pulled through archway, and stopped inside the double garage. Black's Range Rover was not there, and she wondered where he was. He had not called her, either, or picked up when she had phoned him to tell him she'd be late. Something was amiss. She felt it in her bones, so she dialed Black's cell again, and again got no answer.

Inside the house, she was met by the unbelievably elegant surroundings and Maria Christo, who didn't know where Black was, either. The woman hailed from Guatemala and was dark and petite and spoke with heavily accented English. She smiled nearly all the time, always carried a Rosary tied to her waist, and had been asking Claire frequently when they were going to put up the beautiful

Christmas tree. Claire told her yet again that she and Black would decorate it soon and then headed straight up to Gabe's bedroom.

Claire found him in bed, holding Jules Verne on his lap and having a good old time teasing around with Julie Alvarez. The nurse was injecting him with what was probably another potent painkiller—likely the root cause for his very good mood. Gabe and Julie were both smiling, and Claire was relieved that he felt up to having a little flirtation while he recuperated. Jules immediately jumped down on sight of her, and she scooped him up and hugged the wiggling, yapping little poodle.

"Well, Gabe, you seem to be feeling a helluva lot better today," she said, walking up to the bed.

Julie Alvarez was a really pretty woman, now that Claire got a good look at her. The other night, Claire had been so out of it that she hadn't been able to think too straight. Julie was probably in her mid-thirties and had short brown hair cut in a stylish bob, green eyes, and an easy smile. She looked like an athlete, a runner, perhaps, like Claire. Julie also looked like she could give Gabe as good as she got, too. She turned to Claire. "Yes, he's quite entertaining, bedridden or not, I must say. Is he always like this?"

"Oh, yeah. When he's not acting tough."

Gabe said, "Julie's good company. What can I say?"

"So? How do you feel?"

"Not quite wonderful, not quite terrible. I'm alive, that's good enough for me."

"He's a good patient, but that might be because he can't move around much yet and the painkillers are so strong." Julie laughed. "Okay, Claire, if you're going to sit with him awhile, I'll take a little break. You okay with that?"

"Sure, go right ahead. By the way, do you know where Black is?"

Julie nodded. "Nick said he had to go meet Jack Holliday and to tell you that he'd be back later."

Claire wondered if they had one of their little secret-agent-man missions going on, and if she should worry about it, as she watched Julie depart the room. Then she sat down beside Gabriel. "So, how do you really feel, Gabe?"

"I'll be all right. I like that woman. She doesn't take any crap off me. We're gonna get along just fine."

"Name a woman you don't like."

Gabe grinned, then winced when he tried to push himself up to sitting. "Speaking of women, I called Bonnie and she said they're getting ready to move in on the Skulls. She's already outta there and heading home to her office in Miami. I'm glad she's safe. I was worried about her since I wasn't there to protect her."

"Yeah, I saw her at Madonna's funeral. She tried to tell me that they didn't have anything to do with the explosion. At least, that's what I think she was saying."

"She told me the same thing. According to her, they thought I was dead or in jail. They've been looking for my body in the bayous. So, no, I don't think they threw the grenades."

"Well, I hope they keep thinking that. You're out for good, I assume."

"Yeah, got the official word when I reported in this morning. They told me to lie low until they tell me otherwise. Bonnie and I are both gonna have to testify at the trials. But that won't be for a while."

"Best news I've heard in ages."

Gabe lay back against the pillows and twisted around until he found a more comfortable position. He looked a lot better today, not so clammy and gray. His color was coming back and so was his legendary impatience. He shifted, tried to raise his arm, and grimaced with irritation. "God, I hate lying in bed all day and doing nothing."

"Get used to it. Flirt some more with your nurse. You can order anything you want to eat from Black's hotel next door and they'll bring it all the way over here on a heated silver tray. Can't beat that. Just ask for Chef Stephen. So, hey, lie back and enjoy the good life while you can."

"Yeah, Nick already told me all that." He studied her face for a moment. "I like him. He's cool."

"Yeah, he is. Worries a lot about me. Too much."

"No shit?"

They shared a low laugh at that observation and then they got real serious again and real quick. "That was close, Gabe. Too close for comfort."

"Yeah, I never expected anything like that to happen. Getting a knife in my back, maybe, or the hell beat outta me in some back alley, but a grenade blast never even entered my mind. Not exactly the Skulls' style. But somebody wanted to get rid of me."

"Or me. Or Black. It could've been aimed at any of us."

"I'd bet on me. I've testified against a lot of bad guys before this assignment. One of them put out a hit on me, that's my guess."

"Kind of messy for a professional hit man, don't you think?"

"Yeah, I thought the same thing." He watched her face carefully. "Do you think it was you, then?"

"We found a voodoo doll with my face on it, not thirty yards up the hill from that boat, and only a few days before it blew up. Sounds more reasonable to me that I'm the target."

"What about Nick? He got any enemies?"

Claire tried not to look concerned, but she was. It could very well have been him, now that she knew that he played some dangerous games himself. "I don't know anybody who'd want him dead." Which was true, if not exactly forthcoming.

"Maybe somebody who wants you wants him dead."

Claire sighed. "Okay, I had a guy fixated on me once. He's dead, like I told you. Most of the other killers that I've investigated or apprehended are dead or in jail. If this was about me, the killer could have gotten me when I stayed out there by myself that same week. He wouldn't kill all of us indiscriminately. He could've gotten to me when I was alone and not expecting anything."

"None of this rings true to me, Annie. Something's very wrong with how everything's goin' down. You need to watch out. Better yet, take a few weeks off. Take Nick and disappear for a while, like Bonnie and I are gonna do."

Her birth name just couldn't seem to die out, not down in Louisiana. "You've been talking to Black, I see."

"Yeah. He's definitely got your best interests at heart, no doubt about it." He hesitated. "He told me he offered you a private gig, the whole works, your own private investigation business. Told me I'd be welcome to come aboard, the minute you gave the okay. Said he'd pay me the big bucks and it wouldn't be as dangerous as my undercover work."

Claire actually liked that idea. At least, Gabe would be relatively safe, if any of them could ever be bulletproof in their line of work. "So, what did you say?"

"I said I'd think about it. Talk to you. See what you said."

"He told you to try to convince me to do it, didn't he?"

"Not in so many words. I can't see much of a downside to it, though. What's your hang-up about goin' private? You'll still get the bad guys."

"I don't have a downside, really. I just like what I do. I've been unlucky enough to get tangled up with a lot of weirdos and serial killers, that's all. I keep thinking percentages say that things'll get back to normal sooner or later. Not happening this week, though."

"Hey, maybe they will. Like I said, take some time off, enjoy Christmas and New Year's. You've earned it a couple of times over."

When Gabe shut his eyes and kept them closed for a few minutes, Claire knew he was tired, and the painkillers were taking effect. After he dozed off, she tiptoed out and walked down the hallway to the master bedroom. She took a quick shower and washed her hair and put on some soft, dark blue sweats that Black had given her, this time out of the gift shop of his new hotel. *Hotel* was embroidered in flowing gold script down one leg, *Crescent* down the other. Juan had built a nice warm, crackling fire in the bedroom so she sat down in Black's leather chair and picked up her cell phone. Black had called while she was in the shower so she hit redial. He picked up at once.

"Where are you?" he said.

"I'm at home, where you're supposed to be. Remember, we were going to have a nice quiet candlelit dinner outside on the balcony, just the two of us, and then another round of bedroom fireworks like last night. You lose interest in me already, or what?"

"You need to get out here."

"Oh, no. What? Where are you? What happened?"

"No, it's not like that. I'm with Jack. We're heading out to his place on River Road. You need to meet us there."

"Why?"

"We just need to talk to you. It's not too far from the Quarter. We're on our way back from Baton Rouge so you'll probably get out there first."

"What the hell were you doing up there, and why haven't you been answering your phone?"

"We had to check out something. I'll tell you about it later."

"Tell me now."

"I'll tell you later, I said. Just meet us out there. Please."

Claire didn't like that evasive answer very much, and she didn't like the serious tone of Black's voice. Something was up all right, and it probably was bad. Seems like it was always bad. "Okay, tell me how to get there."

"It's an old plantation house, out close to Vacherie. Know where that is? It shouldn't take you long. Remember when I took you to dinner at the Briarside Inn right after Thanksgiving? It's the first plantation after that on the river road."

"You're talking about the one with the high white brick wall around it?"

"Yeah, that's it. It's called Rose Arbor now. It's got an electric gate, which will probably be closed. You're going to get there first, so just wait for us down on the road, and Jack'll open the gate when we get there."

"This better be good, Black. It's raining outside, and I'm hungry."

Apparently, Black was not in a joking mood. "Be careful, okay? We'll see you in a little while."

"Ditto back to you."

They hung up and Claire strapped on her weapons, donned a rain jacket, and headed straight for her SUV, intrigued to say the least, and yes, a little bit wary. But she went through Maria's gourmet, state-of-the-art kitchen and grabbed a handful of miniature Snickers bars out of the freezer and an ice-cold can of Pepsi. She needed sustenance if they were putting off dinner again.

The trip didn't take long, and there was very little traffic. Everybody was snug at home, taking refuge from the stormy weather, and minding their own business, except for her, of course. But the rain was coming down like nobody's business out on the river and her wipers were fighting for their rubberized lives. She knew that the Briarside Inn was a bed-and-breakfast in a beautiful columned antebellum mansion hugging the Mississippi River. The food was good, too, but pretty damn pricey for regular folk like her. She was lucky that Black always insisted on picking up the check.

When she finally reached the fabled river road, only a few minutes passed before she drove by the Briarside. Next up was Jack Holliday's other tawdry little abode, just where Black had told her. Greek Revival, from what she could tell, and palatial, extravagant. Oh yeah, Jack had gotten lots of money somewhere. Probably not as much as Black had, but plenty, nevertheless. Maybe she should ask Friedewald for a raise. After all, she'd almost been blown to bits serving the parish.

The plantation house sat up on a rise with the road between it and the river. The mansion was just barely discernible in flashes of lightning, and Claire pulled in and braked in front of the gate and observed the place through her rain-drenched windshield. It was completely dark on the grounds and everywhere else except for two big electric lanterns affixed to the bricked double entrance pillars. Dusk-to-dawn ones, probably. But the ornate iron gates stood wide open. So she accelerated again. Live oaks, tall and stately and ancient and hung with moss, towered above her car as she drove up a long, curving driveway, but they also could turn into dark, creepy monsters when one was alone among them on the proverbial dark, stormy night. Like at the moment.

Thunder rumbled again, right overhead this time, and then an even bigger deluge opened up and obscured her windshield. She slowed down and watched her poor wipers veritably groan with valiant effort. Well, Black and Holliday had certainly picked one hell of a night to want to talk about something that couldn't be discussed over the telephone.

The road was smooth and well-maintained tarmac, even if it was twisty and turny as the devil and led way back into the woods. It finally came out in a cleared grassy lawn that was about the size of a football field. Maybe Jack's clients practiced there. The rain smelled clean and fresh and full of ozone, but it was coming in off the coast and bringing plenty of thunder and lightning with it. There were lots of flower beds and English ivy climbing all over the oaks and trellises and everything else in sight, and empty concrete urns, which would no doubt be bursting with camellias and azaleas and blue hydrangeas as soon as spring showed up. No cheerful Christmas decorations, though, and no lights, no welcome mat, no wreaths. So, bah humbug, Jack. Something told her, however, that the house was going to be quite the sight to behold, maybe a Louisiana version of the Palace of Versailles.

Seconds later, Claire reached the point where the road curved around a large central fountain that sported gown-draped, stone-sculpted Greek maidens pouring water out of fancy pitchers. When the stormy night cooperated and lightning lit up the place, she got a good look at the house itself.

Wow, what a place, a real-life Tara of Scarlet O'Hara fame. Yes, sir, the sports agent did have a nice little crib out in the boonies. Too bad all the windows were dark. Who wouldn't leave at least one lamp on when he knew he was getting home after dark? Most women would, herself included, but a guy Jack Holliday's size could probably crush the bones of any interloper, even her. Some of the antebellum plantations she'd seen were decayed and dilapidated, old and weathered and neglected, but not this one. This one was grand to be sure and made sure everybody knew it was special.

A veranda, long and wide, stretched out across the ground floor with a matching one right above it. Tall, shuttered French doors lined both porches, about eight or nine on each level, and it looked like those galleries ran around both sides of the house, too. Claire pulled up in front, got out, and shined her flashlight on a tall flight of semicircular red brick stairs that were affixed with an intricate wrought-iron railing that ran up the middle. The newel posts on the gallery's balustrade were beautifully wrought wood and the end post at the top of the steps displayed a large fleur-de-lis that almost looked hand carved.

Eager to get inside and out of the weather, she climbed the steps, tried the door, and found it secured. She tried some more of the French doors and wondered if she could pick the locks, and then decided better of that idea. White wood rocking chairs were lined up along the balustrade and out of the rain, so she sat down in the closest one to wait. Forked white lightning promptly put on a magnificent laser show, streaking and jabbing in and out of the clouds between gaps in the treetops.

Wondering what was taking Black and Holliday so damn long, she sat back and tried not to be creeped out by the fireworks in the sky and the pouring rain and the pitch-black surroundings. One thing for certain, Black probably wasn't the one at the wheel. As fast as he drove, they would have beaten her out there by a mile. But hey, she was a grown woman, an experienced police detective to boot; she could wait outside in a fierce electrical storm that was getting her sopping wet with the best of them. On the other hand, she wished they would just hurry it up, already. After muttering a few choice Cajun curses that she'd picked up from Black, she sat back in the rocker and ate another Snickers bar, trying her best to be patient.

A Very Scary Man

Everything was going so well for Malice. He had been having lots of fun inside his little maze. He was learning new ways to terrify, and there seemed to be a never-ending supply of ingenious props and devices that popped up inside his tormenting-people-loving mind. And he no longer made stupid mistakes. Everybody he took out there eventually died. The length of their lives depended on how much fun they provided to him. The victims who merely cowered and cried for pity rarely lasted more than a day or two. The ones who fought and used some clever ingenuity to get out of his maze impressed and intrigued him a bit, so they often lived for weeks before he tired of them and fed them to the gators. Yeah, the gators around his little island paradise knew they'd get a meal sooner or later, if they just hung around long enough. The little group of them were almost like his pets now. He had even given some of them names: Razor, Hungry, and Bully, who was his favorite by far because he usually dove with as much of the carcass as he could before any of the others could get a bite.

But then, right out of the blue, things started going wrong. He had been keeping careful tabs on his victims that got away, just to make sure they didn't cause trouble for him. That's how he found out that there was a private investigator in town, sniffing around and doing a lot of talking to one of his escaped victims in particular. The one who was the most unstable, at that. She'd spent time in jail, was pretty much a junkie, and promiscuous as hell. So, she'd most likely tell the P.I. anything he wanted to know, especially if he offered her money. Malice didn't think she remembered anything that could identify him, but there was always the possibility she might mention something that could trace back to him.

All of that went on for a time, making Malice nervous as hell, but then when another guy entered the picture, a former football player by the name of Jack Holliday, he really got concerned. Not too long after Holliday got involved, a crack detective out of Missouri showed up and complicated things further. She was not on the case yet, but if the shit hit the fan, she was known far and wide for catching serial killers and probably would be consulted, so he had to make sure she didn't use her expertise to track him down. Damn it, things were getting out of hand and a little too close for comfort, and Malice knew he had to act and act quickly. If he didn't put the brakes on, and put them on hard, he just might end up getting caught.

So, one dark night he just showed up at Madonna Christien's door. She opened it, didn't recognize him as her abductor, of course, so she made the mistake of letting him come inside. As soon as the door closed, he got her around the throat with both hands and wrestled her down on the floor. She struggled desperately, but she was a tiny little thing and didn't have a chance. Once, though, she got in a good kick and ran for the door, screaming and knocking over everything in her path. He was on her in a flash, grabbing her and bending her over and bodily running her head into the wall. That stunned her pretty good, too, but he slammed her head down on her glass coffee table just to make sure, and that was all she wrote.

After she was subdued, he put on his gloves and pulled her up and beat the living daylights out of her when she was only half conscious, just because she deserved to suffer for all the trouble she had caused him. He should've done it all those years ago when he'd first had the chance. Her life had ended up in the garbage can, anyway. She certainly wasn't going to be missed by anybody, except maybe a couple of her johns.

When she finally died, he searched her apartment and found her cute little closet with an altar to Papa Damballah, which was really sort of cool. Maybe she wasn't so stupid after all. Maybe she'd learned something from him. Too bad she was already dead. She might've been a nice little piece to keep confined for his pleasure out at the maze. Except that she'd dedicated her altar to Jack Holliday, too, which might be the reason Jack had been hanging around her so much, but he couldn't take that chance.

On the other hand, it gave Malice the opportunity he needed to transfer the murder rap onto somebody else. Once he found the hurricane glass sitting on that altar, the one with a nice little white placard that labeled it as Jack Holliday's, the rest of his plan began to materialize in his mind. Jack had become a problem, anyway. Now Malice had a way to get rid of him. So he staged the crime scene, placing the hurricane glass with Jack's prints, just so, in the living room crime scene. The struggle had left a mess on the floor, but he made sure there wasn't anything with his DNA on it, picked up the victim, and carried her to his car parked in her garage.

All the way out to the maze, he had fun figuring out all the things he could do to the body before he set it up to be found. It didn't take long to come up with an idea that would get Claire Morgan off the case and out of his hair, too. Once that happened, he was probably home free. Now all he had to do was wash the girl up with some heavy-duty Clorox bleach and get out some sharp needles and embroidery thread. He laughed out loud, more excited than he'd been in ages.

Chapter Twenty-two

Almost fifteen minutes later, thunder cracked like crazy right above Claire and growled like an angry lion on its way north toward Baton Rouge. The rain poured down, rattling the palm leaves and giant elephant ears and the banana trees growing very close to the veranda railing. For some reason, a sudden and strange sense of dread assailed Claire. The old *something wicked this way comes* sensation that always electrified the hairs on her arms and made them stand straight up. She put her hand on her weapon, where it was still snug inside her shoulder holster. She felt very vulnerable sitting out there alone in the dark. Yep, what she needed was to take some deep breaths and chill out.

But she was freaked out big time, didn't like the old place one bit, as lovely as it appeared to be. And she didn't like sitting with her back exposed and vulnerable to possible attackers combat-crawling up behind her. So she stood up and descended the steps and moved a few yards away from the porch. Cold water spattered atop the hood of her rain slicker, but the thick boughs above impeded most of the rain. So she stood out there inside some crouching shadows and tried to figure out what was making her jumpy. She wasn't usually so jittery, so why was she now? Maybe it was getting blown clean off a boat in a grenade blast? Could be.

"Git your hands up! I mean it, girl, I got me a gun pointed straight at you."

Claire nearly jumped out of her skin at the raspy voice coming out of the dark. She had her weapon out in half a second and held it extended with both hands and pointing at the shadowy figure standing on the veranda up to her left. It looked like a man, and it looked like a man holding a shotgun, the butt braced against his right shoulder and aimed straight down at her head.

"Police! Drop your weapon! Do it now!" Her voice meant business. So did the shotgun. It didn't waver. Damn, looked like they had themselves a standoff.

Then her assailant demanded in a cigarette-gruff voice, "Who the hell are you? This here's private property. And you trespassin' and skulkin' around in the dark and sayin' you the po-lice. You think I'm stupid, or somethin'?"

Well, yeah, pretty much. "Okay, listen to me, sir, I'm a Lafourche Sheriff's Office homicide detective. Put that gun down, or I'm going to have to arrest you, understand? Please step out where I can see you."

He didn't appear cowed by her credentials or her threats. "Don' you move till I git the lights on. You hear me, girl?"

Okay, maybe lots of young women liked to trespass on Jack Holliday's estate and steal his underwear, or something. Maybe this was a nightly occurrence and Shotgun Sammy standing up there was sick and damn tired of it. She kept a tight, two-handed bead on his chest with her nine-millimeter as he slowly backed up to the door, opened it with a bunch of jingling keys hanging off his belt, and hit a light switch.

Big lanterns flared on, all up and down the porch. When Claire got a good look at him, she saw a small man, rather wizened and wrinkled, who reeked of tobacco. She could smell it emanating from his clothes from where she stood several yards downwind. He looked to be in his late seventies or maybe even early eighties. Holliday must have a real thing about hiring white-haired senior citizens who weren't friendly to his guests. His haughty butler, the Mighty Yannick, came to mind. The old man had a long white beard, wire-rimmed glasses repaired with black electrical tape between the thick Coke-bottle lenses, and a blue-and-black-checkered flannel shirt underneath denim overalls. In other words, he was Grandpa Jones. Claire took her badge folder off her belt with her left hand and held it up to the light. He was still aiming his weapon at her so she did this slowly and carefully and hoped his eyesight was better than it looked. "I'm going to walk up the steps and show you my badge, sir. Don't you move."

"No need you comin' up here close. I kin see what you got." He lowered the shotgun. Claire waited until he propped it nice and gentle-like up against the wall behind him, and then she sheathed her own weapon.

"You don' look like no po-lice to me, you. You look like a tall, skinny gal that's trespassin' on Mr. Jack's land."

Claire ignored that, although it was rather descriptive and probably not a compliment. "I'm a detective from Lafourche Parish Sheriff's Office, just like I said."

"That don' mean you not trespassin'. What you want here, girl? Mr. Jack don't let nobody come in here wit' out tellin' me. And he din't tell me nothin' 'bout the law comin' out here."

Well, thanks a lot, Jack. "He'll be here any minute and will verify who I am. So you tell me, who are you?"

"Name's Old Nat Navarro. Mr. Jack done tol' me to stop people from openin' up that gate down yonder or climbin' over the wall and gettin' up here close to the house. Don' think you is the first sex-crazy gal to climb that wall and try to get at him. If you a po-lice, why you here? Mr. Jack in trouble wit' the law?"

Okay, she'd give Old Nat Navarro the tall, skinny gal thing. But *sex-crazy?* Come on. And *Old Nat,* what was up with that? The guy looked his age all right, now that she could see him better. She wondered if he used to call himself Young Nat or Middle-aged Nat, and then graduated up to Old Nat when he got some wrinkles.

"Nope, nothing like that, I assure you. He and a friend of his asked me to meet them out here, said that he had something to tell me."

Old Nat scratched his somewhat scruffy white beard. Well, okay, it was really scruffy. "He don' ask many folks to come out here, especially this late. He got a phone he carry 'round wit' him. Why din't he tell me 'bout you showin' up?"

"You got me. He must've gotten a wild hair and not checked in with you. You know, maybe he felt all footloose and fancy free."

"He don't get no wild hairs. He ain't footloose and fancy, neither."

Claire contemplated a witty retort to those remarks, but didn't come up with anything appropriately clever or that made much sense, so she just looked at him.

"Well, why din't you ring the bell at the gate like reg'lar folk do? All you had a do was show your badge."

"I didn't see any bell. The gate was open, anyway." Claire wondered if she was wandering around in some kind of stupid dream, cast down into the briar patch with a shotgun-toting crazy man. All he needed was a moonshine jug hooked on a forefinger and Daisy Mae on his arm.

Old Nat stared a hole through her, as if he didn't believe a word she said. Claire decided to play nice and make some polite chitchat. "Mr. Holliday didn't mention that he had a night watchman. Apparently, he's running late."

"Don' sound like somet'ing a po-lice'd do. Just comin' up here and hangin' 'round in the dark."

Luckily for Claire, and since her attempts at small talk didn't pan out so well, Holliday and Black decided that was the moment to show up. She and Old Nat turned in tandem and watched a slick sports car slow down and turn off the road, and then headlights speared the darkness as it negotiated the curves on its way up toward them.

Holliday was driving, just as she had figured, and he parked underneath the bricked porte cochere. He and Black swung open the doors and climbed out of the coolest, shiniest black Ferrari convertible she'd ever seen. She had trouble believing that Holliday could get his long legs in or out of the expensive sports car, but he managed it somehow.

"Sorry we're late, Claire," Black said, heading over to her. "Have you been here long?"

"A little while, but Old Nat over there kept me company with his shotgun."

"What?" Holliday looked shocked. He turned to his minuscule but heavily armed gatekeeper. "Sorry, Old Nat, I didn't think to call and let you know I had company coming out."

"S'okay. You tell this girl here that she kin open the gate and snoop up here and try to git in the house?"

Holliday and Black both looked at Claire.

"So I tried the front door. Thought I'd wait inside out of the rain. Sorry."

"You be needin' anyt'ing else, Mr. Jack?" That was Old Nat, of course, and still rather grumpy.

"No, we're good. Good night."

Old Nat picked up his shotgun and shuffled off down the gallery with nary a good evening or a "nice to hold a gun on you, tall, skinny po-lice gal."

Nobody said anything until he was out of sight, and then Black got the show on the road. "Let's go inside. We need to talk, Claire. It's really important."

"So you said. Nice place you got here, Mr. Holliday."

"Thanks. It's my grandmother's pride and joy. Old Nat's been out here with her for the last forty years, worked here even before that, I think. He's harmless."

Until he shoots somebody dead on your porch, Claire thought. "I thought the house in the Garden District belonged to your grand-mother."

"That's where she liked to live. She grew up there, her parents owned it, and her grandparents before that, but this was her grand project."

Yeah, and grand hit the nail on the head, too. "Project?"

"She got this back into the family, I don't know, twenty, thirty years ago, I guess. It was falling down, a total disaster. My granddad bought it for her and gave her carte blanche for a total restoration. Said it'd keep her out of trouble." Black and Claire listened politely, both ready to get down to business.

Holliday pushed open the front door, and then stood back and let them precede him inside. And to think Claire had thought his house on St. Charles Avenue was nifty. Carte blanche obviously meant "How many millions do you need?" in Grandpa Holliday's check-book lingo. The place could host prime ministers or royalty, or better yet, Beyoncé and her entire entourage.

The central hallway was floored with shiny black-and-white tiles, wide and long, stretching all the way to the back of the house, where a door probably led to a rear gallery. All the doors had etched glass inserts adorned with giant fleurs-de-lis. A tall, gilt-edged mirror on

their right looked like something Granny had probably picked up at
the Louvre's basement sale. A wide staircase rose in superb splendor
off to their left. A glittery crystal chandelier—with what, about
eight-thousand-plus prisms—hung in the center over a round table
with a white marble top. A giant blue and white spice jar with Chinese
peasants and rivers painted on it—Ming Dynasty, not Pier One; bet
on it—sat on top.

"I'd forgotten how nice this place is," said Black.

Claire said, "And you really live out here, huh? All by yourself?"

"The Garden District's a little too formal for me. Too many
tourists. So I live out here where I can get some privacy."

Claire stared at him. "You don't consider this place formal?"

"Not as much. Grandmother still owns the townhouse, but she
signed this one over to me when she moved to her chalet outside
Paris after she got her ambassadorship. I guess this's as good a place
to live as anywhere. It's mine, anyway. Old Nat's pretty good at keeping people out."

Ambassadorship, is it? Not so shabby, that.

The rain still drummed on the roof and sluiced down the window-
panes. The fresh scent of rain was blowing in through the open front
door. "Make yourselves comfortable. I'll be right back."

Holliday strode off toward the back of the house, and Claire
looked at Black. "This is getting ridiculous. What's going on?"

"It concerns your case. You want to hear this, believe me. He's
been putting it off. I convinced him to get you out here and tell you
the truth."

"Tell me now, damn it."

"Just be patient. Here he comes."

Then Holliday was back, carrying three bottles of beer. Turbodogs, like he'd ordered at the Cajun Grill, obviously his favorite kind
of beer. Whatever he had to tell her, he needed some liquid encour-
agement or thought she needed it. She and Black took their bottles,
but both set them aside on the coffee table in front of them. Jack
took a swig and sat down on a blue velvet chair. Black and Claire
took places on a red brocade antique sofa. Claire was getting a very
bad feeling and didn't intend to wait any longer.

"What is this, Holliday? Am I going to find some kind of evidence against you, is that it? Something you failed to tell us when we interviewed you? Please don't tell me you killed Madonna and Wendy."

Holliday frowned. "Hell, no. I didn't kill anybody."

"Did you lie to us about your relationship with Madonna?"

Then came the hesitation, the dragging of feet, and the looking everywhere but at her. Crap, that did not bode well.

Finally, Holliday came out with it, or part of it. "Okay, just listen. This is complicated."

Claire stared at him and then looked at Black. "I'm all ears. Just fire when ready."

"It's about your case, but it's a personal thing, too."

Personal? "Well, forget the personal. Tell me how it relates to my case."

"I'm going to tell you something about somebody."

Good grief. This guy knew his way around procrastination. She fought a desire to pull her gun and tell him to get on with it or die where he sat, but she tamped down that rather deadly impulse. *Patience, patience.* A virtue that Claire knew very little about. "That sounds like a good start, Jack."

Holliday walked to a desk across the room and opened the top drawer. He pulled out a thick green file folder with an oversized red rubber band around it. He held it up. "I've been working on this a long time. Over ten years, to be exact."

"So what's this got to do with my case?" *Prod, prod, pulllll it out of him.*

"First off, I told you a lie when you interviewed me. I have been to Madonna's house. Several times."

Holy crap. "You lied to the police? That's a crime. What the hell were you thinking?"

"I didn't touch her. I went there for another reason, I swear to God. Something personal. And I did drink out of that glass you found."

"Why in holy hell did you lie about it?"

Holliday stood up and started pacing around the room. Black leaned back and waited. He was the patient one, not her. Claire frowned, thinking this whole conversation was way weird. Then he started to talk as he walked back and forth in front of her. "When I first started playing in the NFL, my mom and stepdad were murdered."

Well, that was the last thing Claire had expected him to say. "I'm sorry, Jack. I didn't know."

"Yeah, it was pretty awful. I went home for Christmas. They lived out in Arvada then. Colorado." He stopped and sat down and leaned toward her as he spoke, pretty eager now that he got started. "It happened on Christmas Eve. We had dinner, sang carols, opened presents, the whole family, and then we went to bed. Somebody broke into the house that night. We never found out who it was. They shot my mom and stepdad, once in the head and once in the heart, with a silencer, execution style, and then they took my two little sisters. Neither of them has ever been found."

Claire was appalled, mostly by the pain twisting Jack Holliday's features. This man had not gotten over the murder of his family, not by a long shot. But the M.O. sounded a lot like the one described by Father Gerard. "What about you, Jack? You were there, too, right?"

"I left the house just after midnight to meet my girlfriend."

"Well, thank God, or you'd probably be dead, too."

Jack's jaw tightened, and his eyes grew hard. "I should've been there. I could've stopped it."

"You can't blame yourself, Jack," Black said in his calm and perfectly modulated shrink voice.

"Well, I do."

"It wasn't your fault," Claire said in her regular and un-modulated cop voice.

"That night? I was changing clothes and getting ready to go meet Amber, and one of the twins, my little half-sis, Jenny, she came into my room. She was three. I can remember that so clearly, every single word we said." His eyes were recalling it now, reliving it, going back to that night. "Jenny and Jill were just beautiful—identical, big brown eyes and this shiny long platinum-blond hair that fell down their backs in ringlets. They looked like my mom. That night Jenny was barefoot and she had on this little red fleece nightgown with a picture of Rudolph the Red-Nosed Reindeer on the front. I'll never forget that gown. It had a nose made out of one of those little red fuzzy pom-pom things. My mom gave them matching gowns to wear on Christmas Eve."

He started prowling around the room again. Claire glanced at Black, and he shook his head.

"Jenny was scared. She said the bogeyman was out in the yard. She said that she saw him hiding out in the trees when she looked out her bedroom window. I was in a hurry, and young and stupid and self-centered, so I told her to quit being a baby and go back to bed, that there wasn't any such thing as a bogeyman. Then I told her that Santa Claus wasn't going to come if she didn't hush up and go to sleep."

His voice actually broke when he said the last part. Claire understood his guilt. She had done things she regretted in her past, was still doing them. "And you think the killer really was outside, waiting?"

"Yes, and so did the police. Mom and Roger were material witnesses to a Mob hit. They were going to testify that coming February. That's what the police believed. But the killer was a real pro. He left nothing behind. The case eventually went cold."

"Jack, I am so sorry that happened to you."

"I got home around three o'clock in the morning. That's when I found my mom and stepdad shot to death in their bed. The back door was open. Jenny and Jill were gone. I called 911, and then the real nightmare began."

"They accused you." Claire realized how that could happen. In fact, that would be proper police procedure. Always check out the remaining family members first. "But you managed to prove yourself innocent."

He nodded. "My girlfriend and her parents vouched for me. I was at their house the whole time."

"But you still blame yourself."

"I could've stopped it. I know I could have. If I hadn't gone out that night, if I had just listened to Jenny and looked around outside, told my parents, let them call the police, they'd all still be alive."

At that point, it occurred to Claire that this was the kind of story that would be hard to hide from the media. "I did a background check on you, Jack. Nothing about these murders turned up."

"My mom had remarried, had a different name. We lived in a

different state. I hadn't played in the Super Bowl yet so wasn't all that famous except at Tulane. The media never got hold of it."

"And they never found the perpetrator?"

"No, but it was Mob related. Mom and Dad were going to testify against a Chicago mafioso. I never could prove it, and the police gave up. The guy left no clues. After that happened, I blew out my knee and couldn't play anymore so I joined the military and flew as a helicopter pilot for several years. After I got discharged and started working as a sports agent, I tried to find the killer on my own, but never could find out anything. So I finally hired John Booker to investigate the murders. Nick put me on to him. He's been working on it for the last three years."

So Jack Holliday hadn't led such a charmed life, after all. He had mourned, lost loved ones, suffered survival guilt and loneliness. Claire knew exactly how all that felt, and all too well. "Has he found out anything? Do you think it's the same guy we're looking for? The one who killed Madonna and Wendy?"

"Yeah, I do. Book finally ran that down. He uncovered other murders around the country with the same M.O. as my parents."

"Good, I need to talk to him. Compare notes. This could be the break that we've been waiting for."

Jack frowned, heaved a deep sigh, and took another swig of beer. "Nick doesn't like you being involved in this, but I can't help it. You're already involved."

Suddenly, something in their serious expressions brought up a new wave of innate wariness that gripped Claire hard, because now she was not quite sure where it was going. But it wasn't going to be good, no matter what it was. "Of course, I'm involved. I want this guy as much as you do."

Black put his hand on her knee. "Listen, Claire, one of the cases Booker turned up concerns Madonna and Wendy."

Claire turned and searched his face. "So Madonna Christien has a credible connection to the murder of Jack's family? How is she connected?"

Jack said, "It's the abduction when she was little, but she survived. Her parents were also murdered when a killer came into their house and took her captive, but she and Wendy got away. The killer marked the inside of their wrists with that voodoo symbol, but they didn't see his face. He wore some kind of mask."

Claire nodded. "Yeah, we saw the tats. Wendy told us about the abduction and so did Madonna's grandmother. It's got to be the same guy."

"Yeah, that's what we think, too. He took my sisters, just like he took Maddie and Wendy. They were just too little to get away from him."

"This is going to complicate our case, but maybe the information Booker's got on the killer can help us. We're getting close now. We found information that this guy is a homegrown assassin or Mob hit man, something like that, and he's probably still around here, waiting for his next contract kill."

Jack said, "We think he's killing off any surviving victims, one at a time."

Everything he said had concrete connections to her case. Claire was getting excited and eager to compare notes. She jumped up. "Let's go. I want to talk to Booker and read that file. I'm calling Zee and getting him in on this."

Black shook his head. "Wait a minute, Claire. There's more."

Claire sank back into the chair. "What? Tell me. Hurry, we need to get going on this. This could be exactly what we've been looking for."

Holliday looked uncomfortable. Apparently, they'd saved the best for last. "You're involved, too, Claire."

"You bet I am. I'm gonna help you get this guy. I can't wait to get him. And the puzzle's coming together. I just found out that this assassin was known to take children out of the home after he hit a family. Don't you see? That ties him to your family and Madonna's, just like you said. We've just got to put together the connections, figure out how the two families were chosen, find the common denominator."

"Your involvement's more than that, Claire," Black said quietly.

Now he had her. What was coming next, she could not imagine. "Okay, shoot, out with it. Just tell me! For God's sake, what's the matter with you two?"

Holliday looked away, looked back, looked everywhere but at her. "He hit somebody close to you, too, Claire."

Relaxing, Claire knew then that he was way off base. "A lot of stuff happened to me in my childhood, bad stuff, but nothing that concerned a sanctioned hit."

Black said, "It's Gabe, Claire."

"Gabe?"

"Booker found out about him. He was abducted, too, when he was young. He and his little sister named Sophie. We think the same guy that took them also took Jenny and Jill."

"No, his parents and sister died in a car crash somewhere down in Alabama a year or so after I left. Gabe survived. I didn't find out about it until years after it happened."

Holliday said, "We think Gabe and his sister were taken by this same man. We found out that he held them for a month, after he shot Gabe's mom and dad to death. Just like my mom and stepdad."

"But that's just crazy. Somebody would've told me. Gabe would've told me."

Black said, "Maybe they had a reason to cover it up. We're sure of our facts, Claire."

Claire got up and did some pacing herself. "Why would they want to cover it up? It doesn't make sense."

Black stood up. "Maybe we should go down to the *Bayou Blue* and ask the LeFevres brothers, or simply confront Gabe about it. See if they'll tell you the truth now. But we're gonna have to talk to them, Claire. We didn't want to do it without telling you first. Gabe survived. He just might have the clues we need to find the killer. If he does, we want them."

Claire stared mutely at them, lapsing into near shock mode. She stared at Holliday and then at Black. What they said didn't make sense, but they were both convinced it was true. Something bizarre was going on. "If this is true, I can't think of a single reason why they wouldn't tell me. Gabe and I are tight. I haven't seen him much through the years, but we've run into each other a few times."

Jack said, "Maybe the killer saw everyone coming back here, saw me talking to Madonna, saw you investigating, meeting up with Gabe, all of that stuff. Maybe that's the reason he lobbed a grenade at you the other night, to get rid of Gabe and you both, since you're investigating him. All that together could be making him nervous enough to try to kill off anybody that might be able to ID him." He paused. "And there's something else."

"Great."

"Madonna didn't seek me out. When Booker told me that she and Wendy had been kidnap victims, I approached Wendy and tried to get her to talk and see what she remembered. When she told me about Madonna, I spent time with her, too, secretly, you know, buttered her up some, I guess you'd say. That's when she started hounding me. Wendy was more sensible. I found out they were scared back then but that they'd seen him with paint on his face and a mask. They were going to let us do an artist's sketch of the kidnapper's mask. Somehow he found out about it, I guess. I don't know. Then all of a sudden she was dead. And then Wendy was dead. And then you and Gabe and Nick were attacked on the houseboat and left for dead."

Trying to absorb it all, Claire had to have time to think about it. And there were lots of people she wanted to talk to. "Okay, I've got it now. Gabe will talk to me, if I confront him. He trusts me. Let me look into this. But I'll tell you one thing. I'm not so sure I believe the part about Gabe. But I'm sure as hell going to find out right now."

"And I'm going with you," Black said.

Jack handed over Booker's file, and they took off in Claire's SUV and headed back to town. "Let's go to the *Bayou Blue* first, Black. I want to know what Clyde and Luc and the others know about all this before I bother Gabe with it."

"Are you okay?"

"Yes, I'm just trying to figure out what's going on. This is all crazy. We're talking crimes that were committed decades apart."

"Take a look in Booker's file. See if that convinces you."

Claire picked it up and used her new phone's flashlight app for illumination. She did not want to do this, but she had to. She opened the green file and picked up the first page and started to read.

Chapter Twenty-three

The *Bayou Blue* looked deserted, both restaurants closed up for the night. The rain poured down in a flood and made it hard for Black to see the road. He pulled in close to the steamboat's gangplank. Claire felt confused, trying to figure out where all this was going and if Gabe had really played a part in Jack Holliday's scenario of the killer's past crimes. Had the murders of Madonna Christien and Wendy Rodriguez really been perpetrated by the same man who'd killed Jack's parents? And why hadn't Gabe told her about that, instead of allowing her to believe his family members had died in an automobile accident? They had mentioned it just the other night.

It was just way too bizarre, all of it. Right now, she was after answers. And she was going to get them from the LeFevres brothers, whether they liked it, or not. The more she had run through the facts with Black during the ride over, the less likely it seemed that everything was connected. Black believed Jack's theory, but she felt there had to be another explanation, mistaken identity or something.

Clyde LeFevres was sitting at the bar in the Cajun Grill, relaxing in a sleeveless ribbed undershirt and khaki pants, white suspenders hanging down at his sides. He was drinking the strong mud he actually described as coffee. When he saw Claire barge through the door in a state of stiff-jawed determination with Black right behind her, he stood up, seemed delighted to see her, waving and grinning, but that certainly wasn't going to last long.

"What you doin' here so late, *chère*? C'mon, let me get you a bit of dis nice strong coffee, yeah?"

"Okay. Sure."

"How 'bout you, Nick?"

"Yes, please."

Keep calm, keep calm, approach the interview like a detective, not a betrayed friend. Claire perched herself on a stool and watched him round the bar and pour all of them a cup from a carafe. "You just in time. Rene comin' in to play some poker wit' us. He be here any time. How you doin', Nick?"

Black chatted with Clyde for a moment, but Claire sat there and said nothing. Clyde placed a thick white mug down in front her and smiled. She only stared at him, mute and disbelieving. How could he have lied to her all these years? Even after she'd moved back to New Orleans and met up with them again, Clyde had not told her the truth.

"What, Annie? You got problems with dat case, dat poor gal got killed down dere on our bayou? Somet'ing messin' you up?"

"Oh, yeah you could say something's messing me up."

Under the bar, Black put his hand on her knee again, tacitly warning her to stay calm. He appeared laid-back enough for both of them. Funniest thing, she did not feel calm. She felt lied to and duped. Clyde leaned both elbows on the bar and leveled worried dark eyes on her face. "What you mean, *chère*? You okay, ain't you?"

Well, okay, since he asked. "I mean that I just found out the truth about how Gabe's mom and dad died. How Sophie died, too."

The stunned look on his weathered face alerted Claire right off that everything Booker and Holliday had dug up on the LeFevres family was true. Clyde tried to cover up his knee-jerk reaction but wasn't quick enough or sincere enough to fool Claire. "What'd you mean?"

"I mean that I know they were murdered and all of you have been lying to me all these years. And I know Gabe was probably a victim of some psycho killer, and so was poor little Sophie." Claire paused there, the idea of such a complicated hoax, so entirely alien to her and to the family she thought she knew so well, that it was absolutely mind-boggling. Her voice clogged with emotion. She swallowed hard and steeled herself. "So now, Clyde, I want the truth, and you're going to tell me, and you're going to tell me right now, and then I'm going to go talk to Gabe."

Clyde looked like he wanted to collapse to his knees and crawl under the bar. "Who done tole you such t'ings?"

"Believe it or not, Jack Holliday told me. He found out and laid it out for me, and now I'm asking you for the truth."

"Holliday found out what?"

The deep voice came from the doorway, and they both turned and found Rene Bourdain walking toward them. Great, now he was going to get involved. She wished he had not shown up. She had enough trouble.

"Jack Holliday found out something about you, I hear that right?"

"This is a private conversation, Rene. Why don't you give me a few minutes alone with Clyde?"

That sounded rude, and the hurt on his face was easy to read and made her regret her short fuse. That upset her, too. Everything was in a steep downhill slide, all right.

Black tried to throw her a lifeline. "How about you and I go down and have a drink at the Creole's bar and let them talk, Rene?"

"Thanks, but I really think I should hear this. Is this connected to the Christien or Rodriguez case, Claire? I'm working those, too, you know."

"Okay, if you must know, everybody's been lying to me about what happened to Gabe's family for years. So Clyde here needs to fill me in on the what and why and when. Right, Clyde?"

Rene and Clyde exchanged a somber look. Somehow Claire knew in that instant that Rene was just as guilty as the rest of them.

"Oh, my God, Rene, don't tell me you've been lying to me, too?"

Frowning, Rene placed his hand on Claire's back. "Just relax, kiddo, take a deep breath. There's a lot more goin' on here than you know."

"No kidding. Well, c'mon, let's hear it. You tell me what really happened and what it's got to do with my case."

Silence. Then Clyde said, "Gabe don't need to know what happened to his family, Annie. He t'inks dey died in that wreck."

"What?" Claire looked at him in disbelief. "Are you telling me that Gabe doesn't know the truth, either? Oh, my God. How could you do that to him?"

"No, he don' know, and it gonna kill him to know de truth."

"Well, guess what? Somebody tried to kill him the other night, and Black and me, too. I think it just might have something to do with this big lie you've been feeding him all these years."

"He okay, right?"

"Maybe. After his dislocated shoulder, concussion, and other injuries heal up."

More silence and exchanged guilty looks. Wow, and now the phrase *family conspiracy* took on a whole new meaning. It was even worse than she had originally thought. Suddenly the story had gone from bad to very, very bad, hard to listen to, hard to accept, then lastly, rotten to the core. Claire debated whether they were right, whether Gabe was better off not knowing the truth. Whatever it was, it was going to change him, maybe forever. She felt something nasty move way down in her gut, like a spider skittering across its web to a moth struggling to get free. Who were these people whom she'd thought she could trust? What the hell was going on? She fought the urge to get out of there and never come back.

Black said, "You guys need to tell her the truth. It's over now. Whatever the reason for the secret, whatever happened, it's over, and she needs to know about it. So does Gabe."

As usual, Black's measured voice and steady presence helped her keep it together. So she took a deep breath, clasped her hands together atop the bar, and looked at each man in turn. "Okay, I'm as calm as I'm gonna get. Let's take this slow and easy, and hey, maybe we can even throw in some truth, if we try real hard. Jack told me that Gabe's mom and dad were murdered. He also said that Gabe and Sophie were abducted as children. Is any, or all of that true?"

"Yes," said Clyde, about as hangdog as a proud Cajun could get. "All of it's true."

"Okay. Okay. Now we're getting somewhere. He also said the same thing happened to his own family. He thinks it's the same predator, the same killer, and that it all ties together somehow. What do you know about that?"

Sighing, Clyde picked up a dishrag and nervously began wiping up nonexistent spills off the granite counter. "I don' know nothin' 'bout Jack Holliday, and nothin' 'bout his family."

Claire turned to Rene. "What about you, Rene? Have you been hiding things from Gabe, too?"

"What we did was for his own good."

"Oh, for God's sake, how on earth can you say that? We're talking about how his parents and sister died."

Rene sat down on the stool beside her. He took her hand and pressed it between both of his. "You need to listen now, just stop with all these questions, and listen to what we say. It was a real ugly thing, what happened to Gabe and his family. It wasn't long after they took you out of their home and put you with a different foster family. Gabe was just a boy, and injured so severely that he didn't remember what happened. One of God's tender mercies to him. So we protected him. Let him grow up without the memory. That's why we hushed things up."

"When was it? How old was he?"

"He had just turned twelve. Like I said, it didn't happen long after they took you away."

"But what about later? When he was a grown man?"

"It didn't matter. It's better that he doesn't know. Truth is, Annie, back then, when it happened, he got hurt, hurt real bad." Claire stared at him, waiting, and the expression in his eyes suddenly turned into naked pain. "That man, that monster that took Gabe? He beat him somethin' terrible, the bastard. When Gabe woke up after we found him half dead in the swamp, he didn't remember the things that were done to him, and we didn't want him to. He was just a kid. It would've messed up his mind even more than it already was over losing everybody in his family. So we told him it was a car crash. We told him that all the injuries he had incurred were from the accident, from being ejected from the car onto broken glass, and what not, and he believed us. He couldn't remember anything. Why wouldn't he believe us?"

There was no arguing with the sincerity on his face. Clyde was wiping his eyes on a dish towel. Weeping. Claire felt her anger begin to ebb, couldn't help it, but she still wasn't sold on their story. "Okay, I can understand that you wanted to protect him. And maybe I won't tell him, either. But I want to know the truth, every single detail, right now. I need to know for my own case. It's important that I know everything."

Clyde's voice got all thick and raspy, and his cheeks were wet with tears. Claire had never seen him sad before, couldn't remember a time when he hadn't been laughing and joking around. She didn't like him this way. "Don't make us do it, *chère*. I cannot t'ink of it without just gettin' sick inside my belly. I don't want him to know. I don't want you to know. You don't wanna know."

Rene took over as Clyde's throat thickened and his voice died away. "Gabe was beaten, very badly, worse than I ever saw anyone able to live through, and then he was dumped in the swamp and left for dead. When they found him, he was unconscious and stayed that way for days. When he woke up, he didn't remember much about it. The doctor said it was a brain injury or maybe he'd locked up the trauma someplace deep inside because his mind couldn't handle what was done to him."

Claire tried to digest that. The same thing had happened to her—at least, the coma and inability to remember things—but it had only lasted for a short time. Unfortunately, she had recalled the bad things, and remembered them anew in frequent awful nightmares. Would Gabe really want to go through the same thing? Did she want him to?

Clyde said, "It happened so long ago. It was the worst t'ing in my life. I had to live with it all dis time. I didn't want Gabe to know. It was terrible."

"Tell me exactly what happened to him."

Rene took over again. "They were on a family picnic out on the bayou. Sophie and Gabe were with them. It was during Mardi Gras week. Gabe was twelve and Sophie was ten. The killer attacked them there. A hunter found Kristen and Bobby lying together on a blanket, Bobby shot in the head and Kristen shot both in the head and in the chest. The children were gone, not a trace. They found their fishing poles about thirty yards upstream."

"Nobody heard or saw anything?"

"No. We think the killer might've been hiding in the bushes, watching them. He probably got the kids when they moved away from their parents to fish, subdued them somehow, and then went back and shot Bobby and Kristen. That's all we could ever figure, and it haunts me to this day that I couldn't find the guy who did that to them." After that speech, Rene looked absolutely stricken himself.

"Anything else? Other evidence found, anything at all?"

"We found some red feathers, like those on some of the Mardi Gras masks but never could trace them to any source. Every shop in New Orleans sells feathered masks. He could've gotten it anywhere."

"Was there an investigation?"

"Yeah, but I petitioned the court to seal it. I've still got the murder file, if you want to take a look. There wasn't much to go on. It's got the crime scene photos, stuff like that."

"I do want to look at it."

"I've got it in a safe at my house. Come by, take a look. Maybe it'll help you understand why we lied to Gabe."

"I will, but right now, I'm going to go back home and talk to Gabe. If he wants to know about this, I'm going to tell him, and you all will just have to deal with it."

They all looked upset about that possibility, but Claire and Black left them there to worry about the consequences of their lies and distortions. Gabe had a right to know what had happened to him, and he was tough enough to take it. As they got back into the Range Rover, she turned to Black.

"What do you think?"

"I think they were telling the truth, all or most of it. I think Clyde was sincere about having Gabe's mental state in mind when they didn't tell him what happened. But I'm with you on this. I think Gabe needs to know. The gaps in his memory could be what sent him into such a dangerous lifestyle. He deserves to know the truth, but that's strictly up to you. You know him better than I do."

After that, he drove straight to their house on Governor Nicholls, and Claire braced herself to tell Gabe. She just hoped he would take it well. It would be a lot for him to absorb all at once, but somehow she knew he would want to know. One thing for certain, she dreaded telling him the ugly details about as much as she had dreaded anything in her entire life.

Chapter Twenty-four

Gabe was in his bedroom, asleep. Julie Alvarez was reading on a Kindle Fire in a chair beside the bed. Black told her to take a break and that they had to speak privately with Gabe. Julie told him that the nurse on duty at his private clinic in the Hotel Crescent had called and said they needed his help with a patient. Apparently, they'd calmed the lady down, but they were waiting for him to order her meds.

Julie looked curiously at Claire but quickly retreated to her guest room and probably some well-deserved shut-eye. Gabe's head rested on the pillows, and his eyes remained closed. It was probably the first time he'd been fully relaxed and off his guard since he'd started playing games with a bunch of savage bikers. He still wore a thin blue hospital gown. Most of the lacerations on his face and arms were covered with bandages that looked white against his dark skin. His arm was still held immobile against his chest with a blue nylon sling.

Claire stood there for a moment, undecided on whether or not she should wake him. Black went to shower and shave and get ready to see his patient. Truth was, though, he knew that she and Gabe needed privacy so he was giving it to them. She sat down in the chair by the fireplace and contemplated what she should do. Okay, did she really want to disrupt Gabe's peace of mind with some horrendous ordeal from his childhood? Just now, when he was finally safe and out of danger and in good spirits? He had a right to know, of course, but he should make that decision. So she just sat there and waited. Gabe didn't wake up for quite a while, after Black had left for the hotel next door.

"Hey, Gabe, how're you feeling?"

Gabe squinted up at her in the semidarkness, all sleepy-eyed and groggy. When he recognized her, he smiled a little. God, he looked so damn good now that he was clean shaven and without that damn braided beard, man-cara, and long hair. Black's barber had paid a house call and made him look human again. He said, "It's nice to wake up to a friendly face, especially yours."

"I'm just glad you're here where we can look after you."

But Gabe knew her way too well. "You look upset. What'sa matter?"

Instead of answering, she said, "Any word on the Skulls?"

"They're working on the arrest warrants as we speak. Drug trafficking and prostitution. As soon as they're charged and find out we were undercover cops, they're gonna send people out lookin' for Bonnie and me. I'm gonna have to go to ground till the trial."

"Don't worry, they won't recognize you now." It was a feeble attempt at jocularity that didn't really pan out.

"What's wrong?" he said again, this time with a frown.

Claire tried to figure out the best way to broach the subject. "Gabe, if there was something in your past that you didn't know about, would you want somebody to tell you, even if it was really bad?"

"This isn't hypothetical, is it?" Gabe had always been intuitive.

"Well, would you?"

"Depends, I guess. What's goin' on?"

"I got some information about the killer I'm tracking." She hesitated, aware that this information might throw him into a tailspin. Gabe seemed to be okay physically and mentally. She was pretty sure he could handle what she was going to say. "It concerns you."

"I've done lots of things while I was undercover. What are you talkin' about?"

She took a deep breath. "You were abducted by a predator when you were twelve. You don't remember it, and everybody's kept it from you."

"That's not true."

"That's what I thought at first, too. But I have it on good evidence now."

"Not that. It happened all right. I do remember it."

Dumbfounded, yes, she certainly was. That was the last thing she had expected him to say.

"They meant well when they covered it up. And I didn't remember for a long, long time. But I had nightmares for years about being held captive and being beaten, and then one night when I woke up covered with sweat and hysterical, it all came back in a rush. My mind just opened up and let me have it. Maybe it thought I was ready."

"So you remember everything?"

"I wish I didn't."

"Can you tell me about it?" She pulled the chair up closer to the bed. "I think the guy who took you is the guy who killed Madonna and Wendy, Gabe. I think he's been killing people around here for decades."

Gabe just lay there and gazed at her. "I thought that, too, sometimes."

"And you never told Rene or Clyde or anybody that you remembered?"

"No, I really didn't see the point in bringing it all up again. It was so long ago. And I knew why they kept it from me, but I've been looking for that guy in the mask. All these years, I've kept my eyes and ears open for the sound of his voice. He disguised it, talked in a hoarse whisper, but I hoped I'd know it if I ever heard it again. I hoped I'd run into him and handle payback in my own way."

Claire knew what that meant and couldn't blame him. "Would you tell me about it? Or would that be too painful?"

Gabe got quiet then and leaned his head back against the pillow. He stared up at the folded pleats in the ornate canopy above him. "I guess so. If you think it's the same guy and it'll help you get him. I don't remember everything, but I remember a lot of it. I've figured out some things that I couldn't recall."

"We're so close now to getting this guy that I can taste it."

Gabe licked his dry lips and shifted positions. When he groaned in pain, Claire winced, too. "We were down on the bayou, havin' a picnic. It was Sophie's birthday. Mama and Papa were sitting on a blanket talking and kissing, you know how they were. He couldn't keep his hands off her, and she'd blush and tell him to stop, not in front of the kids."

"Yeah, I do remember that. They acted crazy about each other, and about us."

"Sophie wanted to catch a fish, she loved to fish, so we walked up the bank a good ways from them. It was warm that day. I remember sweatin' and takin' off my jacket. I went into the woods to find some worms, and that's when this masked man got me and tied me up and put tape over my mouth."

He paused there, and Claire gave him all the time he needed. But all her muscles were tight when she thought of the little children they had been back then. How much fun they'd all had together and how they'd all been devastated when Family Services people had taken her away. Gabe had yelled and cried and held on to the back of her shirt as they'd dragged her out of the house.

"He went out and got Sophie and tied her up, too. Then he walked down the path and shot Mama and Papa. Point blank."

"You saw him do it?"

"Yeah. And I see it to this day. He shot Papa once and Mama twice and then he just walked back to us, like nothing had happened."

Now the pain on his face was visible, and awful to behold. Claire began to have some misgivings about forcing him to tell it. "So you saw his face?"

"No, he put that Mardi Gras mask back on before he got to us, the kind that only covers the top half of your face. Decorated with sequins and red feathers. Looked like a snake. That's when he chloroformed us."

Claire waited while he took a sip of water. "You don't have to relive this, Gabe. I know it's painful."

"You don't know how bad I want to get that guy. I wanted a chance to kill him myself but didn't get it. Not yet, anyway."

"Let me get him for you. I'm going to get him, Gabe. I'll never stop until I do, especially now."

"I hope you do, and I hope you kill him."

"Clyde said he beat you."

"Yeah, he beat me. He liked it. After he got us to his hellhole, he kept us drugged and tied up down in a cellar. But he had this obstacle course thing upstairs, that and a voodoo altar he liked to scare us with. He kept calling it his mini maze of terror. And that's what it was, Annie, that's exactly what it was. It was designed to scare the hell out of us."

"And you don't know where it was?"

"Out on the bayous somewhere. I think there was a river nearby or some kind of water. We could hear the rushing of the current sometimes when it was really quiet. And he got us out there by boat; I remember that because I woke up a little bit while we were still lying in the bottom of that boat. I remember that he had a flashlight and he carried us up some steps to a porch and then inside a dark house." He stopped, sighed. "Believe me, I've looked for the place for years. It's all pretty fuzzy, because I only saw it at night, but it was an old house, a big one, creaky and dark and damp and crawling with roaches and spiders. All the windows were boarded up, and he kept us locked up in some kind of cellar or root cellar, something like that. He made us take pills to keep us quiet."

Gabe stared down at his hands, and Claire watched how his fingers were curling in until his nails bit into his palms. "He got off scaring us. Played all these frightening hide-and-seek games. He'd tell us to hide and maybe he'd let us go home, and then the first one of us he found, he'd take upstairs to what he called his playroom. It had lots of toys and an old four-poster bed. I guess he slept up there. It reeked of cigarette smoke, I remember that. That's where he usually beat me. He put up sheets of plastic on the floor and the wall to catch the blood."

"Oh, my God, Gabe," Claire got out somehow, but she felt nausea pushing its way up her throat at the depravity he'd suffered.

Gabe swallowed down some of his own horror. "He was as brutal as any man could ever be, Annie, an absolute monster. You wouldn't believe how cruel he was."

Claire picked up his hand and held it. "We think he marks his victims with a tattoo. Do you remember anything about that?"

"Oh, yeah, that's very vivid because it scared us so much. He must've gagged us and tied us to chairs, because we already had the tats when we woke up the first time. He bragged about his artwork, told us he did it himself with his own personal tattoo machine."

He turned his wrist over for her to see. "I've still got it, here, on the inside of my wrist. Clyde told me that I'd had it done before the accident, and I didn't remember enough to know any better. I always wear my watch there or a wide leather bracelet to hide it. But I never got that tat taken off. It helps me keep my resolve to find him and kill him."

Claire stared at his wrist. The same snakes and stars. "It's the same thing we found on Madonna and Wendy. He killed them both. Oh, God, Gabe, how many people has he killed and terrorized all these years?"

The muscles were moving under the skin of Gabe's jaw and she could actually hear his teeth grinding against each other. "He left me more memories on my back."

"Rene said he whipped you."

"That's right. I've got plenty of scars to prove it. They told me I got them in the wreck, that I was thrown out of the car onto shards of broken glass and concrete. I believed that for a long time, too."

Gabe turned on his side and pulled apart the back of his hospital gown. Claire gasped, horrified. The scar tissue was raised and pale against his dark skin, some thin lines, other scars the size of a drinking straw. Dozens of them, made by a whip or belt, crisscrossing his back from neck to waist. He had been beaten mercilessly, all right.

"Oh, Gabe, how could anybody do that to a child?"

Gabe lay back again. "He hurt Sophie, too. He chained me up in the cellar and I had to listen to her screaming from upstairs, calling for me to come help her. But he didn't hurt her as bad as he hurt me, thank God. He didn't beat her. He seemed almost fond of her."

Claire remembered Gabe's beautiful little sister with her fine wheat-blond hair and wide and trusting dark eyes. She had still been so little when Claire had lived there. They had shared a room, filled with Barbie dolls and books and jump ropes and a giant dollhouse that Bobby Lefevres had built for Sophie.

"Every single day I look at those scars in the mirror, and I swear I'll find that devil and choke the life out of him with my bare hands."

"Jack Holliday thinks that the man who did that to you and Sophie is the same man who murdered his family out in Colorado. Do you think he could be right?"

Gabe merely shrugged. "Did he mark his sisters with tats?"

"They never found them. Like Sophie. They were just three years old on the night his mom and stepdad were killed in their bed. Jack never saw them again. He's been looking for them for years. He hired a private investigator to find them, and he traced them down here to Madonna, after he found out her parents had been shot in a similar double murder. That's when they discovered the tats on their wrists."

"Well, he ought to stop looking for them. They're dead and gone a long time ago. He always kills the kids he takes. He told me that himself. That he was going to kill us and everybody else he put in his maze. The only reason I survived is because I didn't swallow that last sleeping pill and managed to pry a board off a cellar window and get both of us out."

"Thank God, you made it out alive."

"Sometimes I wonder about that. I couldn't rescue Sophie. I was weak from a beating and not strong enough to carry her out through the swamp. She was still drugged and couldn't keep up after a while, so I hid her, but I shouldn't have. I shouldn't've ever left Sophie out there alone, but when I got a chance to break free, I thought I could get help and get back before he found her. I don't remember much about what happened after that. I vaguely remember wading through the swamp and fighting through undergrowth, trying to find a way out, but I guess I lost consciousness. I don't remember being found or being in the hospital, either."

"Things are coming together now, Gabe. I'm going over to Rene's house and take a look at the file on your parents' murders."

"Be careful. That monster's still out there somewhere. He's probably the one who threw those grenades. If he's killing off surviving victims, he'd want me dead, and you're hot on his trail. Two birds with one stone. Nick was just collateral damage."

"You just rest and don't go anywhere. When Black gets back, tell him I've gone to Rene's house to get the file. I'll be home in a little while. Tell him not to worry. I'll be fine."

"He does worry. He's not going to like you taking off by your-self."

"I know."

"You got a pretty nice thing goin' here. He's good to you. And he's been good to me, and he doesn't know me from a hole in the ground. But I appreciate it."

"Yeah, I know. I'm sorry I had to ask you these questions, Gabe. Bring everything back like that."

"Just get him. For Sophie. I want to get him for her. No telling what he did to her when he found her that night. I try not to think about that part."

"Get some rest. I'll bring the case file in and let you look over it, if you want to."

"Be careful. This guy's good. He's gone a long time without getting caught. And now he's probably pretty anxious, thinkin' that you're getting too close. Just be alert."

"Oh, I will, trust me. I've learned that the hard way."

And that was true. She wasn't going to take any stupid chances. She wanted to live a while longer. But this guy. He was pure evil and they had to bring him down. They would, too; she was sure of it now. His brutal little maze of terror was going to be out of business very soon.

A Very Scary Man

Malice was absolutely furious. Nothing was going according to plan. Nothing. Claire Morgan was still on the case, even after he'd warned her off with that voodoo doll with her picture on it. Why the hell she hadn't been jerked off the case was the real question. He was irritated to damn death about that, and then what did she do? She found another one of his survivors almost at once and paid her a visit, too. It was just a matter of time before she and her partner started putting two and two together and suspecting him.

So now dear little sexy Wendy had to go, too, whether he liked it or not. But he did like it. It was high time that he cleaned house anyway. He had been young and stupid back then when he'd let them get away, and the biggest fool who ever lived to allow them to keep living all these years. There had been countless times in the past when he could have killed Madonna and Wendy without getting caught. Now it had become more risky, but it was something that had to be done. Quickly and efficiently and without leaving any evidence behind.

So he planned out the attack, thoroughly, examining every possible exigency as he'd learned to do. This time he chose just after dark when everybody in Mimosa Circle was either preparing their evening meal or settling down in front of the television set for their favorite primetime programming. He had cased out the place for several nights and found it to be very quiet at that particular time. It would be fairly easy to approach her house without being deemed an intruder. He came in through the woods behind the complex on foot, climbed the fence, and made his way to her place, avoiding streetlights and keeping in the shadows. No one was around except one jogger passing an intersection a good ways down the street, the place very quiet and peaceful. No going up and knocking on the front door this time. Wendy's neighbors lived way too close for that. Besides, Wendy was a lot smarter than Madonna Christien. She wouldn't let him in so easily. But he had no problem getting inside her apartment. He just picked the lock on her back door and cut the chains with his bolt cutter. He had become quite adept at breaking and entering, especially at picking locks, practicing daily until it only took him a few seconds. He entered silently, his bag of voodoo gear in tow.

Once inside her apartment, he looked around and realized that she was upstairs. He crept stealthily up the steps, pulling on his heavy leather gloves. She was in her bedroom, sorting through the clothes hanging inside her closet. She never even saw him coming. He crept up behind her and hit her in the back of her head with one hard fisted blow. She went down in a heap, too stunned to resist his assault, and he took his time beating her to within an inch of her life before he grew tired of it. She had become a problem for him all right, and he didn't like problems. He used the glow of the little night light beside her bed to sew her eyes and mouth shut, a nice touch since he was effectively hushing her up for good.

After that, he had plenty of time to paint her face and molest her body a bit before she died, and then he straddled her waist and strangled her until the bones in her throat cracked and gave way under the pressure of his thumbs. He got off on that sound every single time he heard it. After he was sure she was dead, he spent time cleaning up after himself and setting up the altar downstairs in the foyer. He made it as identical as he could to the one he'd fashioned for Madonna at the LeFevreses' old house. Murder had become as easy as pie for him, a highly enjoyable pastime. He felt better now that she was dead and could tell no tales. Loose lips sunk ships, and all that jazz. So now, he was going to have to remedy that, once and for all, by killing any and all of his survivors. There weren't all that many; he was too good at what he did for that.

Even better, Claire Morgan was still running around in circles. He was fairly certain she didn't know what the hell was going on, and he wasn't leaving her any clues to go by. Let her think it was some voodoo-obsessed crazy, getting off on sewing up lips and eyelids. And maybe this time, when they found a second doll with Claire's picture pinned to it, maybe then her stupid sheriff would come to his senses and assign the case to somebody else. Better yet, he might assign her young and inexperienced partner to run things. That would be even better.

If not, he would just have to kill her, too. He smiled at that thought. Actually that wasn't such a bad idea. He would just murder her, or better yet, maybe he could capture her and throw her inside his maze. Talk about a worthy opponent to pit against his cruel games. It would be quite the interesting challenge to see if she could outwit him. Yeah, he had to find a way to get her out to his little island paradise in the swamp, where they could get to know each other really well. There were all sorts of things he could show her. She wanted to know what his victims suffered? Well, he'd just show her.

Decided on his next course of action, he packed up his gear, wiped down Wendy's place for any DNA he might have left, relocked the back door, and then faded into the night, very satisfied with his night's work. Sometimes murder was just too damn easy for words.

Chapter Twenty-five

It only took Claire a minute or two to drive to Rene's house. He lived in the Quarter, too, in an old home with an inner courtyard like Black's. It wasn't as big and fancy and expensively furnished, but it had been handed down in his family for years. She pulled up and parked across the street. Lights were on upstairs in his living room behind the white wrought-iron balcony that overlooked the street. Underneath Rene's gallery at street level, there was an automatic garage door with a pedestrian portal right beside it, one affixed with a buzzer to ring for admittance. She pressed the button, then stepped back and looked up at the second-floor balcony. A couple of minutes later, Rene leaned over the railing and peered down at her.

"Hey, Claire. C'mon up."

From somewhere inside, she heard a click as he automatically unlocked the door, and she entered a dark hallway, then climbed a narrow enclosed stair to the living area. Rene met her at the top of the steps. He was home for the evening, dressed in a charcoal-gray nylon running suit marked on the back with NOPD in big white letters. He wore scuffed black leather slippers and held a cocktail in his hand, a dry martini with three green olives on a toothpick.

"Well, this's an unexpected pleasure," he said to her. "I didn't expect you to show up so soon. How about sittin' down and havin' a drink with me?"

"No, thanks. I've got a few questions I want to ask you and then I need to see that murder file."

Rene nodded and sipped his drink. Claire walked past him into his living room. It was large and spacious and airy with well-worn, apricot-colored couches facing each other. A black grand piano claimed one corner, and expensive modern art covered the walls. Claire had been there once for a Fourth of July celebration when she'd lived with the LeFevreses. It hadn't changed much at all.

"Nice place, Rene. Looks the same as years ago."

"My mama had good taste. I can't take the credit for the furnishings. Sure you don't want that drink? Martini? I've got more in the pitcher, ready to pour."

"I don't think so." Enough of the pleasantries, already. She turned and waited for him to meet her gaze. "I really need to see that file, Rene. It is here, right?"

Instead of answering her question, he turned around and walked to a dry bar built inside a tall antique rosewood cabinet. He said nothing as he refilled his stemmed glass from a small cut-glass pitcher. He ate the olives, then skewered three more and plopped them into his fresh drink. Claire said nothing, either, just waited. But she didn't like his delay in answering and felt like it was an excuse to think of a reason to deny her the file. Her impatience was simmering, ready to erupt into a full boil.

Rene took a sip and looked at her over the rim of his glass. Then he heaved an audible sigh. "Sit down, Claire. Let's talk about this, calmly and rationally. You got to know how sorry I am about all this. Gabe's like a son to me. Come on, have a drink."

"I said that I don't want a drink. I want to see that file."

"Sit down, please."

Claire sat down on the sofa. Rene took his place on a black leather club chair directly across from her. Apparently, he had been reading when she rang the bell. An open book sat on the hassock in front of him, a thick biography of Andrew Jackson, alongside Rene's black-rimmed reading glasses.

"Okay, what do you wanna see?"

"First off, I want to see the murder file you compiled on the LeFevres murders. I know you buried the facts of the crime at Clyde's request, in order to protect Gabe. But you still have it, don't you?"

Rene still procrastinated. He wasn't keen on discussing the subject. He no doubt felt that he had put it to bed a long time ago and didn't want to wake it up. "I didn't destroy anything. Everything the police came up with I've got right here in my safe. I took the whole thing out of storage after the case was sealed and went cold. Nobody knows about that, and nobody can know. I've come too far in my career to get busted for stealing a police file going back twenty years." He frowned some, obviously perturbed at the thought, and then he drained his glass and leaned toward her. "Claire, I've got to warn you. The photos in that file are pretty hard to look out. I know how much you loved the LeFevreses."

"Go get it, Rene, please. It might help me bring in a serial killer who's been on the loose way too long."

"God, it's just hard to deal with this all over again."

Rene hesitated, wasted more time, the story dragging out as slow as twenty-degree molasses. Claire tried to be patient, but the problem was, she wasn't patient.

"There's something else, too. Something even Clyde and Gabe and the other guys don't know. I've never been able to bring myself to tell them. It's just too ugly."

Claire tensed for the coming blow. Then she realized there couldn't be anything worse than what she'd already heard. Ugly seemed to be the word of the day. So, okay, bring it on, the next chapter in this sordid tale. "All right, let's hear it."

"I uncovered some dirt on Bobby. Something real bad. I didn't like it. You won't, either."

Claire mentally braced herself. She did not like where this was going. She'd been hit with so many curveballs during the last week that she felt like a Major League backstop.

"I hate to say this, but, well, he got himself in trouble, involved with the Mob operating out of Algiers. He went on the take."

As a cop, that hit Claire pretty hard. She found it hard to believe, too. And again Black's black-sheep brother was cropping up in the investigation, which was never good. "I can't imagine that. He was as straight as they come."

"I found evidence of it and confronted him. He begged me not to tell Kristen, but I told him that I couldn't let it ride, that I had to take him in. He wouldn't let that happen. Couldn't stand for her to know he was dirty." He paused again, looked unhappy, and his next words dragged out, his voice heavy with sorrow. "You know what I think happened? I think he killed Kristen and then committed suicide."

Well now, that scenario certainly didn't jibe with what Gabe had just told her. "So now you're telling me that they weren't murdered?"

"I can't prove it, no. But they were killed with a .45 and his service weapon was right there beside him."

"Did the ballistics check out?"

"They were inconclusive, but I think he wanted to end it all and couldn't bear to leave her behind. You know how he felt about her."

Yeah? Only thing was, none of that made a lick of sense. And it sure didn't measure up with Gabe's version of witnessing a masked man kill his parents. "That's not what Gabe saw. And if it was a murder/suicide, who took Gabe and Sophie? And why?"

"Gabe saw the murder? He remembers what happened to him? Why, he never even mentioned it to any of us."

"No, he kept it to himself. He wanted to find the killer and avenge his family."

"So he can identify him?" Rene sounded excited at the idea. "We can get him?"

"No, the killer wore a mask. He thinks he can recognize his voice though."

"Man, no wonder he takes the chances he does. I'm sorry he remembered. It had to have been horrible. The way we found his parents out in the bayous with the kids missing, and all that. We searched out there for days, but didn't find a damn thing until Gabe finally showed up, half dead, his memory gone."

"Yeah, I know all that. Just give me that file, Rene. Let me read through it. Maybe I'll see something that you've always been too close to see."

Rene didn't argue further. He got up and left the room. Claire stood up, too, restless and full of suppressed emotion. All this was coming at her a little too fast and too furiously. Too many angles, too many theories that just didn't add up the way they should.

Moving over to the open French doors, she inhaled the cool night air. Somewhere nearby, she could hear Christmas music. "Jingle Bell Rock." A happy sound. She wished she were happy. She wished this case hadn't come up now. She wished she and Black could put up that huge evergreen tree he'd brought from New York or go shopping at the Riverwalk Marketplace or have some fun groping each other under some mistletoe, something, anything that was cheerful and pleasant. It sure would beat looking at a police file with horrible pictures of dead people she had loved dearly. Somewhere in the distance, she heard the wail of police sirens that drowned out the happy sounds of Christmas. Well, that was just par for the course. She only hoped the NOPD wasn't headed for her house.

She glanced down at the round glass-topped table beside her. It displayed lots of framed photographs. She bent down and looked at each one in turn. Many were of Rene himself, at places unknown, young and handsome, rugged and tanned. A few more were of him in his dress police uniform, both recent and long ago when he had been a rookie patrol officer. Yet another was one with Bobby LeFevres. The two men were posed together beside a black-and-white police car with a third man that she didn't recognize. Grinning arrogantly at the camera, both dark and good-looking and proud. She wondered who the other man was. He wasn't in uniform, but he had his arm hooked familiarly around Bobby's neck. She put the picture down and found a smaller one, in a shiny silver frame, sitting behind the others. She picked it up.

It portrayed a group of young friends, having fun and posing, grabbing each other. Rene, Bobby and Kristen LeFevres, and the fourth person looked like a very young Clyde LeFevres, displaying his usual irrepressible smile. All looked to be carefree teenagers, laughing, as they sat together on the front steps of an old house. Rene had on a maroon and white letter jacket with a football letter and had his arm draped around Kristen's shoulders. Bobby sat one step down, leaning against Kristen's legs and wearing a similar letter jacket with football insignia. Kristen had her fingers entwined in Bobby's thick black hair.

All of them were smiling straight into the camera. Claire marveled at how much Gabe now looked like his dad had back then, both having those ultra-intense brown eyes. Also wearing an identical letter jacket, Clyde was sitting in front of Kristen, smoking a cigarette, turned slightly and looking adoringly up at her. They had all been in love with her, Claire suddenly realized, all three men. And she had been so beautiful back then, with her pale blond hair and clear green eyes and quick smile. She had been beautiful when Claire lived in their home, too. Claire remembered that about her.

She examined the house behind them in the photo, trying to see if it was the one she'd lived in with them and the location of the Christien crime scene. It looked very old, rundown, peeling white paint, some of the wood splintered or boards completely ripped off. Up on the porch behind them, there was a boarded-up front door, but then she saw it, and her heartbeat slowed to a standstill. A fancy fleur-de-lis was carved into the newel post just behind where they sat. She brought the photo up closer to her eyes, and then she held it underneath the lamp, just to make sure she wasn't seeing things. There was no doubt. The carving was the very same fleur-de-lis that she'd seen earlier. The snapshot had been taken on the front steps of Rose Arbor, Jack Holliday's plantation house out on River Road.

"You like that picture, eh? That was back in our first year in high school. We were all freshmen. Except for Clyde, he's a junior in that picture, not long before he went to sea." Rene stood in the threshold of the corridor. He had a large black three-ring binder in his hand.

Claire held up the photograph. "Where was this taken, Rene?"

"We were out at an old abandoned plantation house on the river. We used to hang out there all the time, pickin' up pecans off the ground and sellin' them for change." He laughed. "And then we'd all go to the movies together. All of us guys used to fight over who got to sit by Kristie. Times were pretty simple back then. I miss those guys. The way we were then. We couldn't've imagined what the future was bringin' down the road. Good thing, too."

"Who took the picture?"

"Nat, I guess. I don't remember. He's always been a good friend of Clyde's, older than him, though. Back then he was the caretaker and lived somewhere down behind that house, still does, I think. It's Jack Holliday's now, you know. His family bought it a long time ago and restored it. They call it Rose Arbor."

"Yeah, I met Old Nat out there. Who carved that fleur-de-lis on the banister?"

"Nat did, I think. He likes to carve things, does good work, too, or used to. Don't know about now. He carved Kristie a fleur-de-lis necklace, too. Her mom decided to bury her in it." Rene shook his head. "That was a sad time for all of us."

"Do you remember when the place was restored?"

"No. It's always been a beautiful house place, up there on the hill overlookin' the Mississippi. We had lots of good times out there. Nat was pretty good about givin' us the run of the place. As long as we didn't break out any windows or steal anything off the property, he let us be."

"So he was the caretaker that far back?"

"Yeah. He loves that place."

"Is that the murder file?"

"Yeah, and everything's still here."

Claire took it from him and sat down in a chair beside a bronze floor lamp, the glass shade painted with beautiful pink roses. Rene poured himself another drink, but this time he didn't offer her one. Then he lounged down on the couch where she had been earlier. She put the binder on her knees and opened the front cover. It was mainly composed of graphic crime scene photographs, all right, all of them old Polaroid insta-prints, now faded and curling around the edges. At the back of the notebook, she found some typewritten reports, the paper also yellowed with age.

She stared at the photograph on the first page. Kristen LeFevres. Lying on a red-and-white-checkered quilt, a bullet hole in her forehead. Claire swallowed hard, remembering the woman's warm laugh, her tight good-night hugs, the homemade sugar cookies she always kept in the cookie jar. She had died in a blue gingham, long-sleeved dress with a scooped neck edged with white lace. Yellow flowers were printed all over the skirt. A large yellow rose was pinned in her silky blond hair behind her left ear. There were several strands of colorful Mardi Gras beads around her neck. The dress had a large bloodstain in the bodice where the assailant had shot her in the heart.

Somewhere in the deepest reaches of her mind, a misty picture tried to rise up and take form. Kristen, strolling along a bayou path holding Sophie's hand, her shoes crunching on the tiny white shells. She had turned around and smiled back at Claire and Gabe. They had gone on lots of picnics when she'd been there, all of them together, always on the edge of the bayou.

The second picture was of Bobby LeFevres. He was dressed in a white sweatshirt and jeans with the same Mardi Gras beads around his neck. He lay on his side, his service weapon on the ground beside him. Had he really used it to kill himself and his wife? Had Gabe's mental and physical abuse played tricks on his memory? His legs were sprawled apart, one arm bent and pinned beneath his torso. His eyes were open, as if staring at the camera lens. Blood was dried in streaks down over his nose and mouth from a bullet wound to his forehead.

Claire stared at him a long time. After carefully examining the placement of Bobby's body and the gun, she realized that it was entirely possible that he had shot himself. On the other hand, she felt fairly certain that he had not. The man she remembered could never have killed his wife, never. They had been inseparable. If he had been standing when he'd shot himself, the gun could have fallen out of his hand and landed where it was depicted in the photo, as Rene had surmised, but percentages were against it. She tried to make sense of it all, bring all the parts together into some kind of plausible scenario. She glanced up at Rene. He was watching her closely, his glass propped on his knee.

"I don't believe he killed her. I think the same guy who took Gabe killed them both, just like Gabe said. He said he saw a masked man do it."

"And it could've happened that way, sure it could've. I know that. But it was a long time ago, and Gabe was just a boy and probably in total shock if he saw it all go down. Then right after that, we think he might've been drugged. There's no evidence to prove what happened one way or the other. Believe me, I tried my best to find a clue, something, anything. I'm just telling you what might've happened. I don't wanna believe he killed Kristen, any more than I wanted to believe he was dirty, but I do think it's possible. I've kept all this to myself all these years to protect the family, especially Gabe."

Claire picked up the next photograph. This one was of Gabriel. He didn't look much older than he had when she had been with his family. Dark and striking and good-looking, even then. He was lying unconscious in a hospital bed. He had two black eyes, horribly swollen, bandages everywhere, and he wore no shirt. His naked torso was practically skin and bones, indicating he'd been starved, with awful stripes cut into his chest where he'd been flogged. A second picture was a close up of his back, with stripes and crisscross patterns that indicated he'd suffered blow after blow after blow. How could he live with what had been done to him? It was too horrible to imagine.

There were more pictures of the crime scene from lots of different angles. The blood on the quilt, the fishing poles lying on the bank, a Folgers coffee can full of bait worms found in the bushes near the abduction point. All of which verified Gabe's version of the crime.

Rene said, "Gabe was barely breathing when they found him on that bank. All covered in blood and algae and mud. The doctors told us it was a miracle that he survived—just take a look at his wounds. Most of them were infected, too."

"Who could do something so inhuman to a child? What kind of sick and twisted mind could do it?"

"I've run into my share of psychotic killers and so have you, from what I've heard. But I haven't seen anybody else like this guy. He has to be a sadist, some kind of a pedophile, and a child killer. Whoever he is, he's probably long gone."

Claire looked up at him. "Do you mind if I take this file with me? I want to read the reports and think everything through."

Rene did not look thrilled, but he finally agreed. "Okay, just don't let anybody else see it."

When Claire stood up to go, binder in hand, Rene hugged her tightly, but all she wanted was to get away, go off somewhere by herself and figure out what the hell was going on. The killer, the man who had done such unspeakable things to Gabe, was still walking around, still getting away with his heinous crimes. She knew it, felt it in her bones. He was their killer. They had to catch him, and they had to do it before he struck some other innocent family.

Chapter Twenty-six

Across the street from Rene's house, Claire got into her vehicle and sat there in the driver's seat, thinking about everything Rene and Gabe had told her. Then she opened the binder, using her flashlight app to scrutinize the photographs and reports again. One by one, she sorted through them, studying each one in minute detail. Ten minutes later, she leaned her head back against the seat and shut her eyes. She was so tired; she needed to get some sleep. But she couldn't quit thinking about the terrible things that Gabe had endured all those years ago after she left his house in the bayous.

Surprisingly, her mind kept returning again and again to a particular photograph, as jarring and terrible as the images she'd just seen had been—the one of the LeFevreses and Clyde and Rene sitting on the steps at Rose Arbor. Something about it struck her as odd, something wrong, something out of place, something that didn't sit so well in her mind. It seemed way too much of a coincidence that they had been photographed on the front gallery of Jack Holliday's family's mansion, and possibly by Jack Holliday's current caretaker, the ever weird and armed-to-the-teeth Old Nat. But the snapshot had been captured many years ago. Gabe had said he and Sophie had been held captive in an old house. Could it really be the same one? And was it just a coincidence that Jack had been implicated in her current cases and lived in the house the killer had used as a lair? How could that have happened? Most of all, why did that picture bother her so much?

But it did, and continued to do so, and yeah, enough that she gripped the steering wheel, wrenched a sharp U-turn and headed for

River Road and Rose Arbor. Maybe Jack knew something about the history of the house that could provide her with a clue, something he had either intentionally or unintentionally left out. Who had owned the house before his grandmother? Nat Navarro? And had he really carved that fleur-de-lis in the banister? And when? The carving was not professionally done. It was a nice rendering but slightly rough in spots, probably the work of an amateur, maybe even dug out with a pocket knife. Why? And why had Jack's grandmother left it there when she'd renovated everything else in the house? It was certainly out of place when every other feature was pristine and beautiful and restored, and meticulously so.

The photograph was the key, she knew it, especially after Rene's talk about his high school friends. Plagued by suspicions and doubts, she tried to figure out the root of her misgivings. It bothered her more than even the pitiful images of Gabe, abused and whipped and heartlessly discarded in the swamp like a dead dog. She kept thinking about him, wondering how he could bear such destructive memories. Now that she understood just how bad a time he had gone through, she was surprised he'd ended up on the right side of the law instead of becoming a drunk or an addict or a felon or a real drug-dealing biker.

Feeling guilty about taking off, she called Black and explained where she was going and asked him for the code to Jack's entrance gate. He said he'd call Jack and they'd meet her there. Five minutes later, he called back with the code and permission for her to enter the house but asked her to wait for them. It was still dark when she reached the spiked gate at Rose Arbor, the hour very late now, and the gate was closed. She decided not to step on Old Nat's toes again by barging onto the property. He'd appreciate the courtesy, no doubt, and she'd appreciate not getting shot. So she climbed out of the Range Rover and pushed the bell. Nobody answered.

Claire had the distinct feeling that Old Nat was already creeping around in the dark under the canopy of live oaks and zeroing in on her head with his trusty shotgun. Probably enjoying it, too. The two of them just didn't quite cotton to each other, in Zee's vernacular. Well, that was just too bad. She had some questions to ask him, and he was going to answer them, like it or not.

So, without further ado, she punched in the code and watched
the gates whir themselves open. She drove through and watched it
close securely behind her. Once up the drive and at the front portico,
she saw no fancy, six-figure-window-sticker vehicles sitting around
the driveway, no limousines, either. Nobody home. Well, good.

Picking up the murder binder, she got out of the car, climbed the
steps, and shined her flashlight on the newel post. The fleur-de-lis
was still there, whittled into the wood, just like in the old Polaroid.
Whoever had done it was pretty good. It occurred to her that Bobby
LeFevres, or Rene, or Clyde, or Kristen or anybody else, including
Old Nat, could have wielded the knife that had carved it. She sat
down, focused her flashlight, and stared at the design.

After a moment, she walked up to the front door. It was unlocked
so she breezed inside as if she owned the place. She had permission.
She wasn't going to steal his fancy antique furniture or priceless
Ming vase. She flipped on the light and the chandelier flared. She
stood there a moment and looked around with fresh and determined
detective eyes. Could this really be the old house where Gabe was
held captive? It looked as if Rose Arbor had been restored pretty
much along original antebellum architectural lines. Slowly, methodically, she walked from room to room, not quite sure what she was
looking for. But Gabe had said that he had been held in a cellar so
a cellar she was going to find. Off the kitchen, she found a large
butler's pantry with glass-fronted cabinets, and it was full of the most
beautiful gold-edged dishes and crystal goblets, each etched with
the letter H with lots of curlicues and flourishes. More priceless stuff
handed down from Granny Holliday.

Moving through all the downstairs rooms, she turned on the
overhead chandeliers one after another, pulled open doors, looking
for something, anything, that would help her. Some instinct told her
that she had to search this house, compelled her, even if she had to
rip it apart, board by board. And she had learned to follow her instincts most of the time.

Finally, she hit pay dirt on her return visit to the butler's pantry. A
small door was hidden by a curtain, and she discovered that it opened
onto steps descending into what appeared to be a root cellar. There
was no basement in the house, but the first floor was built up off the

ground about twelve feet. She flipped on the light switch at the top of the steps. The steps went down halfway and then took a sharp right turn. She inched down cautiously, an unsettling sense of unease descending over her. She pulled out her weapon, just in case, and stepped down onto the floor, her finger right alongside the Glock's trigger.

Was this it? Where Gabe and Sophie had been held and tortured? It was extremely dank inside that musty, cold, and nasty place. She could smell mildew and dirt and mold, but there was little else to see. The bricked walls had been whitewashed, but the floor was dirt. She peered up into the floor joists above her head and wondered where all the spider webs were. Holliday must have one hell of a good housekeeper on staff. There were a couple of small windows, rectangular and high on the walls. How would it have felt to be imprisoned there, a monster coming down the steps in some kind of hideous mask with a whip in his hand? She thought of little Sophie, who was so sweet, so little, and how hard it must be for Gabe not knowing what had happened to her.

When a deep voice suddenly spoke behind Claire, she nearly came out of her skin. She dropped the binder, and jerked around, both hands gripping her weapon out in front of her. To her shock, it was Yannick the Snooty Butler, of all people, the all-around indispensable servant at Jack's grandma's house in the Garden District. This time he wore a distinctly startled expression on his face. He quickly raised both his hands, palms out, in a whoa-don't-shoot-me-dead sort of way.

"Good heavens, put that gun down," he choked out, real shaky like, and his manner wasn't nearly as haughty as the last time they'd exchanged pleasantries. Deadly weapons had a way of disarming stuck-up butlers, she guessed.

Claire lowered the weapon and sheathed it in her shoulder holster. "I'm sorry, sir. You startled me."

"What are you doing down here, miss?" Yannick glanced around, puzzled. "Do you always pull your gun on people like that?"

"Yes, sir, when they sneak up on me. What're *you* doing out here in the middle of the night? I thought you worked in town."

"I'm here to oversee the night custodial service that cleans this house. They come at night and are gone by dawn so as not to disturb Mr. Jack. They're upstairs and ready to go to work."

"How did you know I was down here?"

"I saw your vehicle and called Mr. Jack and asked him if he was expecting company tonight. He said to tell you that he and Dr. Black are on their way. The door in the pantry was standing open, and the light was on." He gazed curiously at her. "I must say, Detective, that I'm surprised to find you down here in Mr. Jack's root cellar with a gun in your hand."

Then Yannick gave her that wary look that people usually reserve for when they happen upon machete-wielding escapees from mental institutions. He didn't seem concerned enough to hightail it out of her scary company, though.

"How long have you worked for the Holliday family, Yannick?"

"For many years, even before Miss Catherine bought this place. Well, I think I'll go upstairs now and wait on Mr. Jack."

Apparently not wanting to answer any more questions and without further ado, Yannick turned on his heel and headed up the steps. Since the shadowy cellar made her jumpy, she picked up the binder and followed him. Inside the kitchen, she met up with him again. This time he was busily instructing a small army of cleaners, all of whom were dressed in matching black uniforms and holding various feather dusters, brooms, mops, dustpans, and cans of Pledge. They all stared at her as if she were some kind of armed alien apparition, so she hurried past them when she heard Black's voice call her name from out in the foyer. She met up with Black and Holliday under the giant, sparkling chandelier.

Black said, "So, what's up now, Claire? Why are we here?" He observed her face a moment, and then frowned and said, "Are you all right?"

"I just need permission to take a look around this house."

"Looks to me like you already have," Black said on a wry note.

"Why?" asked Jack.

"I'm following a hunch. Case related. You know how I am. A dog with a bone."

"Why don't you just tell us what's going on?" Black again.

Claire frowned. "I need to talk to Jack, ask him some questions."

Jack said, "Okay, what'd you want to know?"

"I want you to tell me about the history of this house. Everything you know about it."

"Why? Does this have something to do with my sisters? Do you have a new lead?"

"I think maybe Gabe and Sophie were held right here in this house, probably down in your root cellar."

Jack actually gasped, a soft but audible intake of breath.

Black said, "Here? How do you know?"

"He kept them in *my* root cellar? *This one*? Here at Rose Arbor? Oh, my God."

"Gabe told me that he remembers a dark place like a cellar with a dirt floor and it was inside an old boarded-up house. I think this is that place. If this guy held Gabe down there, Jack, he might have held your sisters down there, too."

"But how? My grandmother lived here for years. She would've known about it."

"It wasn't her house then, and I want to know whose house it was. Would Yannick or Old Nat know who owned this place that far back? I need to interview both of them. See what they can tell me. My gut tells me that I'm on to something pertinent to the case."

"Both of them have worked for my grandmother for years. I sort of doubt if they'll know who had this place before that. But we can ask them."

"This is tied together. I think you were right. I think the same guy who killed Gabe's parents and took him captive killed your parents, too. I think all this is happening now, Madonna, Wendy, the attempt on Gabe's life, all because he's getting rid of witnesses. He's killing anybody who got away and might be able to identify him or lead authorities to him. Maybe he found out you were questioning Madonna Christien about her kidnapping, panicked, and got rid of her."

"How the hell did you figure out that it was this house?" Black said.

"It's a hunch. I saw a picture of Bobby and Kristen at Rene's place tonight, taken back when they were young. Rene said Old Nat was out there with them, and I saw the fleur-de-lis carved on the newel post and recognized it."

"The one outside at the top of the steps?" said Jack.

"Yeah. I can't prove it, but I think this is the house. I've also seen the file on Gabe's parents' murders. It's right here." She held it up. "Rene took it and kept it at his house to protect Gabe and his family."

Black said, "He's going to be in big trouble if that gets out."

"The LeFevres family asked him to keep it quiet. They didn't want Gabe's past to be publicized, didn't want him to find out how bad it really was. So he got the department to seal it. He took it out of storage later."

"Let me see it." Jack was not asking; he was demanding.

Claire handed it over, and he moved into the adjoining formal parlor and sat down at a desk. She and Black followed him, and Claire watched his face as he sifted slowly through the photographs. His jaw tightened when he saw the picture of Gabe's bloodied back. He handed the folder to Black.

"I want this animal. I want him dead. The deader, the better."

"Well, join the crowd, Holliday. Gabe's been searching for him for years with blood in his eyes. He thinks he's still around here, in the bayous, murdering people and snatching their kids. So do I."

Black looked up from the file. "I've got an idea, Claire. Something that might help."

Usually his ideas were right on target, so Claire jumped on it. "What?"

"Let me hypnotize Gabe. See what we can pull out of his memory. It worked on you not so long ago. It might work on him. Maybe he'll remember the killer's face or something his mind is blocking out. Maybe he'll remember the fleur-de-lis."

Jack said, "Would Gabe feel up to that? After all he's been through?"

Claire nodded. "I think Gabe would do anything to get the guy who put those scars on his back."

Black said, "I have all the equipment we'll need back at the house. Gabe's still there. Let's go see if he'll agree to it."

Everybody was all for that, and they headed out again to the French Quarter. Claire decided her interview with Yannick and Old Nat could just wait. She only hoped Gabe was up for a visit to his nightmarish past.

Chapter Twenty-seven

"Are you absolutely certain that you want to do this, Gabe? I have to warn you that it could bring up some things that you probably don't want to relive."

"Yeah. I've been dealin' with stuff I don't want to relive my whole life."

Nicholas Black sat in his desk chair inside his large home office on Governor Nicholls Street. It was equipped with all the video equipment needed to record Gabe's private session, which would allow him to remain in the house, since he was still suffering dizzy spells from his concussion. Gabe was lying in front of him on a tufted brown leather couch. Jack Holliday and Claire sat and watched from a nearby conference table. Nick remembered only too well the night he had put Claire under hypnosis. Lots of revelations had come out of her mouth, ones that had scared the hell out of both of them.

Tonight, however, Nick only hoped that he could pull something out of Gabe's subconscious mind that could help catch the sociopath who had been haunting his life for so many years. That's what he needed to do, because Nick was pretty sure that Gabe was experiencing post-traumatic stress and a good deal of suppressed anger issues as well. And now, after having talked at length and one-on-one with Gabe not an hour ago, he was absolutely positive Gabe was suffering a heavy dose of survivor guilt. But why wouldn't he? After what he had lived through, he certainly had good reason to suffer those syndromes and more. But he also feared that Gabe might be a time bomb, ready to go off at any moment. After all this was over,

Gabe needed serious therapy, and Nick was going to make sure he got the treatment he needed

"Just a heads-up, Gabe. Everybody isn't suggestible to hypnotism. You may be in that group. This may not work at all."

Gabe stared up at the ceiling. "I want to do this. Let's get started."

"I can instruct you not to relive any scenario where you or your sister is being beaten or abused or hurt in any way. I can have you only focus on the parts where you're with or around your abductor, when and where he took you, that sort of thing. It'll be as if you're watching a movie, not like you're experiencing it again. You won't feel pain or fear or panic. Understand?"

"Whatever. Just get on with it."

"Close your eyes and try to relax."

Gabe heaved in a couple of deep breaths, shut his eyes, wiggled around a bit, and then lay still. Nick wondered if Gabe could withstand new memories of the trauma. It would not be good for him to be reminded of the abuse he'd suffered. Gabe had managed to survive the horror of what had happened to him somehow and become the decent man that he was. Nick didn't want to mess that up. He had to be careful about what he pulled out of him.

Nick took a cleansing breath himself and then began the session. He spoke softly and told Gabe how relaxed he was, how he was floating around on clouds, going back, back, back into the past, but he wasn't at all sure Gabe was going to be suggestible. Claire had been easy to hypnotize, to her own chagrin.

As it turned out, it didn't take long for Gabe, either. A half an hour later, Nick had managed to regress Gabe back to his childhood years and then to the abduction itself. "You are okay, Gabe. Nobody is going to hurt you. You are just watching what happens in that cellar. Tell me what you see."

Gabe shifted around on the couch, as if uncomfortable, agitated. "It's very dark. Cold and damp and it smells funny. There's a boy in there. He's shivering and trying to keep warm. He's got his hands over his ears. The masked man didn't find him this time but he got his little sister. He got Sophie. She's upstairs with the monster now, screaming and crying and calling for him to come help her."

"How did he capture the boy and Sophie?"

"He got them out on the bayou. He killed their mama and papa."
Gabe stopped, and despite Nick's instructions that he wouldn't feel
the pain, he let out a muffled sob. Nick glanced at Claire, and her
face looked absolutely stricken. She cared deeply for this man. It
was an awful thing for her to have to watch. He had tried to persuade
her to wait outside, but she wouldn't have any of it.

Nick leaned forward, spoke soothingly. "Remember, Gabe, it's
just a movie you're watching. You are not there with them. You are
not suffering. You are not afraid. You are just watching what happened to them a long, long time ago. It isn't real. Remember that, it
is not real."

Gabe quieted, tears still wet on his cheeks. "Okay."

"Where are they now, Gabe?"

"They're still in the cellar, and the windows are all boarded up.
It's so dark they can barely see each other. He keeps them down
there, but they can hear him when he's coming back to scare them.
They can hear him walking on the floor above them and making the
boards creak."

"Are they tied up? So they can't get away from him?"

"No, he didn't tie them up, but there's a bolt on the outside of the
door. Sometimes he forces them to take pills that makes them go to
sleep." Gabe started shivering again and gave a low moan.

"You are not there with them, Gabe. Remember, you are just
watching them from a distance. You are safe. You are perfectly fine.
Nobody's going to hurt you."

Again, Gabe settled down, but his breathing was coming fast and
hard. "They are so scared when he comes for them. He's really mean
and he hurts them. They try to hide when he opens the door at the
top of the steps because he makes them go upstairs and that's where
he hurts them."

Nick glanced at Claire and Jack again. Neither one of them was
handling Gabe's suffering very well. He should have insisted they
wait outside. He didn't need for them to go to pieces, too. Jack, especially. Right now, Jack's hands were clenched so hard on the top
of the table that his biceps were rigid. Nick turned back to Gabe.
"What happens to them when he takes them upstairs?"

"It's dark up there. There are sheets and blankets over furniture and the windows are covered with boards. They hear mice and rats scuttling around and spiderwebs stick to them when they try to run, but they can't see anything."

"Where is this house, Gabe? Do you recognize it? Do you know how to get to it?"

"It's close to a river. He takes them there in a boat. He tapes them up and then he puts a cloth over their face. It smells awful and makes them go to sleep."

"Do you know how to get there?"

"No, it's dark when he drags them out of the boat. The boy hears the tree branches rustling and crickets singing, but he feels sick to his stomach from the cloth and he can't stay awake."

"What happened when the boy first woke up?"

"He's scared because his arms are tied up over his head on the ceiling beam, and his little sister's taped to a chair. He can see where the man tattooed him. It hurts him real bad and it's bleeding. When he twists around on the rope enough, he sees that he did it to the girl, too. Then the man in the red mask comes back and he's hitting the boy with a whip that has lots of knotted ends on it. He hurts him awful bad. He likes to hurt him. He laughs when he hits him with his whip. He doesn't like the boy as much as the girl."

Nick took another deep inhalation. Hell, he didn't want to hear the rest of this story, either. "Tell me about the little girl. What happened to her?"

"She stops yelling and crying for the boy after a while. Then it gets all quiet, and the boy's afraid she's dead, that he shot her with a gun like he shot their mama and papa."

"Did the man ever tell them why he had them? Why he was doing the bad things to them?"

"He says the boy ruined his life. He says they're bad kids and he's got to punish them. He says he's their daddy now and they better get used to it." Gabe started getting restless again, kicking out with his legs.

"Did he ever take off the red mask?"

"No. He changes it sometimes, but usually it looks like a snake with feathers on it."

"Does the boy know the man?"

Gabe was quiet for a few seconds, while they all held their breaths.

"Sometimes, he thinks he does, thinks he knows the voice somehow, but then he's not sure."

"Does the boy ever see his face without the mask? Even a glimpse of him?"

"No. He always wears it. He whispers and growls and screams at them."

"What else did he do?"

"He paints his face to look like a skull and he makes a place with lots of candles around and ties them to chairs and makes them watch him kill animals. He pushes them into dark tunnels and makes them crawl through, and then he jumps out and scares them, or grabs them and shakes them or hits them with the whip."

"Oh, God," Claire muttered from across the room. She stood up. "I don't think I can listen to this."

Claire now looked absolutely ashen, but it was Jack's face that troubled Nick. Jack looked like he was going to kill somebody with his bare hands.

"Do either of you want me to stop?"

"No, don't. We've got to do this. We've got to get him." That was Jack, through gritted teeth and rigid with determination. He didn't look so hot.

Claire nodded, too, but she didn't look quite as sure as Jack. Nick looked back down at Gabe, who had quieted now and was lying completely still.

"Did they ever get outside the house? Can you see them escaping?"

"The boy gets up on his toes and tries to pull the boards off the window. He can't do it, because he's kinda sick, but then he finally he gets one off. He opens the window and pushes the little girl outside. And then he squeezes out, too, but he has trouble because he's bigger and he feels so weak and tired 'cause the man beat him and his back's bleeding. He takes the girl's hand, and they run as fast as they can. It's so dark in the woods, and bugs are bitin' them all over, and she's still sleepy from the pills she took. They stop runnin' away when they get to a brick wall. It's too high! They can't climb over it!"

Gabe was becoming agitated again, his voice loud and frightened.

Nick said, "You aren't there, Gabe. You aren't there. You're just watching them, like a movie." When Gabe grew quiet again and his breathing calmed, Nick said, "What do they do then?"

"The boy grabs her hand and they run beside the wall, and then they see the cemetery and the white crypts, and they get scared. The girl sees a white cross in the moonlight, and she runs to it and thinks Jesus has come to save them. It's on top of the crypt, and the boy pushes her inside and tells her to hide there, to hide and not make a sound and he's gonna go get help and come back and get her. Then he runs as fast as he can into the swamp and tries to find somebody to help them."

When Gabe stopped his narrative, Nick hesitated, afraid to push him too far. "Did the man catch the boy?"

"He catches up to him and gets on top of him and chokes him and hits him in the face with his fists and hits him so long and so hard that the boy can't move anymore. Then he pushes the boy in the water and leaves him there in the dark."

"What happened to the little girl? Did she stay in the crypt?"

"He doesn't know! He doesn't know! He's got to get some-body and go back and get her! He's got to find her before the man gets her!"

When Gabe cried out and writhed restlessly on the couch, Claire ran to him and put her arms around him. Gabe clutched her and wept hard, wracking sobs into her shoulder. "Bring him back, Black! Bring him out of it! He's had enough."

Nick waited until Gabe calmed down a little, then he started to bring him out of the trance. "Gabe, listen to me. You aren't going to feel the pain, or the fear, or the cruelty committed against you or your little sister. You will not feel that, you will not remember that, you'll only remember how you escaped and if you ever saw the man's face or a fleur-de-lis carved into the porch banister. You will no longer feel guilt at surviving, Gabe. It was not your fault what hap-pened to your sister. It was not your fault what happened to your parents. None of it was your fault. You will know you did everything you could to save your sister, but the man was bigger and stronger than you. You did all you could. You were just a child. You will be able to talk to us about what you can remember, without feeling rage or sadness or hopelessness or helplessness. I'm going to wake you up now. When you open your eyes, you'll feel good. You'll feel safe and calm and relaxed and all the guilt you've been carrying on your shoulders all these years will fade away. I will count backwards from five, and you'll wake up and feel free and wonderful and whole again. Do you understand me, Gabe?"

Gabe nodded. Black began to count, and Gabe opened his eyes on cue. Claire said, "It's okay, Gabe. It's okay now. You did fine."

Leaning back against the sofa, Gabe said, "He wore masks the whole time. I never saw his face. He whispered in this terrible scary voice when he talked to us. He played cruel games with us. I got away, but Sophie didn't."

"Can you remember anything about the house, Gabe? Anything at all?" That was Jack, pushing him, distraught and appalled because he now knew what his own sisters had probably endured.

Claire said, "Did you see any kind of carving outside the house?"

"I saw the fleur-de-lis. I saw it when he was carrying me over his shoulder that first night and his flashlight moved across it when he climbed the steps. Is that what you're talking about?"

"You were held inside Rose Arbor," Nick told him. "I think that's pretty obvious now."

Gabe looked around at them. "Where's that?"

Claire said, "Jack owns it now. That fleur-de-lis is still on the post out front. I noticed it myself. It's big and hard to miss when you walk up the front steps."

Nick stood up. "Okay, now we're getting somewhere. Is there a cemetery on your property, Jack? Maybe we can find something out there." He hesitated and glanced at Jack and then at Gabe. "There may be graves out there. You both understand that?"

Jack looked repulsed, probably realizing he'd been living in the house where his baby sisters might have been tormented and murdered. But his face was set in stone. Claire shivered but looked determined.

Jack said, "I know exactly where that cemetery is. It's got the white wall around it, and it's close to the swamp, just like Gabe said. I duck hunt down there sometimes. The crypts are up on a slope that

overlooks where the river overflows and floods the low-lying land
at the back of our property."

"How do you feel?" Nick asked Gabe, handing him a bottle of
water.

Gabe took it and drank deeply before he answered. "It's strange.
Like a dream I was walking through. Not Sophie and me but two
little kids. I don't remember him hurting me anymore, the pain, I
mean."

"That's good. That's very good."

"Are you up to going out there, Gabe?" Jack asked.

Nick could tell Jack was going, come hell or high water, with
Gabe or without him.

"Yes. I'm going. Maybe I'll remember more once I'm there."

That was all they needed. Nick took his car and drove, and nobody
said much of anything all the way out to Rose Arbor. He stopped at
the front gate, punched in the code, and drove up to the house. When
they got out, Gabe looked up at the dark mansion. "It was here?" he
said, looking at Claire.

"Yes." She turned her flashlight up and focused it on the newel
post.

Gabe moved up the steps and ran his fingers over the deep
grooves. "This is what I saw."

Jack went inside and turned on the porch lights and foyer lights
and then flipped on a floodlight out at the fountain. When he came
back outside, Nick asked him how far it was to the cemetery.

"About a quarter of a mile, I guess. It's pretty much overgrown
woods and swampy areas now. Some of the crypts out there date as
far back as the 1700s."

They started off with Jack taking the lead. Gabe was able to keep
pace, probably due to an adrenaline surge and his need to know. The
night had gotten colder, and their path around the side of the house
was dark. They had flashlights, and they followed Jack down through
a stand of live oak trees. As they skirted the perimeter of his property,
both sides of their path were overgrown with dead and tangled vines
and thickets and wild ivy growing out of control. Lots of the gray
Spanish moss hung down and brushed their hair like ghostly fingers.
Startled birds fluttered out of their hidden beds in the bushes and

took wing up into the tree branches. Nick knew when they had neared the swamp because of the smell of the stagnant water and the sound of a nutria rat splashing into the water.

Up ahead of them, Jack stopped and shined his flashlight through the trees, a cone of smoky white light focused on a crumbling cemetery wall. "There. See the crypts? Some are destroyed, but a few of them are still standing."

They all focused their flashlights on the area that he indicated and swept them around like searching beacons at a movie premier.

"Does this look like the place, Gabe?"

He nodded. "Sophie tripped right here and fell down. That's when we heard him coming and panicked. So I dragged her up and we ran up there to the cemetery to hide."

Gabe started across the damp ground, and the rest of them followed, watching where they stepped on wet, spongy dirt that sank a bit under their weight. Then they saw the pale, ghostly crypts in the gloom. Many were crumbling from centuries of wind and rain and hurricanes. Others were covered with weeds and fallen branches. Gabe made his way up the incline to the closest crypt. It sat atop the ground and was about six feet high and eight feet long. He knelt and tried to tear away the weeds with his good arm until he uncovered a rotted wooden door.

"This is where I hid Sophie. Right here." His voice clogged tight, and he couldn't say anything else. He sat down on the ground, as if spent.

They gathered around him and focused their lights on the crypt's door. With some effort, Jack shoved back the rusty bolt on what was left of the splintered wood.

Gabe started to scramble inside, but Claire stopped him. "Let me, Gabe. You've done enough."

Bending down, she flashed her light around the interior and then moved into the dank dark place where poor little Sophie must have crouched in terror so many years ago. Nick squatted down and saw that there was nothing inside at all, no coffin, no moldering corpse, thank God. Before he could stop him, Gabe pushed past him and crawled in behind her. Nick and Holliday watched from the door and held their flashlights where they illuminated the interior. Claire and Gabe were brushing away leaves and gravel and scraping away dirt in search of anything that could help them. After a while, Claire glimpsed something buried in the dirt because she dug it out and held it up against the light. It was a necklace, crusted with grime from decades in the crypt when the water seeped up and turned the ground into mud. She brushed off the dirt as best she could and held it up to the light by its broken chain. When Gabe saw it, he grabbed it out of her hand and squeezed it in his fist. "Sophie got this crucifix the day he took us. For her birthday."

Claire put her arms around him, and they all watched as he gripped his little sister's necklace and wept for the innocent little girl that he had left behind in that crypt all those many years ago.

Chapter Twenty-eight

Their emotions were scraped absolutely raw, and it took some time to get themselves back under control, but they had to. Claire was certain now that they were standing on a serial killer's dumping ground. No telling how many bodies were buried under the moldy dirt of that ancient graveyard. Once Gabe was calm enough and Black was talking through it with him, she got on her phone and called Russ Friedewald. Jack told her that Rose Arbor was located inside St. James Parish so Russ would have to call his counterpart there and arrange a two-department task force to search for other victims. After she'd run their findings past him, Russ immediately ordered in the entire parish forensics team and all available detectives, replete with floodlights and recovery equipment.

By the time the sun came up, and a rolling blanket of ground fog wisped like smoke over the surface of the still green water and crept silently among the centuries-old crypts in the crumbling cemetery, the task force had already gathered and uncovered three small human skeletons. Everybody on scene feared they would find more before the day was done.

Black helped dig, and so did Jack, who wore a dead expression on his face. One that Claire couldn't stand to look at. Gabe had returned to the house, tired and too weak to help, unable to stand on his feet any longer. They toted buckets of cold dirt from the sunken graves amid the crypts, and she knew why Jack looked so determined. They all knew why.

Even so, when another skeleton was discovered, that of a young child found in a shallow grave only feet from where Gabe had left his sister, Jack was still not prepared when Nancy Gill brushed dirt off a scrap of rotted cloth. Tattered red fleece with the face of Rudolph on the front, the tiny red pom-pom still attached to his nose. Claire's heart ached when Nancy carefully lifted the shredded remnant of the nightgown with gloved hands and placed it on a sheet of evidence paper.

Jack stood as if frozen and stared down at his little sister's garment with such mute and terrible anguish that Claire took hold of his arm and tried to turn him away from the grave. "You should go inside, Jack. Let us do this."

Jack didn't answer. He didn't seem to hear her. Nobody said anything out of compassion for his shock and pain so the chatter of awakening birds was the only sound in the cool, early morning quiet. Suddenly, he fell to his knees beside the tiny skeletal remains, his fists clenched on his knees. Then he looked up at them again, and his eyes were so ice-cold, so deadly, that he was frightening to behold. His muscles were flexed into rock, and he was quivering with suppressed rage.

Concerned, Black put his hand on his Jack's back. He kept his voice very low. "You need to go back to the house, Jack. Just like Gabe did. You've seen enough. You've done enough. Come on, I'll go with you. We'll talk about it there."

"I'm not going anywhere."

Nancy and Claire exchanged worried glances, and after a moment, Nancy began digging again. Claire helped her, but Black stayed close to Jack, apparently afraid he was going to lose it at any minute. Ron Saucier staked out the new grave site, and then he slowly and methodically and expertly extracted a second small skeleton. It was the other twin, buried in her matching, ragged Christmas nightgown, an innocent child who had barely lived three years on the earth before a real-life bogeyman had crept into her house and taken her away forever. Now everything was eerie, dreadful, and intense, with everybody on the scene quiet and respectful of Jack's burgeoning grief.

Then, abruptly, after about ten minutes of watching Saucier and Nancy carefully remove the remains, and without a word to anyone, Jack stood up, turned around, and headed at a quick clip back to the house. Black watched him for a moment, glanced at Claire, and then went after him. After a little while, Claire walked back to the house, too, and found Black inside the foyer.

"How is he?"

"Not good, but he's holding up, I guess. I tried to prepare him for this when he hired Booker, but he was so determined to find out what happened to his sisters that he didn't realize how hard this was going to hit him. I think we need to stay with him. He's in the library."

Rose Arbor's library was downstairs, in the back and on the south side of the house. It was a large rectangular room with windows facing the backyard swimming pool. Polished cherrywood paneling and bookcases lined three walls. Jack was sitting behind a huge mahogany desk. His elbows were propped on the glossy surface, his face buried in his palms. A large Tiffany lamp, its edges decorated with open-winged dragonflies, was switched on and threw a circle of light on his hair. A large book lay on the desk in front of him.

Black motioned Claire over to a chair in front of the desk, but he remained standing. Claire could tell that he was very concerned about his friend. "Jack? Are you going to be all right? Can we get you anything?"

Holliday raised his face, and she knew instantly that he wasn't all right. Far from it. His eyes were red and swollen, his expression empty and forlorn. His words came out hoarse. "Now I know what happened. He probably did the same things to them that he did to Gabe and his sister. I can't stand thinking about it. It makes me sick to my stomach to think what they went through, the awful things he did to them. They were just babies, Nick. Innocent little babies."

Claire sat there and remembered her own dead child and what had happened to him and left the comforting to Black. Her own pain overtook her quickly, thinking about her darling Zach, with his blond curls and huge blue eyes and happy laugh. She tried to push it back behind the thick wall she'd constructed to keep herself sane. But this time she couldn't quite pull it off. Zach had only been two years old when he died in her arms. She shut her eyes and forcibly willed the image out of her head. Oh, God, she still missed him so much. She missed him every time she saw a toddler in a grocery store or heard a lullaby or saw a Pampers commercial or smelled Johnson's Baby

Powder. She would never get over it, never. She clasped her hands tightly together and tried desperately to force down the terrible grief overwhelming her.

Black said, "He's a monster, Jack. Rest assured, they'll get him. Sooner or later, they will get him."

"I should've believed Jenny when she came to me. I should've checked outside because he was out there, in our yard, just waiting for us to go to bed."

"Nobody could've known your sisters were in danger, not in their own home, in their own beds, on Christmas Eve. Your parents didn't know, either. Nobody knew. Don't blame yourself. It's not your fault. Jack, listen to me—it's not your fault."

Holliday did not respond, but it was easy to see that he was struggling with guilt and remorse, much as Gabe was. All their lives, they'd been affected by the murders in their families, senseless murders committed by the same savage killer. Decent people always blamed themselves. Claire had blamed herself for a lot of things, too, for many years until Black had come along and helped her work through some of it. But not all of it, not all of it.

Claire hesitated. She took a deep and bracing breath. It was going to take Jack months to come to terms with this horrible crime, maybe even years. She knew that full well. Right now, she needed to tell him what he wanted to hear. The more he heard it, the better off he would be. "Black's right, Jack. We're very close to him now. He's gonna pay for destroying your family. Hear me, Jack? He's not getting away with it, not anymore. We will get him. He won't ever do this to another little kid."

"I'm going to kill that fuckin' bastard. I want him dead. That's all I want. I want him dead. I want to do it myself and make him suffer the way they suffered."

"Yeah, we all do," Black answered in his quiet shrink mode. "But you're not going after him. Claire is on this case, and she'll find him. Just give her time, and she will find him."

"That's right, Jack. It's pretty clear now that this is the same guy who killed Madonna and Wendy, and we're getting close to him. I can feel it. It's just a matter of time."

Jack's jaw was clenched tight, his fists were clenched tight, his entire body was clenched tight. Helplessly, they stood by and watched him endeavor to pull himself together and rein in his thirst for vengeance. It took him a while. Both of them stayed with him, but Claire sat there and thought about the beautiful house around them. How it must have looked before, when it had been abandoned and the sadistic killer had kept children in the cellar and brought them upstairs to torment them, maybe in this very room. She could almost see their frightened faces and hear their terrified screams.

She wondered how many times it had happened throughout all the years gone by. How many little ones had cowered in that root cellar below their feet and heard the monster moving around upstairs and preparing his terrible games? Had he found another lair when Jack's grandfather had bought this house for his wife? Where was he taking his victims now? Was another child out there somewhere right now, screaming for help in some other dank cellar?

"I'm going to take them back to Colorado. I want them buried beside our parents."

"I think that's a good idea," Black said. "I'll go with you, if you want. We can take the Lear so you can have complete privacy."

More silence ensued, while Jack stared off into space. After a few minutes, he spoke again, and more calmly. "I couldn't remember exactly where this was, but I finally found it. Maybe it will help you, Claire."

Claire realized that he was talking about the book lying in front of him. It was an oversized volume, bound in expensive Moroccan leather, a rich maroon trimmed in gold. A filigree clasp held the pages together. There was no title or author's name.

"What is it?"

"My grandmother commissioned a history of this house when she bought it and began the renovations. Somebody owned this place when he kept them here. If this was where he came to commit his atrocities, somebody connected with this house has got to know something, remember something about him."

Claire thought about it a moment. "Yes, and I think Old Nat knows more than we think. I want to question him. He took care of this place for years, as far back as when Gabe's parents were young. Rene showed me a picture of them sitting out on the front steps, a bunch of kids when they were in high school. He said Old Nat was the one who let them hang around out here."

"The old man's been with my grandmother forever. That's all I know about him. He keeps to himself."

"Does he have a family?"

"I don't know. It never mattered to me who took care of this place. He was just here, grandmother's old caretaker. Eccentric, but harmless. At least, I thought he was."

"Is he from around here?"

"I don't know where he's from. Cajun, I guess. Do you really think he could've brought other victims out here?"

"He's had opportunity and he's been around for years. He could even be the killer. Or more likely, he could know who the killer is."

Black picked up the book and started turning the pages. "It says here that the foundation was laid in the mid-1780s. A Frenchman named Louis Bernard, who was a wealthy sugar planter, built this house for his new bride." He thumbed farther into the book. "Looks like it survived hurricanes and fires, and was used by Union troops during the Civil War. Okay, here we go. It says it fell into disrepair in the early 1940s, was boarded up and abandoned and then fell into ruin."

Claire moved closer and looked over his shoulder. Jack just sat and watched them. "Okay, this looks a lot like the picture at Rene's house. It shows the front gallery and the steps. This must be how it looked when your grandfather bought the place."

"Who did he buy it from?" Claire asked Jack quickly.

"I don't know."

"Well, somebody felt secure here, comfortable enough to lock up people in the cellar without any fear of getting caught."

"Here we go," Black said, "It says here that Jack's grandfather bought the property from a French family who moved down to Haiti. Says they just abandoned the house and immigrated to the islands."

Black looked down at Jack for a moment. Claire thought Jack looked way too shaky to stick around for this kind of discussion.

Apparently, Black did, too. "Okay, Jack, you need to go upstairs and lie down. Gabe's up there. I can give you something to help you rest. Let us handle this for now. When you're ready, we'll tell you everything you want to know."

"No way."

Claire frowned, but then she said, "I think everything points to Old Nat. He's been around for decades, and it sounds like he might've been squatting out here until your grandmother hired him on. And he overreacted way too much to my coming up to the house that first night. What was he afraid of? Do you think he's capable of murder, Jack?"

"I don't know him, like I said. He's always been out here, taking care of things. Just like Yannick's been doing over on St. Charles Avenue. He does his job, then he goes home, I guess. I don't keep up with either one of them."

"Where does he live?" Black asked.

"Back behind the property. Down close to the swamp. It's out in the other direction from the cemetery."

Claire said, "I'm going to go down there and talk to him. You two stay here."

"Yeah, right," said Black.

Claire didn't mind Black having her back. He was up to it and fully capable. And always armed, too, at least since he'd met her, which was always a plus. She trusted him implicitly. But Jack. Jack was teetering on the verge of completely falling apart. And he'd already vowed to kill the murderer.

"You're way too emotional, Jack. Back off. Leave it to the police."

He shook his head.

Claire tried again. "I think this guy is still killing, Jack. I think he's trying to manipulate us, right now. I don't know for sure it's Navarro, but I think it could be. Whoever he is, he also killed Madonna and Wendy, probably because they got a glimpse of him or heard his voice a long time ago. Like I said before, I need to interview Navarro, and I want to interview Yannick, too. There's something off with both of those guys."

They watched Jack walk to the back window and stare out over the heated swimming pool and winter garden. He spoke with his back to them. "Why now? Why would he start killing his surviving victims now?"

"It's like you said. He found out you hired Booker, and the two of you were getting too close to finding him. You talked to Madonna about this, right? Maybe he was afraid she remembered something that incriminated him. He had to feel threatened if he knew you had found her."

Claire did not want to wait. They were so close now, she knew it. "Think about it, Jack. Madonna dies, murdered and dumped down there where I recently started working, her tat identifying her as his victim. Then he goes after Wendy, two victims who got away. Then Gabe. All victims of his. Maybe he thought they'd find a way to ID him. He's clever. He's gotten by with one murder after the other for years. And he's still close by. He has to be to know all this stuff."

Jack turned around and faced her. "Old Nat's probably down at his house, right now. I'll get it out of him. Just give me five minutes alone with him."

"Yeah, and don't you think it's a little strange that he hasn't come up here to see what's going on? With all these police cars and this kind of commotion happening inside the grounds? He's the caretaker, your security man, for God's sake. He certainly jumped me and held me at gunpoint when I came out uninvited. So where is he?"

That did it. "I'm going with you. No, don't try to stop me, Nick. Nat works for me. He'll cooperate if I'm the one asking the questions. I can't sit here and do nothing. I cannot do it, damn it."

They didn't argue this time. Everything he had said was true.

Jack was chomping at the bit now, something akin to bloodlust in his eyes. "Let's go. I want this guy."

Claire put a halt to that quickly enough. "Zee's got to come along, and you've got to stand back and let us do our job. You don't have law enforcement credentials, either one of you. Stand back and let us handle it, or stay here. I mean it, both of you."

They both nodded agreement, albeit reluctantly. Then they left the house, returned to the crime scene, and picked up Zee. Claire also filled in Sheriff Friedewald, who had just arrived on scene. She told him where they were going, and why, and then asked if he wanted to come along. He okayed bringing Navarro in for questioning, but he elected to stay with Nancy, Ron, and the forensic team as they continued their recovery efforts. Jack stood waiting, with tight lips and tensed muscles, and stared down at the little bones on the evidence paper. Claire looked away from the torn and filthy Rudolph nightgowns, unable to bring herself to think about what might have ultimately happened to Jenny and Jill.

"Okay, Jack, lead the way. Where's he live?"

Jack took off toward the back of the house again, in a big hurry this time, and the rest of them tried to keep up. His strides were long and rushed as he headed past the pool and down through the formal garden behind the house. A bricked pathway meandered to the edge of the woods, and a dirt path brought them back down into the swampland.

"How far is it?" she asked.

"Not far. He's got a shotgun house down here."

Zee said, "What's goin' on, Claire? Who's this Navarro guy?"

She told him the basics and why they wanted to interview him, and Zee frowned but didn't comment further. When they finally reached the house, it was still fairly early in the morning, and there was plenty of ground fog hugging the path and obscuring their feet. They stopped on a little rise that led up to Old Nat's house. Zee and Claire pulled their weapons, held them down alongside their legs, ready. Just to be on the safe side.

Black pulled out his own nine-millimeter semiautomatic from the waistband at the small of his back and shoved a clip home with the palm of his hand like somebody who knew how to handle deadly weapons. And he did. She could attest to it.

"Better put that down, Black. You have a license to carry in Louisiana, I take it?"

"You bet I do, and I'm not putting anything down."

"Hey, no vigilante stuff is going to go down. You understand that, Black? This isn't the O.K. Corral. Same for you, Jack."

Both men stopped. Both men looked annoyed. They'd worked as a team, all right. Claire took a few minutes and listened and watched for movement around the house. It was a shotgun shanty, which she knew was a structure where the rooms were built in a straight line from front to back, so christened because if you fired a shotgun through the front door, the bullet would exit through the back door. Old Nat Navarro's home looked to have three rooms, four at the most, and it was built up about four feet off the ground on stilts. It was old and weathered gray with a rusted corrugated gray tin roof.

Claire turned back to Jack. "If he feels threatened, will he fire on us?"

"I don't think he's here. His truck's gone."

"What kind of truck?"

"Old model Ford, probably ninety-five, rusted white with a green stripe."

"Okay, I'm going first. Get behind me."

The men got behind her, if reluctantly. They started up the rise. Bushes and undergrowth crowded their way, and the path forced them to walk single file. It didn't look like snarky Old Nat had many visitors.

They stopped again at the edge of the cleared front yard. Claire kept expecting some ferocious guard dog to attack, but all was quiet, peaceful even. They moved cautiously toward the front porch, climbed the rickety steps, and stared down at the big pool of blood on the stoop and the smears indicating something or somebody had been dragged into the house. They faded against the wall on both sides of the door, Black and Claire on the right, Jack and Zee on the left. All of them except for Jack had their weapons held in readiness.

"Okay, we've got blood and drag marks and a possible victim inside. That should give us probable cause. Zee, you take the back and make sure nobody runs for it."

She waited while Zee made his way around the side of the shack.

"Let me do the talking," Claire said, keeping a watchful eye on Jack. He was definitely the loose cannon at the moment. "Black, you make sure Jack stays where he is. Hear that, Jack?"

They both nodded. Claire rapped on the door. "Police! Open up!"

Nothing but a blue jay screaming somewhere far away. No sign of life from inside. Nothing. Nada. Nobody home.

Claire knocked again. "If he's gone, we might ought to get a warrant, just to make sure."

"The hell with that," Jack muttered, and before anybody could move, he stepped forward and gave the door a violent kick. But he ducked back, which gave Claire a clue that it wasn't the first time he'd kicked down a door. Oh, yeah, he and Black had done this before, and together, and it probably hadn't been at Tulane University. But there were no shotgun blasts from inside, no sounds of an old man jumping out of his bed and heading for the hills, either.

"Stay out here," Claire ordered Jack. "I mean it."

Claire went in, stood with weapon poised to fire, back to the wall beside the door. It was very shadowy inside, but she could see all the way to the back door of the house. She hit the nearest light switch. Black joined her inside as Zee thrust open the back door and flipped on another light. He began to move through the back rooms, while they quickly searched the front of the house. When he yelled, "Clear," she sheathed her weapon. So did Black. Jack walked inside without an engraved invitation.

"We do have your permission to search this house, right, Jack?"

"You bet. And I own it, every stinking board and nail."

"Don't touch anything. Zee and I will do the search."

So, they put on gloves and protective gear and started looking around, all four of them. There was more blood on the floor, more evidence that somebody had been dragged inside. Who? Another victim that he kept captive? A child? There wasn't much else in the way of evidence, at least not until they converged in the bedroom. It was stark and empty, the bed made tight enough to bounce a quarter off it. It looked almost like a monk's cell. Claire hit pay dirt when she found the closet door locked with an old padlock.

"There could be a body inside there. Do we have your permission to break that lock, Jack?"

Before she could move, Jack had kicked the door open. No body, no blood, no Navarro, but there was a trunk on the floor, a military footlocker painted olive drab.

Zee pulled out a pocketknife and jimmied the lock. It didn't take him but a few seconds. When he jerked up the lid, they all stared down at the contents. Claire knelt down and found some old newspapers, mostly articles about missing children and unsolved murders, neatly clipped and encased in plastic. She sorted through them, and there were so many and from so many different cities that she felt her skin begin to crawl. "My God."

Jack picked up a fistful of trinkets, and Claire realized there were all kinds of jewelry, mainly children's stuff, pink plastic with little kittens or puppies or Strawberry Shortcake. She picked up a handful of colorful beaded necklaces, the kind thrown from Mardi Gras floats. There were pictures of children, most photographed while they were lying unconscious on a bed, eyes shut, portraits in death, or maybe still alive, just before they woke and found themselves in hell. Others were close-ups of his signature voodoo tat on their wrists.

Beside her, Jack was sorting hastily through the photographs, and when he made a strangled sound, she took the picture out of his hands. It showed a beautiful little blond-haired girl, wearing the Rudolph gown, her face waxen and white in death. Another was of her twin, also dead, so little and pale and still. Claire glanced through the rest of them, and then sat down hard on the floor when she found the one she was looking for. She stared down at sweet little Sophie's face, unconscious, long hair hanging down around her face, eyes shut, her arms outstretched and secured to a chair, the monster's trademark snakes and stars tattoo inked on her wrist.

"Oh, God, this makes me sick."

Black took the pictures and studied them, and Zee tossed the jewelry he held back into the locker. "We've got to get forensics back here. This stuff is god-awful."

"It looks like it was Navarro, all right," Black said.

Claire took a deep breath and pulled out her phone. "I'm putting out a BOLO on Navarro and his truck. You sure it's a ninety-five?"

While Claire talked to Russ, Zee picked up a boxed battery-operated tattoo gun. "We got him. We got the bastard. Let's call Rene, too, and have him put NOPD on alert for that truck."

Claire dialed up Rene's cell, got his voice mail right off the bat. He was on another call. "Call me, Rene. We got him. It's Navarro. We've got everybody down here looking for him. We need you to do the same in your jurisdiction. Call me back ASAP."

Then she called the Louisiana State Police and requested an alert and then turned to her silent companions.

Jack shook his head. "This guy lived here with me. We treated him like family, paid him a good salary, for God's sake. And all along, he was the one who killed everybody in my family."

Claire thought about Old Nat, how creepy he had been stepping out in the dark with his shotgun that night at Rose Arbor. He had known all along that she was looking for him. Now she wanted him. She wanted to question him, force him to tell her everything. She had a feeling that there was a lot more to these crimes than the evidence in the trunk indicated, a lot more victims, God only knew how many, and she wanted to know all of it.

Her phone rang. "Rene? You get my message?"

"Yeah, but Nat? That old guy? You sure it's him? I've known him forever. I can't believe he's some kind of serial killer."

"We found evidence in his house that incriminates him."

"What evidence?"

"Pictures of dead children, pictures of Jack's little sisters. There's one of Gabe. And Sophie, too."

"Oh, my God. Don't let Gabe see them. It'll kill him."

"I'm not going to, not yet."

"Anything else?"

"We found his tattoo gun, and there was a blood trail inside the house, which might mean another victim."

"Shit. No body, though?"

"Not yet. We haven't searched the grounds, but we're going to."

"Do you know where he might be headed?"

"I'd guess the airport or the Mexican border. How quick can you get your people searching for him? Chances are he's still in the area."

"I'll put out our BOLO right now. I'll get back to you in a minute. I'd like to see that evidence once you get it catalogued. I can't believe that old man is capable of this kinda sicko stuff."

They hung up, and she put all those children's treasures back into the trunk and tried not to think of the helpless little kids who had last worn them. Souvenirs of murder, items that he'd probably gotten out often to handle as he relived his grotesque crimes with perverted pleasure. He was a monster, all right.

Chapter Twenty-nine

By that evening, the recovery of the skeletal remains was nearing completion. Despite the fact that all Louisiana law enforcement agencies were out looking for Nat Navarro, there had been no sign of him or his truck. And although they attempted at some length to dissuade Jack Holliday from staying the night at Rose Arbor, he refused to leave. So Black decided to spend the night there with him, unwilling to leave Jack alone in the house where his sisters had probably been tortured and murdered. Claire drove Gabe home to the French Quarter and stayed in town with him, as completely exhausted mentally and physically from the day's events as everybody else. Neither Jack nor Gabe was handling the dark awful truth all that well. Black ordered them both sedatives to help them sleep. Gabe took the pills; Jack would not. Gabe had done way too much, and he was paying for it with headaches and dizziness and renewed pain in his arm and shoulder.

Jack Holliday was simply devastated, emotionally, psychologically, every way. He had suffered enough for one day. Even worse, he still wore that deadly look in his eyes, as if he was looking for any reason to beat somebody senseless. He was going through now what Gabe had had years to come to terms with. It was going to take him a long time to learn to live with what had been done to his sisters. Hopefully, those lethal feelings would eventually fade. Seeing his little sisters lying there in front of him in skeletal form must have been the worst thing possible for a protective big brother to bear, especially since he blamed himself for their abduction. Claire had suffered many heartbreaking things throughout her life, but even she could not imagine watching the remains of a beloved family member being dug out of the dirt. It was a living nightmare, and understandably, Jack was not handling it well. All he wanted was revenge, and that was all he would want for a very long time.

Once back home on Governor Nicholls Street, Claire left a heavily sedated Gabe in Julie's capable hands and retired to her own bedroom. She was just so weary that she could barely function herself, but she gave Black a call just to make sure everything was still all right at Rose Arbor. The way things were going, it wouldn't take long for something else horrible to happen. He sounded beat, having been up all night, too, but he told her Jack was sleeping, and that he wished she were there because his bed was big and empty. They hung up, and she showered and put on one of Black's black-and-gold New Orleans Saints T-shirts and climbed into bed with Jules Verne. She didn't last long after that, and her last thought before falling asleep was of the sight of that ragged Rudolph nightgown and the tiny little bones nestled inside it.

Much later, she roused blearily to somebody insistently ringing the doorbell and banging on the front door. She raised herself on her elbows, realized that it was still dark outside, and turned to see what time it was, still groggy as all get out. Then she remembered everything that had happened out at Rose Arbor and jumped up in alarm. Dressing quickly in soft black sweats and Nikes, she armed herself, certain something else bad had gone down, just as she had feared it would. Outside in the wide white marble hallway, she looked toward the guest room where Gabe was sleeping. Julie peeked out the door of another room, but Claire didn't waste time talking to her. She ran to the grand spiral staircase that wound down to the entry hall, hoping they had captured Nat Navarro before he had fled the country.

Juan Christo was already at the front door, barefoot and wearing jeans and a white T-shirt that showed a lot of serious muscles. With a loaded shotgun in his hand, he was gardener no more, security guard mode on and alerted to protect the house and the people inside it. It occurred to her then that maybe Juan was in Black's little covert club, too. She flung open the French door and then the outside louvered street door and found Zee standing there, looking extremely anxious.

"Did we get him?"

"No, but Rene thinks he knows where he's holed up. C'mon, no time, we gotta go, right now. I've been tryin' to call. Why didn't you pick up?"

"I guess I was asleep. I didn't hear my phone ring. Where's Rene think he is?"

"Some kind of fishing camp out in the swamp somewhere."

"I better call Black and tell him where I'm going. Russ, too."

"No time. Rene says Navarro's not gonna stay there long so he's already down at the *Bayou Blue* readying his boat. He says we can get there a lot quicker by water. I already talked to the sheriff. He's okay with us goin' out there."

"Is something wrong?" That was Julie's voice, upstairs. She was leaning over the polished mahogany balustrade and looking down at them.

"No, we've got a lead on the killer and we're going after him. Don't tell Gabe, okay? It'll just upset him. I don't know when we'll be back."

Juan was frowning. "I think Nick's gonna wanna know you're headed out there."

"Yeah, I know. I'll call him on the way to the boat."

She headed out the door and got into Zee's car, where he'd double-parked it out on the street. "Friedewald's okay with this? You sure?"

"Yeah, I talked to him a minute ago. He said to find you and go out there with Rene. Russ's goin' in with Saucier and some guys down in Lafourche from the police-boat dock. Rene told them where to meet up and coordinate before we approach the place. They're bringin' us Kevlar vests for the takedown."

"Sounds like a plan. Let me get my rifle out of the car."

"Well, hurry it up. Rene said he's not gonna wait long for us to show up."

When she got back, rifle in tow, he was already sitting in the Jeep with the motor running. It took two minutes flat to get to the boat with no traffic to fight, and the *Bayou Blue* stood dark and silent in the night. Rene was waiting for them out front, and they parked and ran after him to where his boat was tied up at the *Bayou Blue*'s stern. Rene's boat turned out to be one of those long, sleek racing boats that she'd heard he used in speed competitions out on Lake Pontchartrain, but it looked like it had a shallow enough hull to negotiate the bayous. Clyde had mentioned that he and Rene sometimes took it downriver to the Gulf to fish offshore. It was sleek and fast and powerful and fairly new. It should get them downriver in a big hurry.

Rene stopped under one of the dock's dusk-to-dawn lampposts. He looked excited but pretty nervous, too. "C'mon, hurry it up and get in and put on your life preservers. If he's where I think he is, he ain't gonna stay there long. I just hope to hell I'm right. Friedewald and Saucier and the other guys are comin' in from the other side. Saucier's from down there and he knows where to meet us. If Nat sees us comin', they're gonna intercept him if he tries to run."

Rene had already untied the moorings, and he jumped down inside the boat, moving with swift and controlled energy, aware they were very close to capturing a notorious serial killer. Apparently, he liked to catch the bad guys as much as Claire did. And this was the perpetrator who had killed Bobby and Kristen. Rene had a dog in this fight, too, just like the rest of them. She and Zee quickly climbed down and found seats in the stern while he took the controls and expertly maneuvered them away from the dock and out into the dark swirling river. Then he opened it up and they flew downriver toward the bayous at breathtaking speed.

The boat skimmed and bounced over the waves, almost too fast for Claire's comfort. She held on to a handle mounted on the starboard side. Zee was doing the same thing on the port side, but they were making good time, to be sure. She admired the craft because everything about it was state of the art. If she remembered correctly, Rene had always loved boating and being out on the water. The boat was a beauty, all right, and Black would probably have to buy one for himself, the minute he saw it. She needed to call him, but it was too loud with the roar of such a powerful motor. Rene handled the controls with ease, and he had very sophisticated navigational equipment. There was a GPS system like Black had in his boats at the lake, and there was a satellite phone for when he was out on the ocean. She could see Rene, standing under the canopy, his eyes intent on the river ahead. She hoped he knew the snags and shallows well enough to go that fast. The Mississippi River was a swift and treacherous waterway, even for those trained to navigate with maps and experienced knowledge of the twists and turns and shifting currents. If they hit a sandbar at such high speed, they were all goners.

Claire knew that they would pass Rose Arbor somewhere along the way. She hadn't seen it yet, but it was very dark. At one point, she pulled her way up to Rene and yelled into his ear. "Where exactly is this place, Rene? You sure you can find it at night?" Her words went whirling off behind them in the wind.

Rene nodded and yelled back, but he kept his eyes on where the boat's headlights illuminated the water in front of him. "You know how well I know the bayous, cher. I've been thinkin' about where he might go and then I remembered that he took Clyde and me out to this fish camp once. And guess who went with us? Guy by the name of Al Christien. Madonna's and Rafe's daddy. Turned out he was a junkie, just like his kids."

Claire said, "Okay, just so you know how to get us there."

Rene nodded again, and Claire made her way back to her seat in the stern.

Not long after that, Rene cut the speed and eased the sleek craft off the river and into a narrow bayou, where live oaks dripped with the ever-present spooky gray strands of Spanish moss.

Now that the noise level was down, Zee said, "How far now, Rene?"

"Out pretty deep, but it shouldn't take us long. He's out there. I feel it in my gut."

Zee's nerves were on edge, too. He kept taking out his gun and checking it over. The two men were beginning to make Claire nervous. "Okay, so where're we supposed to meet up with Friedewald? A lot of things can go wrong out here in the dark. We're headed out in the middle of nowhere. I don't wanna lose this guy again. This could be our only chance to take him alive."

"If he's there, we'll get him," Rene said, fierce with determination.

He was a lot more certain than Claire was. She propped the rifle across her knees, as they slowly motored out through pitch darkness, the still night pressing down on them like a physical cloud of black. It felt primordial, as if they were the only ones left on earth. Claire moved up to the cockpit and asked Rene if she could use his sat phone. He nodded, and she punched in Black's number and told him what was going down. He didn't like it, of course, not one bit, and wanted to know exactly where she was and asked her about a zillion other questions, but she didn't give him time to start a harangue and told him not to worry, that they had plenty of backup, and that she'd call him as soon as they got Navarro into custody. Then she hung up, but truth be told, she did wish he were there, he and the rest of his cloak-and-dagger little A-Team.

After that, she just sat silently and worried about Rene's plan. After all, Navarro was a practiced killer and obviously very good at what he did. He would be watching all approaches to the island where he had his camp. The sound of their motor alone would echo a long way over the sluggish water. They should've waited till day-break. It would have been safer, and they could have seen their target better. She was surprised Russ Friedewald hadn't insisted on that.

The moon suddenly came out of the clouds, dappling dim light through the limbs overhead. This helped Claire get her bearings a bit, but it wouldn't provide much light once they proceeded deeper into the bayous. There would be cypress trees overhead, obscuring the sky. They were already entering the narrow bayous, where the gray moss draped down almost to the surface, and Rene had to take the boat between trees and stands of willows. But she knew for a fact that Rene had fished these back bayous practically all his life. She'd just have to trust him to get them there and back safely. Black was pissed off, big time, she had no doubt of that, but he couldn't expect to babysit her night and day. And he couldn't tag along every time she went out on police business. He'd just have to live with it. Hell, maybe he should join the force. He had the skills.

In the dim yellow lamp up front, she could see the boat's prow cutting through the thick green algae smothering the surface. It looked like smooth olive-colored icing. Gnats and mosquitos buzzed and darted around the light like square dancers. She watched an alligator slide off a half-submerged log and sink underneath the water, probably to follow their boat in hopes of a midnight snack. She liked the bayous that had running currents, like the one where the houseboat had been moored, but she did not like these deep, stagnant swamps with their deadly inhabitants. It was a scary place at night. It was a scary place in the daytime.

But Rene was handling the boat with skill, very slowly negotiating their course between cypress knots and mossy logs and scummy water, and the clinging coarse fingers of the moss. Both Rene and Zee appeared completely comfortable now, both of them having been born and bred in the bayous. She hadn't been, and she did not like the way the gators underneath logs and root wads watched them with slitted yellow eyes that reflected and glowed in the boat's light. She just wished they'd get there, already. She wished again that Black had come along. Then she caught herself and shook her head. Was she growing dependent on the guy, or what? She wasn't so sure that was a good thing. Besides, all three of them were armed to the absolute hilt. So was their backup team. Navarro's only chance was to run so they had to be careful not to alert him before they went in.

As they slid through the murky water, she thought of Navarro's little victims. Had they been taken through this same dark water, on their way to hell on earth and a shallow grave? Had they passed some of these tin-roofed shacks built on stilts that Rene took them alongside now and then? Black had a friend who lived out this way, an old man by the name of Aldus. She'd met him once, several years ago, when she hadn't trusted Black as far as she could throw him. She had pretended she didn't know much about the bayous or the swamp at that time to throw him off, just in case he was planning to take her out into the deep bayous and slit her throat or shoot her down. She smiled, thinking how strange all that seemed now, the way they'd met and everything that had happened since they'd been together.

Most of the people who lived this far from the beaten track followed old traditions and spoke with the thick Cajun French patois. Good people for the most part, at least the ones she'd met through Clyde and Rene and Zee and Black—men and women who minded their own business and raised their families, without interference from the crowded outside world. Tonight, so late, nobody was stirring. Not that there were many human beings around. Every shack they passed was dark and silent, as if hiding and waiting for something awful to happen. A sense of foreboding washed over Claire. She took a deep breath and tried to shake it off. She was spooked, all right, and she'd better get over it fast. The fish camp couldn't be too much farther.

She was right. Only minutes later, Rene cut the motor completely and they glided silently through the torpid water. He cut the lights and lowered his voice. "The camp is right up there ahead of us. We need to paddle in the rest of the way. Zee, grab that oar back there and help me."

Claire let her eyes adjust to the dark. The moon was obscured now by the overhanging branches above them, and it colored the moss over their heads with a peculiar silvery glow. Shadows crouched and loomed everywhere like the monsters in her nightmares. She could barely make out Zee's back where he sat only a couple of feet away from her.

Rene was whispering. He sounded excited. "There it is. See it, over there on that island, just to the right? I knew I could find it again."

Zee paddled with steady, deep strokes that matched Rene's. Claire glanced around, still trying to keep her bearings, just in case anything went wrong. She didn't like to rely on others. And to move in this close to their target, without their backup in place was risky in her opinion. She didn't like it. She didn't like anything about this whole maneuver. They should've waited until dawn. Her pulse started pounding, warning her to stay alert and in no uncertain terms. Something else was bugging her, too. Navarro had gotten away with some of the most heinous of crimes, and for decades, so he had to be one clever guy. He'd be looking for anybody approaching by boat. He would be waiting for them. She had no doubt. And she didn't want to run into an ambush by a psychopathic, deadly, criminal genius.

She kept her voice down very low. "Rene, listen, I don't think this's such a good idea. We can't see well enough to take him down. Where are we supposed to meet the others?"

"Be cool, cher. We aren't goin' in yet. We just gettin' a look-see at the place. He may not even be out here. This might be a wild goose chase."

But she wasn't cool with it. Rene had a reckless streak, always had. She remembered that about him. She also recalled times when Bobby LeFevres had gotten aggravated at him for something or other concerning police procedures. But Rene wasn't stupid, either, not by a long shot, and he was a long-tenured, highly decorated NOPD police officer. He wouldn't do anything that would put them in danger.

Claire could make out the roofline of the cabin now. As they glided ever closer, they picked up the sound of music, a catchy Cajun tune drifting out over the water. It sounded like a portable radio. Okay, now that made her feel a little better. The music would block out any sounds they made in their approach, and they were proceeding cautiously and quietly. It also probably meant Navarro thought he was safe and that nobody could find him hidden this deep in the swamp.

Still, her sixth sense was screaming bloody murder in her head, telling her something's wrong, something's wrong, fight or flight, do it, do it now, don't wait. All her muscles were tensed up, ready to be attacked. Zee put aside the paddle and picked up her rifle and held it pointed toward the island. She wasn't the only one who was jumpy about going in after Nat Navarro on their own.

Now the moonlight was filtering through the trees on the small island, just enough to see that the old fishing camp looked like a cabin and a small barn and maybe a shed or two, all built up well off the water on dry land. From what she could tell in the heavy gloom, the house looked gray and weathered and ramshackle, as if it had been sitting out there for a very long time. It had a front yard of sorts. She kept her eyes peeled for a watchdog, or worse, a pack of growling pit bulls. Most swamp Cajuns had coon dogs for hunting. But there was no barking, no people, and no sign of alarm. Just the snappy music, blaring out over the swamp.

To her chagrin, Rene didn't stop. He kept on paddling, hell-bent to take this guy down himself, right now when Navarro wasn't expecting it. That was his plan—had been from the beginning, no doubt—to get the man who killed Bobby and Kristen himself. But they should have proceeded to the rendezvous point and met up with the others. On the other hand, she knew he was probably right in his assessment. The three of them had a better chance of sneaking up on Navarro than a whole crew of law enforcement officers in a flotilla of boats.

When the bottom of the hull finally scraped into the mud of the shallows and lurched to a stop, Claire pulled her Glock nine-millimeter out of her shoulder holster. Zee already had the rifle up at his shoulder and aimed at the front door. She wondered if Zee had ever stormed a house when he'd worked narcotics. She hoped so. Weapon in hand, Rene climbed out first and silently waded past Claire and out onto the bank. Claire sat rigid and on edge, waiting for all hell to break loose.

It didn't. The music played on. All cheerful and happy like they were going to a party with all their friends. Again, Claire's warning antenna stood up and whooped and hollered like crazy. Rene signaled by pointing his forefinger for them to follow him. Zee got out first and waited for Claire to ease into the water and wade up beside him. "I don't like this," he whispered. "Something's not right."

"Rene wants to take this guy down himself. For Bobby and Kristen and Gabe, I guess. I can understand that, but I'm creeped out, too. This is pretty risky."

But it was too late now to change course. Rene was already moving stealthily up toward the house. So she and Zee spread out about ten yards apart and moved slowly toward the front porch, ready for anything.

Chapter Thirty

The minute Claire hung up on him, Nick Black violently cursed under his breath. He tried to call her back but couldn't get through. Why the hell were they going to try to take Navarro down in the dead of night? That was just stupid. They should've waited for daybreak. He finally got ahold of Russ Friedewald on the phone and listened while he told him where the rendezvous point was and that they were well manned and well armed, so they would be fine.

Nick thought otherwise. Jack Holliday was slouched in a chair beside him, just staring at the burning logs. He had refused sedatives or even Nick's urging to go on up to bed, so Nick sat up with him. Now Nick was glad he had. As Nick explained the situation in terse and angry words, Holliday began to frown.

"What the hell are they thinking? They must not know those swamps out there, if they think he can't get away in the dark."

"You still have that boat docked down on the river?"

"Yeah, gassed and ready to go."

"Does it have GPS tracking?"

"Yeah."

"Will it pick up a satellite phone's location?"

"Yeah. It's the best they got."

"Good. We're going in, too. I don't care what they say. Claire called from Rene's phone. We ought to be able to trace its signal and find them easy enough."

Holliday was up on his feet before Nick's words faded. "Let me get my weapons."

"Well, get as many as you can carry. And make it quick."

As soon as Jack got back with the firepower, Nick armed himself, so pissed off at Claire that he could barely contain it. She ought to know better than going into the deep swamp alone at night to apprehend a killer; in fact, she probably did. Why her superiors had decided to do something so stupid was the question. Thank God Jack had a boat handy, because they sure as hell couldn't get out there by land.

The front steps of Navarro's cabin were made out of stacked bricks and old boards, but it was sturdier than it looked. They climbed to the porch without making a sound. The door stood wide open, and Claire could see a flickering light inside, probably from an oil lamp or an electric lantern. She doubted if there was electricity this far from civilization.

Zee already had his back against the wall on the left side of the door, the rifle barrel pointed up but ready to fire. Rene took the other side of the entrance and motioned for Claire to get behind him. She hesitated, her training telling her that one of them should be covering the back door of the house, but she pressed back against the wall close behind Rene. Rene had been a police officer a lot longer than she had. He knew what he was doing. She hoped to God he did, anyway, because she was as uncomfortable as hell with all of it.

Once she was in place, Rene took a quick peek around the door-jamb and then ducked back. He nodded, put a forefinger to his lips. He pointed to the door and then to Zee, and then at each of them, indicating that Zee would go first, then Claire, and then Rene. Adrenaline surged up out of control, her heart thumping wildly, as they watched Rene give the usual silent finger count: one, two, three. Then they burst inside, high, low, high, weapons drawn and out in front, and they found Old Nat Navarro in there, all right. But he was sitting in a high-backed chair, bound and gagged, a neat black bullet hole in the center of his forehead, dried blood covering his open eyes, his thick-lensed spectacles hanging off one ear. Blood and brain matter were spattered all over the wall behind him, and more blood bloomed out like a red chrysanthemum on the front of his white dress shirt. Claire's weapon faltered slightly, and she turned shocked eyes on Rene.

Rene looked pleased. He was smiling. Zee walked quickly over to Navarro, still looking around the room for anybody who might jump them. Before he could turn around again, a gunshot rang out, a deafening blast that filled the small room with noise and smoke and the caustic smell of cordite. Zee was hit somewhere in the back and went down hard on his knees. Wounded and groaning, he fell on his face and didn't move.

Claire went down in a protective crouch, weapon up and searching out the shooter, but it was Rene holding the gun, the barrel still smoking. Stunned, she quickly got him in her sights, her hands shaking out of control—however, Rene had already lunged at her, fast and hard and low. He anticipated her shot and dodged the slug, slamming his gun butt down so hard on her arm that she felt a bone crack. Pain burned up to her shoulder and her fingers went numb. Her weapon dropped to the floor, and then Rene was there, kicking it away. She clawed at her ankle for the .38 snub, but he came at her again just as she got it out, hitting her hard in the temple with his weapon. The blow sent the gun spinning out of her injured hand and dropped her to her knees and straight into Navarro's corpse, overturning the chair. Frantic for cover, she jerked the table's legs, knocking it over and trying to use it for a shield. When the radio and the lantern sitting atop it hit the ground and scattered batteries everywhere, the loud music died and the room plunged into utter darkness.

Claire scrambled on her hands and knees toward the open front door, her mind reeling with confusion, hardly cognizant of her injured arm. She burst through and onto the porch and took a flying leap into wild bushes lining the front of the house. The moon had disappeared behind clouds again, and she staggered into the dark, trying to shroud herself in the deep shadows. She cradled her injured arm against her breast, feeling the pain now, trying to understand what had happened. Rene? Was he the killer? How could that be? And why? Why?

"Time to come out and play, *chère*. We gonna have us some big fun. You all mine now. My favorite li'l girl's come back home."

Oh, God, Rene *had* done it, murdered all those innocent people, all those little kids. Rene was the monster who had gunned down Bobby and Kristen in cold blood and whipped and abused Gabe and killed Sophie. Desperate to get away from him, she moved deeper into the undergrowth at the edge of the small yard, trying not to make any noise as she inched away from his taunting voice. Her forearm was broken; she could feel two bones in her wrist scraping together each time she moved it. The pain was so terrible that she almost passed out.

She ground her teeth together, her chest heaving with shock and nausea and fear for Zee. Oh, God, he might already be dead or lying in that cabin slowly bleeding to death. She stayed hunkered down, trying to think what she could do, how she could get back to her weapons. Or the boat. That was where the sat phone was. She had to call for help. Oh, God, help would never make it in time, not with Rene already stalking her.

Rene was out in the yard with her now, coming her way. He had his big police-issue flashlight and was swinging it back and forth in great arcs of bright light, spearing the darkness in search of her. He was yelling her name. Maybe Russ and the others could hear him. They had to be getting close to the island by now. Or maybe, she thought with renewed horror, maybe they weren't coming at all. Maybe he'd given Saucier the wrong coordinates, maybe they were somewhere very faraway, just sitting and waiting for them to show up. Oh, God, they weren't coming. Rene wouldn't have told them where he was. She had to find a way out herself. But maybe they'd heard the gunshot; it had to have reverberated for miles across the bayous.

Rene had calmed down and was calling out to her. "You just wouldn't let it go, would you, Annie? Just had to keep diggin' and diggin' into Madonna's case. You just had to solve it yourself, right? That's why I put your face on that damn voodoo doll, so you'd back off. Hell, I thought Russ'd pull you off the case right then and there, but no, no, you had to talk him outta it and keep comin' after me. You've caused me more fuckin' trouble than you'll ever know. So, now, here we are, just you and me, and now I've got to get rid of you. But first, we're gonna have some fun together. You owe me that, you pretty li'l bitch."

Claire kept easing back away from his voice. Her only chance was to make it back inside the house and find her weapons, or get to Zee's rifle. She didn't think she could make it to the boat. It was sitting right out in the open. At the moment, it seemed that Rene only wanted to mock her, so she played his game, if only to distract him from going back inside and finishing Zee off. "So you took Gabe? Killed Bobby and Kristen? You told me you loved them. They treated you like family, you bastard."

Before her words faded, she sprinted back toward the rear of the house, hoping Rene would change his course and follow her voice. She had to get her weapons, had to kill him before he killed her. Then his voice floated back to her, this time in a terrible, grotesque whisper.

"I see you, li'l girl. Come to Daddy now. Know what, Annie? I wanted you the most back then when you lived with them. You were the cutest little thing with all that blond hair and those great big blue eyes that seemed to see right through all my lies, and you had lots of spunk in you. You're the one I was gonna take, you and Gabe, not poor little Sophie. That kid didn't have a bit of fight left in her after about an hour with me and my games. But you, Annie, you woulda given me all I could've handled. Too bad they moved you out before I could get you. And now, lookee look, here you are, at my mercy, after all."

Now Rene was moving somewhere between her and the backyard, so she took off at a hard run and headed for the boat, holding her injured arm up against her side. Maybe she could draw him away from Zee. But Zee was probably already dead. Rene had shot him point-blank in the back. Then she realized that Rene was going to blame everything on Nat, and maybe even Zee. Say they were the killers, had done the murders, had killed her before Rene could shoot them dead.

Halfway down to the boat, she heard Rene's footsteps thudding hard on the ground not far behind her. Then a shot rang out, and a bullet whizzed past her head, missing her by inches. He was going to kill her. A second shot rang out and she took a leap off the bank into the cold, stagnant, foul-smelling water and tried to swim under the surface out of his gun range.

Her broken arm was useless, but she kicked her feet as hard as she could and tried to use her good arm to propel her into deeper water. She could hear slugs peppering the water behind her. Somehow she made it to a thick growth of lily pads and hyacinths and came up in the middle of them, her lungs screaming for air, terrified when she heard a splash nearby as something heavy slid into the water. Oh, God, it was a gator, it had to be. She sucked in air, frantically treading water with one hand while struggling to stay quiet, but there was an alligator, several of them, gliding around only yards away, barely discernible in the moonlight.

On the bank, Rene was jumping into the boat. Within seconds, the motor cranked, and he was heading straight at her. When his spotlight pinned her location in the water, she dove again, but the water was barely over her head and her chest hit the thick layer of cold mud on the bottom as the boat went above her, the blades narrowly missing her back.

She surfaced again and pressed herself against the trunk of a cypress tree where the boat or the gators couldn't easily get at her. She gasped for air, one arm hanging limply, and tried to hold on to the rough bark with her other arm, staying almost submerged in the water, but then his spotlight found her again. Rene was upon her within seconds, cutting the motor and leaning over the side of the boat, the oar raised high in both hands. The last thing she saw was the paddle coming down hard at her head and then everything went dark.

A Very Scary Man

Rene had been right about Annie, or maybe he should say Claire Morgan. She had put up one hell of a fight before he finally got her under his control. As he carried her limp body over his shoulder out back to his playhouse, he had to admit that if he hadn't injured her arm with that first blow, she just might have gotten the better of him. He laughed as he dumped her in the corner, where he'd set up his altar in honor of Papa Damballah. His god was with him once again. He'd come out on top, even when he was pitted against two trained police officers. But the real fun had yet to begin.

Quickly he strapped Annie into the chair that he used for tattooing. He bound her good and tight so she could never get loose. He couldn't take any chances, not with her. She was too damn resourceful. That was why he was going to keep her around for a while. Friedewald and the others would never find them. Even if they did, all he had to do was set up the scene in advance. Say it was Nat. Nat had killed Claire and Zee. And Rene had killed him. It would work out just fine, either way. But Claire was going to have to experience his maze of terror before he got rid of her. He'd dreamed for years for a chance to have her in his clutches, and now here she was, definitely at his mercy. He loved it. He absolutely loved it.

Once she was secured in place, nice and tight, and he'd lit all the candles around her, he hurried back to the house. Zee was still lying there and bleeding all over the floor. But he didn't want him to die, either, not quite yet. So he carried him back to the barn and stretched him out on the floor in front of the candles. He pulled off the guy's jacket and shirt and examined his wound. It was pretty god-awful bad, but not fatal. Rene was a good shot, and he'd purposefully avoided hitting any major internal organs, wanting a double helping of victims for his maze.

Dipping up a bucket of water, he sloshed it over Zee. God, the guy was covered in blood. That wouldn't do. Once he had him fairly well cleaned up, he did the same thing to Annie. She was covered in green slime, her clothes sodden and nasty. He'd have to take them off her later, after he'd inked her arm.

Standing up again, Rene moved up to the altar table and picked up his needle and thread. He stood there a moment, looking down at his two playthings, considering whether he should stitch up their eyes and mouths now or wait until later, after he was finished tormenting them. He decided to wait because he wanted to see them terrified and panicked in the intricate metal prison he'd built. Of all the people he'd taken before, they were the most likely to find their way out, but he didn't think they could, not injured the way they were. Still, it would create some amusement for him. That was the important thing.

Putting on his reading glasses and carefully threading a needle, he knelt beside Zee and liberally doused his wound front and back with Betadine. Then he pierced the ragged edges of the torn skin and began a neat row of stitches. It wasn't going to help much, but it would stop some of the bleeding. He turned his young detective friend over and quickly closed up the exit hole. It was larger with more tissue damage, but he managed to do it well enough. He wrapped Zee's torso with gauze bandages and re-dressed him so he wouldn't die too soon from exposure. It was very cold inside the maze, it being metal, and all. He wanted Zee alive in there with Claire so she'd have to worry about getting her partner out, too, before he died. Rene wanted her to suffer. She had caused him all kinds of grief, really rocked his safe little world, and now she was going to die hard.

Once he finished with the wound, he quickly inked his Veve on Zee's wrist. It didn't take long. Rene had lots of practice drawing it by now. But marking Claire was certainly everything he'd hoped it would be. Such a famous detective as she was purported to be, and now she was completely under his power. He laughed and picked up his brand new tattoo gun again. He had taped her arms palms up, just under the elbow, so that he could get to her wrist more easily. He felt around her narrow left wrist, and when he touched the spot where he intended to start, her body involuntarily flinched with pain. So he'd broken a bone, just as he'd intended. Well, good. But he'd have to splint it so she'd have a fighting chance to compete in his games inside the maze.

As he started inking the first snake on her uninjured arm, her eyes fluttered and then opened a little. She was groaning now, and in agony, it sounded like. He stopped and took hold of her hair and jerked her face up so that he could get down into it. "Hello, there, li'l sweet pea. How you feelin'?"

"What . . . ?"

She was much too groggy for him to have much fun goading her, but he put his mouth against her ear so she'd hear him. "Welcome to hell, darlin'. We are just gonna have so much fun after I get your tat on. You ready to fight, huh?"

"Rene? What . . . ?" She tried to move, but he'd secured her far too well for that. She couldn't move a muscle.

"Just sit still and conserve your strength. You gonna need it, li'l girl. So be patient and hold still. We got ourselves all the time in the world."

Rene let her head drop down again and started in on the second snake. He wanted hers to look especially good, not that anybody would ever see it. Chuckling to himself, he hunched over her arm, eager now to get her inside his maze. Oh, yeah, let the games begin.

Chapter Thirty-one

When Claire finally forced her eyes open, she saw nothing but black. The first thing she felt was extreme nausea rolling around in her stomach, as if she was going to throw up. Swallowing it down, she tensed all over, somehow aware that she was in mortal danger. Then she felt the awful pain in her left wrist and moaned out loud with it. She found where it hurt with her fingers and realized there was a splint taped to her arm. Shivering all over, she felt as if she was freezing and realized that her hair and her skin were soaking wet. Then, with shock, she realized that she was totally naked.

Then, in one horrifying instant, she remembered everything that had happened, all of it coming at once—the danger, the fear, the betrayal, that Rene Bourdain was the killer and that he had her in his grip. She lunged up to sitting, terrified, and ended up slamming her head on something metal. It made a ringing sound that echoed down away from her. Wherever Rene had put her, there was no vestige of light; it was just pitch-black, and very, very cold. She couldn't see anything.

Goose bumps rippled, her skin crawled, and she felt around with her good arm and realized that her other arm throbbed, too. She didn't remember injuring it so she felt around on the inside of her right wrist. When she realized what Rene had done, her blood ran cold. The skin under her fingertips was raised up and bleeding and very sore to the touch, and she could feel the curvy outline of the two snakes on her skin, both upright and side by side, just like the ones on Madonna and Wendy and Gabe.

Horrified, she put her hand over her mouth to stifle a groan. Oh,

God, oh, God, he had inked her with his Veve and put her in the maze. She was at his mercy, naked and unarmed. It took some time to slow down her thudding heart and regain control of her nerves, but she finally did it, somehow, and tried desperately to think what she could do. But she couldn't do anything.

Blindly, she felt around on the floor underneath her until her hand slid into a puddle of something wet and warm. She jerked her hand away and felt around on the metal right above her. She realized then that she was trapped inside something low and narrow. Oh, God, what was it? It occurred to her that it might be a coffin. Had Rene buried her alive?

Chills ran up and down her flesh, and she absolutely panicked. She scrambled forward rapidly on her hands and knees and quickly realized that she wasn't in a box. She was in some kind of tunnel, made out of metal that was cold and hard and impenetrable. Where was she? Had Rene taken her off the island and out of the swamp while she was unconscious? Or were they still in the fish camp?

Sitting very still then, she listened intently. That's when she heard the breathing. Oh, God, something was in there with her. Without thinking, she reached automatically under her left arm for her Glock and remembered that she didn't have either of her weapons. She had lost both of them in the initial scuffle. She was so cold by now that her fingers and feet felt numb. She needed to move them, warm them up, but she couldn't bring herself to do it for fear he'd put some kind of wild animal in the maze with her.

So she sat still and tried to adjust her eyes to the inky surroundings. Surely there was light coming through somewhere. She wondered if it was still the same night and how many hours had passed. She froze when she heard a low growl in the dark, somewhere off to her right. Wait, no, it was a groan, somebody in pain. Zee? Had Rene trapped Zee inside with her? She felt around again and estimated her prison to be a hollow pipe about three feet wide and almost that tall. She scooted along in the direction of the sound, feeling ahead of her in the dark with her good hand until she ran into a body. There was another moan of agony, but she couldn't see him. She couldn't see anything.

"Zee? Is that you?" She could feel the liquid wetting her bare knees. Was it his blood? "Zee, answer me! Please say something!"

Another moan was all she got, so she felt along his body. Rene had not stripped him. He was still fully dressed in his jacket and shirt and T-shirt and jeans. All the clothes were sodden, but his skin felt warm and his hair was wet. She felt around on his torso, trying to find the bullet wound. It was bandaged, and she could smell the antiseptic solution. She realized with some shock that Rene must've tried to doctor him.

Why? Why would he do that? Zee was still breathing, thank God, but he was still bleeding, too. That was the wet substance she felt under her hands and knees. As best she could in the cramped enclosure, she got off his jacket and put it on and zipped it up. She had to stay warm and be able to function if she was going to get them out. Zee's skin felt feverish, hot to the touch. He was running a temperature. She leaned close and whispered into his ear. "Listen to me, Zee. Hang in there. I'm gonna get us out of here. You hear me, Zee? Don't you dare die! I'm gonna find a way out."

Zee made no sound except for slow and rasping attempts to breathe. Oh, God, he wasn't going to last too much longer, not without medical attention. Turning quickly, she felt her way down the narrow tunnel. There was no way out. It was solid steel and felt like it had been welded together, but hollow, too, like one long and endless oil drum. It smelled like oil, too, and that frightened her. Rene was obviously insane. What if he had drenched it with some kind of flammable liquid and was going to light a match and burn them alive?

Claire's heart hammered with the worst kind of dread, and she forced herself to go back and lie down beside Zee's lifeless body and try to absorb his warmth and think what she should do. She had to save them both. She was injured, and he was dying. Rene was going to kill them after he finished toying with them, just like he had with all his other victims. She had absolutely no doubt of that. There was not a single sound, inside or out, except for Zee's labored breaths and her own quick, frightened ones.

Okay, if she didn't come back and Black couldn't get hold of her, he would come looking for her. He always did. She still had the St. Michael's medal around her neck that he'd given her, the one with the tracking device inside. Maybe he could pick up that signal. He'd told her to keep it on, just to be on the safe side in case she ever got into trouble. So, okay. He would come. He would find her. He would. All she had to do was keep them both alive until he did. Oh, God, where was Rene now? What was he doing? What was he planning to do to them? He'd said he was going to play games with her, hadn't he? What games? When?

After several minutes trying to regain composure and control her trembling hands, she turned over and inched down the pipe in the other direction, still on her hands and knees. Her broken wrist was in absolute agony, but she couldn't think about that. She had to forget that and use the injured arm anyway. Mind over matter. Just do it. She still couldn't see anything, but she kept one hand out in front of her, moving it from side to side through the darkness, just in case there was something else in there with them.

Every few seconds she would stop and listen for any sound or movement outside the metal tube. She heard nothing at all, just felt her way through the endless cold metal pipe, welded together into a hellish trap. Maybe he had just left them there alone to die of starvation and exposure. Maybe he was never coming back. She kept moving. She had to. How had he gotten them so far inside the maze? They must be near the middle of the tunnel. And there had to be a way in and out. He couldn't have dragged both of them through the narrow tube without a lot of back-breaking effort. She just had to find the openings he used and hope he didn't come back until she did.

Inching slowly along, she realized that the tunnel shot off every once in a while in a right angle, either left or right, but always away from the main pipe. She tried not to make any sound, but she didn't know which way she should to go. There were lots of angled passages that led off to God only knew where, probably to booby traps and other terrible things.

Claire stopped and listened again. No sounds outside, but she had a feeling Rene was out there, waiting around for her to reach a certain spot. He'd said they were going to play. She shuddered to think what that meant. Gabe had described the torture that he and Sophie had suffered. Was that what he was planning? To tie her to a ceiling beam and beat her bloody? Or even worse things?

Okay, get a grip, she thought. *Think, think. You've got to outsmart*

him. She had to keep going, for one thing. Maybe she'd find something, maybe some kind of weapon she could use on him when he
showed up. She was *not* going to let Zee die. How could they all
have been so blind and not seen Rene for the monster he was? But
who would've ever guessed that Rene was a psychotic killer? He
was a cop, had always been in law enforcement, and he had been
a friend to all of them, a trusted colleague. Why would they ever
suspect him?

Crawling as fast as she could, she turned right at the next junction
to see where it led. She had to do something. The tunnel reminded
her of the children's play areas inside McDonald's restaurants, twisting and turning and rising up and then abruptly descending again.
She found an offshoot that appeared to rise about two feet and then
level off, but just as she started up it, she froze into place. Heavy
footsteps sounded outside, coming closer. Then there was a loud
clanking sound like a lever being thrown, and the floor suddenly
dropped out from underneath her. She went down hard into another
dark enclosed tunnel, crying out when her hands and knees cracked
against the unyielding metal floor. Her broken wrist erupted with
pain that sent her woozy for a few seconds. Outside, she could hear
Rene Bourdain laughing. Oh, God, he really was crazy.

"How'd you like my Maze of Terror, *chère*? Fun, ain't it?" he
called out merrily to Claire, as if they were playing a simple game
of hide and seek.

Claire stayed perfectly still and felt around in the dark again and
realized that the new tunnel was bigger, taller, enough so that she
could squat down and move along if she duck walked. That was
better because she didn't have to use her left arm. She hurried along
the new tunnel and tried not to make a sound for fear that he would
drop her down again. Moving barefoot through the dark, her right
foot suddenly stepped off another drop that was built into the tunnel,
and she couldn't regain her balance fast enough and cried out as she
fell and landed hard on her side. She groaned with pain when something sharp bit into her body. Feeling around, she realized she'd fallen
onto dozens of upended carpet tacks and nails.

Biting her lip, she swept them away and pulled the embedded
points out of her skin. Some of the puncture wounds bled and hurt

like hell. She realized now that Rene was only toying with her at the moment, enjoying her fear and the sound of her screams of terror. Her stomach dropped like lead when she realized that he had done this same thing to other people, to children, like Jill and Jenny, and maybe even Sophie.

Leaning back against the tubular wall, she decided to stay where she was. If he was getting off on her trying to find her way out of his little evil playpen, she wouldn't play that game. That probably meant there wasn't a way out, at least not one she could find. Good God, how had he constructed something so intricate and maniacal, a complicated metal labyrinth in which to torture his captives, out in the middle of the swamp? How long must it have taken him?

Inhaling deep, bracing breaths, she strove first to calm herself. Okay, if she didn't move around in his little maze, he wouldn't get his jollies. Maybe that would make him have to come inside and get her. Then, at least she'd have a fighting chance against him. She could hold her own in hand-to-hand combat, even when injured. So she sat still and listened intently and waited for him to make the next move. It didn't take him long.

Suddenly, she heard another clang, and a smaller door opened up right beside her, flooding her in dim, smoky light. Then a long sharp knife jabbed her hard in the side, and she screamed as it sliced through the jacket and into her bare flesh. Rene kept stabbing at her, and she scrambled away until she found the next turn in the tunnel. She took it quickly, crab-walking down it in a big hurry, now very afraid that he could prod her into going anywhere he wanted inside his vicious trap. She fingered her bleeding side and found a couple of shallow puncture wounds, but they weren't too bad. She pressed her palm over them, but she didn't feel much pain. Her adrenaline was rushing through her bloodstream—gushing and pulsing and sending her heartbeat and breathing into overdrive. She had to control her fear. That was the most important thing. She had to remain calm, no matter what he did to her.

He was right outside again, very near; she could hear him. He was whistling a tune. Oh, God, he was enjoying himself. This was what he considered sport. But there were lots of these hidden doors all over the place so there had to be a place where she could get out. Or maybe kick her way through one of the trap doors. She decided that if she didn't stop, he couldn't attack her from outside. She moved as quickly as she could after that, kept on the move, feeling along the cold floor and ceiling for any kind of bolt or hinge, but the seams she found were soldered tightly with metal screws, so tightly welded that she couldn't loosen them with her fingers.

Praying that Black had realized something was wrong by now and would come looking for her, she kept crawling as fast as she could. The broken bone was still making her sick to her stomach, and she sometimes felt like she couldn't breathe deeply enough. Then, suddenly, right in front of her, another trapdoor opened in the top of the tunnel and she could see again for a mere moment. She backed away, afraid of what he was going to do, and then a large, writhing snake dropped down right in front of her. The door slammed shut, and she was plunged into darkness again. She could hear the sound of it twisting around on the pipe, and she backed up as quickly as she could, scrambling to find a junction in the tunnel somewhere behind her, pounding the metal walls with her fist to scare the snake away in the other direction. She squeezed herself enough to turn around and crawl back to the pipe that descended to a lower level.

A good distance away from the angry reptile, she stopped and listened again. She couldn't hear the sound of the snake slithering and sidewinding along the pipe anymore. It must have writhed off in the opposite direction or coiled up where it was, ready to strike anybody who came close. She wondered if it was poisonous, and if it could see in utter darkness. She had a bad feeling that snakes could probably see a lot better than she could. She couldn't see anything at all. She had never been closed up in such complete darkness. She couldn't see her hand in front of her face. And she didn't know if he'd constructed the pipes into a circle and she'd run into the snake again, no matter which direction she chose. She hoped it didn't slither its way around to Zee.

Suddenly, that very thought materialized. Zee cried out and then groaned again, and Rene started laughing. He was tormenting him somehow, probably jabbing him with the knife. But now she didn't know exactly where Zee was, confused by the serpentine meanderings of the tunnels. He must be up another level from her because Rene had dropped her down a level and then she'd fallen on the tacks. So she felt her way along until she found a pipe that ascended. She cringed as the pipe under her seemed to echo and vibrate with her every move. She tried to think straight. Fear was beginning to overwhelm her again. She couldn't let that happen. Rene had to have some kind of scaffolding outside the maze where he could climb around, up and down, and lots of trapdoors out of which he could torment his victims.

Panting hard, she stopped moving after a while, fighting back a burgeoning kind of despair. The darkness was getting to her and the fear of running into the snake. Bud had been bitten once by a timber rattler, and she knew what snake venom could do to a human being. But she had not heard any hollow rattling sounds when the snake landed in front of her, just hissing and its twisting movements atop the metal.

Then suddenly, Rene struck again. A panel in the metal opened up just above her and she was hit with a deluge of something grainy and coarse. At first, she didn't know what it was, and then she felt the scurrying of the insects swarming all over her hair and face and down into the neck of her jacket. Fire ants, she realized with absolute horror—he'd dumped a nest of fire ants on her. She screamed as they began to bite into her skin, couldn't stop herself, and slapped desperately at them, trying to brush them out of her hair and out of her eyes. But it felt like hundreds of them, crawling all over her and inside the jacket. She crawled away from the trapdoor, jerking off the jacket, before he could dump anything else on her. Outside, she could hear Rene laughing.

Scrambling several yards down, she took off down a different tunnel and stopped there in the dark, getting the clinging ants off her as best she could with her fingers and trying to kill them with the palm of her hand. She was trembling all over now, utterly terrified, just as he intended, but she set her teeth again and forced herself back into icy control. The ants weren't going to kill her—bite her, yes, bother her, yes—but they weren't deadly, not if she could get them off of her. He had done nothing designed to kill her yet. He was getting his kicks tormenting her at the moment, and he probably would do so until he grew bored with it. That meant she had a good chance to survive. She just had to keep her wits about her until she found a way out. She shook the insects off the jacket, put it back on, and darted off again, feeling above her for the hinges of trapdoors so he couldn't drop anything on her again, and along the floor for the hinges of drop-offs. She was going to get out. She had to. Zee was lying somewhere in the dark behind her, dying.

Chapter Thirty-two

Nick Black and Jack Holliday were making progress toward their target. They were deep inside the swamp now, and the GPS signal tracking Bourdain's sat phone was blinking steadily, and so was Claire's St. Michael's medal. They were heading right at them. But Nick was scared this time. She and Zee and Bourdain had been gone for a long time. They had never shown up to meet Friedewald and his men. Somebody had them. He felt it in his gut, and he feared it was the voodoo killer they had gone after.

This time he might get there too late. This time he just might find Claire dead, murdered in some horrible way and propped up on a goddamn voodoo altar with her eyes and mouth stitched shut. Or she might already be buried somewhere, and they'd have to dig up her body, like they'd done with Jack's sisters. His heart reacted to that, squeezed by some invisible hand until it felt like all the blood gushed out of it and plummeted down inside his chest as heavy as liquid lead. In that moment, he felt violently ill.

"Look, Nick, up there. See, in the trees?" Jack Holliday said softly from his seat in the bow of the boat.

Holliday was scouting ahead with the night scope on his rifle, but Nick was working the trolling motor and couldn't see anything at first. Then the outline of a small structure sitting out on dry land loomed out of the darkness, directly in front of the boat. As they neared, it looked like several buildings. They were way out in the middle of nowhere now. Nick had fished and hunted in the bayous many times with Jack and other friends, and he'd never been this deep into the swamp. But according to his GPS readings, Claire was on that island somewhere, and he was going to find her. They switched to paddles now, afraid that even the quiet motor would announce their arrival. He dipped the paddle soundlessly into the murky, slimy water.

If Claire and the others were being held inside that house, they had to catch the killer unaware. That was imperative. They eased the craft up against the bank beside a big racing boat that had been run haphazardly onto the bank. Rene's boat? There wasn't another one, not that Nick could see, but it could be beached out back. Neither he nor Jack said a word. They'd been on this sort of mission together before, but it had been a long time ago when life-and-death situations were daily occurrences. Neither had done anything like this in a very long time, but it wasn't a skill you easily forgot.

There were no sounds, other than night creatures. They got out and moved in a military crouch up to the front door. There was an oil lantern sitting on the floor beside the door. Nick gestured for Holliday to go around and take the back. It was very quiet except for the wind, rustling up high in the cypress trees surrounding the house. Nothing was moving inside, no noise, no talking, and they went in stealthy and fast. Old Nat Navarro was on his side, tied to an overturned chair, dead for quite some time, it looked like. There was crusted blood spatter all over the wall, a large pool of fresh blood on the floor, and an overturned table and chairs and an electric lantern and radio with the batteries scattered around. There had been a fight inside that house, all right. And he didn't think it was the old man who'd put up that kind of struggle. But Claire would have.

Jack pointed out a blood trail leading out through the back door, and they followed it across the weedy backyard to another structure that looked like a barn. They stopped again outside its door. Somewhere inside, they could hear someone moving around. They entered quietly, one at a time, weapons up and ready. It was completely dark inside, and they switched on their flashlights and stared wordlessly at a big, elaborate system of pipes and barred cages winding all around the interior, from the floor all the way up to the ceiling. There was a planked walkway threading through it, a sort of scaffolding, with safety railings and steps. Good God, what the hell was it? And then he remembered the killer's maze.

Suddenly, in the extreme quiet inside the building, he heard Claire let out a bloodcurdling scream. Then a man laughed, and Nick's blood ran cold. He headed toward the sound with Holliday right behind him.

After Rene got her again with the knife, Claire decided that her only chance was to attack him. She found the nearest trapdoor above her by feeling for the hinges, and pretended she was sobbing so he'd know where she was, and then inched to one side of where she figured it would open. He would do something with that door, sooner or later. So she waited there a few seconds, muscles quivering, heart beating like crazy, and then, finally, it was thrust open. Before he could drop anything down on her, she lunged up through the hole and grabbed his arm. He had the knife in his hand, and she screamed as he tried to slash her. He started laughing, but he cut it off pretty quickly when she jerked his arm down into the hole as hard as she could. She twisted the elbow backward, bracing her feet on the side of the tunnel and pulling it down at that impossible angle with every ounce of her remaining strength until she heard a crack as his bone gave way. Rene screamed shrilly. The sharp filet knife dropped onto the floor beside her. But she kept hold of him, didn't dare let go, twisting and twisting the broken arm, wanting to hurt him so badly that he couldn't fight back anymore. She ground her teeth together and tried to break another bone.

Rene screamed and yelled, but he managed to get away when he thrust his gun into the hole. She let go of him and grabbed the knife and took off in blind panic, as he slammed the door with a clang. She could hear him screaming at her, and she quickly renewed her search for an escape hatch while he cursed and beat on the pipe, pretty sure he wasn't going to be able to play any more games for the time being.

Then she heard the trapdoor open again, and the gun fired inside with a deafening booming reverberation and the metallic ring of bullets ricocheting all over the sides of the tunnel. She cried out as one grazed her leg. She heard Rene laugh maniacally, and then she heard more shots and yelling. He was going to kill her this time, and she clutched the filet knife in both hands and stayed as far as she could from any of the trapdoors so he couldn't get at her.

Then as she backed away from the running footsteps coming closer on the outside, she went off a drop backwards and fell about six feet and landed on her back on a concrete floor. It knocked the breath out of her, and she struggled to breathe as she looked frantically around the barred cage into which she'd fallen. There was a glimmer of light coming from somewhere now, probably Rene's flashlight, and she could see the rotting body of a woman lying near her feet, and she backed away from the gruesome corpse in horror. She couldn't climb back into the maze; it was too high. Oh God, she was trapped there. When Rene found her, he could just shoot her through the bars as he probably had with the other woman.

Then she heard Rene coming, right above her now, and he jumped down and landed in the darkness right outside the cage, close enough for her to get him with the knife. A flashlight beam hit her in the face, and she started stabbing hysterically through the bars, trying to wound him.

"Stop, Claire, stop, it's me!"

Black's voice. Oh, God, it was Black's voice. She sank down on her knees and couldn't move. She just couldn't move a muscle. Black grabbed the bars and started jerking hard on them, trying to get the cage open and get inside to her. When he finally got the door off the hinges, he grabbed her up and pulled her outside. She lay against him for a moment, unable to speak, and then she said, "It's Rene, Black. He's the killer. He's still here. He's got a gun. He's trying to kill us."

"He took off when he realized we were in here with him. Jack's gone after him. C'mon, Jack might need my help."

"He shot Zee. We gotta get Zee out. He's inside the maze somewhere. He's hurt bad—he's bleeding, Black. We've got to get him out!"

Black gripped her arms, kept his voice low. "You're okay, Claire. We'll get him out, and I'll take care of him. But we've got to make sure Bourdain's down first. C'mon, I can hear Jack yelling."

Black ran for the door, but Claire was just too exhausted. She couldn't run anywhere. She was shaky, her knees were wobbly, but she followed him slowly, guided by his flashlight. When she got outside in the fresh air, she just collapsed to the ground and couldn't move another step. She could see two men fighting down by the boats. The moonlight faded behind a bank of clouds, but she could make out Black running down the yard toward them. Then the moon burst out again, and she could see that Jack Holliday was on top of Rene Bourdain, looking absolutely huge on the smaller man, his knees holding down Rene's arms while he hit him in the face with his fists, first one and then the other, over and over again.

Claire got up and limped toward them and found Black standing there, calmly watching Jack beat the life out of Rene Bourdain. She tried to catch her breath, cradling her injured arm, but she recognized that Holliday was caught up in pure blood lust and blind fury. When she saw the absolute, utter rage possessing him, she knew that he was going to commit murder. She couldn't let that happen. She feebly grabbed at his arm, hung on weakly to make him stop, but he barely felt her weight and she was too tired and dizzy to hold on to him. So Black grabbed Jack's arm and yelled at him to stop. Holliday finally faltered and gradually returned to reality, his bloodied fists still poised in the air over Rene's face, which was now cut and swollen, already beaten beyond recognition.

Claire sat on her knees and breathlessly tried to reason with him. "Jack, we got him. We've got to take him in, question him, find out who else he's abducted and murdered, where their bodies are. I want to know why he did all this. Tie him up. We've got to get Zee out of that maze. He's been shot. Do you hear me? We've got to get him to the hospital."

Holliday rocked back on his heels and stared mutely at her, coming down out of his adrenaline rush of hatred and vengeance, his face still twisted with fury. But he had finally avenged his sisters and parents, and he seemed to realize it. Claire began shaking all over, still supporting her elbow inside her palm. Black must have sensed then that she was seriously hurt, too, and he took off his coat and wrapped it around her, and then he sat her down and examined her injuries. "How bad is it? What'd he do to you?"

"My wrist is broken, but Zee's the one who's hurt bad. Rene

shot him. Jack, tie him up and get him in the boat. We've got to get Zee out."

They left Jack to take care of Rene and found their way back inside the horrific maze. Claire was so exhausted that she could barely put one foot in front of the other, so Black made his way inside the metal tunnels until he finally found Zee. It took him a while, and he had to kill the snake, but he finally dragged Zee out, still unconscious and now half dead. In the light of the boat's headlamps, Black treated Zee's wounds as best he could, but Zee looked terrible, really terrible. Claire was terrified he was going to die. They hurried then, taking Rene's boat and heading out of the swamp. Claire sat propped up against the side of the boat, holding Zee's head in her lap. Halfway back to civilization, Black called on the sat phone and ordered ambulances to meet them at the nearest marina. Then he called Sheriff Friedewald and handed the phone to Claire.

"Where the hell are you, Claire? We've been out here waiting for you to show up. Navarro's gonna be long gone. We might as well forget it now."

"We got him, Russ. It's Rene, Rene did all of it. He murdered Madonna and Wendy, and he tried to kill Zee and me. He's hurt bad, and so is Zee. We've got a couple of ambulances meeting us down at the marina."

While Russ asked her questions, Claire answered them somehow, but her eyes stayed on Jack Holliday's back. He was driving the boat, but his knuckles were cut up and bleeding down his arms. "Black's with me, and so is Holliday. I think my arm's broken, but I'm okay."

Then she hung up and they motored through the dark still water until they hit a big, swift-running bayou, the boat's headlights the only illumination in the night. Black was on the phone with the ER doctors describing the injuries, and Claire sat and stared down at Rene, who had not moved since Jack had beaten him unconscious. He was still breathing, though, and Claire wished he wasn't. He deserved to die for what he'd done to her and Zee and Gabe and so many other innocent victims. She sat there, silent and numb, feeling an uncharacteristic and almost uncontrollable urge to just grab Black's rifle and shoot Rene in the heart and be done with it. Dump him over the side for the gators, the same way he'd done to Gabe and no doubt other innocent little children, whose names they'd probably never know. She focused her gaze on the water ahead of them, and said a prayer that Zee would live through this horrible night, as the moon guided their way down a long, shimmering path of silver lying on the water, as if leading them out of the darkness they had just endured.

The ambulances were waiting on shore, along with the entire Lafourche Sheriff's Department. The EMTs took Rene and Zee out of the boat and placed them on gurneys and put them in separate ambulances. Black and Claire rode with Jack in a third ambulance, and an EMT named Meg put a new splint on Claire's arm and placed it in a sling, bandaged her stab wounds, rubbed ointment on the welts caused by the biting ants, and then gave her an ice pack to hold against her head and dosed her with a couple of strong painkillers. Jack just sat there while Meg examined his bleeding fists, his head leaning back, his eyes closed, seemingly completely relaxed, now that he had captured the man who killed his family. Maybe she would feel good about it one day, too, and feel lucky to be alive. Funny thing, though, at the moment, she didn't feel lucky, not one bit. She felt like an empty shell of herself.

Chapter Thirty-three

Once they reached the hospital in Thibodaux, they rolled the injured men into the emergency room, and Claire and Black stood near Zee's cubicle while the physicians worked desperately to stabilize him enough to get him into surgery. But Claire kept an eye on Rene, too, and made sure they kept both his wrists handcuffed to the gurney. He had gotten away with his evil for way too long. He wasn't going anywhere this time. If she had to watch his every move for the rest of her life, he wasn't getting away with his crimes.

Still receiving blood transfusions and all kinds of IV medications, Zee made it through surgery alive and was transferred to a private room. Claire and Black joined him there, sat beside him, and waited for the doctors to tell them he was out of danger. It took several hours before they felt like they could say that he was going to make it, that he was a strong young man, physically fit enough to pull through. Then she went outside and found out they were transferring Rene to the Lafourche Parish lockup infirmary. Russ had made that decision, charging him with the murder of Madonna Christien with other charges pending as they finished investigating the case. Everything made sense now, a terrible gruesome, horrible sense.

Claire insisted that she and Black follow the ambulance to the jail, not about to let anything go wrong. If she had to babysit Rene until they strapped him to the table in the death house, she was going to do it. Rene was going to pay and pay hard.

Sheriff Friedewald was standing outside the jail as Rene was taken inside in a wheelchair. Gabe was with him. More worrisome, he looked pale and gaunt and had the thirst of murder shining brightly out of his eyes. She stopped him before he could follow after the man who had beat him senseless and left him for dead so long ago. He wasn't wearing his sling. Now she was wearing one. Both of them had injuries that had been inflicted by the man they'd trusted.

"How'd you know we were here, Gabe?"

"Nick called home and told us what happened to you. He told me everything. Are you okay? You look pretty busted up."

"I've been better."

"Me, too. How bad is Zee?"

"Rene shot him in the back, but they think he's gonna pull through, thank God. He's in intensive care. They're taking good care of him, and Black's working on having him transferred over to the Tulane Medical Center in New Orleans."

"That bastard shot him in the back? Look, Claire, I want some time alone with Rene. Can you fix it?"

"No, I cannot fix it, and I wouldn't, even if I could."

"I deserve a chance to talk to him. I wanna know why he hurt Sophie and me. That's all. I just wanna know why."

"Of course, you do, Gabe, but you're a DEA agent. I'm a cop. We're not going to act like vigilantes, no matter how much we want to. I had to stop myself from shooting him dead on the way back here. But I controlled myself and so can you."

Gabe frowned, rubbed the back of his neck, and muttered a few choice curses under his breath. "Will Russ let me talk to him? Privately, in one of the interview rooms? I won't lay a finger on him, I swear to God, I won't."

"He might. If all of it's on tape and you don't assault him. His lawyer probably won't allow it, though."

Inside the jail, they got a surprise when Russ told them that Rene had requested to be interviewed, and he wanted Gabe and Claire to do it. Russ gave them the option, and they grabbed it.

Rene Bourdain was waiting in Interview One, and not in the best shape physically. Friedewald and Black, and Nancy, who'd shown up about fifteen minutes after they had arrived, along with most of the other Lafourche Parish detectives, were in the adjoining surveillance room, watching and filming the interview through a two-way mirror.

Outside the door, Claire stopped Gabe with a hand on his arm. "I got us permission, Gabe, but you gotta promise me that you won't touch him. You cannot hurt him."

"I'm not stupid, Claire. We finally got the bastard. I'm not gonna mess that up and give him a reason to yell police brutality."

Claire wasn't so sure. Gabe's anger was ingrained, had been buried for decades, and he looked like he was going to choke the life out of his tormentor as soon as the door shut behind them. Just like Jack Holliday had nearly done. "Give me your word. Promise me. Please, Gabe."

"Okay, you got it. Now open that door. I want to see him."

Claire opened the door with her good hand. Rene was sitting at the metal table. His hands were cuffed and attached with chains to the arms of his wheelchair. One of his arms was in a cast, and Claire was glad she'd gotten that satisfaction, at least. His face was so beaten and swollen that they barely recognized him. His nose was broken, his eyes were black and blue and nearly swollen completely shut, his front teeth were missing, and the rest of his face was a mess of cuts and black and purple bruises.

"Holliday did that to you, Bourdain? Remind me to buy that guy a drink," Gabe said through tightly clenched teeth.

Rene only gave a strangled sneer, and it made his nose start bleeding again. Close beside her, Claire felt Gabe's muscles tighten up, and he started shaking. She took his hand in hers and squeezed it. Gabe calmed down some, but his arm still felt rigid.

Wiping his nose on his shoulder, Rene said, his voice was slurred, almost indistinguishable because of his cut and swollen lips, "Thanks for comin' in, kiddos."

Claire felt her own anger shoot up inside her, but she forced the resentment down and glanced at the mirrored window. "Okay, we're here, Rene, let's hear what you've got to say."

"Sit down, make yourselves at home. I wondered if this day was ever gonna come, 'specially after you came back, li'l girl." Everything he said took a long time, uttered between labored and hoarse and painful breathing.

"Don't call me that." Angry, too, Claire sat down with Gabe, both across the table from Rene. Gabe's jaw was working, muscles tightening in both his cheeks. He was balanced on the edge of violence. She knew it and hoped he had enough willpower to remain in control.

She hoped *she* had that kind of willpower. She still couldn't believe it. Rene. Rene, who had been like a favorite uncle to both of them, especially to Gabe. He had wanted them both dead. Why?

Claire heaved in a deep breath. "Rene, I'm going to give you your rights. Do you understand that?"

"Well, I should. I've been giving them to criminals since before you was born."

It took him a while to get all that out in his raspy slur, and Claire repeated the familiar words, loud and clear for the video camera, and then she asked him if he understood after each one. Rene Bourdain was a clever man. He had gotten away with horrendous deeds for years. He wasn't going to get off on a legal technicality— no way in hell would she ever let that happen.

Rene smiled at them, as best he could. It was more of a twisted, unpleasant, and disgusting grimace. "Okay, I get it. Here's what I want. I tell you everything you wanna know. You agree to a plea bargain and the death penalty's off the table. Fair enough? I know good and well you wanna know who my victims were and where I dumped them. No way, not until you take off the death penalty."

It took him a long time to say all that, too, and it made his nose bleed down the front of his hospital gown, which didn't bother either of them one iota.

"We've got your little trunk of souvenirs, Rene. That ought to tell us plenty."

Rene actually chuckled a little. "That's just a drop in the bucket to what I've done, *chère*. I've had a long and lucrative career. Oh yeah, believe it."

Claire kept her cool, how she did not know, but it took some time and struggle. So did Gabe, thank God. She had already discussed the terms with Sheriff Friedewald and the prosecuting attorney. They had agreed to set aside the death penalty for life in prison without the possibility of parole, but only if Rene legally agreed to waive any future appeals and if he gave them the names of his victims and their burial places.

Claire gave him the terms, and then she said, "That's provided that you tell the truth and give us enough to make it worth the trade-off.

Frankly, I'd like to see you stood up against this wall and shot dead right here, right now. I'd like to do it myself, Rene."

"Of course, you would. You always were the one with the gumption. Even when you were a little kid. I could see the fire you had burnin' inside you. That's why I liked you the best." He looked at Gabe. "And you had guts like no other kid I ever ran up against. You could take my blows for hours."

"Yeah, and you're the lowest scum that ever walked this earth."

Rene sighed, and then he croaked out some more infuriating words. "I had a good run, almost made it through to retirement. If it wasn't for you, Claire, I'd still be out there at the maze, havin' a good old time."

"Just start at the beginning and tell us everything."

And so he did, if only part of it. He spoke slowly and painfully, but with relish, as if he got off on the murders a second time in the telling.

"Gabe's family was my first, except for the ones I killed overseas. Madonna and Wendy and Jack's sisters, all of them were taken after I hit their parents. There are others, too, lots of 'em that you don't know about. I'll tell you who they are, but not until my lawyer gets this plea deal signed and in writing. I ain't no fool."

Gabe said, "Why start killing us off now, Rene? Most of us have been around all these years without being able to identify you. Why now?"

"Because that bastard Jack Holliday and his P.I. came snoopin' around, getting too close for comfort. I left some messy loose ends in the beginning when I didn't know what I was doing. I had to take care of them, in case they remembered something and put the police onto me."

"So you had to get rid of those two innocent girls, just in case?"

"One of 'em might've ended up putting two and two together. Made me damn nervous." He stopped and looked back at Claire. "Especially after you showed up out of the blue and got involved in Madonna's murder. I was plannin' to take over the case and weed out anything that could incriminate me. I thought I could scare you off with that voodoo doll and you'd hand the case to me, after all the things you've been through lately." He stopped speaking, licked blood off his lower lip, seemed to like the taste of it. His voice was gravelly and hard to understand, but he kept talking. "And it worked 'til you and your partner came up to her apartment and refused to back off. Holliday was askin' questions all around the Quarter, about you, Gabe, about your parents, about what happened to them. It was just a matter of time before somebody fingered me."

"Why did you kill Gabe's parents? Bobby was like a brother to you. You always said that yourself. You told me that."

"Bobby took Kristen away from me, that's why. She loved me first." Rene stopped, and Claire realized that he was getting riled up. He was panting, trying to talk faster but having trouble moving his swollen lips. "We were gonna get married, had made some plans before I got in trouble, but then Bobby moved in on her and took her away from me. I hated their guts, after that. And I hated you, Gabe. I still hate you. You're the reason she had to marry Bobby." He stopped, breathing heavily, bleeding profusely down the front of his shirt now. "He knocked Kristie up with you. That's why I beat you so hard. I waited for the right time, and then I got 'em back for what they'd done to me. And I got you back for causin' it."

He is completely insane, Claire thought, and then she realized he was actually enjoying throwing his crimes in their faces. "Are you the Mob assassin known as the Snake?"

Rene tried to grin, but his mouth barely moved because of the stitches in his split lips. "You turned out to be a better detective than I figured you for. How'd you get that information, anyhow? I thought I had that buried, nice and deep, never to be found out."

"Answer me. Were you the Snake?"

"Yeah, I sure am. How you think I came by all that money, *chère*? Workin' as a cop, like you two? Come on."

"You said you inherited it."

"Yeah, and everybody believed me. Every single word I ever said. It's a gift."

"Why'd you kill Sophie?" That was Gabe, in a tightly reined, icy, awful voice.

"I wasn't going to. I was gonna let you go after a while if you didn't see my face. But then you got away, and she saw me that night, so I had to get rid of her. So it's really your fault she's dead. So now you can blame yourself for that, too, for the rest of your life."

Tired of his rasping, self-satisfied rant, Claire wanted to get up and walk out. She said, "What about Jack Holliday's family? Why them? They lived out in Colorado. Why'd you go after them?"

He leaned back in the chair and swallowed a few times, licked his cracked lips. His jaw was turning a deeper shade of black now. "Jack's stepdad witnessed a Mob hit in Chicago. He was gonna testify. It took a while but I found him. You know what a good detective I am."

"And his little sisters?"

"I like little kids, always have." He stopped again, breathed heavily. "They're always so scared, so eager to do whatever I tell them to. The fear in their eyes excites me. Except for you, Gabe. You always looked at me with such hatred that it was almost scary, even with you tied up and helpless."

"You filthy pedophile freak," Gabe ground out between set teeth. "I wish I'd been the one to find you last night. You'd be floating face down in that swamp right now."

"Yeah, I believe that. You still got that hate inside you. I can see it in your eyes right now. That's why I always thought so much of you."

"I ought to kill you right now. Just choke the fuckin' life out of your rotten body."

"Gabe, stop." It was sickening, horrific, everything Rene croaked out with such misguided pride, but they really were the lucky ones. They were the only ones still left breathing. And Zee, if he survived—and he would, she told herself firmly. He would. He would be fine.

"Who are the others?"

"Told you that I ain't sayin' until I see the signed plea deal in my lawyer's hand. I will say, though, that most of them were the kids of my hits. Couldn't just leave them all alone in the house with the corpses of their mommies and daddies, could I? I've got some compassion. Figured they were better off with me, at least until I had to kill them. That's all I'm sayin' about that until my lawyer gets down here."

"You killed your victims and buried them in the cemetery out at Rose Arbor, is that correct?"

"Most of 'em. I disposed some in the swamp for the gators to feed on. It just depended on my mood at the time."

"How many?"

"Eighteen, or thereabouts, give or take a few. Most of my Mob hits had at least a couple of kids. You were lucky to make it out of there in one piece, Gabe." Rene stopped, hacked out a deep, painful cough before he continued. "Not many did, none of the ones I kept out at the maze. But I didn't know what I was doing the first time. Got careless. My skills weren't so polished back then."

"Madonna and Wendy got away, too."

"Ah, Madonna and Wendy. That was a bit different. I hit Madonna's mom and dad, but unfortunately, somebody happened by when I had them out on a voodoo altar. So I had to leave them behind. That was the first and last time that happened. I wasn't sure if they saw me, or not, so I had to take care of them."

Gabe leaned forward. "You just killed them, after all these years. Just to cover your tracks?"

"They're part of your investigation. Couldn't take that chance. Claire's too good. Although I did throw you off with that phony restraining order I wrote up on Jack Holliday, didn't I, Annie? Sent you running after him, just like I planned. He tried to smile at Claire. He was having trouble breathing now, all the talking making his throat dry. The air was wheezing in and out of his broken nose and making low, whistling sounds. "I've always been proud of you two. Both of you. You're tough. You turned out to be good cops."

"What about the old man? Nat Navarro? How did he figure into all this?"

"He was my mentor back in the day. Introduced me to the lucrative parts of working hits for the Mob. He knew too much, plain and simple. He's the one that let me use the root cellar down at Rose Arbor when I needed a place to keep my kids back when I first got started. We were in the Merchant Marine together and he taught me how to kill people. In the end, he was the obvious one for me to frame because I knew you already suspected him. Worked, too.

I'm surprised you fell for it, but the evidence I planted was damn indisputable."

"I hope you die hard, Rene," said Gabe. "I hope you suffer and then burn in hell."

"Oh, I will, no doubt about it."

Claire glanced at the big mirror, but she didn't really care who heard her next words. "I hope you suffer as much as Gabe and Sophie suffered. I hope you never have another moment of joy or peace in your miserable life."

Gabe got to his feet. He took a step around the table toward his abuser, his face like a stone mask.

Claire stood up, too. "Let's get out of here, Gabe. We got what we wanted. We're finished. Somebody else can take over from here."

Gabe hesitated a long moment, fists balled at his sides, and then he turned around and walked out the door. Claire followed him, but paused and turned around when Rene called out her name.

"I always loved you the best, Annie. That's the truth. Back then, and all over again when you showed up down here. You got in my way, bested me, but I still love you. You'll always be my special li'l girl."

For a moment, Claire understood what Gabe and Jack felt: rage, pure and simple and black and unbridled, gushing up to fill her head. But they were free of him now. He would pay for his crimes for the rest of his life, for all his victims. It was over. Claire walked out to where Black was waiting for her in the hallway. She didn't look back. It was over.

Hours later, when Claire and Black finally climbed the curving staircase of the house in the French Quarter, they took a long, hot, slow shower together, and Black dried her off around her injuries. Then they got into bed and made slow, tender love that lasted for a long, long time. Then they lay in each other's arms and didn't talk about what had happened that day, not a single word. They had seen enough misery and grief and uncovered enough horror and despair. Their thoughts were their own thoughts, none of which were pretty, at least not in Claire's mind. But it felt so good to feel Black's long, muscular body stretched out beside her, and she held on to him, glad to have him with her, safe and sound, his heartbeat steady under her ear. She had a feeling her ghastly nightmares would come back as soon as she shut her eyes and tried to sleep. But Black was always there when she needed him, and she needed him tonight. She loved him for that, and yes, for so many other things, too.

Epilogue

Claire and Black flew back to Lake of the Ozarks on the day before Christmas Eve. Claire had never been so happy to see a piece of land in her life. They were both safe and sound and relatively uninjured. Her arm was better, and she no longer had to wear the sling, just a small splint. The snake tattoo had already been removed, though the residual scar it had left would always haunt her. But her little A-frame cabin was warm and welcoming, and outside, the edges of the lake were frozen over and a blanket of snow covered everything in sight. It was beautiful and pristine and Claire loved being home on her own private cove. She had hated to leave her new friends behind, especially with Zee still in the hospital. But he had understood, and they'd stayed there with him until he was well out of danger and surrounded by Mama Lulu and all his other friends and family.

The same went for Gabe. He was on the *Bayou Blue* with his kinfolks, all of whom were still in shock over Rene's betrayal of their family and his crimes against humanity. It had been a very bad deal, all the way around. She just hoped they could get over it. Gabe's DEA colleagues had rounded up the Skulls, and now they awaited the long, drawn-out trial process. But he said they had plenty of evidence against them on a multitude of charges, so few of them would walk free for a very long time. She hoped he was right about that because he now had a bounty on his head where they were concerned. He promised to come to the lake and see her as soon as he could and that made her happy, too.

Bourdain had been charged with multiple counts of first-degree murder and would never see the light of day outside prison walls, she had no doubt of that. More remains had been found on his island in the swamp. But probably many others had been thrown to the alligators. He was gone for good, except in her dreams, where other killers she'd faced still dwelled and frightened her nightly. Jack had exacted his revenge on the killer of his family, but that hadn't stopped the horror she'd seen on his face when they'd examined the terrible maze in which Rene had probably kept Jill and Jenny and countless other innocent victims and tormented them and terrorized them and eventually murdered them.

It was too dreadful to contemplate, but maybe now Jack could rest and move on, as Claire was determined to do. She could thank Black for that, too. His understanding and ability to talk her through her feelings helped her without it seeming as if he were plundering her head. She loved him. She loved him more than she had ever admitted to herself before.

But Black had changed since that deadly night in the bayous. He had become very quiet and introspective since they had come in from that appalling place, with Zee lying nearly lifeless in the bottom of the boat. He seemed very tired all the time, very stressed and upset. He was still struggling with the dangers of her job, which never seemed to end. He was outside in the yard now, alone, deep in thought again.

Claire walked to the window and watched him for a moment. He was just standing out there in the snow, in his gray parka, jeans, and snow boots, hatless, hands stuffed in his pockets, staring out over the lake. She wondered what he was thinking and was almost afraid to know. He had put his own life in danger for her, and thank God that he had. But she had a feeling that he was tired of it all, the danger she faced so often, the danger in which she dragged him.

Worse, she had begun to worry that he wasn't going to put up with it much longer. He loved her. She didn't question that. He had not confronted her yet or even asked her for her decision about opening her own detective agency, which he'd offered to underwrite. That had been his compromise. Since their latest case, he had been nothing but attentive and loving, but he had said very little. He hadn't even tried to make her talk about it, which was what he usually did. There was always a sadness and worry behind those crystal-blue eyes of his, and she hated that. It was her fault it lingered there. She couldn't stand to see him unhappy, but she couldn't stand the thought of giving up her career, either.

Wanting more than anything to cheer him up, make him smile and show all those killer dimples of his, she threw on her coat and snow boots and walked down to him. She stopped a few yards away, leaned down, and picked up a glove full of snow and packed it into a big snowball. She aimed, threw it, and hit him square on the back of the head. He turned, and she bent to scoop up more snow, but didn't get off the second shot before he tackled her and they went down together in a soft bed of snow. She laughed when he got on top of her and held her face between his cold hands.

"You shouldn't've done that, Claire. Now I'm going to have to make you pay."

But he was smiling now, and she knew full well how he would make her pay. He rubbed some snow in her face, just to get her back, and it felt cold and fresh and clean and good. She smiled at him, her heart so full of so many things that she rarely ever said to him. But she wanted to say them now. She grew serious, her eyes searching his, and his smile gradually faded, too.

Full of emotions, she reached up, cupped his face with her good hand. "Marry me, Black. Right now. I want you to marry me."

For the first few seconds, he looked absolutely astonished. He didn't seem to know what to say. But that didn't last long. He grinned down at her and then he rose above her on his knees and pulled a small velvet box out of his coat pocket and handed it to her. "Okay, if you really want me to."

"No way, Black. That cannot be a ring. I just asked you."

"I like to be prepared. This ring was the surprise I told you about when I got back from New York. I've been standing out here wondering if I should ask you again, or if you'd just turn me down flat again."

"How did you know I was ready?"

"I didn't know. But I wanted the ring handy, if and when you said you were. We've wasted enough time already."

Smiling, Claire sat up and opened the box. The most beautiful square-cut diamond solitaire that she'd ever seen was displayed on black velvet. "Oh, my God, Black. I can't wear this. What if I lose it? I'm always losing things. I can't even keep up with your cell phones. Somebody will mug me and steal it."

"It's insured."

"You didn't need to do this. I don't care about rings. I only care about you."

"If you only knew how long I've waited for this day. We'll have a huge wedding and go anywhere in the world you want for our honeymoon. But I'd love to take you to the Amalfi Coast in Italy. You'd love it there."

"Or we could fly to Las Vegas right now, get it done quick and easy, and spend our honeymoon at the Bellagio."

"Okay, fine, let's go, before you change your mind."

"Oh, I'm not gonna change my mind, no way. I don't like the way Jude sniffs around you all the time. She wants you back, I can tell."

Black grinned and pulled her to her feet. "The Lear is gassed and ready. I can't think of a better wedding anniversary than Christmas Eve."

And Claire couldn't, either. Whether they went to Las Vegas or had a small ceremony at Cedar Bend with all their friends, or a huge affair in the ballroom of his biggest hotel, it didn't matter to her. He could even have the biggest, most spectacular wedding in the world, if he wanted it. She just wanted them to be together and stay together and be happy together. And he was smiling now, happy again, and that was the way she liked it. Maybe things would be different now. Maybe their lives would be less dangerous. Maybe she'd open that agency the way he wanted her to. When Black kissed her again, she put her arms around his neck and let it all happen. Mrs. Nicholas Black. Oh, God, she couldn't believe she'd said yes. She'd once sworn she'd never marry again, never, ever, under any circumstances. But she didn't think about that very long, not with him kissing her the way he was. She closed her eyes and let the magic happen, as it always did when he touched her. Life was good—oh yeah, life was really, really good.

If you enjoyed *Mostly Murder,*
don't miss Linda Ladd's thrilling

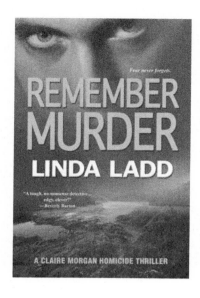

An eKensington e-book on sale now.

Read on for a special excerpt!

Chapter One

Present day

I wasn't sure where I was. I wasn't sure who I was. I didn't care. It was all misty gray and cool and ephemeral, like drifting inside the loveliest, quietest cloud ever created. I was just floating around, softly, swaying gently, and I liked it. It was peaceful and calm, no noise, no bother, no fear. I realized that I was anchored to the ground, somewhere far, far below, at the other end of a shiny silver tether that slipped down through the clouds mounding like giant, fluffy cotton below me. That didn't matter. I didn't want to think about it. I just wanted to be very still and enjoy the soft rocking motions of the gentle breezes. I wanted the clouds to take me higher, up very high, up into the bright white light making the clouds glow above me. It beckoned to me, but I couldn't seem to make myself loosen the silver cord holding me in place so I could float up to that beautiful place.

I shut my eyes and knew nothing more until a man's voice awoke me. It was deep and husky and sounded scared and insistent and determined. I didn't like it, but the voice was familiar somehow, and somehow I knew I had to listen.

"Come on, baby, I know you can hear me. I know you can. You can come back. Just try, try to open your eyes, try to follow my voice back." Then the voice melted away and there was a strangled sound, and I saw a face materialize inside my mind, with blue eyes and black hair, but I didn't really recognize it. I ignored it then and let the rocking lull me to sleep again.

The voice came often and made me weary of listening because I liked the quiet. And then other voices came, not as often as the blue-eyed face, but enough to disrupt my peace and wake me up.

"It's me, Claire, Bud. C'mon, please don't do this to us. The doctors say you can recover, if you'll just wake up. You're in a coma, that's the problem. You gotta wake up to get well. Charlie's here, too. We're all here."

That voice didn't even sound familiar. Neither did the ones that came after his. I slept again, wishing they would just leave me alone and give me the tranquility I wanted. But they didn't, they wouldn't stop, and the voices seemed to go on night and day and forever.

"It's Black, Claire. Listen to me, listen, damn it. You can do this. Everybody's been here to see you. It's okay to wake up. I've got you back home now, and I'm not going anywhere until you open your eyes. You'll be all right. It's over. I've got the best doctors in the world on your case. You're healing just fine. All you have to do is come back to me. You've got to come back. Just do it. Do it, Claire."

I slept some more. The voice would not stop. Now it was reading to me. Shut up and go away, I thought. Leave me alone. That same face loomed in my mind, and he looked vaguely familiar now, but I still didn't know him. I didn't want to know him.

His voice seemed always to be there, always talking to me. "The sheriff needs you, Claire. You love being a detective, remember? You're good at it. You've put lots of criminals behind bars. You got them, all of them. They're never going to kill anybody again. Charlie needs you back on the job. I need you back."

Then a long time later, another voice came in to wake me, slow and drawling. "Listen here, Claire Morgan, this's Joe McKay. What you tryin' to pull doin' something like this? Scarin' us all to death. You get your pretty little butt back here and outta this bed. Lizzie's here with me. She wants to say hi, too."

The more I heard the voices, the closer they seemed. They were dragging me down through the lovely clouds, down to wherever the silver rope was anchored, and I didn't want to go down there. I wanted them to stop. I wanted to stay here in the soft silence so I resisted and tried to arrest the descent and shut my ears and not listen. Why wouldn't they just leave me alone?

Then I heard the voice of a child, very indistinct and far away. Nothing more than a whisper. "Me and Jules is sad you're sick."

A vision erupted inside me, a little blond boy with chubby cheeks and chubby arms and a fishing pole with a little perch hanging on the hook. I didn't know his name, but I knew he needed me. I haven't seen him in so long. I gotta go back and find him. I left him somewhere, but I don't know where. I've got to find him. He'll be scared without me. I know he will.

Somehow I raised myself from that lovely, dreamy, pearly-white, peaceful bed and took hold of the silver rope. I began to pull myself down, hand over hand, down, down, listening for the little child's voice until the other voices came closer and closer. The one named Black, who pestered me so relentlessly, said, "Oh, thank God, she's coming to. She's trying to wake up."

I stopped there for a while, afraid, because the voices were now so near. Then finally, at long last, when they were quiet, I felt ready to face them. I opened my eyes to darkness, but shut them tight again, terror engulfing me. I tried to climb back up into the clouds, but now the lovely silence was gone, and the most terrible dreams came at me like monsters in the night. Then I heard a different voice, a terrible whispering voice, telling me something about an old warehouse on a river, telling me that we were finally together there, that we'd almost gotten away. And then a vision came in a rush, and I was tied to a chair, in a circle with other people, and someone was making the people shoot each other. Oh, God, please, help me. A man stood up and came toward me. He had a meat cleaver in his hand. He was going to kill me, but instead he turned to the man beside him and swung the cleaver hard. I fought desperately against the tape holding me, cringing back against the chair as he approached me with the bloody meat cleaver.

Panting, terrified, trembling in every nerve and fiber of her body, Claire Morgan opened her eyes. She was fully awake now, instantly cognizant of her surroundings. She was in a hospital bed in a dimly lit room that she'd never seen before. She tried to move, but both her wrists were bound to the bed railings! Oh, God, oh, God. Then she saw the big man sitting in a chair drawn up beside her. He was asleep, reading glasses still perched on his nose, an open manila folder in his lap. She didn't know who he was. Was it the man in her dream, the one with the meat cleaver? Did he have her captive again?

Frantic to flee him and the dark room, she pulled and jerked on the bindings and realized that he'd put all kinds of tubes and wires on her arms and chest, ones that led to IV bags on a rolling stand. What was he doing to her? Drugging her? Horrified, she struggled harder against the cloth bed restraints. When alarms on the heart monitor beside her shattered the quiet with buzzes and bells, the guy in the chair jumped up and leaned over her. Her captor grabbed her shoulders and tried to stop her attempts to get out of the bed.

"Claire, oh, thank God. Listen to me, listen, you're okay. Nobody's going to hurt you. You probably had a bad dream. Calm down, I'm here. I'm right here." Then his arms were around her, and he was holding her up tightly against his chest. He held her there, and she wanted to be free. She didn't know him!

"Let me go, let go!"

Her voice came out hoarse and raspy, her mouth dry and parched. She could barely speak. Where was the meat cleaver? Was he going to kill her? A nurse in blue scrubs suddenly ran into the room and to her bedside. She began to adjust the machines. "Oh, my God, Nick! She's awake!"

The man let go of her, but he kept his face down very close to hers. Cringing and pushing away from him, she felt his hand on her brow, very gentle. She tensed all over. Then she realized that this Nick guy was the man with black hair and pale blue eyes. She could see his eyes shining in the dim light. His voice was deep, very low and soothing when he spoke again. "It's me, Claire. Nicholas Black. Do you remember me?"

"No, no, I don't! Why is it so dark? Why am I tied up?"

"Shh, baby, don't fight me like this. I'm taking the bed restraints off right now. See, I'm untying them." He continued to talk to her in that same soft, reassuring tone. Now his voice was beginning to sound vaguely familiar, like the one who talked to her so often. Now he was speaking to the nurse. "Monica, quick, turn on the lights, all of them."

The man, Nick, was holding her left hand now between both of his, trying hard to calm her fears. Her heart raced; she didn't understand any of this. "You've been dreaming a lot, sweetheart, having some pretty bad nightmares. You've been thrashing around, fighting against something. I was afraid you'd hurt yourself so I ordered the restraints. See, they're off now. Nobody's going to hurt you or tie you up again."

As soon as the ties came off, she scooted back away from him as far as she could get. Confused, very weak, she pulled a pillow in front of her, a pitiful barrier against him, trying to understand what was going on. She had to calm down, she knew that, but her heart was thudding so hard that her body shook with each beat. Inhaling deep breaths, she managed to calm down a little bit, but it took a while. Her voice came out hoarse and trembling. "Tell me where I am. What is this place? What's wrong with me?"

"You're okay now. You were hurt in a car accident. You've got a serious head injury. You've been lying here in a coma for a long time."

"I don't remember that," she said, and then added with renewed horror, "I don't remember anything."

"You will, I promise. It's going to take time, that's all." The Nick guy smiled down at her. "How do you feel, babe? Do you want anything—a drink of water, anything at all?"

Claire shook her head and tried desperately to remain calm, and didn't quite make it. "Just tell me where I am!"

"We're at Cedar Bend Lodge. That's where we live. Please, Claire, please just lie back and keep calm. Nobody here is going to hurt you, I swear to God."

Staring up at him, she didn't know what to say. She didn't have a clue to who she was; she didn't know if she could trust what he was saying. She'd never seen him before and never heard of any place called Cedar Bend Lodge. She felt sick to her stomach, like she was going to throw up. Bewildered and mind-muddled, she tried desperately to relax her rigid muscles and lie still. Her heart still thundered. "Tell me who you are. Tell me why I'm here."

"First things first, Claire. You're completely safe, that's the most important thing for you to remember right now. And you've got to trust me. I'm a doctor, your doctor. I've been taking care of you right here in this room since a few days after the accident. What you're experiencing right now is called retrograde amnesia. It's completely to be expected after a head injury like yours." He stopped then, took his own deep breath, and looked upset. "Just don't worry. Trust me, just for now, and I promise you that your memory will come back. The most important thing at the moment is for you to remain calm and quiet and let me take care of you."

Not sure yet whether she could believe him, she did lie still and listen to what he said. She just felt so weak and queasy inside her stomach. She kept the pillow between her and him as he picked up her hand and took her pulse. Then he asked her to remove the pillow so he could listen to her heart. She did, but she didn't want to. He put a stethoscope inside the neck of her hospital gown and listened to her heartbeat and then wrapped a blood pressure cuff around her arm. Then he nodded at the nurse and they started unhooking all the tubes and wires attached to her body. He smiled the entire time. So did the nurse. Claire frowned.

But she did feel more in control, now that the lights were on. She was inside a normal, regular bedroom, a very nice one, large and spacious with beautiful furnishings, not a hospital room. There were no people tied to chairs and nobody held a gun on anybody. Nicholas Black said he was a doctor and he acted like a doctor, and he wasn't going to chop off anything on her person with a meat cleaver so her first wave of panic receded. She watched him pick up a plastic pitcher and give it to her. Her hands were still trembling so much that she had to hold it between her palms, but she took a little sip through the straw. She didn't look at him again, trying to get her thoughts and emotions in order. She still felt uneasy, as if she was in danger from these people.

When she looked up at Nicholas Black again, he was still standing close beside the bed, smiling as if he was very happy to see her awake. "Do you mind if I ask you some questions, Claire?"

Claire? Yes, that was her name. Or was it? She nodded. Something was off with that name, Claire. It didn't ring the right bells. Panic began to well up inside her again, but she mentally forced it back down. She felt mixed up and ill and afraid. But he was trying to help her remember, she knew that, and she wanted to believe that. "I'm not sure if that's my name, or not, doctor."

The tall, dark-haired doctor smiled. "You don't remember your name?"

Something jabbed through the wall of darkness erected inside her head. "You called me Claire, but I'm not so sure about that." Another glimpse came through, thank God. "A name just came to me. Annie, I remember the name Annie." She grimaced, trying to force up more about it. "No, wait, it is Claire. Claire Morgan, I think. Tell me what happened again. I still don't understand what happened to me."

"Your name is Claire Morgan, and it's a very good sign that you remember that. The car you were in went off a bridge into a river, and on impact, you hit your head on the windshield. You've been lying here in a coma for going on three weeks. Eighteen days, to be exact. Do you remember what state you live in?"

Now her mind seemed to be reacting, more things coming back, fuzzy, fleeting, but they were definitely trying to break out of the dark fog. "California. Los Angeles." She thought hard for a few seconds and recalled something else. "I'm a detective. LAPD."

The doctor and the nurse exchanged a quick but significant look that pretty much told her that she'd screwed up that answer. Somehow that scared her, and she shut her eyes to block the uncertainty out. She didn't want to talk to them anymore, didn't want to listen to the questions he was asking, or anything else he said. She wanted them to leave her alone, and let her figure out things on her own.

His deep voice came back, down close beside her ear, and then to her shock, he kissed her cheek. "That's okay, Claire. You just rest. We'll talk later. And in a little while, when you feel stronger, we'll see if you can eat something, and then we'll get you up and walking."

The unknown doctor named Nicholas Black sat back down in the chair beside her, and the nurse named Monica glided out of the room with the kind of silent footfalls that only nurses commanded. Claire Morgan kept her eyes tightly closed after that, and tried to remember who the hell she was and what kind of life she'd had before she'd gone off that bridge and ended up tied to a bed.

Linda Ladd is the bestselling author of over a dozen novels. *Remember Murder* marks her exciting return to the Claire Morgan series. Linda makes her home in Missouri, where she is at work on her next novel featuring Claire Morgan.

Visit her on the web at www.lindaladd.com.

With Every Turn in the Case . . .

After moving from Los Angeles to Lake of the Ozarks, Missouri,
homicide detective Claire Morgan has at last adjusted to the peaceful
rhythms of rural life. Until a grisly celebrity murder at an
ultra-exclusive "wellness" resort shatters a quiet summer morning . . .

With Every Twist of the Mind . . .

One of Dr. Nicholas Black's high-profile clients, a beautiful
young soap opera star, has been found dead, taped to a chair
at a fully set table . . . submerged in the lake. Back in L.A.,
Claire investigated the rich, famous, and the deadly—but she
never expected the problems of the privileged to follow her to
this sleepy small town. Just as she never imagined crossing the
line with her prime suspect . . .

With Every Beat of the Heart . . .

Immersed in the case, Claire finds herself drawn to the charismatic
doctor, spending more and more time in his company—and in his
bed. Now, to catch a killer, Claire will have to enter the darkest
recesses of the human mind. But is Black leading her there to
help her . . . or luring her ever deeper into a madman's grip?

"A tough, no-nonsense detective with a well hidden vulnerable side . . . edgy, clever!"
—BEVERLY BARTON

EVERY
KILLER
HAS THEM...

LINDA LADD

Missouri detective Claire Morgan is eager to get back to work
after recuperating from injuries sustained on her last job. But
the missing persons case that welcomes her home in the dead
of winter soon turns more twisted and treacherous than Lake
of the Ozarks' icy mountain roads . . .

The man's body is found suspended from a tree overlooking
a local school. He is bleeding from the head, still alive—but not
for long. Someone wanted Professor Simon Classon to suffer as
much as possible before he died, making sure the victim had a
perfect view of his colleagues and students on the campus below
as he succumbed to the slow-working poison in his veins . . .

Frigid temperatures and punishing snows only make the
investigation more difficult. And then the death threats begin—
unnerving incidents orchestrated to send Claire a deadly message.
Now, as she edges closer to the truth, Claire risks becoming
entangled in a maniac's web—and the stuff of her own worst
nightmares . . .

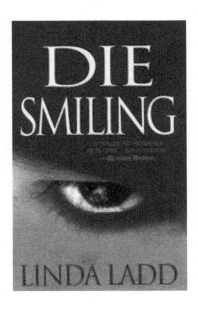

Die Young

Hilde Swensen is a beauty pageant queen with a face to die for and a body to kill for. But by the time Detective Claire Morgan finds her in a shower stall—posed like a grotesquely grinning doll— Hilde is anything but pretty. She's the victim of a sick, deranged killer. And she won't be the last . . .

Die Beautiful

Brianna Swensen is the beauty queen's sister—and the girlfriend of Claire's partner, Bud. She tells Claire that Hilde had plenty of enemies, including a creepy stalker, an abusive ex-boyfriend, and a slew of jealous competitors. But what she doesn't say is that they both shared a dark disturbing secret. A secret that refuses to die . . .

Die Smiling

From the after-hours parties of a sinister funeral home to the underworld vendettas of the Miami mob, Claire follows the trail with her lover Nicholas Black, a psychiatrist with secrets of his own. But it's not until she uncovers evidence of unspeakable acts of depravity that Claire realizes she's just become a diabolical killer's next target . . .

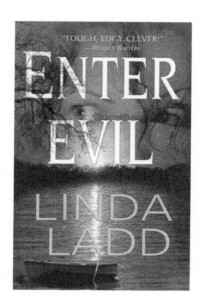

When the Mind . . .

His doctors are the best in the world, his father one of the most powerful men in the state. But they couldn't stop Mikey from succumbing to his darkest demons—the ones inside his head. The ones who told him it was time to end it all.

. . . Plays a Deadly Game . . .

It should have been an open-and-shut case, especially since detective Claire Morgan's lover, Dr. Nicholas Black, recognized Mikey as a troubled former patient. Then Claire finds another body in Mikey's home. Curled inside an oven, charred beyond recognition, the method of murder mind-boggling . . .

. . . of Murder

Claire's only lead is a beaded bracelet, believed to ward off the "evil eye," around each victim's wrist. But by the time she discovers what the dead were afraid of, she's trapped in a mind game of her own—with a brilliant sadistic killer. And this time, there's a method to the madness . . .